*Also by R. Cameron Cooke*

WOLFPACK 351

This is a work of fiction. The names, characters, places, and incidents are either products of the author's imagination or are used fictitiously. Any resemblance to persons, living or dead, events, or locations is entirely coincidental.

ISBN-9781798293584

# WOLFPACK 351

## BY

## R. CAMERON COOKE

## CONTENTS

R. CAMERON COOKE

# 1

# COURAGE

```
FROM:      COMBINED FLEET HEADQUARTERS
           28 APRIL 1943, 0851

TO:        COMMANDER, IJN HAMAKAZE

PRIORITY: HIGH

ENEMY  SUBMARINES  IN  SEA  OF  JAPAN.
HEADQUARTERS  HAS  DETERMINED  IT  HIGHLY
LIKELY ENEMY WILL ATTEMPT TO ESCAPE VIA
SOYA  STRAIT  WITHIN  5  DAYS.  PROSECUTE
WITHOUT  MERCY.  THE  ENEMY  MUST  BE
DESTROYED     AT     ALL     HAZARDS.
REINFORCEMENTS ON THE WAY.
```

## La Perouse (Sōya) Strait

The coastal defenses were on high alert. Illumination flares floated above the dark waters of La Perouse Strait. Flashes rippled along the headlands as shore batteries lobbed shells at any unidentified object broaching the surface. In the deeper water near the center of the channel, two Japanese warships drove on parallel courses, leaving the sea boiling with detonations behind them as one depth charge after another rolled off their decks.

The twenty-five-mile-wide strait connected the Sea of Japan with the Sea of Okhotsk. It was one of a handful of bottlenecks, all controlled by the Japanese, allowing access to that body of water considered to be the emperor's private lake, where the safe passage of his ships was virtually guaranteed. For the first two years of the war, the strait and the sea it protected had been quiet and peaceful, unsullied by the sounds of war.

But now that was no longer the case.

From the darkened bridge of the destroyer *Hamakaze*, Captain Hitoshi Ando read the message affixed to the clipboard while the radio watchman who had just decoded and delivered the message waited patiently nearby. The radioman held a lantern in one hand for his captain to read by, while shielding most of the light with his other hand to keep from distracting the men at their stations.

*The enemy must be destroyed,* Ando read with mild annoyance. What did they think he was doing, inviting them to a geisha party?

This frantic message from the high command was of little use to him. It merely reiterated the obvious. He would perform his duties to the utmost and pursue the enemy wherever he found him, as was expected of all captains of the Imperial Navy. Had Ando not understood the panicked nature in which the message was sent, he might have even considered it an insult.

But, upon further consideration, he decided the message was not entirely useless. It did substantiate the rumors swirling through the private circles of merchant and naval services of late – rumors previously refuted by the high command – that the hitherto inviolate Sea of Japan was now a hunting ground for American submarines.

The Imperial General Headquarters was finally accepting the reality of the situation. They were essentially admitting that the previously released explanations for the recent losses in the Sea of Japan – an assortment of passenger steamers, tankers, and freighters, all blamed on heavy weather when there had been no storms to speak of in weeks – had been yet another coverup.

The communique in Ando's hands demanded action, a shift in purpose for the *Hamakaze* and the other defense forces in and around La Perouse Strait. Up until now, they had been concerned with keeping the enemy out of the Sea of Japan. Now, all efforts would be focused on preventing the enemy's escape.

"Ready stern racks!" A voice intoned from the aft corner of the room. "Four depth charges. Set depth to ninety meters."

Lieutenant Jiro Kawaguchi, the ship's anti-submarine warfare officer, hovered over the shrouded plot table, only his legs visible beneath the drawn curtain as he coordinated the attack. The young officer conversed simultaneously over separate phone circuits with the sonar station and the men manning the depth charge racks and throwers on the main deck.

"Release depth charges!" Kawaguchi commanded with vigor.

Handing the clipboard back to the radioman, Ando crossed to the port bridge wing and looked aft in time to see another cluster of depth charges roll off the racks, plunking into the ocean beyond the destroyer's stern. Ando shifted his gaze to the *Hamakaze's* beam where, in the darkness two hundred meters away, the *Hamakaze's* consort, subchaser *Number 24,* struggled to keep station with the swift destroyer. White splashes appeared astern of the subchaser as it followed the lead of its companion releasing its own depth charges to complete the pattern.

Again, the rumble in the night. Silvery bubbles broached the surface under the dim light of the moon. It was nearly impossible to tell if they were followed by a stream of entrained oil and debris, a sure indication that one of the 160-kilogram charges had found its mark.

It had been nearly four hours since the unidentified submerged anomaly had first been detected by the series of magnetic loops and hydrophones strung along the floor of the strait, alerting the coordinating shore authority to the intruder. Soon after, a myriad of small motor launches equipped with simple sonar sets had drifted along picking it up, too. Pairs of escorts had been vectored onto the suspicious contact, dropping charges at various depths, seamlessly handing off the contact to the next pair. Finally, the contact had been turned over to the *Hamakaze* and the *Number 24* to localize, track, and prosecute.

The two warships had dropped nearly five dozen charges between them, both ships having recently been modified to hold a much larger arsenal of anti-submarine weaponry. Ando, as the senior officer afloat, was in overall command, but he preferred to focus on the larger picture, delegating the subtler points of the attack to Kawaguchi. The young lieutenant had been darting back and forth between the plot table and the bridge-mounted sonar bearing repeater, and often to the signalmen on the semaphore lamps to communicate his plans to *Number 24*.

"Request slower speed, Captain," Kawaguchi said almost impatiently suddenly standing before Ando. "Recommend new course zero-five-zero."

"Very well," Ando replied, nodding to the helmsmen. "One-third speed. Right standard helm. Steady zero-five-zero."

Before the order was rung up, Kawaguchi had already moved back to the sonar repeater, watching and waiting for the operators in the sonar room to regain the submerged contact once the effects of the explosions and the *Hamakaze's* own screw noise had diminished.

Ando observed Kawaguchi eagerly awaiting new information. The young lieutenant's enthusiasm for finding and destroying the enemy was more intense than any other member of the crew. His outward display of emotion bordered on unprofessional, but Ando understood its source. Sometimes, Ando wished that he, too, could feel the zest that Kawaguchi did, that he could find satisfaction in the doldrums of guarding a waterway so far from the main theaters of the war, day after day dropping depth charges on contacts that often proved to be nothing more than migrating whales. This indeed was not the kind of duty Ando had envisioned when he had taken command of the *Hamakaze* almost two years ago.

The *Hamakaze* was a *Kagero*-class destroyer – 2,500 tons, over one hundred meters long, fast and deadly, and built to accompany Japan's great battle fleets as they ranged across the Pacific. Her main armament consisted of three shrapnel-proof gun turrets – one forward, two aft – each containing twin-mounted 127-millimeter 50-caliber naval guns capable of throwing 23-kilogram, high-explosive or armor-piercing shells over 18 kilometers away. With an additional sprinkling of 25-millimeter anti-aircraft guns and two shrapnel-proof torpedo mounts each capable of firing four torpedoes tipped with 500-kilogram warheads, she could take on almost anything the enemy could send at her.

Ever since his days at Eta Jima, Ando had dreamed of commanding such a ship. He had never been interested in the massive, overloaded battleships or cruisers, always tethered to the carrier task forces and destined to serve as flagships from time to time with all the extensive scrutiny that entailed. Ando's heart had always been set on destroyers — light-weight, agile, and often independent speedboats that packed a serious punch. The day he had taken command of the *Hamakaze* had been the happiest of his life. At thirty-two years old, he had reached the epitome of his naval career and envisioned leading his quick ship and its proficient crew through desperate surface battles against the American fleet. Never would he have predicted that the *Hamakaze* would essentially become a guard vessel, her guns and torpedoes silent and unused while her sonar and depth charge racks saw over-employment.

For several months now, much to Ando's dismay, the *Hamakaze* had been patrolling the waters of La Perouse Strait on the cold, northernmost extremity of Japan. Like all destroyer captains, he wished to be with the main battle fleets down in the South Pacific, where the greatest naval battles in history were being fought. Down there, honors were being won by others, while he languished in this seemingly forgotten corner of the war.

Of course, Ando knew that men were dying down there, too. After every major engagement, the names of another one or two of his academy classmates invariably appeared on the casualty lists. The official releases reported great victories with many American ships sunk and few Japanese casualties, but Ando knew such reports were propaganda meant to bolster the Japanese people and maintain the navy's prominence on the Imperial General Staff.

The truth was far less encouraging.

Ando had learned the truth the last time he was on shore leave in Tokyo, when he had dined with several peers whose ships were refitting in the Kobe shipyard before being sent back to the combat zone. The *sake* had flowed freely, as had their grievances. None had been pleased with the direction of the war. They had spoken of shortages, of lacking everything from ammunition, to fuel, to spare parts, to food. They had talked of disastrous fleet tactics used again and again, of nonexistent air cover, and of horrific night gun battles in which destroyers, cruisers, and even battleships – all nearly impossible to replace – were being sent to the bottom with their entire crews.

The outlook had been bleak, to say the least. But Ando still wished to be there, fighting alongside his friends. He wanted to do his part, to engage the enemy in glorious battle, not amble about between two points of land, getting excited whenever the sonar detected a school of shrimp. His officers and crew felt the same way. He had trained them to be warriors, not gatekeepers. Here, searching for submarines day after day, it was far too easy to fall into routine and complacency, and it had been something of a challenge to keep them honed, let alone motivated.

Kawaguchi had been the exception. The young lieutenant's passion for hunting the enemy was second only to his proficiency. His enthusiasm was driven by personal reasons.

"Any success?" Ando asked Kawaguchi who still hovered by the sonar repeater.

"Weak contact to starboard, Captain," the officer stated after a pause. "Sonar reports strange popping noises. We may have sunk it, or it may be —"

"Enemy submarine off the starboard beam!" a lookout on the signal bridge above shouted excitedly through the voice tube.

Ando brought his binoculars to his face. The *Hamakaze's* searchlights clicked on, angling to sweep the dark sea. At first, the powerful beams fell only on a field of empty, green water. But, as the cones of light pushed back the shroud of blackness, they revealed a glistening, rust-streaked object, like a spiny box just poking above the waves. It was the broached conning tower of an enemy submarine. It looked pathetic, really, but Ando knew well the deadly nature of what remained hidden beneath the waves.

"Pass the word to the gunnery officer," Ando said to the nearest man wearing a set of phones. "Submarine bearing zero eight zero, four thousand meters. Load anti-submarine shells and commence firing, all batteries."

Moments later, the night split open. The deck shuddered, and pressure waves rippled through the air as *Hamakaze's* three twin-mount turrets opened up, launching half a dozen lethal projectiles at the floating object. In the darkness off the beam, *Number 24* also opened fire, its single-mount turret flickering like a pop gun compared with the *Hamakaze's* fusillade.

The illuminated patch of ocean came alive with geysers. One shell after another struck the surface and exploded, sending columns of frothing sea a hundred feet into the air. Still somewhat experimental, the flat-headed ASW projectiles were designed with an anti-ricochet shape which, in theory, allowed them to continue on a straight path after entering the water in hopes of hitting a submarine's submerged hull, but this came at the cost of considerable range. Whether the shells performed as advertised, Ando could not tell, since the sub was masked entirely by spray. But he knew he would not wish to be on the receiving end of this barrage. If not scoring direct hits, the shells were certainly rocking the enemy submarine with very close detonations.

"Cease firing!" Ando ordered after the *Hamakaze* and *Number 24* had fired a half-dozen salvos each.

The guns of both ships fell silent. It was time to look and listen again. After the last cascading fountain had dropped back into the sea, the searchlights converged on the submarine's former location but found only an empty, frothing surface. Straining their eyes, the lookouts searched for any debris, an unusual ripple, the minutest stick of a mast, but saw nothing. Once again, the elusive enemy would leave them guessing.

*Not this time!* Ando thought. Frustrated with the tedium of this assignment and bearing in mind the high priority message he still held in one hand, he strode to the chart table.

"Give me a bearing to the last good position of the submarine!"

"Zero seven eight, sir," Kawaguchi replied from the plot table.

"Come right to zero seven eight. Flank speed!"

The ordered bell was rung up on the engine order telegraph, and the *Hamakaze* surged forward, drawing a broad curved line of phosphorescence in the dark ocean, her stacks releasing a torrent of white smoke into the night sky. She maneuvered like a racing yacht, her knife-like bow parting the waves effortlessly. Like most Japanese destroyers, the *Hamakaze* was designed for speed and maneuverability. When her engines were running at maximum, she could easily surpass thirty-five knots. Tonight, *Hamakaze's* engines were up to the task. By the time she steadied on the new course, she was surpassing fifteen knots.

"Time to the submarine's last known position?" Ando prompted.

"Thirty seconds, Captain," Kawaguchi answered after stretching a pair of dividers between two points on the plot. "But sonar won't be able to detect the sub at this speed, sir."

"I do not intend to search for it, Lieutenant." Ando gave a spirited grin. "I intend to sink it. Pass the word to all hands, brace for impact, and ready the stern racks. Depth setting, twenty-five meters!"

A stunned look crossed the junior officer's face before he turned back to the plot table. He probably thought his captain had lost his mind setting the depth charges so shallow, but Ando had a reason for his actions, and years of experience beyond that of Kawaguchi.

For a submarine to risk coming to the surface while being assailed by two warships, one of three things had to have happened. Either its batteries were out of charge, it was running low on breathable air, or it was severely damaged. The fact that the sub was no longer visible meant it had either been sunk by the gunfire, or it had dived again and was lurking just beneath the surface. If the latter was the case, and the *Hamakaze* got there fast enough, the destroyer's keel would slice through the enemy's pressure hull like a *katana* through a ripe melon. Yes, it would mean time in the yards for the *Hamakaze*, but the enemy would be sunk with no uncertainties, and the high command's wishes fulfilled. Even if the submarine managed to go deep in time to avoid the *Hamakaze's* charge, it could only do so by rapidly flooding more water into its ballast tanks, a dangerous maneuver for a submarine that was probably already damaged and struggling to maintain depth control – and one that may result in the same outcome as a ramming.

"Ten seconds, Captain. Nine…eight…seven…"

The bridge fell suddenly quiet. The ship's communications circuits, normally abuzz in combat, fell silent, too. Men grabbed the nearest bracket or any other handhold they could find. Ando did the same, peering through the windows as if he could somehow see the destroyer's bowsprit in the darkness. He imagined the enemy captain struck dumb with horror as he looked through the periscope and saw the *Hamakaze's* sharp bow driving through the waves directly towards him. Every man held his breath anticipating the vessel to collide with the submarine at any moment.

But the impact never came.

"We are over the submarine's last known position, Captain," Kawaguchi reported after what had seemed like an intolerable wait. "It must have gone deep."

"Release charges!"

Four more depth charges rolled off the destroyer's fantail, disappearing in the dark frothing wake. Moments later, the sea erupted astern. Four explosions in rapid succession sent a violent pressure wave through the *Hamakaze* from stern to stem as each 160-kilogram charge went off at its assigned depth.

"Full starboard helm. Stop starboard engine."

The destroyer leaned hard to port as the steersman conned her through a tightly-executed 360-degree turn to the right, returning her within seconds to the last known location of the submarine still effervescent from the underwater detonations.

"One-third speed," Ando commanded. "Look for oil and debris. Lieutenant Kawaguchi, commence your search."

The lieutenant nodded from the plot table while in the middle of talking to the sonar room on the phone-set. As the *Hamakaze* slowed, Ando climbed the ladder to the signal bridge, joining the lookouts there who were scanning the dark sea in every direction. Before long, a piercing whine came from the lapping water below as the *Hamakaze's* echo-ranging sonar transducers began probing the depths. The eerie sound was distant, lonely, like one whale calling to another across a vast empty ocean.

After half an hour circling the area, with both the *Hamakaze* and *Number 24* alternately listening and pinging the depths, neither ship had found any trace of the enemy, and Ando returned to the pilothouse.

"Sonar reports no contacts, Captain," Kawaguchi admitted, almost apologetically. "The water is only 120 meters deep here, sir. It is possible the enemy submarine was destroyed but reached the bottom before its pressure hull failed."

"I am sure that is the case." Ando forced a smile. Of course, he knew the reality of the situation, that the enemy had probably escaped. "We will continue to search for another hour before we report the victory to shore command."

"Yes, sir. Thank you, sir."

One look from Kawaguchi told Ando the young officer was just as wise to the more likely probability, and that they both understood they must give the *Hamakaze's* crew something to keep them going, something to keep them motivated through the doldrums of channel duty.

Ando thought of the irony of it all. The navy grossly understated its losses to the high command, while he grossly overstated his ship's success to his crew. Glancing around the pilothouse, he wondered how many of the crew understood the optimism of the assessment.

But, Ando sighed, they needed a victory, and this would have to do.

# 2

# ADMIRAL GILES

*Eight Days Later*

*Midway Atoll*

Rear Admiral Theodore Giles watched from the pier as the *USS Blueback* crept into the lagoon through the narrow channel separating Sand and Eastern Islands. Under the noonday sun, her camouflage paint seemed out of place on a navy ship – gray sides and a black deck, with all limber holes and cavities white – but it was indeed effective, even from this close distance. As the *Blueback* drew closer, Giles could see how much the paint had faded, the orange flares of rust accenting every nook and crevasse, the marine growth near the waterline, indications of just how long she had been at sea. But it was not until the submarine eased closer to the pier and lines went across that Giles finally saw the extent of the damage, and he could not help but gasp.

His eyes ran along the three-hundred-foot hull and found large dents and ripples in more than a dozen places. The conning tower had been battered, too, one side adorned with a peppering of jagged holes of various sizes left by flying shrapnel. Along the main deck, wooden planks were entirely missing, the splintered gaps now spanned by loose deck plates so that the line handlers would not fall into the dark chasms.

Giles was dumbstruck.

Submarine service was voluntary. Those who patrolled beneath the waves stood on the front lines of the war in the Pacific – indeed, far behind enemy lines. They knew what they were getting into, and were prepared to sacrifice all. It was not Giles's way to feel guilt or remorse for those who carried out the missions he conceived, but the sight of the *Blueback* gave him pause. She had taken a severe beating. Those men who now calmly tended the lines on deck must have experienced an unimaginable horror.

*They all seem so young — so very young.*

But Giles quickly sequestered such thoughts. It did no good to dwell on the cost when so much had been gained. The mission had been a success, a resounding success. That's what he kept telling himself. Didn't the very ordeal of the *Blueback* prove it?

In any event, he was glad he had taken the long flight from Pearl Harbor early this morning to see the damage first hand. He had arrived at the airstrip on Eastern Island aboard the regular R4D supply plane a little less than an hour ago. So determined was he to be on the pier when the *Blueback* docked that he had hardly glanced at his surroundings after stepping off the plane. Even during the short ride on the motor launch across the lagoon to Sand Island, he had kept his eyes focused on the open sea, beyond the frothy reef, where he had just been able to make out the crippled submarine turning into the atoll's narrow channel. But, now, as he waited for the *Blueback* to finish mooring, he finally took a moment to look around.

It had been many years since Giles had been to Midway. It was much busier now, but it still felt like the same surreal escape from the world he had remembered. The remote outpost was little more than a spit of sand in the middle of the largest ocean on earth. The two islands that made up the habitable portion of the atoll, Eastern and Sand, were not much larger than two miles at their widest points. Hangars, barracks, bunkers, and repair shops stood serenely amid a sparse forest of palms while gentle surf lapped against white beaches facing the crystal-clear lagoon. Everywhere the ground was alive with a virtual carpet of squawking albatrosses – or "gooney birds" – who seemed unfazed by the presence of the islands' human inhabitants. Were it not for a few charred frames and piles of burnt wreckage, stark reminders of the massive Japanese air attack more than a year ago, one might even forget there was a war on – a merciless, terrible, world war, the prosecution of which consumed every waking hour of Giles's days and nights.

It had been a year and a half since the attack on Pearl Harbor, and now, finally, the Pacific War was beginning to turn in the Allies' favor. Guadalcanal was now firmly in Allied hands. The Japanese Combined Fleet commander, Admiral Yamamoto, had been killed in a daring air ambush. And an invasion fleet was, at this moment, on its way to take back the Japanese-occupied Aleutian Islands. Even with these major successes, the Japanese were not yet done — not by a long shot. In fact, Giles had never been busier.

His contribution to the war effort was not as simple as that of most flag officers. He did not lead men in major engagements or plan out set-piece naval battles. He was not in charge of any fleets or armies and always had to borrow the resources he used from grudging commanders. The missions he oversaw involved little glory and never made the Hollywood newsreels or Life Magazine. They were the clandestine side of the war, the whispers and gentle nudges that eventually sent the elephant over the cliff. Quite probably, no one in the general public would ever know about them, even when and if the Japanese were finally defeated. Often, even the men who carried out these missions, such as the crew of the *Blueback*, did not realize the missions' true objectives. They were mere pieces on Giles's personal chessboard.

With mooring lines secured, the submarine's crew began to debark. They filed past Giles with haggard, weary expressions, some saluting, some not. They had been through hell, to the devil's swimming pool and back, but none looked eager to celebrate. A hush descended on the pier as a stretcher made its way along the main deck. It was carefully passed across the gangway and then to a waiting jeep on the dock which sped off the moment its unconscious passenger was strapped down. Next, a procession of wounded men was guided off the sub, some wearing bandages, some looking disoriented. They, too, were loaded aboard jeeps and trucks, all bound for the hospital. No sooner had the last injured sailor debarked than the waiting repair crews rushed aboard lugging welding kits and tools like weapons. They were racing against the clock, for the submarine was, essentially, a sinking ship, given a lien on death by her machinery. The *Blueback's* pumps were barely keeping up with her numerous leaks. Should the diesel generators fail, or the batteries deplete, the pumps would go silent, and she would quietly sink beside the pier.

Members of the crew began to file off now, dungaree-clad sailors and officers in khaki, each one stopping halfway across the brow and saluting the colors on the *Blueback's* fantail before proceeding to the pier. The last of these was a slim, tired-looking officer wearing a combination hat with the brim pushed back on his head. His face was almost trance-like, his mind clearly consumed with the state of his ship and crew.

"Commander Lynch, I believe?" Giles greeted him.

The officer appeared to suddenly notice him, came to attention and threw up a sharp salute.

"Yes, sir," the officer said with slight embarrassment. "That's me, sir. Lieutenant Commander Andy Lynch."

"My name is Giles."

"I'm sorry, sir. I was expecting Captain Brewer. Are you the new deputy?"

"No," Giles smiled. "Captain Brewer is still the deputy here. He's over at Eastern Island at the moment. I'm sure he will be back shortly." Giles did not mention that he had arranged for Brewer, who normally met all returning submarines at the pier, to be conveniently summoned over to Eastern Island just as the *Blueback* was arriving in order to get him out of the way. Giles needed a few uninterrupted moments with Lynch to discuss things that were far more important than spare parts and maintenance work orders. "I work with ComSubPac. I was wondering if I might have a word with you."

Lynch seemed somewhat confused, but he shrugged and nodded. "Certainly, Admiral."

"Can I buy you a drink?"

Lynch's face immediately assumed a guarded look, that of a submarine captain reluctant to jump the proper chain of command. "We've just returned from one hell of a patrol, sir. I should probably report to Captain Brewer first. I'm not sure I have time to –"

"I know all about your patrol. I've read your initial report. As I said, I work with ComSubPac." Giles was careful not to say that ComSubPac had sent him here, for he had not. Giles had come at his own discretion. Had the submarine fleet commander known about Giles's impromptu trip, he would have surely done everything he could to stop it. Giles was not his favorite person at the moment.

"I assure you, Commander, one drink will only take a minute."

Fifteen minutes later, they were seated at a small table in the Gooneyville with cold beers in front of them. The Gooneyville was by far the most lavish building on the island, appearing somewhat out of place among the spartan military structures. Before the war, it had been the Pan American Hotel, catering to the ultra-wealthy passengers of the large Clipper planes that had used Midway as a stopover point on the six-day, cross-Pacific, island-hopping run from San Francisco to Hong Kong. Now, it served as a club for officers of the local garrison and visiting submarines.

After two beers and several unsuccessful attempts to engage the *Blueback's* commander in small talk, Giles decided there was no sense in beating around the bush any longer.

"I know that you have much to do, Commander," Giles said. "So, I'll get to the purpose of my visit."

Lynch said nothing but kept his eyes on the admiral as he took a long drink.

"I wished to meet with you, Commander Lynch, because you have unique experience that may help ensure the continued success of this mission."

"The continued success, sir?" Lynch said skeptically.

"Yours was the first boat to run through La Perouse Strait," Giles said, ignoring the bold quip. "You know the enemy disposition there, first hand. I would like to get a gauge for the type of defenses you encountered."

"You said you read my report, sir," Lynch said unhelpfully.

"That was only a summary," Giles smiled to hide his annoyance. "You and I both know summary reports don't convey everything."

Giles had indeed read the summary, but it had contained nothing he did not already know. He knew full well the Japanese had stepped up their anti-submarine measures around La Perouse Strait. Two weeks ago, he had been summoned to the office of a very irate ComSubPac who had presented him with an intercepted Japanese communique, a transmission from Combined Fleet Headquarters to all Japanese commands in and around the home islands. It stated that American submarines had been sinking ships in the Sea of Japan, that they would likely attempt a breakout within a week, and that all available assets were to be diverted from their present duties to prosecute them. The Imperial Navy was allocating land-based aircraft, a squadron of destroyers, escorts, and a plethora of smaller craft to block all the northern passages, primarily the strait in question.

The accuracy of the message had been unsettling, to say the least. At the time of the message's transmission, American submarines had indeed been in the Sea of Japan – four of them, to be precise – and, up until that message, all four had been preparing to make their escape within a matter of days. Obviously, with the Imperial Navy applying a full-court press around La Perouse, the escape plan had to be scuttled, or at least postponed. Naturally, at the prospect of losing four of his submarines, ComSubPac had appeared mad enough to throw Giles out his office's second story window. That was understandable since Giles was the one who had *borrowed* the four submarines to form the wolfpack for this mission, designated *Wolfpack 351*. Giles had sent *Wolfpack 351* to the Sea of Japan. Now, ComSubPac wanted it back.

It had taken Giles some time to calm the submarine fleet commander down, but he had eventually managed it, assuring his fellow admiral that, while the situation looked bleak now, the enemy blockade could only last for a few days at the most. The destroyers and escorts of Japan's dwindling fleet were far too valuable to be kept tied up guarding the remote northern waterways. It was a simple matter of sitting and waiting. After a few days — a week at the most — the Japanese would surely pull them back, the way would be clear, and the wolfpack could make its escape.

That was two weeks ago.

Enemy message traffic intercepted this morning indicated the Japanese warships and aircraft were still there. If anything, they had grown in strength, and they were still covering the passes around the clock.

Low on torpedoes, provisions, and, most importantly, fuel, the subs would soon have no choice but to try to push through. Like a school of fish, they were being driven into a net, and they were running out of time. Even now, by all estimates, their fuel levels were so critical they would need a favoring current to get them to Midway.

The *Blueback* had been the exception. She had suffered a ruptured fuel ballast tank halfway through the patrol, leaving her with much less fuel than the others. Lynch had had no choice but to attempt a breakout, and his submarine had been battered to the point where she would need weeks, if not months, in the shipyard before she was of any use again.

"ComSubPac should receive my official report within two days, sir," Lynch said, blatantly checking his watch.

"I'm afraid that might be too late," Giles said. "I know I don't have to remind you, Commander, that there are still three other submarines out there. Your cooperation will greatly improve their chances of making it home."

"You want my advice, sir?"

Giles got the feeling he was going to get it whether he wanted it or not.

"Abort the mission," Lynch said bluntly. "Order the rest of the wolfpack to scuttle their boats in Vladivostok and seek asylum there. That's their only chance of making it home alive, Admiral. If you send them through that strait, they'll be sunk for sure. The Japs are ready for them."

Giles sighed. While the Soviet Union and the United States were indeed allies on the other side of the world, on this side of the world, a non-aggression pact existed between the Bolshevik power and Japan, an agreement that Joseph Stalin appeared to have no intention of violating – at least not until Germany was defeated. The American submarine crews may have found some comfort in the fact that an *allied* port existed on the north end of the Sea of Japan, but, in all reality, that option was off the table. For a myriad of reasons – some of them diplomatic, some of them political – sending the boats to Russia would never do.

"You made it," Giles retorted.

"Just barely."

"If the others follow the same tactics you used, why shouldn't they succeed, too?"

Lynch looked at him incredulously for a few seconds, then Giles saw the commander's eyes avert to his left breast pocket, where, unlike Lynch, Giles wore no insignia. Having spent his entire career in the fields of intrigue and intelligence, Giles had never been a sea-going officer. Upon this realization, Lynch's demeanor changed visibly, now seeming to regard Giles with a measure of reservation.

"We got lucky, sir," Lynch said. "That's all I can say. There was no skill in it, no clever tricks – just plain, dumb luck."

"Now, I'm sure that's not entirely true," Giles said with a smile. "Come now, Commander, I wish to know exactly how you did it."

"You want to know how we did it, Admiral?" Lynch was almost belligerent now. "I'll tell you how we did it. A hundred miles before we ever reached the strait, Jap planes started showing up. We ducked one plane after another, taking depth bombings nearly every watch. There were times when we stayed down for ten hours only to come up and find them still there, circling overhead, driving us back down with more bombs. When we finally reached the strait, we found it full of escorts, and destroyers, and mines. We spent most of our time deep, rigged for silent running. Long hours with the air conditioning secured. Long hours of foul air and humidity. We skirted one minefield after another, always afraid the FM sonar might give away our position, and it probably did. When we were almost half-way through the strait, the Japs got a whiff of us and never let us go. They sent everything they had after us, passing us off from one pair of escorts to the next. Just when we thought we'd given them the slip, another group would come from a different direction. We took over eighty depth charges in ten hours. Once, we broached and found ourselves on the receiving end of the Jap guns. You saw the damage we sustained. A man can only take that kind of punishment for so long. One of my men just lost it. He went crazy, started going after his shipmates with a wrench. Luckily, my corpsman was able to sedate him before anyone got hurt." Lynch paused. He took a long drink, and his face grew somber. "I lost a man, Admiral. A good man. Buried him at sea a few days ago. Another one of my boys is not expected to make it. And for what? A handful of small freighters? An ocean liner that was probably full of Korean laborers!"

Giles nodded and did his best to smile sympathetically. He waved for the waiter to bring another round of beers. "I appreciate your perspective, Commander. But I assure you, your man did not die in vain. The ships you sank were crucial to the Japanese war effort. They were directly supporting the Japanese homeland. All the intelligence reports still point to that conclusion. The mission has been a resounding success."

"With all due respect, Admiral, the damned mission is a total disaster! A waste of good boats and good men. You sent them where they should never have gone, the one place in the whole damn Pacific Theater where the Japs have the upper hand on us!"

Giles glared at Lynch. He had no interest in establishing his authority over the lower-ranking submarine commander, but there were other officers around, and he felt he needed to send a clear message to the disgruntled captain of the *Blueback* that he was pushing the survivor's privilege a bit too far. Still, if he reprimanded Lynch, would the skipper even care? And who could blame him? After this patrol, what fear could he possibly have for a little dressing down or a demotion?

Reconsidering, Giles decided not to make an issue out of it. It really did not matter what Lynch thought of him. He was a simple, ill-informed, and insignificant submarine captain with no concept of his place in the grander scheme. He did not understand the big picture. How could he? His patrol order had only contained the intelligence Giles had seen fit to include.

Just then, a telephone rang at the bar. The bartender picked it up, and after a brief exchange, raised his voice over the conversation in the room.

"Lieutenant Commander Lynch? Is there a Commander Lynch here?"

Lynch half-heartedly raised his hand, and the bartender came over to the table.

"Excuse me, sir," the bartender said politely. "They want you over at the radio shack, sir. You have an important call from Pearl Harbor."

Lynch nodded, seeming somewhat relieved to have an excuse to leave. He threw back the last drops of beer in the glass and rose from the table.

"If you'll excuse me, Admiral," he said evenly. "I must go talk to the boss. Thanks for the drink."

"Of course," Giles said with a smile. "Give him my love, will you?"

Lynch gave him a grim look before tucking his hat under his arm and leaving the room without another word. If it was indeed the *boss* – that is, ComSubPac – on the other end of that telephone line, then there would certainly be no love for Giles coming back on the receiving end.

Giles watched the doorway long after the submarine commander had departed. He sipped at his beer as he mulled over what Lynch had said.

Okay, maybe Lynch had a point. Perhaps nothing had been substantially gained by sending subs into the

Emperor's private lake. Maybe it had even been a blunder. But it had at least shown the Japanese they could not count on freedom of navigation in waters they had considered their own for so long. Imagine the impact to the morale of the American people if German U-boats suddenly appeared on Lake Michigan and began sinking ships.

Four subs. It had been a lot to ask. ComSubPac had been against it from the start. But he had failed to see the intangible rewards such an operation could achieve. It was the blow to the citizens' fighting spirit that mattered, not the size or value of the ships sunk. Wars were often won by such tips of the scale. From Napoleon's failure to secure the seas around his empire, to Hannibal's failure to keep Scipio off African soil, to the Confederacy's inability to recognize the importance of the rivers snaking through the South, it was always the little things that made the difference in war, seldom the big battles. Aside from the one KIA on the *Blueback* and the near-fatal pummeling it had endured, *Wolfpack 351* had suffered no casualties, thus far. It had done its job, and it had done it well. How many ships had they sunk?

Six confirmed, with two more probable? Sure, none had been combatants, and none had been genuinely crucial to the war effort, but who could weigh the ramifications to the psyche of every factory worker, every shipyard worker, every family member who would fill their letters to their fighting men with stories of ships lost in the Emperor's swimming pool? What effect did such news have on the mind of the frontline soldier?

Still, ComSubPac was not happy. In his narrow viewpoint, yet another one of Giles's far-fetched missions had cost him ships and men. Commander Lynch was surely not the only one ComSubPac was telephoning today. The high-placed admiral would be calling in every favor with every power player he knew back in Washington in an attempt to strip Giles of his power, and send him packing to some quiet, out of the way desk job, such as the naval liaison's office, *in Moscow.* After this blunder, Giles knew even his own connections in Washington would have trouble defending him. They might even join in the collective clamor for his removal.

Could they not see that while his peculiar schemes often proved costly to the executing commands, they saved thousands of lives, if not tens of thousands, far down the road? No, of course not. And even if his career survived intact, the higher-ups would certainly not go to bat for him again. They would never approve any future missions, not unless the submarines still trapped in the Sea of Japan miraculously managed to escape.

Giles lit a cigarette.

There had to be a way to help them aside from sending a message to the sub skippers to say a prayer and hope for the best. If only he had a fast carrier or cruiser group at his disposal, something with some firepower, something to get the enemy's attention, then he might lure their ships and aircraft away from La Perouse Strait and open the barn door for the wolfpack to escape. Unfortunately, in the balance of military value, carrier and cruiser groups were worth much more than three submarines.

*Even a single cruiser could do it*, Giles thought. But he was not about to go pleading to CinCPac for one. He knew the answer he would get.

Then, suddenly, an idea popped into Giles's head.

*A single cruiser! That's it!*

Immediately, his mind began to formulate a plan, a plan that ComSubPac would not like because it involved another one of his boats — a boat that was, at this moment, completing another of Giles's missions. It was the only boat that was equipped to do what Giles was scheming, and it just so happened to be in an ideal location. ComSubPac would not be happy about it, but Giles would convince him — he *had* to convince him.

Putting out his cigarette, Giles rose abruptly. He checked his watch as he marched toward the door. The supply plane was heading back to Pearl Harbor in one hour, and he intended to be on it.

It was time to bring *Wolfpack 351* home.

# 3

# RESPECT

*La Perouse (Sōya) Strait*

The three Japanese destroyers and four escorts, also known as *kaibōkan*, had been trolling back and forth across the narrow passage, each covering its assigned area, but now they broke from that incessant routine. With a measure of smartness, they came together in column, their long, white wakes converging into one. Like cubs wishing to be part of the pack, a half dozen subchasers followed suit, the little craft falling in at the tail of the formation. A pair of *Aichi D3A* dive bombers droned high overhead, circling twice above the swaying ships, before resuming their patrol in the skies above the strait.

With the *Hamakaze* in the van, the impressive flotilla drove toward a small motor launch that had just put off from the shore. On the main deck of each warship, hundreds of sailors in blue uniforms quickly came to attention. Whistles sounded as the launch passed down the formation's port side, each crew, in turn, bringing up sharp salutes. Though each sailor stood like a statue, none missed the small pennant lolling from the launch's bow bearing two gold stars, nor did they fail to see the gray-haired, barrel-chested officer standing in the sternsheets wearing an immaculate blue naval tunic adorned with ribbons. The gray-haired officer returned their salutes, his face emotionless as if set in stone.

As the short ceremony concluded, the fleet parted ways, each warship returning to its patrol sector at top speed – except for the *Hamakaze*. With her impeccably painted sides and superstructure glimmering in the sun, the destroyer hove to and prepared to receive the launch's passenger. Again, whistles sounded, and men came to attention as the gray-haired flag officer ascended the ladder and stepped onto the main deck.

"Request permission to come aboard," the flag officer said in a throaty, deep voice.

"Permission granted, Admiral Yamada." Ando greeted his superior with a sharp salute. "It is indeed an unexpected honor to have you aboard, sir."

Rear Admiral Akira Yamada looked up at the fluttering admiral's pennant that had just appeared at the masthead. His steady eyes ran along the destroyer from stem to stern, eyeing with evident satisfaction the neatly coiled lines, the freshly scrubbed decks, the polished gun mounts, and the resplendent sailors standing in neat ranks all around him. With each breath of the salty air, his countenance visibly softened, as if the mere act of setting foot on a warship again was invigorating to his soul. Within a matter of seconds, Yamada began to look more and more like the vibrant man Ando had known all those years ago when the now-aged flag officer had been his instructor at the Imperial Japanese Naval Academy at Eta Jima.

Behind the admiral, a young lieutenant wearing the gold braid of an aide struggled to the top of the ladder toting the admiral's sea gear, as well as his own. A pair of *Hamakaze's* sailors stepped forward to relieve the lieutenant of the bags — all except for a long item wrapped in fine linen which the young officer kept close to him. Ando caught a glimpse of a pair of squared hilts with ornamental *tsuba* protruding from one end of the wrapping, and immediately realized what it contained – a *katana* and a *wakizashi*, the traditional long and short swords of a samurai. It was an odd choice of gear to bring along on a sea cruise, but Ando dismissed it, assuming they must have some sentimental value to the admiral.

"My executive officer is vacating his quarters, Admiral," Ando said. He then addressed the sailors holding the bags. "Take the admiral's things to the executive officer's stateroom."

"No, Captain," Admiral Yamada interjected with an appreciative smile. "Tell your executive officer to remain where he is. I did not come aboard to upset the combat routine of this ship. My lieutenant and I will bunk with the other officers."

"As you wish, Admiral." Ando bowed, little surprised by the gesture. "Let me show you to your quarters."

Yamada raised a hand. "Let one of your men show the way to my flag lieutenant, Captain. I would prefer to accompany you to the bridge. The situation is grave, and we do not have much time."

Minutes later, the *Hamakaze* was underway again, and the senior officers were assembled on the navigation bridge, gathered around the plot table. They stared across at the ship's new passenger as if he were the latest *yokozuna* of sumo. They were in awe, and it was no wonder. There was not one of them that had not heard of the great Admiral Akira Yamada. Few officers in the Imperial Navy were not familiar with the admiral's famous exploits. During the war with Russia in 1905, Yamada had served as a junior officer aboard the cruiser *Kasuga* and was wounded in that great victory of all victories at Tsushima Strait, where the Russian fleet was annihilated and Japan's naval primacy established. Years later, during the Great War, when Japan's present-day enemies had been her tenuous allies, Yamada had commanded one of several Imperial Navy destroyers assigned to the Mediterranean to escort Allied ships through waters menaced by the dreaded submarines of the Central Powers. One day off Crete, after an Austro-Hungarian U-boat torpedoed and damaged a destroyer in Yamada's squadron, Yamada hunted down and sank the offending submarine, successfully dodging several torpedoes in the process. That daring act had secured his legendary status in the Imperial Navy and had made him the idol for all young cadets entering the academy for decades to come, including Ando and many of those now gazing reverently at the admiral across the plot table.

"First, I wish to commend Captain Ando for performing so admirably with so few resources for so long," Yamada began, returning Ando's bow at the compliment. "You have done an excellent job, Captain, fulfilling the role of commodore while our ships have been arriving over the past weeks, but now that the squadron is fully formed, I will assume overall command."

Ando bowed again. He had been expecting this, and his admiration for Yamada buried any instinctive urge to take offense at the demotion.

"Understand, Hitoshi, I will not interfere in the running of this ship," Yamada said in a friendlier tone now that the awkward moment was out of the way. "And I will count on you to coordinate with the other captains in carrying out my orders."

"I understand perfectly, sir," Ando replied. "And I believe I speak for every man in the squadron when I say, we consider it a great honor to be under your command. It is indeed a rare opportunity for us to serve under such a distinguished – "

"Enough with the platitudes, Hitoshi," Yamada said with a smile. "They overinflate our egos and do little to defeat our enemies."

This prompted a few snickers from the other officers and instantly lightened the mood around the table.

"Yes, Admiral." Ando bowed, pleased that time had not changed the man he had idolized during his years as a cadet.

"Let us get down to the business at hand, gentlemen," Yamada said. "Many of you are probably wondering why the high command has sent me here to take over this assemblage of valiant destroyers. You observed one of the reasons the other night when that enemy submarine slipped by. I only wish I had been able to convince the general staff to allocate more resources here sooner. If I had, the Yankee might have been sunk."

"Excuse me, Admiral," Lieutenant Kawaguchi spoke up, his manner somewhat brazen. "With all respect, sir, the enemy submarine was sunk. The *Hamakaze* scored a great victory."

Ando tensed at the brash disruption and shot a scathing glance in Kawaguchi's direction.

"Admiral, I apologize, sir," Ando said contritely. "Lieutenant Kawaguchi is —"

"Is absolutely right to correct me," Yamada interrupted with a smile. "My apologies to you, lieutenant, and to you all. Of course, the enemy submarine is likely on the bottom. I did not mean to imply otherwise. That kind of fighting spirit is precisely what we need. I encourage you to spread it to the rest of the squadron. A competitive nature will serve us well in the coming days." The admiral produced a piece of paper from his pocket and then turned to a quartermaster who was standing by with a compass and ruler. "Young man, mark these coordinates as I read them. 36 North, 130 East, cargo freighter *Hirokawa Maru*. 38 North, 131 East, cargo freighter *Nissan Maru*. 41 North, 132 East, passenger freighter *Ganges Maru*..." Yamada read off three more coordinates and ship names and then waited for the sailor to finish annotating the chart before continuing. "Observe, gentlemen, the path of destruction left by our enemy, and the reason we have assembled this squadron."

"Surely, sir, the submarine we destroyed was responsible for these sinkings," Kawaguchi said confidently. "The threat has been eliminated."

"I would have come to the same conclusion, lieutenant, had several of these attacks not occurred nearly simultaneously, separated by hundreds of miles. We are not dealing with just one submarine, gentlemen, but several — at least three, by my estimation. They entered the Sea of Japan through Tsushima Strait five weeks ago and have been prowling on our shipping ever since."

Kawaguchi spoke again, frustration evident in his voice. "If that is true, sir, then may I respectfully ask, why our destroyers are sitting here, doing nothing, when they should be in the Sea of Japan hunting the enemy?"

Ando cringed inwardly as he watched Yamada's eyes narrow at the junior officer. The young lieutenant was pushing his assertiveness too far. There was a reason for it, Ando knew, but there was no way Yamada could have known.

"Please excuse Lieutenant Kawaguchi, Admiral," Ando butted in before another word could be said. "I regret to say that his brother served on the *Nissan Maru*. The lieutenant received word of his loss a little more than a week ago, the same day we engaged the enemy sub."

A hush descended on the assembly, and Yamada's irritated expression was instantly replaced by one of sympathy.

"You have my condolences, lieutenant."

"Thank you, Admiral," Kawaguchi managed to utter. His face was red with anger and sorrow, and he was suddenly unable to meet Yamada's piercing eyes.

"I would like nothing more than to find those responsible for your brother's death, Lieutenant," Yamada said. "When this operation is over, you and I will drink to his memory, and to our enemy's destruction." The admiral then glanced around the table at Ando and the others. "But one does not catch a honeybee, gentlemen, by chasing it around the field. You wait by the hive, for there it must return. And here we will wait for our enemies to come to us."

The officers glanced at one another and nodded enthusiastically. Many of them would have agreed with Yamada even if the admiral's plan had called for sailing the fleet across the Pacific and blasting into San Francisco Bay.

"Can we be certain they will attempt an escape here, sir?" Ando asked to address the concerns of the few skeptics in the group and to pre-empt another outburst from Kawaguchi.

"Observe, gentlemen." Yamada placed a finger on the chart. "The first attack, a thousand miles to the south. The next attack, fifty miles to the northeast. Each successive attack moves farther and farther north. And these are just the sinkings. There have been many more torpedo and periscope sightings by other ships and aircraft, all indicating the devils are moving north, toward Sōya Strait – this strait, gentlemen."

"Is it possible the enemy intends to deceive us, sir?" Ando asked. "Would it not be wiser for them to go back the way they came, through Tsushima? It is a much wider passage."

"I have ships and aircraft patrolling Tsushima, as well," Yamada said, reassuringly. "But it is highly unlikely they will go that way."

"May I ask why, sir?"

"A mathematical equation, Captain. Assuming these submarines left the American base at Midway with full tanks, they would have used forty percent of their fuel just getting here, and at least another twenty percent while on station, which puts them at critical levels now.

They cannot go back the way they came, simply because they do not have the fuel to do it. They would have to fight against the Tsushima Current most of the way. It is my belief they intended to slip through the strait a week ago, and the submarine you destroyed was the first to make an attempt. No doubt, when that submarine failed to report in, the American naval command radioed the others to delay until our defenses stood down. But our defenses have only grown stronger, and now the enemy submarines have spent another week wasting precious fuel. They are left with few options."

Yamada looked around the table from one officer to another, as if to impart his own confidence and determination to them all with a single stare.

"They will attempt an escape, gentlemen. They will attempt it here, and they will attempt it within days, if not hours. We will deal with them swiftly and decisively. We will crush them with our superior numbers. We will drive them into our minefields. We will blast them from the water with our bombs and depth charges. The Americans will know that all who dare venture into our sacred sea will meet with destruction." Yamada met eyes with Kawaguchi. "We will avenge our fallen comrades and send the imperialist devils to the bottom! *Banzai!*"

"*Banzai!*" the officers shouted in unison. They were stirred to a frenzy by the admiral's passion and answered him with a fervency Ando had not seen in them since the beginning of the war. "*Banzai! Banzai!*" they cheered, again and again, Kawaguchi the loudest of them all.

After dinner that evening, Yamada and Ando retired to Ando's quarters to discuss the subsequent operation further. Splitting a bottle of *sake* between them, they spent hours poring over the charts and reviewing the assigned patrol areas of each ship in the squadron to ensure maximum coverage of the strait. At first, Yamada was as inspiring and enthusiastic as he had been on the bridge and all throughout dinner. But, as the evening stretched on, Ando began to detect holes in the admiral's confident exterior. The more they drank, the more Yamada seemed only half-interested in the work. Many times, after proposing a new idea, Ando looked up to see the admiral staring off into space, his thoughts clearly elsewhere. Initially, Ando dismissed it as the occasional absent-mindedness brought on by old age, but soon he began to realize it was not a vacant mind that plagued his former instructor, but an overburdened one. Yamada was inundated with too many thoughts, too many worries. His eyelids were heavy, the lines on his face deep. A cloud of despair hung over him, strikingly similar to that Ando had sensed in his own classmates during his last visit to Tokyo.

Ando's suspicions needed no further proof. The tide had indeed turned. Japan was losing the war.

"You have come a long way from Eta Jima, Hitoshi," Yamada said, after one such pause. "You have always been an excellent officer, and now I see you are also a splendid captain."

The comment was quite out of the blue, spoken almost like an apology, as a harsh father might make amends to his son for the discipline that had molded him into a man. It took Ando by surprise. Like all student-instructor relationships, there were times at Eta Jima when Yamada had used a heavy hand with him, but Ando had never harbored a grudge over such trivialities. Or, perhaps, it had nothing to do with their past. Perhaps, something else entirely plagued the admiral's mind. Were the recent events of the war to blame for the admiral's oddly penitent manner?

"Whatever I have become is a reflection of those who taught me," Ando said. "I can only aspire to the successes they have achieved in their careers."

The dull din of a bell sounded, signaling the changing of the watch. Footfalls padded in the passage outside. The sea breeze wafted through the open portholes carrying the voices of sailors chatting merrily about trivial things as they headed for their bunks and a few hours' sleep.

Yamada gave a half-smile as if he cherished the sounds yet was too troubled by weighty thoughts to enjoy them. His eyes drifted to the chart, and he placed a finger on the lines marking the strait. "What happens in the coming days in this 30-kilometer-wide strip of water will decide my own success or failure, Hitoshi. This will be the defining act of my career."

"Surely not, Admiral," Ando protested, trying to cheer up the old sailor. "Certainly, this operation is of great importance, but it must be considered trivial compared to the others you have overseen. You have achieved so many other —"

"If we are not successful," Yamada interrupted bluntly, "I have vowed to commit *seppuku*."

Ando gasped. The image of the two samurai swords carried by the flag lieutenant flashed in his mind as he suddenly realized their purpose. The idea of ritual suicide was nothing new. Many officers, mostly army commanders, had made similar vows in the past as a display of their commitment to the Emperor and their troops. But to make such a pledge over a task that might well produce no tangible measurement of success was madness. Personally, Ando despised the concept as an antiquated tradition that had no place in modern times. In his opinion, the macabre ritual and many others like it were leftovers of Japan's feudal past and the reason for many of the problems Japan now faced.

"Do not worry, Ando," Yamada said, apparently seeing the concern on his subordinate's face. "I do not intend to fail."

Yamada had said it confidently, but Ando was not convinced.

After Yamada had retired to his quarters, Ando downed another cup of *sake* and continued studying the chart, wondering where the enemy subs were at this very moment. With such forces at his disposal, Yamada was poised to make good on his vow. Still, Ando now felt a more significant burden on himself, that he must make no mistakes and advise Yamada properly to ensure his success.

If the enemy escaped, it would mean the death of his mentor and friend. From this moment forward, the consequences of failure would be at the forefront of his thoughts, and that was not a good thing for any captain.

Once again, Ando wished the *Hamakaze* were not here serving as the flagship for this motley flotilla but was instead with the great battle fleets far away in the South Pacific. He felt a yearning for battles in which there were clear victors and clear losers.

Was it the spirit of the samurai that imbued him with such longings? After all these years, he was still his teacher's pupil – and he always would be.

# 4

# NOT ACCORDING TO PLAN

*Aleutian Islands*

*USS Aeneid*

*Drip, drip, drip…*

The drops pattered into a bucket on the deck stirring Lieutenant Commander Henry Weston awake. He never really did sleep at sea, but not because of the annoying drip coming from the loose joint on the pipe running through his stateroom – the joint that always seemed to drip faster whenever the ship was leaning to starboard. Nor because of the uncomfortable 72-inch by 30-inch bunk in which he lay, the best accommodations on the ship. He never could sleep at sea because this was *his* ship, and he was the captain.

Rolling over, Weston glanced at the course and depth repeaters mounted on the bulkhead.

Periscope depth. That was normal.

Course changing slowly to the right. That was not in itself alarming. That would explain the slight tilt of the deck.

Speed, seven knots. That was not normal. She should be crawling along at no more than four knots, a silent shadow lurking in the frigid waters where the North Pacific met the Bering Sea.

A check of the clock on the bulkhead confirmed Weston's suspicions. The turn was early by at least twenty minutes.

Something was wrong.

The expected knock sounded at the door to his stateroom, and the curtain was drawn aside without waiting for an answer.

"Captain." A head poked into the darkened room, the bristles of a closely cropped neckline lit by the red light in the passageway beyond. "Excuse me, sir. The XO requests you come to the conning tower ASAP."

Weston had already sat up. He eagerly received a steaming cup of coffee from the sailor and downed several gulps of the potent mixture. "Thanks, Romero. Trouble?"

"The XO sees lights on the shore. It looks like the distress signal, sir."

"I'll be right up."

Romero nodded, took the half-drained cup, and left the room. As Weston shook himself awake, willing the caffeine to revive him, he tried to get his bearings.

How long had it been since their passengers had debarked? Only six hours? It seemed like weeks ago. The ship seemed so quiet now.

Stepping out into the long passageway running between the officers' staterooms, Weston heard heavy snoring emanating from the darkened cavities on either side. Most men who were not on watch were in the rack, getting some much-needed rest after the strain of the last forty-eight hours. That was not the case with the ship's yeoman who could be heard typing away in his office at the far end of the passage, generating one report after another.

Weston did not head aft immediately. More out of instinct than anything else, he first poked his head through the watertight door just a few steps forward and glanced inside the torpedo room. Even now, he had trouble adjusting to the modifications. Where he would typically see rack upon rack of twenty-foot-long torpedoes, there were now dozens of wood and canvas bunks, stacked four-high and crammed into tight rows. A similar set of beds filled the after torpedo room as well. The extra accommodations were only temporary, having been added just before the submarine left San Diego, almost two weeks ago. Now the bunks were empty, their occupants no longer aboard. The room seemed barren with only the regular watch section and a few dozing off-watch sailors. A cluster of torpedomen lounged near the bronze torpedo tube doors at the distant end of the room, conversing quietly. Weston gave them an acknowledging nod before ducking out again and heading back down the passage to the control room.

Condensation beaded on the bulkheads. The dehumidifiers were acting up again. Grounds had been abundant. The electricians were working overtime to isolate them before they caused a fire. Such problems were especially irritating to Weston since the submarine had only recently undergone a four-month modernization at the Mare Island naval shipyard, during which nearly everything from the diesel engines to the galley stove had been replaced.

*They could make her over all they wanted to,* Weston thought with a smile, *but she was still an old girl.*

When the *USS Aeneid* was christened back in 1927, most of her present-day crew had been in grammar school. She was one of a forgotten class of oddball submarines, the V-boats, made to answer the growing need for long-range submarine cruisers that could operate for extended periods across the vast Pacific should the U.S. ever find itself in conflict with the increasing power in the Far East. The *Aeneid* was built during the latter stages of the V-Boat project and was designed to accommodate larger quantities of fuel, torpedoes, mines, and ammunition than any of her predecessors. She was enormous, dwarfing all previous and succeeding U.S. submarine classes. Even now, she was larger than the new boats coming off the docks, displacing nearly twice the tonnage of the new Gato-Class, wider by the height of a man, and longer by sixty feet. She had been designed with only six torpedo tubes, four forward and two aft, but she had gained four more during her recent interval in the yards — two external tubes forward and two aft, along with external storage for additional torpedoes, and a new torpedo data computer mounted in the conning tower.

Weston remembered how his crew had beamed with pride at the upgrades, and how Gallagher, the chief of the boat, had boasted that *Aeneid* "could now shoot torpedoes as good as any boat in the fleet." Their spirits had just as quickly deflated when they had learned that, for their first mission out of the yards, their brand-new external storage tubes would not be used for torpedoes, but for deflated rafts and equipment. It seemed the *Aeneid* had been modernized only to fall back into the same odd jobs she had been tasked with before, ferrying raiders and commandos, while the fleet boats were off sinking enemy ships by the dozen.

With the war in its second year, word had already made it around the submarine fleet to avoid the V-boats at all costs. Every officer angling to attain command someday pulled every string he could to ensure he was not assigned to a V-boat, and the sailors avoided them like plague ships.

Having grown up in Royal Oak, Michigan, Weston often likened commanding the *Aeneid* to the plight of a hockey coach who must give one of his players a shortened stick and then try to convince that player he was still a vital part of the team. Commanding such a ship was a careful balancing act between keeping up crew morale and trying to carry out each mission with enthusiasm.

Weston entered the hushed control room which was bathed in the same red night lighting as the passageway. The lieutenant and sailors at the diving station glanced at him before returning their attention to the gauges and the giant wheels before them. Stopping at the chart table, Weston placed a finger on the pencil mark just left by the quartermaster. The chart displayed the *Aeneid's* current position in the waters southwest of an island roughly shaped like an armadillo with a saddle on its back.

"How far are we from the shore?" Weston asked.

"Six thousand yards, Captain," the quartermaster answered after measuring off the distance with a pair of dividers. "Two thousand yards from the 30-fathom curve." He pointed to a small cluster of pencil lines that intersected at a spot near the coast. "These are the bearings the XO's been passing us. That light's coming from the shore, sir, near the landing beach."

After a brief study of the chart, Weston grabbed the ladder rungs. "Very well. I'm heading up."

In the cramped conning tower, one level above, Weston was greeted by Lieutenant George Townsend, the *Aeneid's* executive officer, who immediately stood aside so that his captain could take the periscope handles. All of the normal watchstanders were there. Kendrich, the stocky steersman from Philly. Finkelman, the sound operator, a skeleton-thin farm boy from Ohio.

Reynolds, the periscope assistant, a sun-tanned, all-state track star from Los Angeles. They were the best at their jobs — the first string, so to speak. They were not supposed to be on watch with this section, and Weston suspected they had volunteered to take their posts when the buzz about the lights made its way around the ship.

There was also another man in the conning tower, a young man in his mid-twenties with close-cropped hair, squeezed into the back corner and trying to stay out of the way. He fidgeted periodically on one foot. His other foot was shoeless and wrapped in a bandage. The young man's trim-cut, olive drab army combat uniform seemed out of place among the motley attire of the sailors, yet he appeared more interested in what was going on in the world above than anyone else in the room.

"What's the status, XO?" Weston said to Townsend as he pressed his face to the eyepiece. In his first two sweeps around the azimuth, he saw only blackness. Even with the red lighting, it would take several seconds before his eyes adjusted to the dark.

"We hold a light, bearing zero five zero, skipper," Townsend replied only inches away from his ear. "And gun flashes further inshore."

"Gun flashes?" Weston raised an eyebrow.

"Yes, sir. We think it's only small arms fire, but there's been a lot of it. The bearing to that light puts it on the beach, right where our boys landed. It's blinking two short, two long, followed by three short, three long."

"Damn."

"Yes, sir."

"How long until sunrise?"

"Two hours, ten minutes."

After taking his face away from the lens long enough to align the periscope with the right bearing, Weston found the light.

"Yes, I see it now."

It was flashing consistently, a small pinprick of light against a field of black. It repeated the same pattern over and over again, eliminating any possibility it was some mindless soldier waving a flashlight in the direction of the sea. It was the distress signal. There was no doubt about it. It meant the mission was a failure. More than that, it suggested the mission might very quickly turn into a disaster.

With his eyes now adjusted, Weston could see the dimmer flashes inshore, as well. They were haphazard, sometimes appearing in many places at once, sudden flurries followed by long intervals of nothing.

"Those gun flashes are in the hills just beyond the beach, XO?"

"Yes, Captain. They've been getting closer to the shore."

Weston did not have to take his face away from the scope to see the dismay on Townsend's face. It was evident in his voice. The gun flashes and the distress call portended doom for the *Aeneid's* recently debarked passengers.

Six hours ago, more than one hundred U. S. Army scouts had debarked from *Aeneid's* awash decks aboard rubber rafts loaded down with weaponry, provisions, explosives, and radio equipment of every kind. It had been a grueling, overcrowded, journey to get them here – ten days from San Diego to American-held Dutch Harbor to top off fuel tanks, then three more tumultuous days crossing the Bering Sea tossed by a maelstrom fiercer than any experienced by most of the older sailors. The *Aeneid* now sat just off the Japanese-held island of Attu, a thirty-mile-wide, volcanic wasteland, devoid of trees, and known to contain an airstrip and harbor from which enemy aircraft and ships could sortie at any moment. Weston had orders to remain on station until he received either an *all-clear* signal from the scouts ashore or the signal to *abort* – and he had just received the latter.

He knew those twinkling lights ashore represented hundreds of bullets slicing through the night air. They meant one hundred American boys were likely in serious trouble, and while Weston knew that was part of the reason for his executive officer's apprehension, he knew there was a personal element to it as well. Townsend had a close friend somewhere amidst that storm of flying lead. Major Nash, the hard-nosed army officer leading the scouts ashore, was like a brother to Townsend, both having grown up in the same rural Virginia town. Pure coincidence had reunited them when Nash and his scouts had reported aboard the *Aeneid* for this mission. At every pause in the days of vigorous training around San Diego, and the subsequent cruise to the Bering Sea, the two old chums had reminisced about everything from football games to former girlfriends, subjecting Weston and the rest of the *Aeneid's* officers to an endless stream of rip-roaring stories and private jokes during the wardroom meals.

Weston did not have to see Townsend's face to know his executive officer was more than a little concerned – and he was not the only one.

Two steps away, in the back corner of the confined compartment, the young army officer with the bandaged foot seemed even more wrenched with apprehension, staring down at the deck plates, his fists balled in frustration.

"Not according to plan, is it, Lieutenant MacCullen?" Weston asked him.

"No, sir," the army first lieutenant replied, his jaw clenched tightly. Clearly, he wished he was ashore with his comrades, facing whatever they were facing, but he had not been allowed to accompany the landing.

The situation ashore was tenuous, and there was no telling what impact it would have on the overall operation, of which the scouts were only a small, preliminary part. One year ago, the Japanese had seized Attu during their failed Midway campaign as part of a feint meant to draw the American carrier forces north. Now, the small, central Aleutian island was about to change hands again. Two days behind the *Aeneid*, beating their way westward through white-capped seas, was a fleet of lumbering transports carrying ten thousand troops of the U.S. 7th Infantry Division. If all went as planned, the invasion force would land on Attu, wipe out the enemy garrison there, and secure the airfield and harbor.

The operation had been a closely guarded secret, kept even from the troops in the transports who, until recently, thought themselves headed for combat in the sweltering jungles of the South Pacific. The mission of the *Aeneid* and her army passengers was the first phase of the operation. The company of scouts was to land unnoticed on the deserted southwest side of Attu three nights before the main invasion force arrived, and this they had done without a hitch. From there, the scouts were supposed to have ventured into the island's interior, setting up positions in the mountains to deny the high ground to the retreating Japanese come D-Day.

But something had gone terribly wrong.

"Talk to me, Lieutenant MacCullen," Weston said sternly. "I need to know what's going on. Why do I see gunfire? Your team was supposed to avoid engaging the enemy and hide out in the mountains until D-Day."

"That's right, sir," MacCullen confirmed with a measure of hesitation. "I don't know what could have happened. Maybe they came across a Jap patrol."

Clearly, there was an inner turmoil going on inside MacCullen's mind. Weston could read the young army officer's face as easily as he could a diesel engine technical manual. It was apparent he was suffering from a watershed of guilt. Weston had seen it before in his own peers, other submariners who had received transfer orders only just before their boats left on fatal patrols – blind strokes of luck that had saved them from dying with their shipmates.

"They may have run into more than they bargained for, sir," Townsend interjected suddenly. "Major Nash expressed some concerns with me privately before he left. He thought the Japs had two or three thousand troops on that island, twice the official estimate. It wouldn't be the first time intelligence miscalculated enemy strength. If that's the case, we have no time to lose."

Weston nodded, detecting the increased anxiety in Townsend's voice. No matter how well his executive officer tried to remain professional and objective, there was no question he was worried about his friend on Attu. Weston could feel Townsend's eyes watching him expectantly, as he continued watching the dark shore . If Major Nash and his scouts had indeed run into more trouble than they could handle, considerations had been made for such an event. Clearly, Townsend wanted to execute the contingency plan immediately, but there were other things Weston had to consider, like the safety of a 2,700-ton submarine and her eighty-eight-man crew.

He had to be sure.

As he watched the shore through the small lens, waiting for one final confirmation, Townsend all but fidgeted beside him. Then, after what seemed an interminable wait, he finally saw it again – the distress signal, flashing for the third time. There could be no doubt now as to its authenticity.

"Sound general quarters," Weston commanded, much to Townsend's visible relief. "Prepare to battle surface!"

# 5

# THE RETREAT

The fourteen-bell gong rang throughout the *Aeneid*. The narrow passages, barely wide enough for two men to squeeze past each other, came alive with sailors rushing forward and aft. Within two minutes, all hands were at their stations.

"Battle surface!" Weston ordered as he donned a heavy bridge coat, gloves, and a woolen cap.

Compressed air blew the ballast tanks dry, propelling the *Aeneid* to the surface in a matter of seconds. Weston was the first up the ladder, cracking open the hatch and gaining the bridge with white water still streaming from the scuppers. He was followed by a train of men, some wearing binoculars, some bearing freshly oiled machine guns and jingling belts of ammunition. More men appeared on the darkened decks below. They scurried fore and aft and immediately began preparing the submarine's unique surface arsenal for battle.

The *Aeneid* had been built at a time when the big-gunned ships, not aircraft carriers, were considered the kings of the sea, and its peculiar design was a result of that thinking. Where most subs had only a single main deck topside, the *Aeneid's* conning tower was bracketed fore and aft by a second, elevated deck upon which were mounted two cruiser-quality guns, one forward and one aft. They were large guns for a submarine, each situated on an exposed wet mount, each measuring a caliber of six-inches, and each capable of throwing a 106-pound shell nearly thirteen miles. They would have been the envy of any destroyer captain – of the First World War. Like much of the navy's arsenal at the outbreak of hostilities, the *Aeneid's* big guns were ideal for fighting the last great war at sea but bordered on useless in the present war. There were, however, a few occasions when a submarine had a use for such heavy artillery – this being one of them.

As the white seas crashed against the hull, two dozen gunners worked feverishly removing the watertight plugs and restraining brackets to prepare the big guns for battle. A line of men stood by to receive the giant shells and forty-pound bags of gunpowder lifted from the magazine two decks below by hydraulic ammunition hoists. On each gun, men rapidly spun the azimuth and elevation training hand-wheels as if competing to win a prize at a state fair. Within seconds, both twenty-six-foot-long barrels were angled over the port side and elevated to point toward the darkened shore.

"Both gun mounts ready, Captain," a lieutenant junior grade reported from the darkness behind Weston. A sailor wearing a phone headset stood beside him.

"Very well, Mister Berry. Load with high-capacity and stand by."

The light signal on the beach was still there, still flashing the same distress call. It was much easier to see now from the higher elevation of the *Aeneid's* bridge. The darkened coastline was alive with gun flashes, some of the reports now audible above the icy wind. With Townsend on the plot providing recommended course corrections and fathometer updates, Weston conned the ship to a position just two miles away from the shore.

"What's the depth here, XO?" Weston said into the intercom.

"One hundred sixty feet beneath the keel, Captain," came the reply over the speaker.

"All stop."

The big submarine's momentum began to fall off rapidly as she drifted parallel to the coast. Weston noticed MacCullen fidgeting a few paces away as he trained his binoculars on the distant land battle. The army lieutenant was doing little to favor his bandaged foot.

The light signal on the beach continued unabated.

"Give them the reply, Yates," Weston ordered a gray-haired sailor who was in the process of mounting a searchlight he had just hauled up through the hatch.

"Aye, aye, sir," Yates replied with a toothy grin. "It'll be flashing in no time."

Weston allowed a small smile. Petty Officer Yates, the quartermaster of the watch, always approached any situation, no matter how dire, with a measure of joviality.

Often referred to as Old Yates by his shipmates, the middle-aged sailor had been in the navy longer than any other man aboard, Weston included. He was tough as nails and salty as Davy Jones. A sordid history of barroom brawls and other more notorious shore leave infractions had kept him from ever being promoted up to the goat's locker, but every sailor on the ship regarded him with something akin to reverence.

Within moments, Yates had the light powered and ready for operation. Training it toward the beach, he cranked on the shutter to send the reciprocal code, informing those ashore that the *Aeneid* was prepared to pick them up.

"Keep sending it, Yates."

"Aye, sir."

Townsend appeared on the bridge. He had left his plot table in the conning tower clearly out of concern for his friend ashore.

"Mister Monk has taken over for me on the plot, Captain," Townsend said, after a questioning glance from Weston. Upon receiving an approving nod,

Townsend commented, "No telling how many of our boys are out there. They've probably got wounded with them. It'll take some time to pull their way past the surf."

"I'll give them time to reach us, XO," Weston said reassuringly.

"We could move in closer, sir."

Weston raised his eyebrows, somewhat surprised at the suggestion. More often than not, Townsend was the one to reign in his ambitious ideas.

"Our last star fix is over twenty-four hours old, XO. We're working on a DR track based on land fixes taken several hours ago. And I'm not sure how good those fixes were since our charts of these islands aren't exactly what I would call reliable. If we end up on the rocks, the Japs can add a submarine to their bag as well as a company of Army scouts. I'm sorry, George. We can't take the risk."

Townsend nodded dismally and turned his gaze back to the shoreline. MacCullen, too, seemed disappointed at Weston's decision, but the army officer said nothing. This was Weston's boat, after all – his crew, his men.

"Well, if anyone can make that pull, Major Nash can," Townsend said with a sigh, glancing at MacCullen as if to bolster the lieutenant's dwindling hopes and his own.

Weston knew Townsend understood. Over the weeks preparing for this operation, they had both familiarized themselves with the lessons learned from last year's operation in the Marshalls. In that operation, *Aeneid's* sisters *Argonaut* and *Nautilus* had ferried marine commandos to raid Japanese-held Makin Island, hoping to draw Japanese forces away from the Solomons before the invasion of Guadalcanal. While the Japanese garrison on Makin was largely destroyed, the marine raiders only narrowly escaped. The two submarines, waiting in clear shallow waters to pick up the marines, were forced under by several enemy air attacks, any one of which could have turned the entire operation into a disaster.

"That light on the beach has stopped, Captain," Yates reported as he continued to flap the shutter on his lamp.

"Very well. Keep flashing the signal. We've got to give them something to steer by."

Presumably, the absence of the light signal meant no one was left on the beach to send it. Whether that was because the scouts were now loaded aboard their rafts and paddling out to sea, or they were all dead, there was no way of knowing. Indeed, someone was still ashore, because the gun flashes had not ceased in the hills beyond. If anything, they had increased in intensity.

The men on the *Aeneid* waited in silence, those on the guns standing frigid at their exposed stations. It began to snow again, as it had off and on all night. Thick flakes stuck to the lens of Weston's binoculars momentarily blurring his vision. It left him wondering how well the soldiers in the rafts could see Yates's flashing signal lamp. The lamp was the only beacon guiding them to their salvation, and it was woefully inadequate amid this blinding snowstorm. It would be nearly impossible to make out from a low rubber raft bobbing between wave crests.

"Open your shutter, Yates," Weston said. "Forget about the signal. I want a constant beam sweeping the ocean to port. Search for them. We've got to guide them home."

"Aye, aye, sir," Yates replied somewhat incredulously, but he did not hesitate to switch the lever to the fully open position. Instantly, the signal lamp was transformed into a search lamp, projecting a defined cone of light through the falling snow.

"Thank you, sir," Townsend said lowly.

"Don't thank me just yet. The Japs will be watching, too. We're sitting ducks out here."

The light completed a dozen long sweeps across the dark waters off the port side. No rubber rafts fell under its beam, but it certainly alerted the enemy ashore. Within minutes, shells were falling into the black waves around the *Aeneid*, prompting every man on the bridge to instinctively duck behind the fairwater. The detonations were too small to have come from naval guns or fixed emplacements. Even in the snowstorm, muzzle flashes were visible in several spots just inland from the beach. The shells were not landing close to the *Aeneid* yet, but it would not be long before the enemy gunners corrected their aim and found the range.

"Army light artillery. Probably 75-millimeter field guns," Weston surmised out loud. He turned to the naval lieutenant beside him. "Well, Mister Berry, this will be your first combat as the ship's gunnery officer. Are your men up to it?"

"Yes, Captain," Berry answered confidently.

"Your targets are those flashes on the shoreline. Knock 'em out or make them take cover. Commence firing when ready."

"Aye, aye, sir."

"All hands," Weston keyed the 1MC circuit to alert the compartments below. "Engaging with main batteries to port."

Berry murmured a few words to his assistant who quickly relayed the orders to the gun decks, and the *Aeneid's* batteries went into action.

*Ka-blam!*

The forward gun fired, its elevated barrel spewing a fiery tongue of yellow flame and sending a shudder through the deck plates. The tracer round floated away into the darkness like a glowing orb. Berry watched the fall of the shot and then passed adjustment orders to the gun captains below. This process repeated several times until, finally, when the correct range had been ascertained, Berry ordered the gun crews to fire for effect. Now, both guns began shooting in succession, one gun erupting every few seconds. Explosions dotted the shoreline as the high explosive, hundred-pound shells detonated one after another. The brief flashes of light revealed columns of smoke rising high into the air where fires burned ferociously on the beach. At first, Weston thought some of Berry's rounds might have found their mark but then realized the flames were too close to the shore and were likely coming from the scuttled remnants of the scouts' equipment.

Yates continued to sweep the searching beam back and forth, finding nothing but dark curling surf. Shells continued to land around the *Aeneid*, one coming close enough to douse the forward gun crew with the icy sea.

"Where the devil are they?" Townsend said to no one in particular, frustration evident in his voice.

But, then, one of the lookouts sang out from the periscope shears above.

"There they are, sir! Two hundred yards off the port bow!"

Every man's eyes converged on the spot as a black, slickened object emerged from the darkness. Under the searchlight, they could clearly see four men rowing, fighting desperately against the waves to steer the raft toward the *Aeneid*.

Townsend was already on his way to the main deck, nearly slipping on the snow-covered ladder rungs as he shouted encouragement to the weary paddlers, his calls lost in the din of the guns.

"Cease firing, Mister Berry," Weston said. "We don't want to hit our own people."

The guns fell silent, and Weston watched the main deck up forward as Townsend shuffled along the slick wooden surface leading a cluster of sailors bearing coiled lines. As the sporadic fire from the shore continued, some shells landing dangerously close to the approaching raft, Weston began to consider what must be done now as the company of beaten soldiers returned. Space must be prepared for the wounded. The ship's corpsman would likely have dozens on his hands, some of which were bound to be severe. The scouts had carted their own medical supplies ashore, which meant the ship's woefully inadequate supplies would be stretched thin. The thousands of pounds of water that had been pumped into the variable ballast tanks to compensate for the departure of one hundred men and their equipment would have to be pumped back to the sea to keep the *Aeneid* trimmed for diving.

The morbid thought suddenly occurred to Weston that the compensation would not be precisely equivalent since some of the scouts were probably dead and left behind on Attu. But, how many?

"Mister Hudson." Weston keyed the intercom circuit to talk to the ship's diving officer in the control room, two decks below. "Line up to pump from auxiliaries to sea. Stand by for an estimated weight."

"Already lined up and pumping, Captain," came the reply.

Weston smiled. Hudson was proficient at his job.

Bringing the binoculars to his face again, Weston scanned the circle of ocean lit by the searchlight. Still, he saw only one raft rowing toward the *Aeneid* where he had expected at least a dozen by now. Was this one raft so far ahead of the others? Or was it...

A cold feeling crept up Weston's spine as he watched the weighted lines tossed to the approaching raft. The first two lines were out of reach, but the third fell close enough for one of the men in the raft to grab it and tie off. With a half-dozen of the *Aeneid's* sailors pulling on the other end of the line, the boat began to move much more swiftly through the waves. As the raft finally brushed up against the submarine's side, night turned into day. The sea all around was suddenly lit up, the barrels of the guns casting long shadows upon the green water. High above, a brilliant light descended slowly, illuminating the falling snowflakes and the black and gray hull as if the *Aeneid* were on display inside a giant snow globe.

"Damn!" Weston cursed.

The source of the light was an incandescent flare from an enemy star shell, its slow descent retarded by a parachute. Under the flickering white light, Weston saw the men in the raft negotiate the Jacobs ladder, the able ones first passing the wounded to the waiting hands on the deck, before climbing the ladder themselves and casting the raft adrift. As the drenched evacuees were bundled below by Townsend and his men, Weston counted nine in total – nine scouts out of the one hundred six landed on Attu.

"Did you see the major?" Weston asked MacCullen who had been watching the events below closely but who had remained silent.

"No, sir," MacCullen replied, his tone not quite as somber as Weston might have expected. The army lieutenant appeared to be fixed in thought, perhaps in a mild state of shock.

On the deck below, Weston saw Townsend converse briefly with one of the survivors, then look up at the bridge to meet his gaze. Even in the fading light of the flare, the despondent expression on the executive officer's face was evident. A single shake of Townsend's head confirmed Weston's worst fears.

There would be no more survivors coming from the shore.

"Permission to go below, sir," MacCullen said, snapping out of his malaise as if suddenly realizing that he was perhaps the only officer remaining in his unit and that he must see to the surviving scouts.

"Granted."

The lieutenant had just disappeared down the hatch when a shell buzzed over the bridge, close enough for Weston to feel it part the air. Every man ducked instinctively.

"Should we return fire, Captain?" Berry asked expectantly.

"No," Weston said, mentally putting the weight of the heavy losses in its proper place. He still had a ship to get out of harm's way. "Secure the guns. Secure the deck. Prepare to dive."

As the gun barrels were realigned with the hull and the men on deck scrambled below, Weston looked back at the flickering coastline, pondering the number of American soldiers, either dead, wounded or captured, that he was leaving behind.

The mission was a total failure.

"Deck secured, sir," Berry reported. "All hands below."

Weston keyed the microphone. "All ahead full. Right full rudder. Steady two two five."

The *Aeneid's* bow crashed through the waves as she came over to the new heading. Water streamed over the deck that had been covered with men only minutes before. Weston was steering her toward the deeper water away from the shore, but the enemy had not yet abandoned their efforts to sink her. Another star shell appeared overhead, lighting up the sea again, but there was something different about this one. It seemed much more powerful, more luminous, as if it had come from a different source.

Directing his binoculars to the southeast. Weston spied the promontory masking the southern side of Attu from view. The Japanese had a port and an airstrip there. If danger were to come from anywhere, it would come from that quarter.

"Man the SJ radar," he ordered. "Perform a full sweep. Focus your search off the port beam."

The mission orders had called for complete radio silence around Attu. That meant no transmissions from the radar, the concern being that the Japanese might have listening posts that could use the signals to triangulate the *Aeneid's* location. Triangulation was highly unlikely with the directional SJ surface search radar, but those had been the orders. Now that the Japanese were apparently alerted to the *Aeneid's* presence, there was no sense in keeping the best set of eyes on the bench.

The radar mast squeaked in its housing as it began to rotate, controlled by the radar operator down in the conning tower who would be dialing in voltages and staring at the circular oscilloscope trying to discern the sources of the different spikes displayed. The heavy snow and the nearby landmass were surely not helping.

But Weston did not have to wait for the report from the radar operator. His suspicions about the new star shell were abruptly confirmed when two geysers appeared less than one hundred yards off the port beam – large ones. One of the impacts spawned a ricochet that bounded half the distance to the *Aeneid's* hull and then struck the water again, creating another geyser almost half as high as the first. The ensuing detonations were ear-shattering. These projectiles were substantially bigger than the previous ones. They had not come from light field artillery.

They had come from naval guns.

"Bridge, SJ radar contact bearing one one five, range ten thousand yards, closing rapidly!" the radar operator's voice squawked over the speaker.

"Lookouts below!" Weston ordered. "Clear the bridge! All ahead flank! Diving officer, give me a sounding!"

Out in that black night, some five miles away, was an enemy warship closing on the *Aeneid's* position. Their only chance was to get deep and hide.

After a long pause that seemed like an eternity, Hudson's voice came over the speaker. "Sounding twenty fathoms, sir!"

*Damn!* Weston cursed inwardly. They had driven over a shallow spot. No wonder Hudson had taken so long reporting back. He had probably taken two or three soundings just to confirm the unwelcome readings. There was less water beneath the keel than the *Aeneid* was long. But there was no time. It would have to do.

"Crash dive!" Weston said as the last lookout brushed past him. After pulling the diving klaxon twice, Weston dropped down the hatch, pulling the hatch shut behind him just as the thunderclap of another explosion split the air outside.

# 6

# CRASH DIVE

On a submarine as old and as cumbersome as the *Aeneid, crash dive* was a relative term. A long interval of silent waiting passed as every man in the conning tower watched the needle on the depth gauge teeter back and forth between fourteen and eighteen feet as the submarine refused to go under.

Keeping the old boat in trim was a never-ending challenge, and Weston began to wonder if Hudson had overcompensated by pumping too much water off the ship. He could hear the diving officer's angry voice in the control room below, demanding why it was taking so long to flood several thousand pounds of water into the variable ballast tanks.

Another explosion smacked the sea nearby, jerking the hull to one side. Perhaps it was the shockwave of the enemy shell that finally got the *Aeneid* started on her downward journey because the depth gauge suddenly began to move.

"Forty feet..." Hudson announced triumphantly. "Forty-five ...fifty..."

The needle moved faster as the big submarine passed sixty, then seventy feet, and every man breathed a sigh of relief with the comforting knowledge that the masts were now beneath the waves.

"Level off at one hundred feet," Weston called down to the control room.

That would leave barely twenty feet between the keel and the sea bed, but, Weston figured, if the *Aeneid* continued on a southeasterly course, away from Attu's coast, the water should only get deeper.

Townsend ascended the ladder into the conning tower and took his position at the plot table, his face expressionless. Weston shot him an inquisitive glance.

"They ran into an ambush, sir," Townsend reported bitterly. "They were heavily outnumbered and outgunned." He paused, took a breath, and then added soberly, "Major Nash is dead. Killed by a Jap sniper several hours ago. Only a few scouts made it back to the beach. The rest are either dead or got separated and cut off. We brought nine men aboard. One has already died of his wounds. Two more are serious. The rest are shaken up. Sergeant Greathouse is the highest-ranking survivor."

The compartment was starkly silent as each man absorbed the news. They had spent the last several weeks with those commandos, living literally on top of one another, closer than most siblings would ever want to get. They had grudgingly grown accustomed to those smiling, laughing, confident soldiers. Now, nearly every one of the scouts was gone – dead on Attu.

Weston placed a consoling hand on Townsend's shoulder. "I'm sorry, XO." Weston leaned in and spoke in a near whisper. "I'll understand if you want to send Lieutenant Monk up to take your place."

"Not a chance, Captain," Townsend replied determinedly.

"High-speed screws, Captain," Finkelman, the sound operator, reported. "Sounds like a destroyer. Bearing one one five. Getting louder. Drifting slightly to the right."

"How far to good water, XO?"

"There's a sharp drop-off two miles to the south, sir." Townsend measured the distance on the chart with a pair of dividers. "At six knots, we can be there in twenty minutes. Recommend course one eight five."

"Very well. Steersman, come left to one eight five. All ahead standard."

Evasive maneuvering against a prowling destroyer required a measure of dash, of which the *Aeneid* had none. With a maximum submerged speed of seven knots, which would quickly deplete her batteries, she had but one option, and that was to drive straight for deep water and hope for the best.

As the destroyer drew closer, Weston risked ordering the submarine a few feet deeper, using only the dead reckoning indicator position and the depth markings on the chart. He did not dare use the fathometer, lest the sound pulse be detected by the listening destroyer.

When the *Aeneid* was half-way to the line penciled onto Townsend's chart, a faint, eerie whine echoed outside the hull, as if some far-off mermaid were playing an underwater flute. Every man in the room exchanged anxious looks.

"Echo-ranging, Captain," Finkelman confirmed their fears. "The tin can's slowed. He's looking for us. Bearing one two five, still drifting to the right."

In such shallow water, it would not be difficult to find the *Aeneid's* three-hundred-seventy-foot steel hull. If Weston turned her away from the destroyer, he might succeed in presenting a narrower aspect to the pinging transducer, but he would also be steering away from the deep water that was their only chance of escape. A torpedo shot was out of the question. Any warship alerted to the presence of a submarine would be expecting such an attempt and would frequently change its course and speed to avoid it.

The sonic pulses continued probing the depths as the *Aeneid* crawled along at a snail's pace, and her crew prayed for a miracle.

Then, the dreaded report came.

"Destroyer's shifted to high frequency, sir. Bearing one four zero. Constant bearing now. I think she's found us."

Weston picked up the second set of headphones at the sound panel and put one speaker to his ear. The *swish-swish-swish* of the destroyer's screws and the pinging sonar pulses were steady and clear. Finkelman did not even have to adjust the direction of his hydrophone to remain focused on the noise, its source was so close. It was only a few hundred yards away and heading straight for the *Aeneid*.

"Right full rudder!"

As the steersman acknowledged, Weston crossed to the plot table. "How deep can we go, XO?"

"We're pushing it now, sir. I estimate only thirty feet beneath the keel. And we can't put her on the bottom."

The tactic of setting the boat down on the sea floor such that the *Aeneid's* sonar return would blend in with everything around it was not an option in these waters. The volcanic island of Attu was surrounded by an infinite number of submerged rock formations, many uncharted, any one of which might tear a hole in the *Aeneid's* keel as she attempted such a maneuver.

"Steady on two five zero. We'll head back south once she's passed over us."

That was optimistic, and everyone knew it, including Weston. It was highly unlikely the destroyer would drive over them without leaving a few souvenirs.

"Pinging's stopped, Captain. She's speeding up. She's right on top of us!"

It was standard procedure for a destroyer to increase speed before dropping depth charges to prevent getting caught in the subsequent explosions, especially if the charges were set to go off shallow.

"Multiple splashes, sir."

"Pass the word to all compartments. Brace for depth charge attack."

Time seemed to run slower as all hands waited out the descent of the hurtling barrels, each packed with a three-hundred-pound explosive charge. A flurry of clicking noises sounded outside the hull, the sound of the sinister weapons' arming mechanisms.

"God help us," uttered someone down in the control room.

The next instant, the *Aeneid* was rocked by half a dozen massive detonations.

# 7

# LIVES AT STAKE

## *Pearl Harbor, Hawaii*

The black U.S Navy staff car drove along the jetty where a half dozen submarines sat at their moorings. A tangle of hoses, electrical cables, and scaffolding left nearly nothing of the hulls discernible as repair crews worked feverishly to get the hunters ready for sea again. The car rolled to a stop outside the headquarters building for Commander Submarines Pacific Fleet. The passenger door opened, and Admiral Giles exited toting a satchel in one hand. He walked briskly up the steps, mindlessly returning the salutes of the sailors and officers passing by as he shook off the aches from the six-hour flight from Midway.

Purposefully avoiding engaging any acquaintances in conversation, he made his way directly to the office of the chief of staff, for he knew his plan would have a better chance of approval if he convinced ComSubPac's right-hand man rather than going to the submarine admiral himself. Besides, he was sure ComSubPac would refuse to see him, anyway, and would likely order the marine sentries to throw him out. The chief of staff, on the other hand, was a different story, an old associate of Giles's — not so much an old friend as one who owed him a favor for an incident earlier in their careers.

"Good morning, Sam," Giles said robustly as he stood in the door frame of the chief of staff's office. The stars on Giles's collar had gotten him past the yeoman in the antechamber without any questions.

Captain Samuel Kent looked up from his desk, at first annoyed at the unexpected intrusion, then visibly disturbed when he recognized it was Giles.

"Well, Admiral Giles, this is an unexpected pleasure," Kent said without a trace of conviction. Wearing a forced smile, he rose from his chair but did not bother to come around the desk to greet Giles.

"May I sit?" Giles asked after shaking Kent's hand across the desk.

"Actually, Admiral," Kent checked his watch, "I have an important meeting with the shipyard supervisor in precisely – "

"It will take only a minute, Sam." Giles preempted the expected brushoff. "And I'm sure you can spare just a minute for an old shipmate."

Kent met eyes with him. The meaning was clear. The card Giles held over him, the card from their past, was being played right now.

"Alright, Admiral," Kent sighed. "But I can only spare five minutes."

"Good enough."

The chief of staff now came out from behind the desk, walked over to the open door, glanced outside, and then closed it, as if he did not wish to be seen meeting with Giles. Clearly, Giles was persona non grata around here.

"What do you need this time, Teddy?" Kent said when the two were again facing each other over the desk.

"I want you to propose a plan to the admiral for me, regarding *Wolfpack 351*."

"No, no, no, Teddy." Kent shook his head. "I'm afraid that's out of the question."

"Why?"

"You have to ask? One fleet submarine beat to hell, and three more trapped in the Sea of Japan. We've got a major disaster on our hands, Teddy, thanks to you. I'm still at a loss as to how you convinced the old man to go along with this whole operation in the first place. I was against it from the start."

Giles smiled. That had required a little behind-the-scenes manipulation, as well, he mused. Kent was not the only one he had known for a very long time. Having been in the service for nearly three decades, Giles knew most of the fleet commanders, just as they knew him. Many had been his classmates at the academy. They did not like him. They never had. Even at the academy, he had never been welcome in their circles, dismissing him as a snobbish bookworm, one who did not fit the mold of a fighting sailor. All these decades later, most still had the same opinion about him.

Because of those perpetual attitudes and the nature of Giles's present work, he often came across as brusque, if not downright rude. He did not have to use tact when appropriating resources for his missions, because his own orders were typically signed by men who spent most of their working hours in the company of the president. That fact, coupled with his self-assured nature, had made his face dreaded and loathed in a dozen command headquarters across the Pacific, including this one.

"The mission is not yet a disaster," Giles said, doing his best to sound obliging. "If we can get those subs out of there, and I believe we can, it can still be a success."

Kent sighed. "ComSubPac has no desire to hear any more of your harebrained suggestions, Teddy. He doesn't trust you. He doesn't want to hear your voice. He doesn't even want to hear your name. I sure as hell am not going to be the one to wake the dragon. Who knows what he'd do if he knew I was meeting with you right now."

"There are two hundred lives at stake, Sam."

"There were two hundred lives at stake when you proposed this operation."

"Look, I know this may not have produced the results we wanted – "

"You mean, the results *you* wanted, Teddy. You've always had your own agenda. You've always been on independent ops, answering to the devil knows who back in Washington. Well, ComSubPac is fed up with it. And, quite frankly, so are the rest of us."

Giles chose not to argue with Kent. He was not at liberty to discuss with anyone the impetuses driving the secret operations he fostered, nor did he expect Kent to understand them. Kent and his kind were primarily concerned with putting weapons on targets, controlling the seas, seizing territory from the enemy, as all good combat commanders should. Giles's concerns – or at least those of *his* superiors – were of a more subtle nature, but no less critical to the national interest. He usually met such a challenge to his efficacy with poisonous arrogance, but this time he decided it was wisest to make an exception.

"Alright, I admit there is some truth to what you say," Giles conceded, as an act of appeasement. "But you have to believe me, Sam, my only concern now is getting those boys home in one piece. I have no other motive."

Kent looked at him skeptically. "I'm telling you, Teddy, as a friend, and just between you and me. The admiral's not about to listen to anything you have to say, for the simple reason that your days around here are numbered. The top brass is calling for your head."

Giles assumed a grim expression though he knew that would never happen. His top brass was higher than theirs. Just as he knew Kent was not really his friend.

"Then let it be your idea, Sam." Giles offered. "I don't care what you tell him, but you have to run this by him. It's the best chance our subs have of getting out of there."

Kent grimaced. "I don't know…"

"Do you have any other plans?"

121

Kent did not answer right away. His eyes darted to the papers on his desk, before looking back at Giles. "The staff is mulling over a few ideas. Nothing solid yet."

Giles knew that meant they had nothing.

"I want you to take a look at this," Giles removed a folder from his satchel and placed it on the desk.

"What is it?"

"My plan, the best chance we have of bringing them home."

"Their best chance would involve a carrier task force, but of course –"

"Of course CinCPac has none to give you right now," Giles finished his sentence, a glimmer of his curt manner shining through before he sat back in his chair and continued in a milder tone. "That's the beauty of my plan. It doesn't call for a carrier task force. It doesn't even call for a cruiser group. The old man won't even have to go ask for help because my plan calls for just one sub. One of his own boats – the *Aeneid*."

"Now just a damn minute!" Kent raised his hands. "You seriously want me to ask the admiral to give you another submarine for one of your ludicrous ideas?"

Giles ignored the outburst and the insult. "Think about it, Sam! The *Aeneid* should be finishing up her mission in the Aleutians today. That puts her halfway to Japan already. You know we're running out of time. She's just what we need to throw off the Jap defenses around La Perouse."

After staring at the paneled wall for several long seconds during which Kent appeared to be contemplating the idea, he finally sighed. "The *Aeneid*, huh? Commander Henry Weston, if memory serves." He looked at Giles. "I'm not concerned about Weston. He's as good as any skipper in the fleet. But the *Aeneid*? Do you really think that old cow's up for anything like that?"

Giles smiled. "As a matter of fact, she happens to be uniquely equipped for my plan. Just take a look at it, will you?"

Kent sat back in his chair, looking browbeat. He opened the folder and half-heartedly flipped through the pages, giving the first few a cursory glance. "Oh, alright. I suppose I can review it this afternoon."

"Thank you, Sam." Giles smiled appreciatively, and then rose and extended a hand across the table.

"You know, Admiral Giles," Kent said, just as Giles opened the door to leave. "Even if I do like it, the old man still might shoot it down."

"That's why I came to you first, Captain Kent." Giles met eyes with Kent as if to remind him there was still an outstanding debt between them, then smiled. "I know he'll listen to you."

# 8

# ROCKS AND SHOALS

*North Pacific*

*USS Aeneid*

The *Aeneid* cut across an azure sea capped with white spindrift. It was a sunny day in the cold northern Pacific, with only a few patches of cumulus dotting the sky. The aroma of fried chicken wafted through every compartment, the midday meal having been doled out to the oncoming watch section, with more being prepared for those coming off watch. The crew had returned to their normal sea routine going about their duties in a casual fashion as if they had not been on the receiving end of a depth charge barrage less than twenty-four hours ago.

Weston stood on the aft portion of the bridge enjoying a cigarette after a long morning spent penning after-action reports. He purposefully chose a position farthest from the watch officers and lookouts to allow them to converse without worrying about their captain eavesdropping. The jagged mountain peaks of Attu were now well beyond the horizon astern, but those terror-filled moments in which they had brushed closely with death would live in their minds for some time to come.

In one grueling hour as the submerged *Aeneid* had crept toward the deep water, the Japanese destroyer had dropped four successive patterns of depth charges. The last one had been exceptionally close and had sprung leaks in many compartments. Weston had thought the next pattern would surely do them in. But as the enemy warship had closed in for the kill, two loud explosions unlike those of the depth charges had sounded overhead. The explosions had been shallow, very near the surface. Within moments, the destroyer had ceased echo-ranging and had departed the area at high speed, its screw noise quickly fading in Finkelman's earphones.

It was not until several hours later that the mystery was finally cleared up. After ordering the *Aeneid* to periscope depth to ease the sea pressure on the many leaks, Weston cautiously raised the periscope, fully expecting to find the destroyer still there, engaging in some kind of ruse. Instead, he found a most welcome sight. Dawn had broken over the world above. The storm had cleared, revealing the freshly powdered mountains of Attu rising beyond the cresting waves. A cluster of tiny black dots flew through the sky around the island's snow-covered peaks. At first, Weston thought they were enemy aircraft, and he came very close to ordering the submarine deep again. But, after switching to high power magnification, he recognized the familiar fuselage and wing configuration of navy F4F Wildcats. These friendly planes were equipped with bomb racks and had undoubtedly come from the escort carrier accompanying the invasion force. With D-Day only hours away, they were taking advantage of the clear weather to knock out some of the Japanese defenses on the island. Weston soon lost sight of them, but, not long after, Finkelman reported distant explosions on the last known bearing of the destroyer, and a corresponding column of black smoke appeared on the horizon. Weston could only conclude that an earlier flight of aircraft had attacked the Japanese destroyer while it was in the middle of its depth charge run, prompting it to break off and high-tail it for Attu's harbor where it might gain additional protection from the anti-aircraft batteries there. The billowing cloud of smoke and the absence of any screw noise was a good indication the enemy warship had not made it. The Wildcats had undoubtedly stopped it dead in its wake.

The rest of that morning had been uneventful. The *Aeneid* had slinked away while her crew quietly made repairs. When Weston finally ordered the quartermaster to plot a new course for Pearl Harbor, some of the passengers were not happy – one passenger, in particular, Sergeant Greathouse, the senior scout to have survived the foray ashore.

"We can't leave yet, Captain," Greathouse had said with urgency after knocking on Weston's stateroom door early that morning. "We've got to see if there are more survivors. I'm requesting that you turn this boat around, sir."

A big man, Greathouse's bulk seemed to take up nearly the entire stateroom. He was an imposing figure, used to giving orders to his soldiers and having them followed immediately. His request and his manner were entirely out of line, but Weston did not make an issue out of it. The fresh blood on Greathouse's green fatigue shirt indicated the sergeant had just come from the crew's mess where he had spent the night assisting the corpsman in treating his wounded men.

"I understand your concerns, Sergeant," Weston replied sympathetically. "But that goes against the approved plan. You know as well as I, we can't be anywhere near Attu when the fleet arrives. Six hours from now, any sub caught in the vicinity of that island is a fair target for our aircraft and escorts. If any of your men are still alive back there – and I pray there are many – then they know this, too. The contingency plan calls for them to hide out in the mountains until the invasion force arrives, and then to make contact with friendly troops as soon as practicable. I understand how you feel, but we can do no more for them. I've already sent a sitrep to ComSubPac. They'll pass the word on to the 7th Division to look out for them."

Greathouse was clearly incensed by that answer but said nothing and turned to leave the room.

"Sergeant." Weston stopped him.

"Yes, sir?"

"I'm always interested in what any man on board has to say, but, in the future, when you have a complaint or a recommendation, be sure to observe the chain of command. Go through Lieutenant MacCullen first."

"The lieutenant, sir?" Greathouse seemed somewhat shocked at that idea.

"Yes. He is the senior man now in your unit. You must keep him in the loop." Weston paused after a look of mild contempt crossed the sergeant's face. "Is there a problem, Sergeant?"

"No, sir." Greathouse replied formally. "No problem. Will that be all, sir?"

"Yes, carry on."

After Greathouse had left, Weston realized the disdain exhibited by the sergeant had not been aimed at him, but at MacCullen, and he suspected it was rooted in the fact that the army lieutenant had not gone ashore with the others. Now that Major Nash and all the other officers were presumed dead or captured, MacCullen was the *de facto* commander of the scout company – a company of only eight men. And it appeared there was already a rift growing in the new command structure of the gutted company. The tension had been apparent earlier that morning during the burial ceremony for the army scout who had succumbed to his wounds.

It had been a succinct, quiet affair, with the surviving troops assembled on deck for a final salute to their fallen comrade as his wrapped body slid into the sea. Lieutenant MacCullen had stood noticeably apart from Greathouse and the others, and there had been no interaction between them before or after the ceremony. The few times Weston had seen MacCullen since, the army officer had been sitting in the wardroom drinking coffee and reading a tattered dime novel. An odd thing to be doing at such a time, but Weston had been too absorbed with other matters to question him about it.

Now, with the brisk wind blowing through his tousled hair, Weston took a long draw on the cigarette and exhaled slowly as he considered how he would deal with this new problem.

On the gun deck below, several sailors were passing armfuls of stacked lumber through the conning tower side hatch and tossing it over the side. They were clearing away the temporary bunks that had been used by the scouts. It was a somber duty, almost like another burial at sea, but it was necessary to make space for moving around the few torpedoes the *Aeneid* had brought along on this voyage.

Weston had detested seeing his ship transformed into an undersea version of Noah's ark, but now, as he watched the trail of floating wood merge with the frothing wake, he wished he could see every one of those scouts crowded back aboard, overrunning the mess decks, smiling and joking and being an overall nuisance as they had been for the last few weeks.

He did not envy MacCullen. The young lieutenant had lots of letters to write. It would be a gut-wrenching task for any commander, let alone a junior officer who was probably already dealing with an enormous amount of guilt.

If MacCullen did feel guilt, then he was not alone. Weston felt it, too. Not the guilt of a survivor, but that of a commander who had left good men behind and who would always wonder if it might have gone another way had he done things differently.

Had the mission been a success, those who had dreamed it up would have been lauded as military geniuses. Now that it had failed, it would forever be considered a rash and foolish idea. Weston wondered who would be blamed for the disaster. Too many lives had been lost to not lay the fault somewhere. Would the crafters in Washington assume some of the responsibility, or would they levy all the blame on Major Nash? The dead were always the easiest scapegoats.

*Who knows?* Weston thought. *Maybe they would even blame me.* Such things had happened before. Whatever happened, Weston was content that his men had performed admirably under extremely hazardous conditions. He was proud of them. Eight men were alive today because of them. If those in the high circles of power wished to relieve him of his command to save face, then so be it.

Townsend had voiced similar sentiments. He had come to see Weston that morning shortly after Greathouse.

"I want to submit a statement, Skipper," Townsend had said in a huff. "A written statement for the record, that Major Nash and his men went ashore ill-equipped and ill-advised as to the forces arrayed against them. Shitty intelligence is to blame for this disaster, not the scouts!"

Townsend was intent on making sure his dead friend did not take the fall.

"I understand your feelings, XO," Weston had replied compassionately. "I share them. But why don't you put that statement on hold for a while?"

"You know they'll try to hang this on him, Captain."

"It goes with the territory, George. And it's a fight you can't win. Intelligence reports are estimates, not fact. Every commander knows that, including Major Nash." Weston paused, thumbing a finger at himself. "Including me. Any problems Nash had with the intelligence he should have voiced during the planning phase – as I'm sure he did. Your friend knew the uncertainties. He was willing to live with those uncertainties to take the fight to the enemy, and he did just that. It's over now, George. Let Nash be remembered for his heroics, for the brave thing that he did, not as the victim of some elaborate snafu."

It had taken a little more convincing to cool Townsend down, but he had eventually agreed to pigeonhole the letter, at least until the *Aeneid* arrived at Pearl and he had spent some time ashore. After a few days of R&R at the Royal Hawaiian, if he still felt the same way, Weston had promised to gladly forward his letter up the chain of command.

Inwardly, Weston agreed with Townsend's intentions, but he was more concerned for his XO's career than he was with seeing the proper heads roll. The top brass often came across as open to any and all criticisms from the frontline forces, but Weston knew better. Many flag officers smiled outwardly while holding a grudge inwardly, often exacting payback when they sat on the command boards that decided whose stars would rise and whose would fall.

Townsend was a good executive officer and a natural leader, the kind of leader who worked tirelessly to get the job done and bring his men home safely. The submarine service needed more like him. Weston did not want any hasty vent of frustration to interfere with his exec's chances of commanding his own boat someday.

The *Aeneid* was scheduled to arrive in Pearl Harbor in ten days. Typically, Weston would be looking forward to some much-needed rest ashore, but the Attu mission had left him somewhat rankled. He suspected many of the veterans among the crew felt the same way. There were few things submarine sailors cherished more than shore leave, but pride in their ship was one of them. It was bad enough returning to port with no sinkings to their credit. Failing a special mission, coming home with their tail between their legs, was beyond the pale.

"Captain, sir." Berry, the officer of the deck, was suddenly beside him. "Radio reports a message coming over the Fox broadcast. It has our callsign. Lieutenant Monk has been notified."

"Very well." Weston flicked the cigarette into the waves. "I'll go below."

Dropping down the hatch into the conning tower, and then down the next hatch, Weston stepped off the ladder into a control room that was nearly empty. With the diving station secured, there were only a few hands on watch. They quietly acknowledged him and went about their duties. In one corner of the room, an ensign sat on a locker trying to stay awake as he studied a three-inch-thick diesel engine technical manual that lay open on his lap.

Weston smiled. The learning never stopped on a submarine.

A stocky officer dressed in khaki trousers and an untucked white t-shirt ducked out from the radio room, his dark hair tousled and straight from the bunk. In his arms, he struggled to hold a bundle of ticker tape fresh from the coding machine.

"Captain!" The lieutenant said excitedly when he saw Weston, his energy clashing with the dark circles under his eyes.

"What do you have for me, Mister Monk?"

"It's an Ultra message with our number, Captain! It's marked urgent! We've got new tasking!"

A mix of concern and exhilaration flooded Weston's mind as he took the tape – concern that the *Aeneid* in her present state might not be up for whatever this message called for, and exhilaration that she might not return to Pearl Harbor with her tail between her legs after all.

# 9

# THE MISSION

"Our return to Pearl Harbor has been delayed, gentlemen," Weston announced to the assembled officers and chiefs, addressing the question he knew was at the forefront of their thoughts. "There is a critical task that needs doing, and there's no boat close enough to do it – except us."

The faces looking back at him were a mix of excitement and gloom. The cramped wardroom was filled beyond capacity with every seat around the booth table filled, some men standing in the pantry, and some even standing out in the passage. All of the officers and chiefs were there, except for those on watch. Even Lieutenant MacCullen was there, hovering near the back of the pantry. It was the first thing he had seemed to take interest in since leaving Attu.

"It's just like us to get stuck with the bad deals," one of the junior lieutenants grumbled, gesturing casually across the room at Lieutenant MacCullen as if the army lieutenant were the human manifestation of their most recent "bad deal."

MacCullen did not crack a smile or even acknowledge that he had been the butt of the lieutenant's jibe. His mind seemed to be elsewhere.

"Someone back at ComSubPac was kind enough to think of us again. Eh, Captain?" Monk said.

"If you find out who it is, Skipper, let me know," a boyish-faced ensign chided from the corner. "I'll send him a Christmas card."

A hush descended on the room as every eye turned to focus on the young officer who would have looked more proper in a fraternity sweater than a naval uniform. The ensign was initially pleased with his own jest, but his grin quickly faded when he noticed the glowers from the others in the room, none of whom believed he had enough time in the boats to be so candid with his thoughts.

"Get qualified, Weaver!" Monk scolded with mock sourness.

The assembly chuckled at the ensign's red face. Fresh from NROTC and submarine school, Ensign Weaver was the newest addition to the *Aeneid's* wardroom. Having only just joined the ship days before it shoved off from San Diego, he had yet to complete the necessary qualifications to stand watch on his own. Until he did, he was of no use to Monk and the others.

"I'll keep that in mind, Mister Weaver," Weston said with a mild smile. He allowed the levity to last a few moments longer before he spoke again. When he did, his tone was grave. "I'm afraid this mission is a bit more personal than the others, gentlemen. Some of our brother submariners are in a pickle, and it's up to us to get them out."

Any remaining smiles abruptly vanished. He had their full attention now. Even those disgruntled about the change of plans seemed suddenly interested.

"Three of our own boats have penetrated the Sea of Japan, right under Tojo's nose. They're there with one purpose – to send the Japs a clear message that they aren't safe anywhere on the deep blue sea, not even in their own backyard. That no matter where they send their merchant ships, their tankers, or their troop ships, an American sub is sure to be there waiting to sink them. And our boys have been sending that message loud and clear. Many a *maru* that once sailed the Sea of Japan are now rotting in Davy Jones's locker." Weston paused as astonished looks were exchanged around the room. The failure at Attu had shaken their confidence and had left them demoralized. Any news of success, albeit several thousand miles away, was most welcome. "Our boats have been hunting there for the last several weeks. They've done a bang-up job, but they're running low on fuel, and now it's time for them to go home."

Weston pointed to the small-scale chart laid out on the wardroom table. It displayed the northwestern reaches of the Pacific Ocean, the east coast of Asia, and the many outlying island chains and smaller seas, including the Sea of Japan. Reaching over, Weston used one finger to draw an imaginary line from the *Aeneid's* present position, three hundred miles south of the

Aleutians, to the Japanese island of Hokkaido, the northern extremity of Japan proper. His finger stopped on the narrow gap formed by Hokkaido and Sakhalin, the next island to the north.

"This is their only way out – La Perouse Strait."

"Sounds French," Monk said.

"The Japs have another name for it," Weston said. "But no matter what you call it, it's not friendly to submarines. The water is shallow, and the current is strong. The strait measures just twenty miles wide at its narrowest point, but you can cut that number in half for a submerged submarine. The water is too shallow everywhere except for a ten-mile-wide channel right down the middle."

"Doesn't sound too bad," Hudson commented dismissively. "Like going through the English Channel, isn't it?"

"Kind of like that, Joe, except there's no friendly side of this channel. The Japanese own the land on either side, and they've placed a fair number of shore batteries on both promontories to ensure anything trying to run through on the surface is given a proper reception. They've also laid minefields along both coasts narrowing the gap of navigable water even further. The strait itself is thirty miles long, but once you're through that you've got another forty miles before you get to deep water. And then there are the sentry ships. They're covering the strait around the clock. The Japs have summoned every coastal defense craft within a thousand miles – at least one squadron of destroyers, escorts, and smaller ships, along with several squadrons of land-based aircraft."

"Sounds like Tojo doesn't want our boys to leave the party," Monk commented.

"Whether he does or not, they're leaving. Four days from now, all three boats are going to attempt a breakout through La Perouse no matter what they encounter. Even if the whole damn Jap fleet is there blocking the exit, our boys are going to drive through it." Glancing around the room, Weston could see by their expressions that they all understood. There was no need to state the obvious, that the three submarines with over two hundred American sailors aboard would either slip through the enemy defenses or die trying.

Weston moved his finger along the map several hundred miles north of La Perouse Strait and across the Sea of Okhotsk to rest on a small dot of an island in the Kuril chain. "*This* is where we're going, gentlemen."

"Matsuwa," Hudson read off the tiny label while squinting. "That's a long way from La Perouse, Captain. What's there?"

"A small airfield with a few hangars. A small garrison. Not much, if you believe the intelligence reports. The planes there patrol the northern stretches of the Kurils."

"Sounds like a nice, quiet, out of the way place."

"It is." Weston nodded. "And that's precisely why we're going there."

Puzzled looks appeared on many of the faces gazing at the chart.

"Three days from now, we're going to hit Matsuwa with a naval bombardment, targeting the airfield, fuel depot, and any other structures or planes we can manage to knock out. We're going to stay there long enough to let the Japs see us, long enough for them to see that we're a submarine. With any luck, the garrison on

Matsuwa will radio our position back to combined fleet HQ, and they'll send the whole fleet after us."

"You mean the fleet guarding La Perouse, Captain?" Monk asked hesitantly.

"That's right. If all goes as planned, the enemy will be drawn away from La Perouse allowing our boats to escape."

"So, what you're saying is, we're the bait," Monk voiced the thoughts of every man in the room.

"Yes," Weston replied succinctly. "We will be the bait. We will be the bait so that our comrades in the Sea of Japan can escape."

A quiet murmur passed through the rear ranks in the pantry and passageway, and Weston waited for the mumbling to cease before he spoke again.

"And that brings me to our second objective. It would do no good for our boats to escape the Sea of Japan only to be sunk a few hours later when they pass through the Kurils into the Pacific. The planes at Matsuwa are critical to the defense of the Kurils. That's why it's imperative that we put that airfield out of action. Not permanently, but for at least forty-eight hours, just long enough to keep the skies clear while our boats make it through the Kurils and beyond aircraft range."

As expected, Berry's eyebrows came together in a troubled expression. The gunnery officer was evidently not confident his guns could do something even a cruiser would have trouble accomplishing. Weston nodded to Townsend who quickly unrolled another chart and laid it on top of the first one. The new chart displayed a larger scale portrayal of the central Kuril Islands and a more detailed view of Matsuwa. The island was similar in shape to a pistachio. Bunched up topographic lines represented the steep slopes of a volcano that took up the entire north end of the island, while the southern end of the island was much more level. Here, fresh pencil marks had been scrawled onto the chart, a series of boxes and lines showing the location of the Japanese installations.

"You might have noticed, Matsuwa is a small island," Weston continued. "Just seven miles across at its widest point. The airfield sits on the south side of the island, about half-a-mile inland. These markings were added by the XO based on the supplementary intelligence reports that came with our tasking, so take them for what they're worth. But we know the intel can't be too far off. We know the airfield has to be on the south side of the island because that's the only place with land flat enough to support one. As you can see, there's plenty of deep water to the east for our approach. Assuming there are no minefields, I intend to take the *Aeneid* in within three miles of the shore. That will put the airstrip and its support structures well within the range of our guns and give us the easiest escape route."

"Deep water's a relative term, Skipper," Hudson said, always the concerned diving officer. "This chart shows the fifty-fathom curve at five miles."

Weston gave a mild grin. "It's deep enough for our purposes, Joe."

"Pardon me for asking, Captain," Berry finally spoke. "But what exactly are we supposed to accomplish? My guns can bombard those structures, put a few holes in the runway, maybe even knock out a few planes on the ground, but there's no guarantee we'll put the whole airstrip out of action."

"You're right, Mister Berry. That's why the airstrip is not our primary target." Weston placed a finger at a place on the chart where Townsend had placed a large X. "According to intel, a single fuel depot serves the whole airfield. It is located here. If we take out the fuel tanks, the planes can't do much flying. They'll be grounded until more fuel can be brought in from the mainland, a process that will hopefully take a few days — days that our boats will use to reach the safety of the Pacific. The fuel tanks are our primary target, gentlemen. If we get lucky and knock them out early on, we can try our hand at the runway and the hangars, but they are secondary targets to the fuel tanks. Is that understood?"

Berry nodded, eyeing the *X* on the chart as if he were already mentally calculating the elevation angle the *Aeneid's* six-inch guns would have to use to strike the inland target from three miles off shore. While the gunnery officer looked agreeably challenged by the problem, many of the others seemed skeptical. They had a right to be justifiably cautious after the snafu on Attu. There was no telling how large that fuel depot was, how many tanks were there, or how well they were protected by earthworks or some other means. Weston shared the same concerns, though he did not show it. It was his job to get them to perform, even when the situation was not an ideal one. A simple general order had come down from on high, and now he was expected to make it happen, regardless of incomplete information, degraded equipment, and teetering morale. Any green midshipman could command men through a well-orchestrated, fully-resourced, clockwork-like operation, but operations like this one required a true leader. Weston knew this was where he earned his pay, where he either measured up to, or fell short of, the trust the Navy Board had placed in him when they had given him this command.

"This is the silent service, gentlemen," Weston addressed the murmuring crowd, his tone deadly serious. He felt he needed to emphasize once again exactly what was on the line here. "We don't know which boats these are that we're helping, but you can bet your dolphins they're manned by some of the same fellas you split a bottle with at the club, or sailed with in another command. They were your classmates in sub school or at the academy. If you want to know what they look like, just take a look across the table from you. Right now, they're probably sitting around in their own wardrooms, just like you guys, thinking of the mess they're in, only they're in it much deeper than you. They're in enemy waters, low on fuel and food, with every Jap warship and plane looking for them. Their chances of getting out are practically nil. If I were in their shoes, I'd be praying for a miracle. Well, gentlemen," he glanced around the room, meeting every eye, "I intend for *us* to be that miracle. When you signed up for submarines, no one told you it was going to be easy. We're here to do the tough jobs no one else can. We're here to sink Japanese ships without mercy and strike fear in the hearts of every enemy sailor that shoves off on a voyage no matter how short or insignificant. Our submarine brothers that are trapped in the Sea of Japan have been doing just that for the past several weeks. Now it's time for us to do our part. I want you all to pass this on to your divisions. They need to know what's at stake. Understood?"

"Aye, aye, sir," several of the officers and chiefs said as the whole group collectively nodded.

"All departments are ready, Captain," Townsend confirmed. "We've got plenty of reserve fuel on board. No critical systems are out of commission. My only concern is our wounded. The corpsman's been doing the best he can to keep them stable, but I'm not sure what this delay will do to them. With this diversion, it will be at least another week, maybe two, before they're seen by a proper doctor. I didn't get the chance to talk to the corpsman before this meeting to get the scoop on their present condition. Perhaps Lieutenant MacCullen can speak to that."

Weston looked around at the army officer. "What do you say, Lieutenant? Can your wounded men handle a few more days at sea?"

MacCullen stammered, looking somewhat taken off guard.

"I-I don't know, sir," he finally replied.

"What do you mean, you don't know?" Townsend snapped accusingly, his expression suddenly hardened. "They're your men, aren't they?"

Weston was surprised by the caustic tone used by his normally unflappable executive officer. It was uncharacteristic of Townsend to dress down a subordinate in public, let alone a passenger from another branch of the service. Weston had known Townsend long enough to sense that this reprobation went deeper than a simple annoyance at the army lieutenant's unpreparedness. There was something personal in it, as if the executive officer was venting anger at the young lieutenant – anger that had been building for quite some time. Could it be that Townsend blamed MacCullen for the disaster on Attu, perhaps believing that the army lieutenant's unanticipated absence from the landing force had somehow thrown the company's command structure into disorder? Could it be he blamed MacCullen for the death of Major Nash?

At that moment, Weston noticed something different about MacCullen. His foot was no longer bandaged. He now wore standard army-issue boots on both feet. Weston raised his eyebrows. He was not stunned, just mildly surprised, and he now understood the reason for Townsend's crossness.

"I'll have to check with Sergeant Greathouse," MacCullen answered calmly, seemingly unfazed by Townsend's grilling. "I will get you an answer, sir."

"In the navy, a junior officer is expected to know the state of his men at all times," Townsend said bitterly. "I would assume the army has the same standards."

"As I said, sir, I will get you an answer." MacCullen's face was emotionless, his tone tinged with slight annoyance.

"That will do, lieutenant!" Weston interjected, heading off the heated reply that was sure to come from Townsend. He briefly met eyes with his XO to silently communicate that this was not the time nor the place for such an exchange, and Townsend held his tongue. "Now," Weston continued, gesturing to the recognition manual on the table. "Let's take a look at the types of enemy planes and patrol craft we can expect to encounter..."

Hours after the meeting had adjourned, when Weston had retired to his stateroom to make a dent in the bottomless stack of paperwork piled on his desk, there was a knock at his doorframe.

"Yes?"

Townsend's head poked through the curtain. "You wanted to see me, Captain?"

"Yes, George. Come on in." Weston gestured to the fold-down chair on the bulkhead. "Close the curtain and have a seat."

"I've updated our track to Matsuwa, Captain," Townsend said after waiting patiently for Weston to finish reviewing and signing the report before him. "It's on the chart in the control room when you're ready to approve it."

"Thanks. I'll be up there, shortly."

Townsend nodded, and then ventured, "What did you want to see me about?"

Weston sighed heavily. He had to get this out of the way. "It's about Lieutenant MacCullen, XO."

At the mere mention of the army officer's name, the executive officer's expression soured. "You think I was too hard on him. Is that it?"

Weston shrugged. "Certainly, I believe we are obligated to do something if the lieutenant is not doing his job – considering there are no other army officers aboard – but I also believe we should cut him the same amount of slack we would Monk, or Berry, or any of our own officers."

"He didn't know the state of his men, Captain – his *wounded* men. I doubt he's even started writing the letters to the families. What the hell has he been doing with his time?"

"I'd expect our own ensigns to make similar mistakes. MacCullen is young. He's learning."

"If it were up to me, he'd be relieved of all duties from this day forward," Townsend said succinctly. "Sergeant Greathouse can take over. He seems to be doing MacCullen's job now, anyway."

"Isn't that going a bit too far, XO?"

Townsend looked at Weston thoughtfully, as if hesitating to say what was truly on his mind. "It may interest you to know, Captain," he said finally, "that Nash didn't have many good things to say about Lieutenant MacCullen. This is not the first time MacCullen conveniently stayed behind while his unit engaged in combat. Last year, in North Africa, when he was in a different regiment, a similar sort of thing happened. Did you know that?"

Weston said nothing but indicated that he was listening. It was best that he first understand the exact nature of the rumors being spread about the army lieutenant.

"Nash told me the whole story," Townsend continued. "Or, at least, some of it. The regiment was out-gunned and retreating from a panzer brigade. MacCullen's platoon was assigned rear guard. They were ordered to make a stand against the Germans so that the rest of the regiment could establish a better defensive position some miles to the rear. The panzers attacked, and MacCullen's entire platoon was wiped out – all except for MacCullen. He turned up at regiment HQ some hours later claiming that he had tried to coordinate covering fire with the artillery but his radio was down." Townsend shook his head in disgust. "A pretty convenient excuse for leaving the frontline, if you ask me."

Weston nodded calmly. "Major Nash told me the same story."

Townsend looked at him astonished. "Well, Captain, don't you think it's a bit odd that MacCullen is the common denominator in two massacres?"

"No disrespect to your friend, XO, but I believe Nash allowed that North Africa story to gain more traction than it should have. It's all hearsay, rumors passed from one soldier to another, from one side of the world to another." Weston raised a hand before Townsend could reply. "Let me tell you something, George. One of the best captains I ever served under was drummed out of the service after his sub collided with a freighter in a dense fog off Long Island. The accident was entirely his fault, and he admitted to such at his court-martial, but I think the navy made a mistake in getting rid of him. He was one hell of a leader. I would have followed him into battle, any day of the week."

A quizzical expression crossed the XO's face. "But he was found at fault, Captain."

"Come on, XO. We've both been in those waters before. We both know how thick the fog can get. We know that sometimes the only thing keeping you from running aground or hitting something is pure luck. Some things are simply out of your control. I wasn't there on the bridge of that sub that night. I don't know what really happened. Just as I don't know what happened in North Africa. There's only one man that knows what truly happened, and that's Lieutenant MacCullen."

"Did you see his foot today, Captain?"

Weston met eyes with him. That was one subject he had hoped to avoid. "You noticed that, too, did you?"

"It's the quickest damn recovery from trench foot I've ever seen. I can't imagine what his men are thinking right now. He was faking his injury, plain and simple."

*So*, Weston thought, *Nash had failed to fill Townsend in on that little detail. It would have been much easier if he had.*

"Listen, XO. I think it would be best if –"

"There's no two ways about it, Captain. MacCullen chickened out!" Townsend's face was flushed with anger. "Maybe if that coward had gone ashore, Nash would have had the help he needed to manage the company. Maybe if that coward had done his job, my friend and all the others would still be…they'd still be…" Townsend choked up, the death of his friend too recent, too painful.

"Listen, George," Weston said hesitantly. "I've got to tell you something. It's about a decision Major Nash made regarding Lieutenant MacCullen." Weston paused allowing Townsend a few moments to collect himself. "I'm not sure why Nash felt I should know about it. Probably because I was the senior officer aboard. In any event, I did not agree with the decision, but I was not about to meddle in army affairs. Nash wanted me to keep it a secret, and I've respected his wishes. But, considering the circumstances, considering Nash was your friend, I think you need to know about it."

The sorrow on Townsend's face was slowly eclipsed by a look of keen interest. "Go on, Skipper. I'm listening…"

# 10

# RETRIBUTION

"Battle stations torpedo!" Reynolds's voice intoned over the 1MC announcing circuit, followed immediately by the fourteen-bell gong.

A ship had been spotted in the world above, and the air was alive with anticipation. As Weston leaned on the handles and peered through the periscope, he heard the bustle of sailors rushing to their stations. A few feet away, Reynolds marked a board with a grease pencil as each compartment reported in over the phone circuits. In less than a minute, the expected announcement came.

"All compartments report battle stations manned and ready, Captain."

"Very well," Weston replied. He did not take his face from the eyepiece. Now that the ship in question was hull-up, he was finally getting the chance to see it. Up until now, it had been nothing more than two tiny sticks – the ship's masts – poking above the western horizon. With the newcomer's broad hull now silhouetted by the yellow glow of the setting sun, Weston easily confirmed its identity.

"She's a freighter, alright," he announced to the others in the cramped conning tower. "Medium-sized. Two masts. Cranes fore and aft. Probably headed for Kiska."

*But what the hell what she doing here?* Weston thought. Japanese shipping had been scarce in the Aleutians for the past several months, ever since an inconclusive naval battle off the Komandorski Islands had forced a sizeable enemy supply convoy to turn around and head back to Japan. With Attu in the process of being invaded by Allied forces, the freighter's presence made even less sense. Perhaps word of the invasion had not yet reached the ears of that merchant captain. Perhaps it had, and the Empire had sent him anyway, expecting him to deliver his cargo despite the danger.

For the briefest moment, Weston half-considered letting the freighter go. With only eight torpedoes aboard, and a rigid timetable to meet under the new tasking from ComSubPac, there was little tactical reason to attack the *maru*. Allied aircraft covering the Attu operation would undoubtedly spot the freighter long before it ever reached its destination and swiftly reduce it to a flaming hulk. And then there was always the risk of an undetected escort popping up out of nowhere. Prudence would dictate going deep and remaining undetected. As many reasons as there were to pass up the freighter, there were other reasons not to – reasons that did not always make sense to those ashore pushing miniatures across large maps.

"All ahead one third," Weston ordered. "Right fifteen-degree rudder, steady on course two six zero."

The steersman acknowledged the order, spinning the giant spoked wheel to bring the submarine around. The turn would place the enemy ship just off the port bow. If Weston's intentions were not yet evident to the crewmen around him, his next order certainly removed any doubts.

"Make tubes five and six ready for firing in all respects."

There were many smiles in the crowded compartment as the order was enthusiastically relayed to the torpedo room. Weston had decided to use the *Aeneid's* external tubes – tubes that were outside the pressure hull and thus not capable of being reloaded submerged – but the torpedomen would still have to perform a myriad of electrical and mechanical checks on the weapons from the forward torpedo room.

They needed this attack, Weston reasoned with himself. Not just the torpedomen, but the entire crew. With morale as low as it was, they needed this attack more than they needed food or water. The new tasking had raised their spirits somewhat, but the dismal outcome of the Attu mission was still hanging over them like a dark cloud. The last thing Weston wanted was to head into a new mission with a crew that was doubting its own abilities and its own luck.

Hunters were only happy when on the hunt. The men of the *Aeneid* needed to get back into the business of sinking ships. They needed to be submariners again.

"Stand by for observation." Weston steadied the reticle on the forward mast of the distant ship. "Bearing, mark!"

"Two four four," Reynolds announced.

"Range, mark. Revise mast head height to fifty feet."

"One one double-oh," Reynolds read the indication off the stadimeter scale on the back of the periscope.

"Angle on the bow, starboard five five. Down scope!" Weston slapped up the periscope handles.

As the glistening mast slid down into its well, the *Aeneid* lurched to one side from a large swell, forcing Weston to grab hold of a pipe stanchion to keep from losing his footing. He watched the needle on the depth indicator briefly tip above fifty-four feet and then stabilize once again at sixty.

"Watch your depth, Joe," he called down to the control room, though he knew it was not necessary. Hudson was well aware of the depth excursion and was already ordering more water flooded into the auxiliary ballast tanks to counteract the suction forces of the tossing seas.

One step away from the periscope well, Townsend maintained a pencil depiction of the tactical situation on the small DRT table, plotting each observation relative to a tiny ball of light representing the *Aeneid's* position. The ball of light was projected onto the paper from beneath the glass sheet on which it rested. The light automatically moved along the chart driven by a continuous dead reckoning calculation maintained by an intricate mechanical device that used inputs from the submarine's speed log and gyrocompass.

"Good set-up, Captain," Townsend reported. He had already plotted the freighter's projected track on the chart and had marked each future position in ten-minute intervals.

Weston exchanged glances with Townsend and gave a slight nod of acknowledgment. The revelation Weston had shared with him not four hours ago had come as something of a shock to the trusty second-in-command. But, like the veteran submariner Townsend was, he had taken the information about his late friend in stride and had carried on with the execution of his duties as he always did, as he did now, working the plot table elegantly and efficiently like a fine craftsman.

Both men shifted their gaze to the aft corner where Lieutenant Monk spun dials on the bookcase-sized torpedo data computer, also referred to as the TDC. Monk appeared slightly flustered as he entered data from the most recent observation adding to that he had entered earlier as the freighter had come over the horizon.

"How's it looking, Stu?" Weston asked impatiently. "Come on. We're not dealing with Tokyo Bay up there. It's only one ship."

"That last observation checks, sir. She's holding steady on course." Monk was clearly doing his best to ignore the ribbing, and he raised a finger to politely hold off any more questions from his captain until he had worked out the final corrections.

Monk was adept at handling the TDC, but it had been several months since he had used it to track a real target. The device would have amazed any submariner of the Great War and was still considered a luxury item by the

*Aeneid's* old guard. Using a series of mechanical gears and wheels, the TDC determined the precise gyro angle necessary at the point of firing to place the submarine's torpedoes on a collision course with the target. The angle setting was electrically transmitted to the gyroscope spindles on the weapons resting in their tubes and was continually updated as the target drew closer. When the whole process worked as designed, the torpedoes would receive their final gyroscope settings at the time of firing, launch from their tubes, turn to the set angle, and from there drive on a straight path to hit the target. But, no matter how fantastic the TDC was, no matter how capable Monk was at operating it, the device was only as good as the data it had to work with. If the periscope observations were poor, the calculated angles would be inaccurate and possibly send the torpedoes off in the wrong direction.

"Any day now, Stu," Weston prompted, watching the clock on the bulkhead.

Another thirty seconds passed before Monk finally announced, "We have a solution light, Captain. Course zero two eight, speed six knots. She should be on bearing two five four now."

"That checks with the sound bearing, Captain," Finkelman reported from the sound gear.

"Let's have a look, then." Weston raised both thumbs to Reynolds, who then pressed the actuator to raise the periscope. Weston met it at the floor, spinning it around as it came up. After two quick sweeps of the violet sky and the dimming horizon, he steadied the lens on the merchant. The freighter now took up much more of the periscope's field of view. "There she is, just chugging along like she's out for a pleasure cruise."

Weston marveled at how, even now, almost two years into the war, some Japanese merchant captains did not follow standard anti-submarine procedures. Even a simple, unpredictable zig-zag pattern, when properly executed, was enough to wreck a torpedo firing solution. Maybe the enemy captain did not have enough fuel on board to waste it on a zig-zag routine, or perhaps he just wanted to get to Kiska and get the hell out of these waters.

"Forward torpedo room reports, tubes five and six ready for firing, Captain."

"Very well. Set torpedo depth to ten feet. Open doors on tubes five and six."

As the order was passed over the phones, Weston heard Hudson's voice down in the control room ordering water pumped between tanks to compensate for the change in trim.

Switching to high power magnification, Weston could clearly make out the ship's markings. Had there been anyone on deck, he would have surely spotted them, too, but it was far too frigid for anyone to be strolling outside. The Japanese lookouts would be hunkering in their perches, bundled in parkas and hoods, most of them more concerned about keeping their ears and noses from freezing than watching for enemy periscopes.

"Doors are open on tubes five and six, Captain," Reynolds reported.

"Final bearing and shoot," Weston announced, steadying the reticle on the freighter's pilothouse. "Bearing, mark."

"Two five six."

"Down scope!"

"Matches!" Monk announced, confirming that the new bearing fell in line with the calculated solution.

"Fire five…Fire six…"

Townsend pressed the button on the torpedo firing panel twice, each time initiating a violent shudder through the deck as a twenty-foot-long, one-and-a-half-ton Mark 14 torpedo was launched into the sea. Weston felt his eardrums tighten as the impulse air vented inboard.

"Tubes five and six fired electrically," Reynolds announced.

"Both torpedoes running hot, straight, and normal," Finkelman reported.

"Torpedo run, seven hundred yards," Monk said as he carefully watched the needle on his stopwatch. "Thirty seconds to impact."

As the two torpedoes sped toward the freighter at forty-six knots, each man in the compartment counted down the interval in his head. The periscope had just finished its lazy descent into the well when Weston gave Reynolds the thumbs up again. Weston grabbed the handles expecting to have enough time to do a quick safety sweep of the horizon the instant the lens broke through to the surface, but his sweep was interrupted by a sharp 'Whack!' reverberating through the water and vibrating through the deck plates beneath his feet. He spun the periscope around to point at the freighter again and saw what he had expected to see, a column of water rising into the sky – *half-way to the target!*

"Looks like number six was a premature," he commented irritably, drawing the expected moan from the others in the room.

Premature detonations were not unheard of. In fact, malfunctions with the Mark 14 torpedo had become something of a norm, often with much more disastrous results. Prematures, duds, and run-unders had left more than one captain cursing the Bureau of Ordnance. There were even documented incidents in which the Mark 14's gyroscope or rudder had failed, sending the weapon in a deadly circular run back at the firing submarine.

But the men of the *Aeneid* did not have long to ponder the setback. Unofficial communications over the phone circuits hardly had time to spread the bad news before another distant explosion rumbled through the hull.

This detonation was not premature. Weston looked to see the freighter shudder as if it had run onto a rock, and now a new column shot skyward, this one filled with flame, smoke, and debris. The torpedo had struck just beneath the freighter's bow, savaging the hull there and sending the forward mast toppling into the sea.

"A hit!" Weston announced.

A cheer resounded through the submarine as if all the tension of the previous minutes were suddenly released in a moment of euphoria. The failure of the other torpedo was instantly forgotten.

As the smoke cleared, Weston could see the extent of the damage, and he gestured for Reynolds to hand him the 1MC microphone.

"This is the captain," he said, keying the talk button and hearing his own voice echo up through the hatch from the control room below. The ship-wide announcing circuit could be heard on loudspeakers in every compartment throughout the submarine. "I'm looking through the periscope right now at a medium-sized enemy freighter. No,…correction. She used to be an enemy freighter. Now she's a wreck headed for Davy Jones' Locker." He let the resulting cheers and laughter diminish before he continued. "She's down by the bow. Her superstructure is spewing out black smoke like the smelter of an ironworks. I see Japs running around on deck, but there's nothing they can do. Their ship is on fire, and it's slipping further beneath the waves every second. Now she's tipping up. I can see her screws now, still spinning, but high and dry. She's going down fast. Crates and equipment are sliding off her deck. Gentlemen, I'd say this cargo's not going anywhere but to the bottom. Chalk up one more *maru* for the *Fighting Aeneid*. And that means a combat pin for every man when we get back to Pearl."

Again, cheers. Weston wondered how long those cheers would last. It would be a long voyage to the Kurils, and then to Midway to offload their wounded, and then finally to Pearl Harbor. But, for now, they were cheering. The attack on the freighter had served its purpose. Morale had been restored.

"Secure from general quarters. Section Three take the watch."

# 11

# NO MERCY

Weston had just finished his first cigarette after the attack when the close-cropped head of an army scout appeared at the hatch from the control room. It was Lieutenant MacCullen. He ascended to the conning tower followed immediately by Sergeant Greathouse. The room was still cramped by any sensible measure but it seemed spacious to Weston now that general quarters had been secured and half of the watchstanders had gone below.

"You wanted to see us, Captain," MacCullen said. He stood awkwardly distant from Greathouse, as much as one could in such a confined space. It was clear there was tension between the two men.

"Yes, gentlemen." Weston gave a thumbs-up to Reynolds who immediately pressed the actuator to raise the periscope. "I called for you, because I wanted you both to get a front row seat." After making three quick turns around the azimuth, Weston focused the lens on the burning freighter and then gestured for MacCullen to take the periscope. "Have a look, lieutenant."

The army officer hesitated at first but then peered through the eyepiece. He stared at the devastation only briefly, as if he was not sure what to make of it, but then stepped aside, saying nothing, his face as expressionless as it had been before.

"Care to have a look, Sergeant?" Weston said, turning to Greathouse. The words had hardly left Weston's mouth before the big sergeant took the scope and eagerly pressed his face to the eyepiece.

Greathouse was apparently much more satisfied at the sight of the destruction than was the lieutenant. He grinned with delight as he twisted the periscope handles, changing the magnification several times.

"Ah, that's nice, sir," Greathouse said finally, still looking after a long minute. "This makes my day, sir. You and your boys have done well."

"Thank you, Sergeant," Weston said guardedly. He was about to tell Greathouse it was time to move on when the sergeant suddenly changed the magnification back to high power and rotated the periscope slightly to the right.

"See something?" Weston asked expectantly.

"There are lifeboats out there, sir."

"Yes, we have noted them in the log," Weston replied. He then placed a hand on one of the periscope handles. "I think that's long enough, Sergeant. I'll take it back now if you don't mind."

Greathouse took his face away from the eyepiece, looked at Weston for a long moment, and then shrugged and stepped aside.

MacCullen had already left the conning tower, descending through the hatch in the deck without another word. The lieutenant either had little interest in the freighter's destruction, or he did not wish to share the same room with Greathouse any longer than he had to. Evidently, the new company commander was having trouble interacting with his senior NCO. Before Weston could return his face to the lens, he caught the knowing glance from Townsend across the room who looked at him as if to say *I told you so.*

Several minutes passed, and Greathouse made no move to go. Instead, he hovered near Weston's elbow as if hoping to get another turn on the periscope.

"Shouldn't we sink those lifeboats, sir?" Greathouse asked in Weston's ear, speaking quietly such that the others could not hear. "No sense in leaving any of them bastards behind to tell the tale. Put me and my boys topside with a few Tommy guns, and we'll take care of it, sir."

Resisting the urge to tell the sergeant he was out of line, give him a brief lecture on the rules of war, and then send him below, Weston addressed him without taking his eyes from the lens. "They will be left to the mercy of the sea, Sergeant. Believe me, in these latitudes, that's no mercy at all. The poor devils will likely die of exposure within a day or two."

"That's good," Greathouse said, more to himself than to anyone else, his tone distant as if he were briefly back on Attu with his company. Perhaps he believed the suffering of those Japanese merchant sailors up there was somehow retribution for his lost comrades.

After another sweep around the horizon, Weston signaled for Reynolds to lower the periscope. He pulled a box of cigarettes from his shirt pocket and drew out his second since the attack.

"The smoking lamp is lit for five more minutes," he said, offering one to Greathouse. "Better smoke 'em while you can."

The sergeant gladly accepted it.

"How are your men, Sergeant?" Weston asked, after lighting both cigarettes. "How are they holding up?"

"Fine, sir," Greathouse replied taking his first long drag and then gazing at the smoldering cigarette as if it had regenerative powers. "They're ready to get at the Japs again. Not counting Burns and Gomez, of course."

Weston had heard that the severely wounded Burns and Gomez were still confined to the rack and would likely remain there until the *Aeneid* returned to port.

"I'm sure Lieutenant MacCullen filled you in on our change of plans," Weston ventured.

Greathouse nodded. "Yes, sir. He did."

Weston sensed a bitterness in his tone and could not decide whether it had to do with the delay in returning to port or the mention of MacCullen.

"After we finish our business in the Kurils, we'll head straight for Midway at top speed, where the eight of you will debark for a plane back to Hawaii. I know it's not enough for your wounded men, but it's the best we can do."

"I understand, sir. Thank you, sir." Greathouse's brows furrowed. "If you don't mind my asking, I'd like to make one request."

"Certainly."

"I'd ask you to arrange for Lieutenant MacCullen to go back on a different plane, sir. The boys and I would rather not ride with him."

Weston raised his eyebrows. "That is an unusual request, Sergeant."

"I know it is, sir. I appreciate that. But if it's something you can manage, I'd be most grateful."

"He's your own officer, Sergeant."

"Begging your pardon, sir, but he's not mine," Greathouse corrected him in a respectful tone. "My platoon leader was Lieutenant Hawthorne, and he's dead back on Attu. None of these boys who survived belonged to Lieutenant MacCullen's platoon, either."

"I see," Weston replied, though he was not sure he understood at all. What did it matter that MacCullen was from another platoon? They were all from the same company. They had all trained together in the weeks leading up to the operation. It was clearly a made-up excuse. After another niggling glance from Townsend, Weston surmised he knew the real reason for the sergeant's request. Weston looked Greathouse in the eyes. "Does this have anything to do with Lieutenant MacCullen not going ashore with the rest of you?"

The sergeant nodded hesitantly. "I won't lie, sir. It upsets the boys to see him, especially when his pretty little foot was bandaged up not twenty-four hours ago."

Greathouse paused before adding, "I know what he is, sir. I won't share a plane with the likes of him, and I don't expect my boys to, either. Burns and Gomez might still die of their wounds. It's an insult to them whenever he shows his face."

"Come now, Sergeant. With all due respect to your wounded men, that's complete nonsense."

Greathouse looked at him sideways. "I've got friends in The Big Red One, sir. That's where Lieutenant MacCullen came from before he joined our outfit. They warned me about him. I know his type, sir. I've known it from the day he reported to our unit. All the other sergeants and me, we knew about him. I voiced my concerns to Major Nash, just as I am to you now, sir. Now, the major is dead, and so is most of our company."

"Surely, you don't think the operation failed because MacCullen stayed behind."

"I'm not saying it did, sir. Could have been a hundred reasons why things went bad on Attu. But it doesn't change the fact that the sight of that bastard with his foot all healed like nothing ever happened upsets my boys, and I won't have it, sir. Not after what they've been through. I don't even want him in the after torpedo room where my boys are bunking. I told him as much, sir."

Weston clenched his jaw in frustration. This really was getting out of hand. When he spoke again, he was firm and direct. "He is your officer, Sergeant, the de facto commander of your company. I expect you to treat him with the respect due his rank, no matter what your personal opinion of him is! Is that clear? I'll have no more of this ridiculous behavior!"

The sergeant had come to attention for the brow-beating, staring straight ahead as if he were a marble statue. "Yes, sir," he said heartily, though Weston knew he was cursing him inside his head. "Will that be all, Captain?"

Weston nodded. "Dismissed."

As the big sergeant fit his large form back down the hatch, Weston's anger quickly subsided. He could not blame the sergeant or the other scouts for doubting

MacCullen's courage. The commandos led a life of honor, bravery, and commitment to each other. They were a unique, close-knit tribe whose success depended on identifying the bad apples quickly and rooting them out. Greathouse was only doing his job.

For a moment, Weston considered telling the sergeant what he had told Townsend – the secret Major Nash had entrusted him to keep. Weston glanced once again across the room at Townsend, who looked up at him briefly, and then went back to his chart work. The revelation had not seemed to change the XO's opinion of MacCullen. Perhaps it would not sway Greathouse, either.

No, Weston decided, he would keep his word to the late major and not tell the sergeant or anyone else. It would do little good, anyhow. With any luck, the *Aeneid* would complete her mission and then make port at Midway two weeks after that. And then, MacCullen and Greathouse and the rest of the scouts would no longer be his problem.

# 12

# HONESTY

*La Perouse (Sōya) Strait*

*IJN Hamakaze*

The *Hamakaze* heeled over to starboard drawing a long white line in the blue waters east of La Perouse Strait. Having just completed a full sweep of its assigned sector, the swift destroyer turned nimbly through one hundred and eighty degrees in just under a minute and steadied on its new course.

"Standard speed," Ando said into the voice tube on the exposed signal bridge. The new course had placed the wind just off the bow, forcing him to remove his cap or lose it over the side.

The muffled acknowledgement came from the pilothouse below, and the *Hamakaze* rapidly slowed to twelve knots, once again ready to search the strait with all sonar equipment probing the depths and fresh lookouts posted to scan for enemy periscopes.

"Next planned zig in ten minutes, Captain," the navigation officer's voice reported.

"Very well."

As the *Hamakaze* began yet another leg of its seemingly endless search routine, Ando saw a pair of merchant vessels several kilometers away crawling out of the strait in single file. They were older ships, coastal steamers, neither displacing more than five thousand tons. Both rode low in the water filled to capacity with coal and other precious resources desperately needed in the factories in the south. They moved along at a snail's pace, slowly, lazily, in sharp contrast to the swift warships crisscrossing the strait behind them. Droning above the lumbering ships, a flight of patrol aircraft kept a bird's eye view on the waterway.

Ando took in a deep breath of the salty air and let it out slowly. This was the third day the fleet had spent monotonously scouring the same patches of ocean over and over only to come up with nothing. And yet, his men went about their duties as smartly as if the routine had just started. He would have liked to take credit for it, to claim that his crew's commendable performance was merely a result of his leadership, but he knew better. They had a different inspiration this time.

A living legend walked among them.

On the other side of the bridge, Admiral Yamada conversed quietly with Lieutenant Kawaguchi. Like the rest of the *Hamakaze's* two hundred forty crewmen, it was clear that the young officer idolized Yamada, hanging on every word that fell from the admiral's lips as if the legendary flag officer were a *Rōshi* imparting some sage-like wisdom. For his part, Yamada seemed to relish the attention, even thrive on it. In the three days since he had assumed command of the squadron, a new man had emerged to replace the aging admiral. Where Yamada had earlier moved about with a measure of feebleness, he now seemed invigorated, his step as sprightly as that of a junior officer, the lines of stress that had marred his face all but melted away.

"I do not wish to interfere in your day-to-day running of the ship," Yamada had told Ando on the first day after a brief tour of the main deck that had ended on the *Hamakaze's* raised prow. "I will see to the squadron. I trust you to handle the ship." Taking in a full breath of the salty air, the admiral had brandished a genuine smile as he had gazed back at the full length of the destroyer. "Ah, Ando! The sights and smells of a ship at sea are medicine to my soul. You have no idea how much I have missed it. You will please understand if I make my way around this fine ship of yours in the coming days. Do not worry. I have no need of an escort. I wish to see your men in action, to hear their raw thoughts uncensored by the presence of their captain."

True to his word, over the past three days, Yamada had not interfered in the ship's internal matters. He had primarily left Ando alone, seldom visiting the bridge and spending most of his time in the spaces conversing with the off-watch sailors. Beyond establishing specific patrol zones for each ship and issuing a few general orders to the squadron, Yamada had been mostly hands-off, content to let the captains do their jobs. Ando was thankful for that, as he was thankful for Yamada spreading general encouragement throughout the crew. Despite the fact that the searches had thus far produced nothing, the crew seemed convinced the American submarines would eventually be found and sunk. Ando, on the other hand, was not so sure, and he wondered if the admiral was setting up the crew, and himself, for a big disappointment.

There was indeed nothing wrong with inspiring men to achieve more than they thought they were capable of, provided a measure of pragmatism was used, but Yamada's behavior in the past days had been anything but pragmatic, and Ando was beginning to wonder if the admiral's *harakiri* vow was clouding his judgment. Of course, one might question the judgement of anyone in modern times making such a vow.

In Ando's mind, it was utterly foolish.

Admittedly, the samurai code of *bushido* had its uses in warfare, often producing devout, committed warriors ready to die for the emperor. That had been suitable for 12th century Japan, but in 1943, in the ever-evolving age of modern warfare, the samurai code fell woefully short.

In these times, especially in naval warfare, proper planning, advanced technology, and a healthy measure of flexibility were more often the keys to victory than a warrior's sacred honor.

In his experience with Yamada, Ando had never remembered him to be so devoted to the ancient codes. Perhaps in the admiral's old age, as he watched the high command lead his country down paths from whence it could never return, the old ways gave him a certain level of comfort — a measure of certainty in an uncertain world.

Despite his new-found interest in the old religion and his overly optimistic outlook, Yamada's strategy for catching the Yankee subs was sound. He had separated the fleet into three divisions, placing them at strategic points along the forty-kilometer-long passage in staggered lines of battle that would present progressively stronger forces to the enemy subs the farther they managed to penetrate the strait. The subchasers had been posted at the western approaches, the *kaibōkan* near the halfway point, and, finally, the destroyers at the eastern exit, all waiting with guns bristling and depth charge racks loaded. Patrol aircraft circled overhead incessantly. At any given moment, no less than twelve dotted the skies. Add to this grids of minefields reaching out from the shore, and underwater magnetic loops waiting for any sizeable metallic object to pass by, and the enemy was facing an imposing, if not impenetrable, obstacle.

With this network of defenses, Ando had anticipated finding at least one of the enemy subs. But, after three days, there had been no confirmable detections, and he was beginning to think it was all a hopeless endeavor.

*Where were the enemy subs? Had they somehow slipped through Yamada's net, or had they headed for one of the other outlets far away to the south? How long would Yamada keep the Hamakaze and her sisters here listening to bubbles while other, more critical duties were neglected?*

Ando turned his attention back to the merchant ships. They had reached the open sea now, their smokestacks belching out thick columns of black smoke as their boilers built up steam. They would have to push hard on the next leg of their journey, though the most the lumbering craft could make was eight knots, and that was in a calm sea. They were at the beginning of a thousand-mile run down Japan's Pacific coast through waters prowled by enemy submarines, and they were going without an escort. Only through some miraculous stroke of luck would both make it through unscathed.

Steadying his binoculars on the pilothouse of the leading merchant, Ando could see the figures within going about their duties. Just shadows behind the glass. Nameless faces that had been written off by the high command. He wondered if those merchant sailors over there realized they had been deemed expendable. But, of course, they did. Despite what the high command wished people to believe, at this point in the war, the merchants all knew the risks. They simply did their duty, for the Emperor, for the homeland, just as the *Hamakaze's* sailors did theirs.

Still, Ando could not just let those brave merchantmen go to their deaths when it was perhaps within his power to head off such a tragedy. Surely, one escort would make no difference here.

"Forgive the intrusion, Admiral," Ando said, interrupting the conversation between Yamada and Kawaguchi. "But might I have a word with you, sir?"

Kawaguchi instantly picked up on the hint and bowed to Yamada. "If you will excuse me, Admiral. I must be about my duties. It has been a pleasure talking with you."

"Of course, Lieutenant," Yamada said with a smile, returning Kawaguchi's salute. "What is it, Hitoshi?" Yamada said to Ando after the lieutenant had left the bridge. "I can see the concern on your face."

"It is nothing of great importance, Admiral. I was just observing the freighters heading out to sea without an escort and was contemplating the hazards they will face. The thought occurred to me that we might send one of our destroyers, or perhaps one of our *kaibōkan*, to accompany them. We could easily adjust our search patterns to accommodate all sectors. From the inactivity we have experienced thus far, I believe it would have an insignificant impact on our blockade."

Ando had tried to keep his tone even and emotionless, but something in his delivery must have communicated his dissatisfaction with the current mission because he saw the admiral's eyes suddenly bristle with annoyance.

"As I have told you before, Captain," Yamada replied curtly, clearly angered by the suggestion. "I have allocated half of my patrol aircraft to that end. The merchants will be escorted, but compromises must be made. As you well know, resources are limited. We must choose one front and concentrate our forces there if we are to be successful. If we attempt to cover all fronts equally, we will lose everywhere. One *kaibōkan* and its 120 depth charges might make the difference between sinking the enemy submarines and letting them escape. And they *must not* be allowed to escape!" Yamada paused and looked away at the merchant ships as if waiting for his fury to subside before he spoke again. "How long have you been captain of the *Hamakaze*, Hitoshi?" Yamada said almost too calmly. "What has it been, two years now?"

"One year and ten months, admiral," Ando replied guardedly.

"That is a long time to carry such a burden. The strain of command takes its toll on everyone. I certainly remember how it affected me when I was in your shoes." Yamada then looked at him squarely. "If you are finding it difficult to understand the importance of our mission here, Captain, then perhaps you are overdue for an extended shore leave."

Ando swallowed hard. The threat had been made plainly enough. They were harsh words coming from a man he so admired. Ando's first instinct was to acquiesce and apologize, to assure the admiral of his commitment to the mission, but he resisted, for it would have been a lie. In the service to his country, in his responsibility to the men he commanded, Ando's sense of duty always took top priority. No matter how much he respected or felt beholden to his old teacher, honesty must always come before loyalty.

"Forgive me, Admiral, but I must speak plainly." Ando kept his voice low such that the nearby signalmen might not eavesdrop. "I believe this to be a vain pursuit. We are tying up valuable ships here when they are needed elsewhere. Our sailors and their families at home depend on us to use their lives for meaningful purposes."

"And you believe sending a *kaibōkan* to escort two freighters is more meaningful than what it is doing here?"

"Yes, sir, I do."

"And for the *Hamakaze* and the destroyers?" Yamada prompted. "Surely, you have devised a better use for them, as well?

There was a measure of ridicule in the admiral's tone, but it did not dissuade Ando from his present course. Derisive or not, he had the admiral's ear, and he had many ideas of how their ships might be better employed – one of them, in particular, he had been contemplating for the last two days.

"With respect, Admiral, I believe I have."

"Oh?" Yamada said icily. "Please, continue, Captain. I wish to hear this grand plan of yours."

"You and I have both seen the reports coming in from Attu over the last few days," Ando said, unfettered by the admiral's scornful manner. "The Americans have landed troops there. The island is expected to fall within weeks, if not days." Ando pointed to the gray shapes of the destroyers *Asakaze* and *Yamagumo* cruising a few miles off the beam. "Our destroyers have nearly full fuel tanks, Admiral. We could leave the *kaibōkan* and the subchasers here to continue the search for the enemy submarines and send our destroyers on a high-speed run to Attu."

"You do indeed have grandiose ideas, don't you, Hitoshi?" Yamada chortled. "But have you forgotten? There is already a large carrier fleet assembling in Tokyo Bay to deal with the American invasion force. That is one of the reasons we have so few ships and planes here."

"That fleet will not sail for several days," Ando countered. "Once it does, it will take a full week to get within striking range of Attu. At flank speed, we can be there in three days."

"And do what precisely, with a mere three destroyers and no air cover?"

"Weather reports from Attu indicate heavy cloud cover and unsuitable flying conditions. It is very likely we can approach the island unnoticed, using the other islands as cover to mask the Yankee radars. We can then pounce on the enemy transports and supply ships at night as they sit at anchor. Our long-range oxygen torpedoes will allow us to strike them before they even know we are there. We will launch wave after wave, wreaking havoc among them, just as our destroyers have done in the Solomons time and time again. We can then use our superior speed to withdraw before daylight. The Americans will believe they have been attacked by a much larger force and, following their standard doctrine, will withdraw to protect their remaining ships." Ando tried to suppress his enthusiasm as he described the script he had carefully worked out in his head, but he could hardly stand still at the prospect of such an action. "Then, Admiral, if conditions permit, we can take the wounded off Attu and make it back to friendly waters before the Americans know what has happened, even before our own fleet has sailed from Tokyo. We will have dealt the Americans a severe blow and saved the lives of many soldiers. It will be a great victory! It will be glor..." Ando stopped himself.

"Glorious, Captain?" Yamada said with a small smile.

Ando bridled internally at the admiral's quip, but outwardly he continued to exude the same confidence as before. "The submarines here are an unknown, sir. It is quite possible they have already slipped past us, or that they have headed back to Tsushima, or that they have found refuge in Vladivostok. In any event, we do not know when or if they will ever appear. The invasion fleet at Attu, on the other hand, is there. It is a firm target that we can attack and destroy."

For a long moment, Yamada said nothing. He stared across the water at the lumbering freighters, his face contemplative, the smug smile all but vanished, as if he was actually considering the plan. Ando had expected an immediate and outright snub, but now he got the sense that Yamada liked the idea. And for the first time Ando realized that, at least inwardly, Yamada was not convinced hunting for submarines was the best use of his ships. The order had, after all, come directly from the high command, including the direction that Yamada should commit *seppuku* if not successful. Yamada was merely following his orders. He was following them with vigor and inspiring his men to do the same – as any good flag officer should.

Suddenly, a wave of guilt swept over Ando for presenting the admiral with a mental quandary. The last thing the aging flag officer needed was an over-eager subordinate itching to take away his assets and trying to tear down his resolve. Ando immediately wished he could take back everything he had said.

"It is important that we are victorious here, Hitoshi," Yamada said earnestly. "It will not be a glorious victory as we might have had at Attu, but it will be far more significant. Worth sacrificing those two freighters. Yes, even worth sacrificing the men on Attu."

Ando was perplexed by this reply. "I am not sure I understand, Admiral."

"Japan is starving, Hitoshi. Our factories lack the raw materials needed to meet production demands. To put it simply, we are consuming war supplies faster than they can be replenished. This can be blamed on one thing, and one thing alone — the enemy's submarines. The Americans are slowly choking us to death. In the last two years, their subs have sunk over two million tons of shipping. Countless valuable resources — oil, rubber, and other goods for sustaining the war effort — resources that were our primary reasons for driving into Indochina, are now strewn across the ocean floor. We cannot keep up with such losses."

Ando gasped. He knew the enemy submarines were taking a significant toll on the merchant fleet, but he had no idea the proportions were on the order of a strategic disaster.

"You will keep this to yourself, Hitoshi," Yamada eyed him grimly. "The high command does not wish such news to reach the ears of the people. There is no need to start a general panic. They will feel its impact soon enough."

"We are building more merchants, are we not, sir?" Ando asked hopefully.

"Not fast enough to replace the losses. And there are not enough *kaibōkan* or destroyers to adequately escort our remaining convoys." Yamada sighed heavily. "At present, there is no viable solution for dealing with the Yankee submarines. And so, there can be only one final outcome."

Ando suddenly felt foolish about his proposed plan. What was the loss of a few soldiers on Attu next to the strangulation of the Empire? And he felt sudden anger at those in the high command who had let affairs get this far out of hand. Japan had submarines, many of which were far superior to the Americans' subs, but the old guard in the imperial staff were still set in their old ways. They viewed Japan's submarines as fourth-rate ships, behind battleships, cruisers, and destroyers. Submarines were there to support the main battle fleet and were to save their torpedoes for capital enemy warships. Why were they not being employed in the same manner as the Yankee submarines? Why were they not ranging along the coasts of North America, Australia, and New Guinea, sinking everything that steamed by?

"We must have a complete victory here, Ando," Yamada said in a tone that lacked his earlier passion. "Sinking one or two submarines will accomplish nothing. Three or four, however, will achieve a great deal. By concentrating so many of their submarines in one area, the Americans have handed us a golden opportunity. We can strike a serious blow here and now, a blow that will ripple across the Pacific. Though it may sometimes seem like the enemy has unlimited reserves, they do not. The loss of so many subs will necessitate a redrawing of their patrol zones. This will thin out their blockade for perhaps several weeks, maybe even months, allowing more of our ships to get through. Those few ships will mean an increase in production of war materials - new advanced planes and ships that could make the difference in the next major fleet engagement, or tanks and artillery pieces that could tip the balance in Burma and China. Perhaps most important of all, the Americans will never again risk sending their submarines into the Sea of Japan. Our shipping routes there, at least, will be protected, allowing raw materials and goods to be transported from the mainland unhindered." Yamada turned to Ando half-smiling. "Hunting submarines is often an unrewarding endeavor. We may never know for certain that we sank any. But the enemy will know. The admirals in Pearl Harbor and Washington will know, and that is all that matters."

Something in Yamada's tone left Ando uncomfortable. "Regarding your vow, Admiral. Surely, probable sinkings will be enough to satisfy the high command. Surely, they will not demand hard evidence for the destruction of three enemy submarines."

Yamada did not respond, but his eyes indicated that was not the case.

*That was it then*, Ando thought. *The high command expects nothing less than complete and verifiable victory.*

"You know, Hitoshi, I, too, would like nothing more than to take this squadron to Attu and face our enemies in a glorious battle." Yamada paused looking wistfully out at the sea. "But, as you said, we must use the lives of our men carefully. We must make certain their sacrifice contributes to ultimate victory in this war."

Ando bowed to his old teacher, suddenly embarrassed. "You are right, sir. Forgive me for ever doubting our purpose here. I will be committed to this mission with my whole heart from this point forward.

Yamada smiled. "I have known you a long time, Hitoshi. You have an honest nature, and you are very poor at lying."

# 13

# THE FOG

*North Pacific Ocean*

*500 miles east of the Kuril Islands*

*USS Aeneid*

Two days after the encounter with the freighter, the *Aeneid* entered waters within range of the enemy airfields in the Kurils. The standard precautions were taken. The lookouts were doubled. Water was brought into the auxiliary tanks so that the submarine might crash dive faster should the need arise. The SD radar operator kept his face glued to the oscilloscope display, anticipating that small, green spike that might indicate a plane was somewhere within the radar's reach. The farther the submarine drove into Japanese waters, the more the tension rose among the crew. But those tensions were somewhat relieved when, late in the afternoon of the same day, a bank of fog appeared on the western horizon and quickly rolled over the sea to encompass the *Aeneid*, reducing visibility to a few hundred yards.

"Let's bring another main engine on the line, Stu," Weston ordered Monk who was on watch as the officer of the deck. Both men leaned against the bridge rail straining their eyes to see into the thick blanket all around the ship. "If we can't see the Japs, then they can't see us. Let's use that to our advantage and make some headway."

"Aye, aye, Captain." Monk leaned over to the intercom. "Maneuvering, prepare to place another main engine on propulsion. Steersman, all ahead full."

The orders were acknowledged, and soon the murmur of the engines shifted to a higher octave. The vibration in the deck plates increased as the green wake stretched farther astern and grew more vibrant. Within a matter of minutes, the speed log showed the *Aeneid* moving through the water at nearly seventeen knots.

Weston smiled as he pictured Chief Hoffman moving from one stifling engine room to the next, barking orders to his grease-covered men above the clamor of the four 1,600 horsepower diesels. The massive engines – dubbed Moe, Larry, Curly, and Shemp by the machinist's mates – generated enough power to propel the *Aeneid* through the water at eighteen knots on a calm day, with enough left over to charge her batteries and drive all her lights, pumps, galley range, radio, radar, and sonar equipment. The diesels were the heart of the submarine, and the skilled men who nurtured them were cut from a different mold than the rest. If the other men were made of iron, then the machinist's mates were made of steel. Daily, they withstood conditions worse than most POW camps, seldom getting to see the light of day, spending most of each voyage confined to the stifling, oily, deafening engine rooms with little awareness of what was going on in the world above.

As night fell, the *Aeneid's* wake began to glow as a phosphorescent green tail stretching several hundred yards astern. It could have easily been seen by any patrolling aircraft within twenty miles, had it not been for the thick blanket of mist shrouding the sea. Though dazzling to observe, the abundant plankton in these waters was an eternal curse to submarines, practically an invitation for any aircraft in the vicinity to attack. Even with the fog, Weston was reluctant to maintain the *Aeneid's* present speed. But the ship had a schedule to meet, and every opportunity to run fast had to be taken.

It was a standing policy aboard the *Aeneid* that either Weston or Townsend be awake whenever the ship was in enemy waters. Thus, Weston had been on the bridge for most of the day and well into the early evening, only going below to briefly eat and sift through reports. Now, with a new section having just relieved the watch, he was ready to go below for some much-needed sleep. Like clockwork, Townsend emerged from the hatch in the deck. Having slept a few hours in the afternoon, the XO was ready to take over for the overnight watch. They performed the standard turnover, going over the chart in the red-lit control room, discussing where the *Aeneid* had been, where she was projected to be in the next twelve hours, what navigational hazards they expected to encounter, what maintenance was being performed, and several other things not in the night order book.

Finally, with Townsend taking his place on the bridge with the OOD, Weston headed below. On the way to his stateroom, he stopped by the empty wardroom to grab a leftover roll from the evening's dinner. Farther down the corridor, the never-ending *rat-tat-tat* came from the ship's office where the tireless yeoman never seemed to stop. That yeoman was meticulous, Weston mused. The *Aeneid's* records would certainly stand up to any scrutiny should she be subjected to a surprise inspection someday.

Drawing the curtain to his stateroom shut, Weston stripped down to his t-shirt and settled into his bunk. The speaker on the bulkhead next to his ear intoned the voice exchanges between the officer of the deck on the bridge and the steersman in the conning tower, the volume level set so that he could just hear it above the muffled purr of the diesels. Again, the same thoughts roiled within his weary mind, the same thoughts that tormented the captain of any ship before trying to sleep.

*Have I trained them well enough? Will they know what to do when things go wrong?*

No sooner had Weston drifted off to sleep than he was abruptly awakened by Monk's agitated voice blaring over the speaker.

"Torpedoes off the starboard beam! Hard left rudder! Port, stop! Starboard, ahead full!"

Weston bolted from his bunk, his legs moving by themselves. He had already groped his way to the control room and was climbing the ladder by the time he was fully awake. Passing through the conning tower, he knew he did not have to say anything to Sullivan who was intently hovering over the SJ radar station. The attentive sailor had already trained the radar to sweep the seas off the starboard side. By the time Weston emerged on the darkened bridge, Sullivan was already reporting over the speaker.

"Bridge, SJ radar holds no contacts."

"Keep checking!" Monk shouted into the microphone, the panic evident in his tone.

Weston took up position beside him scanning the seas to starboard. Townsend was there, too. He did not acknowledge Weston but kept his binoculars glued to his face. Up in the periscope shears, the starboard lookout focused on the same spot, his torso leaning out over the circular ring that kept him from being catapulted into the sea each time the ship rolled. The *Aeneid* was already leaning over hard to starboard, her phosphorescent wake curving sharply astern. Torrents of white spray were thrown upon her main and gun decks as her bow dipped and crashed into the black swells rolling from the south.

"I hold the torpedoes visually, Captain," Townsend said.

At that moment, Weston involuntarily met eyes with Yates as the older sailor handed him a set of binoculars. The gray-haired quartermaster looked back at Weston uncertainly, his face grave. Weston knew that for Yates to look like that, the situation had to be serious.

Quickly putting the binoculars to his face, Weston strained his eyes to find the incoming weapons, but not without a certain measure of skepticism. It would not be the first time a nervous OOD was spooked by spindrift or a curling wave. But when Weston finally found the objects in question, he swallowed hard.

A few hundred yards off the starboard bow, two long phosphorescent streaks glowed bright green just beneath the black waters. They were similar to the *Aeneid's* own plankton-energized Wake, only much thinner – and they were moving much faster.

*They were torpedoes! And they were heading straight for the starboard bow!*

Like glowing fingers, they reached out for the submarine's hull, drawing closer with every breath. But the *Aeneid's* bow was already coming over to the left, and, after only a few seconds of observation, Weston could tell that the green wakes would miss by nearly one hundred yards. They would not have missed had the *Aeneid* continued on her original course. Monk's quick thinking had saved the ship.

"Good work, Stu." Weston clapped Monk on the shoulder.

Monk looked shaken and embarrassed. "Actually, Captain, it wasn't my –,"

"Good work indeed, Mister Monk!" Townsend interrupted wearing a wide grin. "That was swift thinking."

Still somewhat shame-faced, Monk shot Townsend an uncertain look and then turned his attention back to the sea. Townsend did the same, assuming a straight face and bringing up his binoculars as if to avoid his captain's suspicious gaze.

Weston chuckled inwardly. He could deduce what had really happened. Though Monk was a veteran on his third patrol, no one was ever truly ready for the first time they spotted torpedoes coming their way. More than likely, Monk had frozen and had simply done as Townsend had ordered him to do. It had been Townsend's quick thinking, not Monk's, that had saved the ship. Weston saw no reason to call either man out on it. Certainly, Monk would never forget what to do should he ever face a similar situation in the future.

"Keep an eye out for that enemy submarine," Weston called up to the lookouts. "If the SJ didn't pick him up, then he's probably submerged. Look for his periscope." Weston was about to remind Monk to use a zigzag course for the next few hours when a sudden exclamation came from Townsend.

"What the hell?" The executive officer was once again gaping at the torpedo wakes.

Weston brought his binoculars to bear again on the glowing streaks and gasped in disbelief at what he saw. Somehow, the torpedoes had changed course. They had turned and were once again heading straight for the *Aeneid.*

"Continue the turn, Lieutenant!" Weston ordered. "All ahead flank!"

Monk quickly passed the orders over the intercom, and the ship continued to steer left, now having turned almost one hundred eighty degrees away from her original course. But still, the torpedoes followed, changing direction once again to account for the *Aeneid's* maneuver.

They were now mere seconds from impact.

Weston snatched up the 1MC ship-wide announcing circuit. "Sound collision! All hands brace for impact!"

Now ignoring their sectors, the lookouts' attention turned toward the impending doom. Like his men, Weston watched helplessly as the slim green wakes closed from astern. The behavior of these weapons had left him baffled. He knew of new torpedoes under development, self-guided weapons equipped with a listening sonar to home in on a ship's screw noise. But they were months, if not years, away from deployment to the fleet. Had the Japanese already developed such a device? Perhaps they had obtained it from their German allies.

*But none of that really mattered now*, Weston thought. The weapons did exist. They were here. And there was no way the *Aeneid* could get away.

Then, as Weston watched forlornly, he saw something very odd. The wakes of the two torpedoes converged and separated several times, weaving in and out, repeatedly crossing each other's paths as if they were set at different depths. The course corrections were subtle, smooth, and quick – too subtle, smooth, and quick for any mechanical device.

Weston suddenly felt like a fool.

Pressing the talk button on the 1MC microphone, he spoke calmly. "This is the captain. I have the conn. Secure from collision. All hands stand down. All ahead standard. Rudder amidships."

Monk and Townsend and every other man on the bridge gaped at him with white-faced horror, but no one said anything. As the *Aeneid's* speed fell off, the two green wakes were soon lost amid the foam churned up by the submarine's screws.

"Bridge, answering all ahead two thirds," the steersman reported, the uncertainty in his voice matching the expressions of those on the bridge. They were all clearly convinced the torpedoes would hit at any moment.

But Weston replied calmly. "Very well." He then flashed a smile at the men around him and gestured at the water below. "Be sure to get a good look at them, gentlemen, as they go by. You don't see this sort of thing every day."

"As they go by?" Monk said incredulously, clearly believing his captain had gone mad.

An instant later, a bright streak emerged from beneath the hull, passed up the port beam, then took up a position just beyond the bow. It then proceeded to zip to the right and left, in and out of the submarine's bow wave. Soon another streak joined it, then two more, then three, all weaving back and forth across the bow while matching the *Aeneid's* speed.

"Well, kiss the gunner's daughter!" Yates exclaimed with a toothy grin. "They're just dolphins!"

A collective disbelief pervaded on the bridge and in the lookout perches as the realization set in that they had all been tricked by mother nature. The pulsing tails of the dolphins had stirred the bioluminescence in the water just as the spinning propellers of torpedoes would have done. Suddenly overwhelmed with relief, the men began to laugh and point at the frolicking animals who put on quite a show for them, zipping this way and that, some leaping from the water and crashing back into the sea like schoolchildren at play.

It was a common enough occurrence to encounter dolphins at sea. Weston could not count how many times he had seen schools of the sociable creatures leaping from the bow waves of the various ships he had sailed in his career. But this was the first time he had ever encountered them in the dark while traveling through plankton-infested seas. He would certainly never forget it. The glowing dolphins looked like something from another world, like the spirits of ancient shipwrecks beckoning the living to join them in their watery graves. Weston could only imagine what the ancient mariners must have thought. Such phenomena no doubt gave rise to many of the sea legends of old.

"Sorry, Captain," Monk said. "I had no idea."

"Nor did I, Stu," Weston admitted. "Not until a minute ago. We were both hoodwinked by a couple of fish. You still did the right thing. I'd rather turn away from dolphins all night than get hit by one torpedo."

"Thank you, sir."

"You can thank me by relieving me of the conn." Weston looked sideways at Townsend whose white-toothed grin stood out in the darkness. "I'm going to get some sleep."

"Aye, sir," Monk replied. "I relieve you, sir."

"I stand relieved." Weston began heading toward the ladder but stopped short when he noticed that the lookouts were still directing their attention toward the dolphins, cheering the sea creatures on instead of watching their sectors.

"Don't worry, Captain," Monk said. "I'll take care of it."

At first, Weston nodded, but then he paused. The *Aeneid's* crew had been through a lot since departing San Diego all those weeks ago, and perhaps the most challenging part of the voyage still lay ahead. From the officers to the chiefs, the electricians to the torpedomen, the auxiliarymen to the firemen, the cooks to the stewards, every man had done his duty and had done it well. Weston had no complaints. He would give his life for every last one of them.

"Give them a little time, Stu," Weston said quietly with a smile. "Let them relax for a couple more minutes. Heaven knows, they deserve it."

# 14

# HUNTERS AND PREY

*Sea of Japan*

*USS Sea Dog*

Coordinates *46-degrees 24-minutes north, 140-degrees 2-minutes east* lay open and vacant as dusk fell over the mirror-like sea. The position marked a remote area in the Sea of Japan far from any shipping lanes. Whales often spouted in these seldom-hunted waters, but the two objects broaching the surface this evening were not whales.

Two disturbances formed a mile apart, two separate spots where the ocean boiled. First, the triangular bows appeared, then the masts, then the rust-streaked conning towers, and finally the wooden decks and black, steel hulls of two American submarines. Flashes were exchanged between the darkened bridges as the boats approached each other. After a few skillful maneuvers, they were running on parallel courses with only a few dozen yards of black water separating them.

"Ahoy, *Sea Dog*!" Came an amplified voice from one bridge.

"Ahoy, *Finback*! Good to see you, Tommy!" Commander Fred Prewitt, captain of the *Sea Dog*, answered. He withdrew the megaphone from his face for a moment and forced a white-toothed grin, knowing his counterpart on the other submarine was probably looking back at him through binoculars. Prewitt then returned the megaphone to his lips. "What's your status?"

"All fish expended," came the reply. "Low on food. Fuel level critical. How about you, Fred?"

Prewitt cursed under his breath before lifting the megaphone again. "Two fish left over here. The rest the same as you. Time to go home, don't you think?"

"I agree. You think the Japs will leave the back gate open for us?"

"About as much as I think Rita Hayworth will be waiting for us on the pier in Pearl." Prewitt turned to the officer beside him, suddenly business-like. "Tommy's out of fish, XO."

"Looks that way, skipper," the *Sea Dog's* executive officer replied drearily, rubbing the scraggly, five-week-old beard on his chin. "God help us."

"Amen to that." Prewitt smiled encouragingly at his second in command, a devout Presbyterian who diligently read the Holy Bible every night and often prayed with members of the crew. Prewitt was not much of a praying man himself, but in times like these, he appreciated any invocation on his behalf. "The plan doesn't change, then. We go out in the original order." Prewitt turned to the man standing ready with the signal lantern and pointed at the hand-written message on the XO's clipboard. "Send it, Smitty, just as it's written there."

"Aye, Captain," the signalman replied. The XO held a red-filtered flashlight to the clipboard such that the sailor could read each of the encoded characters and convert them into a series of long and short flashing lights.

As the shutter on the lantern flapped, Prewitt held his binoculars steady on the other submarine. The lighting was dim, but he could make out the signalman on the other bridge jotting down the characters as Smitty sent them. The signalman disappeared for a moment, presumably having descended into the conning tower to decode the message, before returning and presenting it to his captain.

Prewitt watched as the *Finback's* captain, *Tommy*, read the message then looked up and raised the megaphone again.

"Understood, Fred! Will do. Just make sure you don't wait too long."

Prewitt waved back. "Don't worry about us, Tommy. We'll be along."

"I'll have a cold beer waiting for you at The Gooneyville! Good luck! Godspeed, my friend!"

"Same to you!"

Final gestures were exchanged between the clusters of men on each bridge, some friendly, some crude, all in the spirit of camaraderie. They were two crews, thousands of miles from home, adrift in a sea controlled by their enemy.

The two submarines parted in opposite directions. They would open the distance between them by several dozen miles before turning southeast and heading for La Perouse Strait, some one hundred miles beyond the horizon. Though both submarines shared the same destination, they would arrive at the strait staggered by two hours, the *Finback* arriving first, per the orders Prewitt had just given to his counterpart via signal lamp.

"How about that, Skipper?" the XO said to Prewitt on *Sea Dog's* cigarette deck as they watched the other submarine disappear astern. "Between three boats, ours is the only one who didn't shoot off all her fish."

"What are you trying to say, XO?" Prewitt replied good-naturedly. "That we haven't been aggressive enough?"

The XO smiled. "That's one accusation I don't think could ever be levied at us, Skipper. Three freighters sunk and one probable is a respectable score for our humble boat."

"You failed to mention the four prematures, the dud, and the three run-unders," Prewitt added bleakly.

The XO's smile faded as the frustration of those attacks came to mind, perfect set-ups ruined by faulty torpedoes. Had those torpedoes run true, the *Sea Dog* would have added three more enemy ships to her tally. "Hopefully, we won't need to use those last two fish, Captain." The XO clasped his hands together and looked up at the stars. "Lord, help us not to use them."

Prewitt was not sure that was the way he would have worded it, but he gave his hearty endorsement, anyway. "Amen to that."

Soon the black shape of the *Finback* had dissolved into the darkness beyond *Sea Dog's* wake, and Prewitt let out a long sigh, trying not to think about the three crews, the two hundred forty men, whose lives hung on his decision. As the senior captain in *Wolfpack 351*, it was his responsibility to coordinate the withdrawal from the Sea of Japan, and, despite some misgivings, he was reasonably confident the plan he had devised was the soundest, considering the constraints with which he had to work.

He forced himself to be optimistic. Tomorrow night, if all went as planned, the wolfpack would slip out through La Perouse Strait and be half-way across the Sea of Okhotsk by sundown of the following day. If they made it to the Pacific, they stood a fair chance of making it home. Sure, there would still be two thousand miles of open ocean to cross before reaching Midway, but the water was deep, and the SD radar would give them ample notice should any long-range patrol planes appear.

But it was difficult for Prewitt to remain hopeful when he knew how high the odds were stacked against them. Should the Japanese catch their scent as they passed through the strait, an untold number of destroyers, escorts, and aircraft would be unleashed on them, dropping an inexhaustible supply of depth charges and bombs. In that event, the *Sea Dog's* torpedoes – the last two weapons in the wolfpack – might find some employment. But, in all truthfulness, her two fish would be of little use against high-speed destroyers.

Though the crew outwardly exhibited indestructible confidence, every man knew what was coming. They had exacted great punishment on the enemy over the past several weeks, torpedoing ships from one end of the Sea of Japan to the other. Now came the payback.

Prewitt had often overheard his men comparing the hazardous run through La Perouse Strait to that faced by German U-boats going through the Strait of Gibraltar, but that comparison fell somewhat short. Gibraltar was extremely deep, a trait that had allowed so many U-boats to pass through undetected, whereas La Perouse was shallow, sounding less than thirty fathoms in many places. That meant that a submerged submarine must cruise several fathoms above that depth to account for chart errors and undiscovered geological changes. Should a submarine be caught in that shallow water during daylight hours, its dark shape would be clearly visible to any searching aircraft. It was less than ideal, but it was the only means of escape. And, like his men, Prewitt just wanted to get on with it, to get it over with. He wished they had made the attempt two weeks ago, but he had received orders from ComSubPac to wait.

It seemed ComSubPac was reluctant to send its boats through that gauntlet after the *Blueback*, the first boat in the wolfpack to attempt the breakout, had stirred up a virtual hornet's nest and had been savaged by a massive depth charge attack. The *Sea Dog* had been some two hundred miles away from the strait at the time, but her sonar had clearly monitored the tumult, a seemingly endless repetition of underwater detonations echoing across the cold depths. Prewitt remembered how it had sounded, like a burgeoning sea mount rumbling far in the distance. The fate of the *Blueback* was still unknown to rest of the wolfpack. Did she make it home, or was she a lifeless hulk on the sea floor? Perhaps ComSubPac knew. If it did, it had not seen fit to tell the *Sea Dog* and her sisters.

For the last week, the three submarines had monitored the VLF waves, waiting for guidance. Like the other boats, the *Sea Dog* had spent her time meandering aimlessly in seldom traveled waters, submerging during the day, and surfacing to recharge batteries at night. She had drawn giant circles in the sea as the crew waited the interminable wait, like condemned prisoners anticipating their turn before a firing squad. As they had watched fuel levels and food supplies dwindle, scuttlebutt had begun circulating that ComSubPac had written them off.

Then, finally, the long-awaited message had come, addressed to all three submarines.

FROM:     COMSUBPAC

TO:       WP351A / WP351B / WP351D

EXIT LA PEROUSE STRAIT NO EARLIER THAN 2000 15 MAY AND NLT 0200 16 MAY. DIVERSION PLANNED TO DRAW OFF ENEMY FORCES. CO *SEA DOG* IN OVERALL COMMAND. *SEA DOG* RENDEZVOUS WITH *PINTADO* 2100 13 MAY AT COORDINATES 46-24N, 140-02E. *SEA DOG* RENDEZVOUS WITH *FINBACK* 2100 14 MAY AT SAME COORDINATES. COORDINATE DEPARTURE SEA OF JAPAN.

And so, the wheels had been set in motion. Prewitt had devised a plan of escape, which he had communicated to the *Finback* this evening, and to the *Pintado* during a similar rendezvous last night.

The plan was straightforward. Tomorrow, before reaching the range of Japanese shore radars, all three submarines would surface and charge batteries as best they could while avoiding enemy aircraft. At dusk, they would approach the strait submerged. When the black of night had fallen over the sea, they would start the perilous run. Rather than pass through the strait one at a time and risk another delay should one boat draw an attack, Prewitt had decided on an all-or-nothing approach. All three submarines would run through the strait nearly simultaneously, staggered by two-hour intervals. They would have roughly ten miles of separation between them to allow for maneuvering. *Pintado* would lead the underwater procession, followed by *Finback*, and finally, the *Sea Dog* would bring up the rear. As the last boat in line, *Sea Dog* ran the highest risk and would undoubtedly receive the heaviest shellacking should one of the other boats set off the enemy defenses. She would be driving straight into a swarm of alerted destroyers and escorts with no option to turn back.

Prewitt had intended all along for his boat to go out last. He could not bring himself to place another captain and crew in that dreaded position. The fact that *Pintado* and *Finback* had expended all their torpedoes now gave him a logical justification for it – something to assuage the few members of his crew who were not happy the *Sea Dog* had drawn the short straw.

No one underestimated the formidable nature of the task before them. Even if the current ran in their favor, the excursion would take nearly fourteen hours – fourteen hours creeping along at a turtle's pace while rigged for silent running, the refrigeration plant shut down, the air growing stale, battery voltages diminishing. It was possible that, should the Japanese detect them, the sheer number of submarines might overwhelm the Japanese ASW screen by giving them too many contacts to track. But, then, Prewitt mused, there was little chance of that. If the reports from ComSubPac were accurate, La Perouse Strait had become a rendezvous for half the Jap fleet. They would have ample resources to deal with three American submarines.

"I wonder what the diversion is, Skipper," the XO said suddenly.

"What?"

"The diversion mentioned in ComSubPac's message. I wonder what it is." The XO's face was silhouetted in the moonlight as he stared out at the sea. Like every other man on the *Sea Dog*, it was clear that he, too, was apprehensive about the next forty-eight hours.

Prewitt smiled. "I'm hoping for Halsey's carriers, XO, but I'll settle for anything."

Again, the XO's hands clasped together, and again he tilted his head to view the twinkling heavens. "Lord, let it be a good one."

"Amen to that."

# 15

# MATSUWA

*The Kuril Islands*

*USS Aeneid*

"Matsuwa, gentlemen," Weston announced as he steadied the periscope lens on the land mass rising out of the sea ten miles ahead of the *Aeneid's* submerged bow.

At this distance, the only part of Matsuwa he could see was the steep cinder cone of the volcano on the north end of the island, its pyramid-like peak shrouded in a veil of clouds. It stood some five thousand feet above sea level giving Weston an excellent visual reference with which to guide the *Aeneid* closer to their objective. The southern end of the island containing the Japanese airfield was too low in elevation to be visible yet and was still beyond the horizon.

Switching to high power magnification, Weston focused on two dark objects in the distance rising into the mid-afternoon sky.

"Two more aircraft," he said. "Mark this bearing."

"Two five zero," Reynolds read off.

"Range, ten thousand yards."

The quiet chatter among the others in the conning tower ceased, and Weston knew they were all wondering if the new aircraft would present a threat.

"They just took off from Matsuwa," he said, attempting to put them at ease. "Looks like they're heading south. They won't be a problem."

Pulling his eyes away from the mesmerizing volcano, Weston performed a sweep of the entire horizon and then did another turn around the skies. Visibility was good, with scattered clouds above. Satisfied there were no other contacts, he took a few seconds to stand upright and relax the sore muscles in his back before putting his face to the eyepiece again and focusing on the distant island.

The last two days had been tedious and tiresome. The *Aeneid* had run submerged during the day – long, silent hours running on the battery in which barely twenty miles was traversed between each watch relief. The only break in the monotony had been the enemy patrol planes, which had been sighted more frequently with each passing hour. Most had been too far away to be of any danger, but that would not last. As the *Aeneid* drew closer to the airfield on Matsuwa, so would the risk of detection. The water around the island was relatively clear – clear enough that it would not take a keen-eyed pilot to sight the submarine's black shape lying just beneath the surface, or the feather of spray produced by her periscope. The watch officers would have to be on their toes and perform their safety sweeps at more frequent intervals.

Aside from the aircraft, the activity around Matsuwa had seemed unnervingly scarce. The only contacts had been a small group of sail-driven sampans and a single Japanese patrol craft earlier in the day. The patrol vessel had never come closer than five miles, just a stand of masts on the western horizon, driving south at a moderate speed, never deviating from its course. It had disappeared from view and the sound of its screws had quickly faded in Finkelman's headset.

*Perhaps it was on its way to join the enemy forces around La Perouse Strait,* Weston thought. Wherever it was going, it had not come back. It was somewhat unsettling that, in the coming hours, the *Aeneid* would try to entice that patrol craft, and all other anti-submarine forces in the area, to converge on Matsuwa.

"Alright, XO," Weston said. "Let's start piloting using the landmarks we discussed."

"Aye, Captain." Townsend took up his parallel ruler and pencil at the plot table.

In the preceding days, they had carefully reviewed the chart of the area and had picked out two conceivable spots from which the *Aeneid* could hurl her six-inch shells at the airfield and view the fall of the shots without running onto a shoal. They had also picked out several prominent land features they would use to triangulate the ship's position. Determining the *Aeneid's* precise location would be crucial for tonight's operation. If they captured a few good fixes before sunset, the DRT plotting table would have a solid position to use as the starting point for its dead reckoning trace.

"I hold peak number two, XO," Weston said as he steadied the periscope reticle on a jutting shoulder of rock about half-way up the southern slope of the volcano. "Bearing, mark."

"Two six eight," Reynolds called out.

Weston then rotated the scope to the right until the volcano's misty peak filled the field of view. "Peak number one is partially obscured, but I'll take a guess at it. Bearing, mark."

"Two seven six."

"The southern headland is still over the horizon," Weston said, referring to the third chosen landmark, a jutting cape that was the southernmost extent of the island.

"That two-point fix puts us eight miles out, Captain," Townsend reported after marking the intersection of the two lines of bearing on his chart.

They continued plotting fixes for the better part of the next hour, refining the *Aeneid's* position as it slowly approached the quiet island. When the entire island was finally visible, Weston stopped passing bearings to perform a closer inspection of the coast. The flatter portions of the island were emerald green, shrub-covered lowlands. In high power magnification, he saw a steep berm rising from the shoreline all along the rocky east coast. Poking up from beyond the berm were flag poles and the tops of several buildings. The metal lattice of a radio tower stood among the structures. The command building was likely nearby, though Weston could not see anything more than the roofs of the buildings. Somewhat separated from the structures, a brightly colored windsock stood out stiffly in the breeze, presumably marking the end of the runway. Weston assumed planes were parked just beyond that berm, but he could not be sure. Nor could he see the fuel storage tanks the intelligence reports had placed at the west end of the airstrip.

"It's just like we figured, XO," he said with mild disappointment. "Both of our objectives are completely masked from this side of the island."

"There's also shoal water here running out nearly three miles from the coast, Skipper, assuming our charts are correct," Townsend replied. "That rules out this location."

"I concur. Down scope." Weston slapped up the periscope handles. "Take her down to one hundred feet. Steersman, come left to one eight zero. XO, plot a course for the deep water off the south side of the island. Let's have a look from over there."

Moving to the south side of the island would take the submarine, just barely, into the Sea of Okhotsk. Weston tried not to let his disappointment show. He had hoped to remain on the Pacific side of Matsuwa for the entire operation. Bombarding the island from there would have afforded an easy withdrawal route to the Pacific. Performing the bombardment from the Sea of Okhotsk side, on the other hand, came with many hazards. It was possible the Japanese had hydrophones and magnetic loops strung along the sea floor between Matsuwa and

Rasshua, the next island to the south which Weston could neither detect nor avoid. Should a few escorts show up and things get hot, he might be forced to evade to the west, which would take the *Aeneid* farther into the Sea of Okhotsk and closer to more Japanese air bases. And then there were the mines…

The *Aeneid* spent the next two hours maneuvering to the south and rounding the southern promontory with periodic checks at periscope depth. There were two or three hair-raising moments on the journey when the fathometer soundings jumped up several dozen feet shallower than what was annotated on the chart. Such an error was not completely unexpected, since the chart bore the date April 1ˢᵗ, 1922. But it forced Weston to order the *Aeneid* higher and higher until the conning tower was only inches away from broaching the surface. Some skillful maneuvering and a risky interval of continuous soundings on the fathometer eventually saw them safely beyond the shoal water and finally to a point less than three miles off the southern coast.

"We're in deep water now, Captain," Townsend reported cautiously, still not trusting the accuracy of the chart. "There's fifty fathoms beneath the keel in most places around here, and we should be in a good position to see the airstrip."

"Very well, XO. Go to periscope depth, Joe. Be ready to go down fast."

Weston was already spinning the scope around by the time the lens broke the surface. After three full sweeps of the sky and the sea, he breathed a little easier.

"No close contacts," he announced, then steadied the lens on a black shape to the west. He had seen the object during his first rounds with the periscope, but it had been too distant to raise any alarm. "I hold a small freighter to the west." He announced, then began scanning the area again for any escorts he might have missed. When he was satisfied that there were none, he turned his attention back to the freighter. "Stand by for observation. Bearing, mark."

"Three zero zero," Reynolds called out.

"Use a thirty-foot masthead height." Weston flipped a switch on the side of the periscope, and the freighter in his field of view split into two images. One image remained stationary while the other moved up and down as he adjusted the periscope elevation angle. Carefully rotating the periscope handle, he moved one image until it was on top of the other, keel-to-mast. "Range, mark."

"Seven oh double-oh," Reynolds read off the range from the stadimeter scale on the opposite side of the periscope, which automatically solved the trigonometric equation using the freighter's masthead height and the angle formed by the horizon and the tilt of the periscope lens.

Seven thousand yards was about what Weston had expected. The freighter sat off the southwest coast of Matsuwa presenting its starboard broadside to the *Aeneid*. It rode the gentle swells with no sign of getting underway anytime soon. Its single stack did not emit even a wisp of smoke.

"She's at anchor," Weston said. "Just sitting there, quiet as a church on Saturday. I put her at five thousand tons. She'll make a fine target when the fireworks go off tonight."

Even from this range, Weston could see the anchor chain clearly. It stood out from the freighter's blunt bow at a large angle, a clear indication of how strong the current was here. Weston made a mental note of that. Townsend would have to compensate for the current so that there would be no errors tonight.

Switching to high power, Weston saw clusters of sailors idling on the freighter's deck. They chatted and smoked, the attentiveness of their normal sea routine all but abandoned. He noted the rust streaks near the scuppers, the sparse paint job, the patches on the hull, and soon concluded that the vessel was in a deplorable state. Everything from the pilothouse to the anchor chain looked old. It was probably from the era of the Great War and had been consigned to carrying provisions, parts, and mail to the Japanese garrisons in the Kurils. The five-hundred-mile voyage across the Sea of Okhotsk from the Japanese homeland was probably all the little ship could manage.

Comfortable that there was enough spindrift on the surface to adequately conceal the *Aeneid's* periscope from those lounging sailors, Weston rotated ninety degrees to the right until Matsuwa's southern coast filled the field of view. The coast was not as rocky here as it was on the eastern shore. There was even a short, half-mile strip of sandy beach. From the shoreline, the landscape sloped upward gradually, allowing him a clear view of the grasslands and foothills running all the way up to the base of the mountain. Most importantly, he had a nearly unobstructed view of the Japanese base. All the buildings were clearly visible now – four hangars and a half-dozen outlying buildings that probably filled the roles of barracks, headquarters, infirmary, and mess hall.

"Mark this bearing," he said as he steadied the reticle on the largest hangar.

"Zero one two."

"That matches with the chart, skipper," Townsend reported. "That's the air base."

Weston was encouraged by that information. It meant the intelligence reports had at least some truth to them. But something was wrong. He could see the buildings clearly, even several flags fluttering in the breeze. He could see the tailfins of a dozen or more aircraft, all well-separated and parked within individual earthworks. But what he did not see was any fuel tanks. If the intel was correct, then the tank farm should be visible just beyond the west side of the runway. He could see the west side of the runway clearly, but there was nothing there, only empty fields.

"Recommend a safety sweep, Captain," Reynolds said quietly. The sailor was closely monitoring the clock on the bulkhead, keeping track of the time between scans of the full azimuth.

Weston did not respond, nor did he take his eyes from the scope. He knew it was time to check the other sectors, but he was frustrated and intrigued. He allowed himself another half-minute focused on the land, reducing the magnification to get an all-encompassing view of the areas around and beyond the enemy base. It took only about ten seconds for his eye to catch sight of something among the foothills farther inland, something that did not fit in against the gorges and crevasses of the mountain beyond. A few hundred feet up the sloping terrain, a long line of green foliage ran about a half a mile east-to-west, marking a summit of some kind. The line was almost perfectly horizontal, perfectly straight – too straight to be natural.

Weston suddenly realized he was looking at a series of man-made earthworks constructed atop a natural ridgeline. As he watched, a small dot appeared below the summit and began weaving its way down the hillside slowly moving towards the airfield. In increased magnification, Weston saw that it was a standard army truck. He could not make out the road the vehicle followed and assumed it was hidden by the knee-high shrubs that covered most of the island's lowlands. The road must have been well-constructed since the truck appeared to have no trouble moving at a moderate pace downhill.

Of course, Weston concluded. The fuel tanks were up there. They had to be. They were hidden in one of those crevasses beyond the earthworks. The truck was bringing fuel down to the airfield. What else would it be doing up in those foothills? Why else would the Japanese have placed a good road there? With the tide of the war turning against them almost everywhere in the Pacific, their island garrisons were beginning to fear attacks from ranging carrier and battleship squadrons. The Japanese had moved the fuel tanks far up into the hills, deep within one of those shadowy volcanic fissures, where a battleship's shells or a dive bomber's payload would have trouble scoring a decisive hit. They had then fortified it further by adding works of their own. If the fuel depot was there, then it was definitely beyond the reach of the *Aeneid's* guns.

That was a problem – *a big problem.*

Weston checked the clock on the bulkhead. Five hours to H-Hour. Five hours until they were to wake up the Japanese on that small, peaceful island. Sure, the *Aeneid* would have no trouble creating a diversion. But if the fuel tanks were not destroyed, the whole point of the diversion might be for nothing. With the airfield on Matsuwa operational, the wolfpack might escape the Sea of Japan only to be sunk as they attempted to pass through the Kurils.

"Down scope." Weston closed the periscope handles in frustration. "Make your depth one hundred fifty feet. Pass the word for all officers to meet in the control room."

# 16

# PLAN IT WELL

The chart table in the center of the *Aeneid's* control room was much larger and more accessible than the one in the conning tower, and thus was a better place for discussing plans that involved land masses and shoals. The submarine's officers crowded around the table and looked on as their captain explained the tactical situation.

"We have a predicament, gentlemen," Weston said. "The enemy's been busy on Matsuwa. They've moved their fuel depot farther inland, up in the foothills of the mountain. By my guess, about three miles from the airfield. The fuel tanks are completely hidden from view. Considering the distance and higher elevation, they are essentially unreachable by our guns — even with Jorgenson and Trott in the gunners' seats." The mention of the *Aeneid's* most proficient gun crew drew smiles from most of the assembly, all but Berry who studied the chart with a concerned expression. "If we had a more versatile ammunition loadout," Weston continued, "we might have been able to set off the tanks with airbursts, but our simple high-capacity rounds aren't going to cut it."

Berry was jotting down numbers on a notepad as if to check the calculations. Weston silently hoped the young gunnery officer would find something he and Townsend had missed when they had run the math only minutes before. But when Berry had finished, he put down his pencil and dolefully nodded his head to indicate he had reached the same conclusion.

"I am looking for ideas, gentlemen," Weston said. "We can bombard that airfield all night long. We can destroy the planes there and pockmark the runway with blast craters, but unless we knock out those tanks, that airbase will remain in operation. The Japs can fly more planes out here and use this as a base of operations to hunt our boats as they run through the Kurils."

Weston then noticed that MacCullen was there, too, his cropped head peering between the shoulders of two of the others. Weston made eye contact with the army lieutenant who seemed antsy, practically fidgeting, as if he wanted to say something but was holding his tongue, the verbal lashing Townsend had given him in the last meeting evidently still fresh in his mind.

"Do you wish to add something, Lieutenant MacCullen?" Weston offered.

"It can be done, Captain," MacCullen replied briskly. "My men can do it."

Most of the faces around the table looked bemused by the suggestion. A few of the junior officers sniggered, but the army lieutenant appeared unfazed.

"Please elaborate, Lieutenant," Weston said, silencing the others with a single look.

"There are still two rafts on board from the Attu operation – the spare rafts," MacCullen said. "We also still have our spare explosives. One raft will be sufficient to take my team and the explosives ashore. We'll infiltrate the fuel depot and destroy it, and the remaining raft can be used to take us off."

"Your team?" Townsend interjected. "You have eight men. Two of them can't even walk."

"Leaving seven to do the job," MacCullen replied matter-of-factly. "Including Sergeant Greathouse and myself."

"Are they all even from the same platoon?"

"This is just the kind of thing we've trained for, sir."

Townsend shook his head, apparently not satisfied with that answer. "I don't like it, Captain. There's not enough time to prepare. It's too risky. We don't need another disaster on our hands."

Weston detected an element of distrust in Townsend's tone and suspected anything MacCullen proposed would be met with the same reaction. Though the executive officer's reservations were likely prejudiced, they were not entirely misplaced. It had taken weeks to train for the landing on Attu, weeks of surfacing and offloading the boats again and again, weeks of adjusting the loadout of every raft, finding the right balance of equipment, men, strength, and skill to ensure each craft made it to the shore safely. While the few surviving soldiers had been a part of that training, it was unlikely they had crewed the same raft.

Still, MacCullen did have a point. The scouts were army commandos. They were used to adjusting to any situation. In their withdrawal from Attu, these same survivors had successfully rowed one raft at night, against the surf, with wounded men aboard. And that was something.

"I want to hear the lieutenant's plan," Weston finally said in a tempering manner. "Go ahead, Mister MacCullen."

Townsend deferentially crossed his arms and remained silent while MacCullen nudged his way between two of the officers to reach the table. He placed a finger on the beach along the south side of the island.

"There is a good beach here," MacCullen said. "That's where we'll land. The Japs are likely to have pillboxes and listening posts there, but they aren't expecting an invasion, so I doubt they'll be manned. In any case, we'll be landing in darkness and that should be enough to get us ashore undetected."

"What if they are manned?" Weston asked.

"The Imperial Army is like any other army. They don't waste their best troops occupying insignificant islands far from the action. This garrison is probably comprised of wash-ups and second-rate troops. They've spent the whole war twiddling their thumbs, and nothing has happened. They've grown complacent. I doubt they will be vigilant enough tonight." After an acceding nod from Weston, MacCullen continued. "My men and I will land undetected and march inland to the fuel depot. It's a four-mile march uphill, and we'll be loaded down with gear, but we should be able to cover that ground in less than two hours, allowing time for ducking any Japanese patrols we might encounter. We don't know the size, number, or spacing of the fuel tanks, but we'll have the six spare M37 demolition kits with us. That should be enough to do the job no matter what we encounter. I'm counting on the volatility of the fuel to assist in the demolition."

"Very bold," Weston said with raised eyebrows. "Of course, once you blow up that depot, the Japs will be combing the island for you — and it's a small island.

There's no way you'll make it back to the beach without running into trouble."

"I don't intend on this being a suicide mission, Captain," MacCullen said with an uncharacteristic grin. "If we time our attack to coincide with your bombardment of the airfield, the Japs won't suspect an infiltration, at least not initially. They'll think you got lucky and landed a shell in one of the fuel tanks. My team will then head north." He ran his finger along the chart to the jagged northern coast of Matsuwa. "We'll have to skirt around the mountain, and that will slow us down, but our load will be considerably lighter. The east side of the mountain appears to be more level than the west, so we'll go that way if we can. I anticipate a march of no more than five miles."

"That's a long haul across very rugged country," Weston said skeptically.

"No more rugged than Attu, sir. I estimate it will take two hours — at most, three." MacCullen grinned awkwardly. "As I said, we're trained for this sort of thing."

Weston nodded, though he still thought the lieutenant's assessment was a bit too optimistic. The dozens of crevasses formed by lava flows of the past centuries were an unknown. The chart did not provide precise elevation data. Any one of those gorges could prove to be an insurmountable obstacle.

"Once the *Aeneid* has finished its bombardment," MacCullen continued. "It will drive around to the north side of the island and send the remaining raft to take us off. With an H-Hour of 2200, I expect a 0600 rendezvous on the north coast would allow for any hazards either of us might run into."

Weston marked off the distance around the island with a pair of dividers to check the feasibility of such a timetable. Exchanging glances with Townsend, he could see that the XO was still not thrilled with the idea or the man who would have to lead it.

There was some comfort in the fact that Sergeant Greathouse would be there, keeping an eye on MacCullen at every turn, though Weston was still concerned about the friction between the two men. It had not abated over the past two days. Weston wondered if Greathouse even knew what MacCullen was proposing. He wondered if the sergeant would flat-out refuse to follow MacCullen on this operation.

"What if the depot is well-guarded?" Townsend asked skeptically. "You say these are second-rate troops, Lieutenant, but we just don't know. There might be a whole regiment of crack troops there. There's no way of knowing."

"Whatever they have there, we will handle it," MacCullen replied confidently.

"Suppose everything goes as planned ashore. If any escorts show up before we take you off that island, we'll have to leave you there – all of you."

MacCullen looked at him squarely. "That is an eventuality we understand and are prepared to face, sir."

Townsend slammed his fist down on the chart. "That's just the kind of bravado that got your company wiped out on Attu, Lieutenant! Unknowns are just that – *unknowns!* You have to assume the worst case! Otherwise, men die!"

Clearly, the loss of his closest friend was still fresh in Townsend's mind. Weston did not have to ask his executive officer's opinion about the operation. It was evident he would vote no. But, Weston mused, it was not up to Townsend. It was up to him. He would be the one to send those seven men ashore, possibly to their deaths, and it seemed to weigh more heavily on him than the Attu operation had. The Attu landing had come from on high. He had merely been following orders there. Now, with the *Aeneid* under strict radio silence, he was the one who would have to make the call – and bear the responsibility for failure or disaster.

There were many unknowns. The plan was risky. It was downright insane. But it was the only plan they had. Were the lives of these seven soldiers a fair trade for the lives of two hundred plus submariners trapped in the Sea of Japan?

The men around the table stared across at Weston, waiting for his final decision. Most, like Townsend, appeared apprehensive about the answer they knew he must give, while MacCullen looked eager to get started with preparations.

*If only there were more time*, Weston thought. Normally, such an operation would spend weeks in the planning phase. But they did not have weeks. They did not even have a day. The wolfpack would begin running through La Perouse Strait tonight. The *Aeneid* would have to make her noise within a few hours if she was to be of any help to them.

After taking a deep breath, Weston finally nodded. "Alright, Lieutenant. Draw it up for me and meet me back here in one hour. The XO will help you with any information we have on the tides."

Townsend closed his eyes and nodded, clearly disappointed, but resigned to give his full support now that the decision had been made.

"Plan it well, gentlemen," Weston said, looking around the table at all of them. "Check your calculations, and then recheck them. Coordination is the key. Once the shellacking starts, once things are set in motion up there, there's no turning back." He paused before adding, "We're going to give the Japs one hell of a reason to come after us. Let's just hope they take the bait."

# 17

# NO MORE WAITING

*Sea of Japan*

*West of La Perouse Strait*

*USS Sea Dog*

Commander Prewitt squeezed the periscope handles as he looked through the lens. The sun was beginning to set on the world above. He could see Cape Soya to the south with its emerald green hills bathed in the last light of the day and a handful of structures where there was a small seaport village. The cape marked the entrance to La Perouse Strait. It was the northernmost point of Hokkaido, the northernmost point of Japan proper.

Dark clouds hovered above the cape threatening a storm. That was promising, Prewitt thought. Heavy weather would be a hindrance to the Japanese ships guarding the strait and would likely ground any patrol aircraft.

Rotating the periscope to point at the entrance of the strait, Prewitt saw the masts of two ships poking above the horizon. They were single-masted ships, probably subchasers, and undoubtedly the source of the echo-ranging the *Sea Dog's* sonar had been monitoring for the last few hours. The two vessels cruised back and forth across the entrance like guards outside the gates of Buckingham Palace. Prewitt could visualize the racks of depth charges on their decks, ready to turn the waters of the strait into a boiling cauldron. They were yet another menace he would have to deal with in the long hours ahead.

Despite having already been forced deep on two occasions by patrol planes that had come too close, the *Sea Dog* had arrived at the strait right on schedule. Several land fixes had been taken and the dead reckoning trace updated with the most accurate position possible. All the necessary calculations had been made. The ship was ready. The crew was as ready as they could be.

It was time to run the gauntlet.

As Prewitt continued to watch the masts of the enemy warships and listen to the sonar audio on the speaker, he pondered what his counterparts aboard the *Finback* and the *Pintado* must be thinking right now. They would have already started their runs and would be within reach of those probing sound waves by now, praying the next pulse did not find them and that they were not driving straight into a minefield.

The *Sea Dog* would now follow them. Moving along at four knots, seven if you counted the current, the *Sea Dog* would enter the strait just as the sun set. Like her sisters ahead of her, she would ride the great Tsushima Current like a giant conveyor belt with everything shut down except the essential machinery. If all went well, the current would spit the three submarines out into the Sea of Okhotsk undetected and they would have enough battery power remaining to get well clear of the Japanese defenses before sundown the following day. If all did not go well…

"Down scope!" Prewitt said, unable to hide his frustration. "Take her down to one hundred twenty feet."

As the deck tilted downward, Prewitt cursed himself for ever expecting anything different. What had he been hoping for, a miracle? Had he thought the strait would be open and clear, that they might sail on through like they were on a Sunday pleasure cruise? No destroyers had been sighted, and that, at least, was encouraging.

As Prewitt stood there, leaning against the bulkhead, the sonar pings abruptly ceased.

"Those escorts are recalibrating their sonar equipment, Captain," the sound operator reported without any prompting.

"Good. Maybe it'll give our boats a chance to make some headway. I'm sure the Japs will start up again soon."

"I'd be willing to bet on it, sir."

"While we have the opportunity, train your gear on the strait. See if you can hear anything, no matter how faint."

"Already on it, sir." The sailor minutely adjusted the wheel controlling the steerable hydrophone. After a few minutes listening down one bearing, he nodded grimly.

"I'm picking up something, fading in and out. It sounds like warship screws. Intermittent pinging, too. Very faint. There are definitely more warships out there, Captain. At least three that I can make out, probably more. Sounds like destroyers and escorts."

*Damn!* Prewitt cursed inwardly. It was as he had suspected. The destroyers and escorts were waiting in the waters on the far side of the strait. The pair of subchasers patrolling above were probably a ruse, a line of pickets just light enough to entice a desperate sub commander to enter the strait, only to find hell waiting for him on the other side.

Prewitt could only conclude that ComSubPac's diversion, whatever it was, had not worked. And now the wolfpack must trust in prayers and luck to get them through. Chances were slim that all three boats would make the seventy-mile run undetected. If one boat was attacked, it was possible the other two might use that opportunity to get away, like wildebeests sacrificing one of their own to escape attacking lions. Then, of course, there was also the dire possibility that each submarine would be sunk in turn as they came through the channel – the entire wolfpack annihilated in one night.

If only the *Sea Dog* had the fuel to spare, Prewitt thought. If only there were enough food, he would turn her around and wait for another day to make this run.

But there could be no more waiting.

Prewitt grabbed the portable microphone from the bulkhead and pressed the switch to activate the 1MC ship-wide announcing circuit.

"This is the captain." He spoke enthusiastically, doing his best to mask his trepidation. "In just a few minutes, we'll be entering La Perouse Strait. It's a long run, as you all know. We'll be rigged for silent running the whole time. All we've got to do is get through it, gentleman. After that – after we've left the last enemy escort behind us – it's an all-expenses-paid pleasure cruise to Midway. Of course, the milk's powdered, and you might have to scrub a deck or two on the way. But the beans are free and so is your bunk." Light laughter echoed through the control room hatch. At least a few men were uplifted by the joke – a very few. "In ten days, we'll all be sunning on the beach, drinking cold beer, playing softball, and frying up more Mahi Mahi than you can eat. So, stay sharp. Silent running. Move around as little as you have to. Keep the chatter to a minimum, and keep those sweat rags handy. That is all."

After Prewitt hung up the microphone, the watchstanders around him avoided his gaze keeping their eyes on their panels. The men who stood their watches in the conning tower tended to know him better than the others. They knew when he was merely acting confident for the sake of morale.

"Recommend coming left to zero eight five, Captain," the executive officer said from the plot table.

"Very well. Steersman, left handsomely. Steer zero eight five."

The *Sea Dog* was going in.

# 18

# MACCULLEN'S RAIDERS

*Matsuwa Island*

Greathouse shined the flashlight on the face of the dead Japanese soldier. The soldier could not have been more than eighteen. He was feeble, thin-shouldered, and clearly not frontline caliber. Undoubtedly, he had been assigned to the Matsuwa garrison because he could not stand up to the rigors of combat in Burma or the South Pacific. On this night, he had made the unfortunate decision to go stargazing in the foothills of the mountain unarmed. He was looking up at the night sky when Greathouse had come up behind him, easily putting him in a chokehold and driving his serrated bayonet into the struggling soldier's spine. The wide-eyed youth had died without a sound.

"Well, that takes care of that," Greathouse said, wiping his blade on the dead man's uniform.

"Hide the body, Sergeant," MacCullen ordered from the dark brush where the rest of the squad remained hidden.

Greathouse grunted, not pleased with being wet-nursed as if this were his first combat, especially by the likes of Lieutenant MacCullen.

*Who the hell does he think he is? Major Nash?*

Before burying the body, Greathouse rummaged through the dead man's pockets, coming up with a few one-*yen* notes, a service card, and a crinkled photograph of a pleasant-looking Japanese family all dressed in traditional kimonos.

"Not much on this bastard."

"Put it back, Sergeant!" MacCullen snapped. "All of it!"

"Say again, sir?"

"You heard me. I said put it back."

"With all due respect, sir, this bastard's a Jap. He's a dead Jap, at that. He's got no use for these things now. You think his kind would show us the same courtesy? You think they respected the bodies of the boys we lost on Attu?"

"Use your head, Sergeant. If the Japs capture us and find that loot, we'll all be strung up and used for bayonet practice, or worse."

Greathouse eyed the young lieutenant defiantly. "I never considered on us being captured, sir."

"You must think of your men first. They could be executed because you robbed the dead."

Greathouse grimaced at the condescending tone and gave MacCullen an obscene gesture knowing it was too dark for the lieutenant to see it. "The Japs won't capture us, sir. The Japs won't capture me, I can tell you that. I'll die first and take a dozen of them with me. How about you, sir?"

"Put it back, damn you!" MacCullen said impatiently. "Bury the body and get back under cover!"

Begrudgingly, Greathouse obeyed. After the dead soldier had been sufficiently covered in the loose lava rock, Greathouse returned to the squad where they all waited and listened to ensure the soldier had no companions.

The young Japanese soldier was the first they had killed since landing on the island, and Greathouse had been eager to do it. He felt no remorse. He would gladly kill another dozen in the same manner if the opportunity presented itself. It would take many more to even the score from Attu – and he would even the score, as long as the damn lieutenant didn't foul things up.

Greathouse looked over at MacCullen who briefly shined a covered flashlight on his wrist to check the time, ever concerned about keeping to the schedule. Greathouse was not happy about being placed under the bastard of a lieutenant for this raid. He had never liked MacCullen. Even before the Attu operation and the lieutenant's miraculous trench foot recovery, Greathouse had thought him the worst officer in the company. Now, the son of a bitch was the company commander. As much as Greathouse did not like the present arrangement, he had no choice but to accept it. The *Aeneid's* captain had made sure he understood that, in no uncertain terms, shortly before the scouts had departed the sub.

"Give him your full support, Sergeant." Weston had said, after pulling him aside to speak with him privately. "Treat him as you would Major Nash. He is your commanding officer now, but you have the experience. Help him to make the right decisions over there. I'm trusting you, Sergeant."

Like a good soldier, like a good sergeant, he had accepted the commander's directive.

Of course, coddling a new platoon leader was not anything new to Greathouse. Many times in the past, he had helped young lieutenants who didn't know shit from Shinola learn how to stay out of the way. He had done what most good infantry sergeants do. He had kept the incompetent officers appointed above him unknowingly corralled and occupied while he personally led the platoon in battle. He had no personal grievance against the officers. They were good men, for the most part. But they were also idiots, except for a few, such as the late Major Nash.

MacCullen, however, was a different animal entirely. He was clever. He was an aloof glory hound. But he was also a coward, and that was a dangerous combination. Such men devise elaborate plans and then let others take the risks executing them. On the voyage to Attu, Greathouse and the rest of the sergeants in the scout company had heard of the lieutenant's exploits in North Africa, and his mysterious reassignment to the scouts. Greathouse had not been surprised. He had suspected there was some dark secret in the lieutenant's past from the moment he had reported for duty.

Fully expecting MacCullen to come up with some last-minute excuse for staying behind on this mission, just as he had at Attu, Greathouse had been somewhat surprised when MacCullen had appeared on the dark, pitching deck of the submarine ready to board the raft with him and the five other soldiers. The lieutenant had not stayed behind this time. He had come along, fully dressed out for combat and leaving no uncertainties as to who was in charge. From the start, he gave orders in a detached, imperious manner, like some cadet fresh from West Point, but none of it fooled Greathouse. It was all an act to cover up ineptitude and fear. Greathouse was sure of it. The bastard had probably just not found a good enough excuse to remain aboard the ship, that's all.

The night landing had gone better than expected. The *Aeneid* had surfaced a mile offshore, and the deck hands and commandos had set about preparing the raft, resorting to their extensive training for the Attu operation.

"I'll stay on the surface until I see your signal from the shore," Weston had told MacCullen and Greathouse as they stood on the *Aeneid's* gun deck.

The unarmed, clean-shaven naval officer in his heavy bridge coat had contrasted sharply to the commandos who wore slouch hats, painted faces, and combat fatigues, with M1A1 Thompson sub-machine guns slung over their shoulders, and dozens of spare magazines and grenades adorning their chests like armor.

"If you get into trouble," Weston said, "fire off two green flares, and I'll cover your withdrawal. Don't be heroes. Once you get over there, if you find yourselves in over your heads, abort the mission and head straight for the pick-up location."

But Greathouse knew that he personally would never retreat again, even if Lieutenant MacCullen ordered it.

No sooner had the raft shoved off from the submarine loaded with the seven heavily armed commandos and packs filled with explosives, than an incident occurred in which Lieutenant MacCullen's incompetence had nearly blown the whole operation.

Paddling steadily toward the shore in the darkness, the commandos had kept their eyes focused on the foamy, white rollers a few hundred yards from the beach and had not expected to have to worry about any threats behind them. But before they made it half-way to the white water, a dark shape suddenly materialized out of the night, coming straight at them from astern. It was a vessel of some kind, the gentle break of the seas clearly visible at its bows. At first, Greathouse thought it was the *Aeneid*, but then he heard the creak of timbers and the snap of sails and rigging, and his eyes finally made out the silhouette of a sailing craft. He quickly realized it was a fishing sampan, creeping along the coast, darkened and silent, traveling in a northwesterly direction. As the sampan drew closer, so close that its oddly-shaped, junk-rigged sails blotted out the stars above them, Greathouse looked across the raft to MacCullen for orders, but the lieutenant appeared to have frozen. At least, that was what Greathouse believed happened. Taking charge, Greathouse hurriedly ordered the men to ship their oars and lie flat in hopes that the nighttime fishermen had not yet seen the raft.

Greathouse smelled the heavy aroma of piled fish and heard quiet voices conversing in Japanese. Every commando kept his weapon pointed at the passing craft, ready to fire should a single head appear above the bulwark. MacCullen was the only exception. Instead of his rifle, he clenched the flare gun in one trembling hand, his eyes blinking rapidly as if in panic, as if he might fire off the distress signal in the next instant.

"No!" Greathouse whispered harshly. "Not yet, sir!"

MacCullen shot him a scathing glance in reply, but he did not fire the flare gun. After the sampan had sailed away and was no longer a threat, MacCullen wasted no time in reprimanding Greathouse for what he had determined to be stepping over the line.

"I did not intend to send up a flare unless absolutely necessary, Sergeant," MacCullen said contemptuously, loud enough for the others to hear. "In the future, you will leave such decisions to me. We're lucky those Japs didn't hear you."

At that moment, Greathouse considered using his oar to knock the bastard overboard, but he held both the paddle and his tongue and turned his attention back to the approaching coastline.

They managed to bring the unwieldy craft with all its cargo through the surf without capsizing and finally to a skidding halt on the darkened beach. There, they quickly offloaded the supplies, punctured the rubber flotations, and buried the deflated craft in the sand. As expected, there were several Japanese pillboxes on the heights above the beach, but they were found to be unoccupied – all but one. The commandos peered through the dimly lit gun aperture of that pillbox to see a group of wine-drunk garrison troops smoking and playing cards. The distracted soldiers seemed oblivious to anything transpiring down on the beach, so the commandos left them to their *sake* and card games undisturbed and headed inland, giving a wide berth to the airfield, only visible as a cluster of darkened buildings to the east.

The trek into the island's interior had been rapid. The low country was, for the most part, open ground, the gently sloping land containing only shin-high vegetation sprouting up through a seemingly endless plain of lava rock. Making good time, they had reached the foothills of Mount Matsuwa within an hour and had stopped to collect their bearings. MacCullen carried with him a hand-drawn map copied from the *Aeneid's* charts which he consulted often, Greathouse eyeing his every move, uncertain if the lieutenant knew where the hell he was going. But, either MacCullen had gotten lucky, or the map was good, because they had soon smelled the aroma of aircraft fuel on the breeze. It grew more pungent the higher they climbed, telling them they were close to the valley containing the fuel depot.

MacCullen had brought them to a halt when, by his estimation, they were within a half-mile of their objective. And it was then, as they had prepared their weapons and explosives, that they had heard the crunching footfalls of the solitary Japanese hiker moving along the lava rock towards them.

Without waiting for orders, Greathouse had killed the Japanese soldier outright. And now MacCullen seemed slightly annoyed that he had done so.

Greathouse did not care if he had ruffled the lieutenant's perception of the command hierarchy. Even though he had taken great pleasure in killing that soldier, there had been good tactical sense in it. If the fuel depot was only a half-mile away, then it was very feasible the soldier had come from there. Had they remained hidden and let the soldier pass by, he might have doubled back and come upon them as they were preparing to attack the depot, and might have raised the alarm.

With his own weapons checked and ready, Greathouse took a moment to look out at the glittering expanse of ocean in the distance. He wondered just where the submarine was hiding out there. It was probably lurking a few hundred feet below the surface, listening and waiting, not far from the dark void which Greathouse knew to be the anchored freighter.

"Fifty minutes to H-Hour," MacCullen said looking at his watch under a light. "The road should be just ahead. Move out. Same order as before."

In the lead, Greathouse looked back at the five soldiers comprising their small team. Martinez, the sniper. Wilcoxon, the only one with more than a scout's basic training with explosives. Houston, Myers, and Bell, regular scout riflemen. Though Greathouse knew them all to some extent, Houston was the only one from his own platoon. It was not a bad offering. It certainly could have been worse. It would have been better still if they had left Lieutenant MacCullen back on the sub.

They moved out, each man holding his weapon at the ready while toting a demolition kit on his back. It did not take long to reach the road. It was constructed of gravel pulverized from the abundant lava rock. Running alongside the road and slightly elevated was a pipeline stretching off into the blackness in both directions. Presumably, the pipeline was used to port fuel to and from the depot. Judging by its size, it could deliver fuel at a considerable rate, beyond that needed for most airfields.

Turning left, the scouts followed the road uphill, three men on one side, four on the other. They kept their eyes peeled for foot patrols and their ears listening for the sound of approaching vehicles. The road led them to the entrance of a narrow canyon, and there it forked. One fork led into the canyon where they suspected the fuel depot was, a suspicion further confirmed by the fact that the pipeline ran in the same direction. The other fork headed north climbing farther up into the foothills.

"I wonder where that goes?" Greathouse said, gesturing to the other road. "The map we got from the navy boys doesn't show any Jap facilities up that way."

"Who knows what's up there?" MacCullen shrugged. "The intel is old. Our business is in the canyon. We go this way, as planned."

The squad followed the road into the confined canyon and were soon engulfed by cliff walls on either side. The Japanese engineers had cut through the rock where necessary, widening the gorge to accommodate the trucks that used the single-lane road.

Before long, the commandos heard the low putter of a generator up ahead and then came to a place where the canyon widened considerably. Finally, they rounded a bend and saw the fuel depot several hundred feet ahead, a small forest of about a dozen large and small tanks nestled into the end of the canyon.

"That's a lot of fuel for a few squadrons of planes," Greathouse whispered.

"The smaller ones are for aircraft fuel," MacCullen replied. "The bigger ones are for fuel-oil used by ships. No wonder the Japanese moved the tanks up here. Matsuwa must be a refueling stop for ships headed to the Aleutians."

A few lights shined amongst the tanks. There was no reason for the little depot to be under blackout conditions because the canyon walls adequately hid it from the ocean, and an air attack was highly unlikely. There were also no fences, and that was to be expected since the depot was in a remote place on a remote island.

"Martinez," MacCullen said lowly. "Get into position."

With a glance at Greathouse and then a nod, Private Martinez shouldered his sniper rifle and began to make his way up the canyon wall. There was a ledge there that would afford a good view of the installation.

The rest of the squad watched the facility for several long minutes. There was no visible activity. A small shack stood at the entrance where the road led into the facility. The building's only door opened onto a small veranda bordering the road such that the truck drivers could check in with the facility attendants. There was a light inside the structure, just visible through the open windows.

"There can be no more than a handful in that hut, Sergeant," MacCullen said. "Select two men and take care of them. Leave the others here to unpack and prepare the explosives. We'll cover you."

Greathouse regarded him doubtfully. "I recommend we watch the place a little longer, sir. If there are sentries about, they may not have had time to make their rounds yet."

MacCullen glanced at his watch and shook his head. "No time to wait. H-Hour is in twenty minutes."

"A few minutes won't matter that much. The *Aeneid's* supposed to start the barrage, anyway. Our explosives aren't supposed to go off until ten minutes after they fire their first shot."

"Yes, I know that," MacCullen said irritably. "Just follow your orders, Sergeant. We will not be late. Is that clear?"

"Better late than dead, sir. If Major Nash were here, he'd have us-"

"Well, he's not, Sergeant!" MacCullen snapped. "I am here, and Major Nash is dead! Now do as you're told!"

Greathouse eyed MacCullen, not liking the tone he had used when he had said the major's name. *Here's the coward again*, Greathouse thought. *I'll bet if he had to go take that hut himself, he'd want to watch and wait a little longer.*

"Yes, sir," Greathouse finally said stiffly, knowing any further argument would be useless. "Bell and Wilcoxon, you stay here with the lieutenant and get the fireworks ready. Houston and Myers, drop your packs and come with me. No grenades, now, you hear? And watch where you're aiming. We don't want to set this place off ahead of time, and us with it."

Within moments, the three commandos were creeping forward toward the small structure, their Thompsons at the ready. As they reached the hut, Greathouse had difficulty seeing into the darkness beyond it. A dim light affixed to a post just beside the small building washed out nearly everything but the immediate surroundings. The windows of the hut did not have glass, but simple hatch-like weather shutters which were slightly cracked open. A lively female voice came from within, speaking Japanese. Greathouse quickly realized it was a radio broadcast when the voice transitioned to soft orchestral music with a decided Japanese influence. The soothing tune made Greathouse want to drift off to sleep, but he quickly shook himself back to alertness. He hoped the music was having the same effect on whoever was inside the hut.

"Houston," he whispered. "Check the window."

The soldier slithered on his belly until he was just below the opening, removed his hat, and then carefully peered inside. Even in the dim lighting, Greathouse could see that the private was meeting with some frustration. Houston moved from one side of the window to the other until, finally, he crawled back to Greathouse.

"Can't get a clear view, Sarge. That shutter's blocking the way. If I try to move it, the Jap's inside will see it for sure."

Greathouse nodded. "You take up position over there by that pump station. Stay out of sight. Myers, you cover me from here. I'm going to try to flush them out."

A tin can sat on the wooden rail surrounding the small veranda. Greathouse belly-crawled over to the raised platform, got into position, and then nudged the can off the rail with the muzzle of his rifle. The resulting thud and clang were loud enough to be heard above the din of the generator. A clump of paper chits spilled out of the fallen can onto the planks of the platform, evidently the receipts for fuel deliveries.

Crouching just at the edge of the veranda, Greathouse waited with his weapon pointed directly at the door, waiting for it to open, for some startled Japanese soldier to come out and receive a face full of lead. But the door remained shut, and there were no sounds of movement within.

Cursing under his breath, Greathouse knew there was only one option now. He turned and signaled for Houston to stay put and for Myers to join him at the veranda.

"You take the window," he murmured to Myers. "I'll go in the front door."

The private nodded, squeezing his rifle in anticipation, and then slinked away to a position just beneath the window. Greathouse carefully stepped onto the veranda, but the wooden planks instantly creaked under his boots. He immediately discarded any notion of approaching the door unheard, and instead rushed the door in two steps, bashing it in with a strong kick. It gave way easily, nearly coming off its flimsy hinges. Leveling his sub-machine gun, he burst inside, ready to spray the room with .45 caliber bullets.

But, to his surprise, the single-room structure was empty.

In one corner, a radio stood upon a small table, its speaker still playing the soft music. Nearby, a kettle simmered on a small stove. A long table sat in the center of the room upon which a ledger lay open with a pencil left in the binding. Next to the accounting book sat two cups of tea, still steaming.

Someone had been here very recently, Greathouse concluded. They must have just stepped out when the squad approached – which meant they would likely return very soon.

"Myers, get away from the hut!" he said through the window. "Get back behind cover! Fast!"

Myers' boots crunched outside as he ran for cover. Greathouse made for the door but stopped abruptly when a gunshot rang out. It sounded like a pistol. Then, Japanese voices were shouting outside. There was more gunfire, this time it sounded like a burst from a Thompson cut short by two more reports, both of them rifles. Then the gunfire stopped.

Greathouse was convinced that Myers had been hit. He chose not to exit the structure but instead crouched behind the half-closed door, waiting and listening.

The voices that had first spoken loudly and with alarm were suddenly hushed. Several footfalls drew closer and then stopped just outside the hut. Frantic murmurs were exchanged in Japanese. Greathouse imagined the enemy soldiers hovering over Myer's body, examining it, identifying him as American.

Had the Japanese simply gotten lucky in sighting Myers, or had they been watching the squad the whole time?

Greathouse did not dare move. The ramshackle hut was so crudely constructed that any move he made would be heard by those outside, even over the murmur of the distant generator.

Then the voices fell suddenly silent. Evidently, the Japanese had made a decision. The boards on the veranda creaked outside as someone stepped onto the platform. Slowly the footfalls made their way toward the door.

*Where the hell was Houston?* Greathouse thought urgently. *Where was Martinez with his sniper rifle? And where the hell was the damn lieutenant?* Didn't they see he needed covering fire? Or maybe they had already been taken out by the patrolling enemy soldiers.

Greathouse quietly brought the Thompson from his hip to his shoulder and leveled it at the slightly ajar door. At any moment, he expected to see the muzzle of a gun thrust through the opening to spray the room.

If his comrades could not help him, he would have to help himself.

*Rat-tat-tat-tat-tat!....Rat-tat-tat-tat-tat-tat!*

Greathouse's Thompson broke the silence with a crescendo of automatic fire. He held down the trigger, sweeping the area around the door. The .45 caliber bullets passed through the thin wall practically unimpeded leaving a pattern of holes that snaked from one end to the other. Greathouse continued firing until the thirty-round magazine was expended. Before the last of the spent shell casings clinked to the floor, he had replaced the magazine with a new one.

As the smoke from the hot barrel curled into the air before his face, he heard a gasp, then a whimper coming from the other side of the bullet-riddled door. Moments later, a heavy thud sounded on the platform. Whoever it was, had been eliminated.

There was no reason to remain silent now. Greathouse upended the table, flipping it onto its side. The cups fell to the floor, shattering and splashing hot tea onto his boots. He crouched behind the makeshift barricade only just in time to avoid a bullet that penetrated the opposite wall and zipped over his head, missing him by inches. Then, many guns began firing outside – *Arisaka* bolt-action rifles, by the sound of them. The Japanese soldiers were shooting blindly into the hut. One bullet burst through the table leaving a blossom of splinters only a few inches from Greathouse's right ear. Another struck the stove and ricocheted around the room.

Realizing that the table offered little more protection than the walls, Greathouse crouched lower and lower as the fire intensified until he was practically flat on the floor. He considered tossing a grenade outside to distract the enemy long enough for him to make a mad dash and hopefully find some better cover, but Myers or one of the others might also be out there, wounded or captured. And then there was the possibility that a piece of flying shrapnel would set off one of the nearby fuel tanks and start a chain reaction sending them all sky-high. Of course, that would kill him and everyone within several hundred yards of the depot, friend and foe alike. But at least the mission would have been accomplished.

For himself, Greathouse was not concerned. He had forfeited any last cling to life after seeing his comrades slaughtered on Attu. But, if MacCullen and the others had avoided capture and were still out there, they still might execute the mission as planned. Greathouse decided it would be best if he just kept the enemy busy for as long as he could.

Another two shots pierced the wall, and then two more. More Japanese voices shouted excitedly, at least half a dozen now. It seemed a whole squad had converged on the hut.

At that moment, Greathouse made up his mind. He would fight and die right here. No matter what, he would not be taken prisoner.

The radio in the far corner caught his eye, hopefully, the only means of communication between the fuel depot and the airfield down by the coast. A long burst of .45 caliber bullets smashed the transmitter and receiver assemblies into sparking and smoking wrecks, silencing the music for good. The Japanese outside answered with another fusillade of rifle fire.

Again, Greathouse replaced his magazine with a full one. There was no sense in conserving ammunition now. More bullets crisscrossed the room. The Japanese were firing from multiple sides, forcing him to lie flatter to avoid being hit.

As the projectiles whizzed past him, Greathouse considered this was no way for a soldier to die. He quietly resolved that, after the next fusillade, he would jump to his feet and dash outside killing anyone he saw.

As he mentally steeled himself for his final, suicidal charge, he heard more gunfire outside, but these reports were unlike the others. They were distant but distinctly familiar.

Did he dare to hope?

The rifle fired again. Yes, there could be no doubt about it now. It was an M1903 Springfield, and it could only belong to Private Martinez.

The Japanese voices were a mix of confusion and alarm. Their *Arisaka* rifles continued to fire sporadically, but they were no longer shooting at the hut. Then came a steady crescendo of typewriter-like reports – Thompson sub-machine guns, several of them.

Within seconds, it was all over.

Emerging from the doorway, Greathouse saw three writhing bodies on the ground. Even in the dim lighting, he could make out the distinct gray-green uniforms and puttee leg wrappings of Japanese soldiers. Four more figures were running away towards the tanks, firing their weapons blindly behind them as they ran. Greathouse went down on a knee, brought his Thompson to his shoulder, and fired at the retreating enemy. The closest one fell into the gravel spasming, his back peppered with

.45 caliber bullets. Muzzle flashes flickered to Greathouse's left, and another enemy soldier fell. Another crack of Martinez's Springfield rifle knocked the helmet off one soldier and blasted a spray of dark matter out of the side of his head. The soldier's gun dropped, his legs went limp, and he collapsed, dead.

Only one Japanese soldier reached the cover of the tanks alive.

The next moment, the scouts emerged from the darkness. Houston and Bell chased after the fleeing enemy, while Wilcoxon riddled the Japanese bodies on the ground with his Thompson for good measure. Shortly after the firing ceased, Lieutenant MacCullen arrived bearing the demolition kits.

"Didn't think you were going to make it, lieutenant," Greathouse said, making no effort to mask his irritation. As he rushed over to inspect Myers' still form on the ground, he could not help but add, "I was wondering if you went off looking for HQ." Greathouse was too incensed to say any more. He turned his attention away from MacCullen to solemnly confirm that Myers was dead, shot twice — once in the abdomen and once in the head. Greathouse removed the private's dog tags, then stood up to discover MacCullen one step away from him, staring harshly into his eyes. The lieutenant looked mad enough to murder him.

"What did you say, Sergeant?" MacCullen demanded as the echoing report of two sub-machine guns indicated Houston and Bell had dispatched the final enemy soldier.

Greathouse wanted to tell him, tell him to his face how incompetent he was, what a poor excuse for an officer and a leader he was, that his hesitation probably got Myers killed. He wanted to tell MacCullen that he was a coward, hiding behind his rank. Instead, he took a deep breath and got control of his rage.

"Nothing, sir," Greathouse replied neutrally. "I'm just riled up after dodging those Jap bullets."

MacCullen's venomous eyes displayed no acceptance of Greathouse's explanation. "You don't have a high opinion of me, Sergeant. That is obvious. Your impertinence has gone unchecked for too long. When we get back to the States, when this unit is reconstituted, and replacements are recruited, I will see to it that you are not among our numbers."

Clenching his grip on the stock of his weapon, Greathouse felt the burning desire to knock the lieutenant out cold, but he did not. Wilcoxon was only a few feet away, and Houston and Bell were already hustling back to join them. It would do no good to beat this asshole here and now, in front of the troops. It would only disrupt the mission.

"That's the last of them, Lieutenant," Houston reported. "We checked all through the depot. No more Japs."

"See to the explosives, Sergeant," MacCullen spat. "On the double!"

"Yes, sir," Greathouse answered with forced obedience.

Without another word, MacCullen turned on his heel and walked toward the hut. Had the lieutenant remained another few seconds, Greathouse's temptation to lay him flat might have risen beyond his control.

Greathouse glanced at his watch. Only four minutes to H-Hour. Only four minutes before the *Aeneid* rained hell down on Matsuwa. They would be hard-pressed to plant the charges in time.

"Let's get these damn explosives set!" he commanded Wilcoxon sternly, still frustrated by the death of Myers and angry at MacCullen. "We got enough?"

"We got enough, Sarge," Wilcoxon replied after a long pause, his tone indicating there was something else on his mind. "We can set the charges on the small tanks and open the drains on the big tanks. If we flood the area with fuel, the fire should do the rest."

"Then hop to it!"

"Yes, Sarge," Wilcoxon said uncertainly. He hefted the packs, but then paused and looked back at Greathouse.

"What the hell's wrong with you?" Greathouse demanded.

"The lieutenant didn't freeze, Sarge," Wilcoxon finally answered in a hushed voice. "I hate him as much as you, but I got to say, he called it right."

"How's that?"

"There was a Jap foot patrol coming up the road, and another coming into the depot from the opposite side. The lieutenant ordered us not to fire until the Japs were all together in a group. Otherwise, we'd have been shooting in both directions. And he repositioned us so that our fire wouldn't hit the hut, where you were. He told us to hold our fire until we could be sure we'd hit all the Japs and miss you."

Greathouse was taken aback by the revelation. If it all happened just as Wilcoxon said it did, then the private was right – MacCullen had done the right thing. He took a long look at the lieutenant who was some distance away studying the map under the light outside the hut.

Had he judged the bastard too harshly? There was still the incident in Africa, and the feigned trench foot at Attu. Those events alone were enough to prove the asshole was a coward. How did they reconcile with Wilcoxon's comments? Still, as much as Greathouse hated to admit it, MacCullen had successfully gotten them this far. They had reached the objective and had neutralized the enemy guards, losing only one man in the process. Maybe MacCullen had gotten lucky.

"Well, what the hell are you gawking at?" Greathouse snapped at Wilcoxon who was still standing there, open-mouthed. "Get those damn explosives planted before I plant my boot in your ass!"

"Yes, Sergeant."

# 19

# DIVERSION

*Off Matsuwa*

*USS Aeneid*

The *Aeneid* broke the surface of the dark waters south of Matsuwa. She came up quickly, white water cascading from the conning tower and gun mounts as high-pressure air blasted thousands of pounds of seawater from the ballast tanks to make her instantly buoyant. Moments later, crewmen were swarming over her bridge and decks. The gun crews in their gray helmets raced to the giant guns, removing the barrel brackets and preparing them for action. Shells weighing one hundred pounds each and silk powder bags weighing forty pounds each were hauled by the straining men from the ammunition hoists to the weapons. The metal seats mounted on either side of each gun were soon occupied, the gunners spinning the elevation and azimuth wheels until the long, glistening barrels were pointed toward the dark island.

From the bridge, Weston watched the carefully choreographed preparations with satisfaction.

"Load high-capacity ammunition. Fuse setting super-quick." Berry ordered the gunners below through his phone headset. Seconds later, the gunnery officer reported eagerly, "Both guns ready to fire, sir!"

"Very well," Weston replied, glancing fore and aft at the two guns now angled at 90-degrees off the port side.

The *Aeneid* was creeping along at one-third speed, running parallel to the coast, such that both guns could simultaneously engage the enemy installations on Matsuwa. Several miles downrange, the island appeared dark and lifeless, devoid of light and activity. The Japanese had done an excellent job blacking out the airfield. Berry's guns would truly be firing in the blind. He would not have had a prayer of hitting anything had he not spent most of the afternoon taking additional fixes on those distant targets in the light of the day, carefully marking their locations on the chart. Using that information, Berry would direct the guns to fire at a pre-determined set of coordinates, each denoted by a different combination of azimuth and elevation. The script had been jotted onto a notebook which the lieutenant now studied under the subdued glow of a red-lensed lantern held by his assistant.

Berry and his gunners were ready to go. But before Weston gave them the go-ahead to unleash the *Aeneid's* arsenal on the unsuspecting airfield, there was another task that had to be attended to first.

Weston depressed the 7MC talk button. "Open outer doors on tubes nine and ten."

"Outer doors on tubes nine and ten are open, sir," came the muted reply from Townsend over the speaker a few moments later.

Weston crossed to the aft TBT and rotated the large lenses to point directly astern. Sitting just a half a mile beyond the *Aeneid's* churning screws was the small freighter, still anchored as it had been earlier that day. It was nearly as dark as the island, but enough moonlight glistened off its superstructure for Weston's purposes. He placed the reticle onto the center of the dark shape.

"Bearing, mark."

"Two eight two," came Townsend's voice over the speaker. "That checks with her last position, Skipper. That freighter hasn't moved an inch."

Weston nodded in the darkness. "Range one thousand yards. Set depth to ten feet."

"Ready, Captain."

"Fire nine!...Fire ten!"

The deck shuddered beneath Weston's feet. A flurry of large bubbles appeared in the submarine's wake and as the 3,000-pound weapons were launched from their tubes. Moments later, effervescent trails appeared on the surface, leading off into the darkness.

"Torpedoes running hot, straight, and normal," came the report over the intercom.

Every man on deck, from the bridge crew to the gun crews, stared into the darkness astern. The wait seemed like minutes, but only a little over thirty seconds had passed when a violent eruption appeared, a brilliant flash of light lifting the veil of darkness off the sea for a few moments. Every man not temporarily blinded saw the small freighter shake as six hundred pounds of Torpex exploded just below the waterline. Seconds later, the mighty thunderclap reached their ears, deafening even from one thousand yards away. As the rumble was subsiding, the second torpedo hit, driving an enormous fireball and a column of water up through the very bowels of the ship. Masts and crates were blasted into the sky. By the time the maelstrom of debris had splashed into the sea, the dying freighter had broken into two halves. As the oil fires raged on the wrecks and on the surface, each half rapidly filled with water and sank. Human cries of terror were just audible across the night sea, some of them high-pitched, like the screams of women.

In a matter of seconds, it was all over. Only burning flotsam remained.

The men on the *Aeneid's* deck cheered, one sailor on the bridge even being so bold as to slap Weston on the back in congratulations. But Weston took a moment to consider the grim reality of the sinking, and the possibility that there had been women aboard. The same merchant sailors he had observed that afternoon lounging on deck had just suffered horrifying deaths, crushed or blown apart in their bunks, incinerated or hurled hundreds of feet through the air, or now drowning. Weston found himself considering the victims more and more often as the war progressed. The terrible price of victory.

But he had to put that out of his mind. There was work to be done.

"Scratch one freighter," he said into the 1MC microphone with forced enthusiasm, drawing more cheers from the compartments below.

Turning his binoculars onto the island, Weston expected the shore batteries there to open up at any moment. The freighter's destruction had undoubtedly stirred the local garrison. He could imagine soldiers, airman, and mechanics scrambling from their bunks as sirens blared. If they had not woken up yet, they were about to get a wake-up call from hell.

"Mister Berry, you may commence firing."

"Commence firing, aye, sir." Berry keyed the microphone on his headset. "Number one gun mount, fire!"

An instant later, the forward gun discharged, illuminating the deck in a bright flash, its earsplitting report deafening every man not wearing ear protection. The submarine shook violently as its slender hull absorbed the energy of the cruiser-sized gun. Berry's lips moved, but Weston could not hear what he was saying. Then the second gun fired, shaking the hull again.

Doing his best to ignore the concussion of the big guns, Weston raised his binoculars to watch the fall of their shots. The luminous tracer rounds floated toward the dark island like harmless fireflies, gaining altitude as they flew over the water. It was difficult to conceive that those floating fireflies were in fact 105-pound high-capacity shells. The tiny balls of light descended into the darkness, each one exploding in turn in what appeared to be a muffled flash, but which was, in reality, a massively destructive blast and instant death for any enemy troops nearby.

There were no secondary explosions or fires after the first two rounds hit. They had apparently not struck any of the buildings, though it was possible they had carved large gouges in the runway.

Berry fed the new azimuth and elevation settings to the gun crews. Again, the guns fired, spewing tongues of flame into the night sky, the surface of the water shuddering under the concussion. The second salvo found its mark. The shell from the number two gun exploded with a great dash of flame that eventually settled into a roaring fire. At least one of the structures was burning, and the ensuing light exposed the shadows of the hangars and some of the other buildings.

Weston recalled what he had seen earlier that day, how the radio tower stood on the east side of the air base. Berry had orders to avoid hitting the tower at all costs, even if it meant half of his shots falling harmlessly into the countryside to the west. The tower would have to be spared for the ruse to work. Word of this attack must make it back to the Imperial Navy general staff, or the mission would be pointless. Those last shots had fallen a little too far to the east for comfort. Weston turned to Berry to remind him of this, but he could see that the young lieutenant was already jotting down corrections on his notepad, undoubtedly to shift the aim of the guns to avoid it.

With new directions, the gunners rotated their barrels ever so slightly to the west, allowing enough room for error in the wind and the roll of the sea, and then resumed the barrage. Three salvos later, another shell found its mark, this time striking a hangar, setting it ablaze. The fire burned so fiercely that Weston could see the skeletal frame of the structure through his binoculars. The tail fins of several planes were also visible, jutting up from behind dugouts and bathed in the red glow of the fires. Figures ran to and fro in a panic, some seeking to douse the flames, others seeking shelter.

"That's enough damage to the buildings, for now, Mister Berry," Weston said. "Shift your fire to the runway."

"Aye, aye, Captain."

As stirring as it was to see the structures catch fire and blown to bits, it was the runway that presented the greatest immediate threat. It was crucial that it be damaged to the point that it could not be used for several days. There was a momentary pause in the barrage while Berry issued new orders to the gun crews.

During the lull, a secondary explosion erupted near the wrecked hangar, probably a fuel truck or an ammunition store cooking off. Liquid flame leaped from one building to the next, lighting up the whole installation.

The barrage commenced again, sending round after round into the darkness between the coast and the burning buildings, where the runway lay. These explosions were not as dazzling as those that had struck the buildings. A flash of light, a dark cloud which was probably pulverized lava rock, and then darkness again. Berry spoke calmly into the microphone, carefully coordinating each shot, ensuring they were well spaced such that the recoil of one gun did not disrupt the aim of the other. The *Aeneid's* guns were like a well-oiled machine, a factory of death, delivering round after devastating round upon the airstrip.

There was no way to tell how much damage the guns had inflicted. When the giant battleships and cruisers of the surface fleet engaged in a shore bombardment, they often employed floatplanes launched from onboard catapults to provide a bird's eye view of the damage. Lacking such a perspective, Weston would have to trust in mathematics and probability, that if the *Aeneid's* shells were scattered over a specific area, allowing for uncertainties in range and wind effects, a certain percentage of those shells were likely to impact the runway. He was resolved to increase those odds by firing until the *Aeneid* had run out of ammunition, or the Japanese forced him to do otherwise.

But then, something changed in the firing sequence. The number two gun skipped a salvo. The number one gun continued as before, but when it was number two's turn again, it again remained silent.

Weston looked at Berry who was talking heatedly to someone over the phone circuit.

"The ammunition hoist for number two has failed, sir," Berry reported anxiously. "The gun captain believes

313

the worm wheel drive assembly has failed. It'll take a few hours to repair."

Weston grimaced, unable to hide his frustration. "Then serve both guns with the forward hoist!"

"Aye aye, sir."

Berry relayed the order, and Weston leaned over the rail to watch a dozen helmeted sailors form a line along the side of the conning tower from the forward hoist to the aft gun deck. They all knew what to do. The failure of a single hoist was a contingency they had all trained for. Those endless hours of seemingly meaningless drills were now paying off. Soon bags and shells were being passed aft, and the guns were firing again, but at a reduced rate — two rounds in the space of time they would have normally gotten off three.

Weston was gripping the rail, pondering the bind they would be in should the forward hoist fail, when a bright light suddenly appeared in the sky over the shore. It streaked in a high arc and then slowed considerably, almost coming to a complete stop. Thirty seconds later, it was joined by a second light, and then a third.

"Star shells, Captain," one of the lookouts reported unnecessarily.

The Japanese coastal defenses had awoken. The brilliant flares descended slowly, lighting up the shoreline and the sea for several hundred yards around, but the *Aeneid* remained safely outside the reach of the light. The second salvo of flares, however, was much closer. They appeared in the sky off the stern, a few seconds apart, and clearly illuminated the submarine's decks exposing the dozens of bustling sailors as if in daylight. Within moments, the flares had all fizzled into the sea, but they had been close enough. The Japanese gunners would have surely spotted the *Aeneid* by now, and Weston prayed that the intelligence was correct and that the enemy had light coastal defenses on that island.

The answer came moments later when two distinct columns of white water rose from the dark sea a half-mile off the bow. They were the first and second impacts of a skipping shell. Ten seconds later, another round struck the surface slightly closer than the first. Based on the size of the splashes, Weston deduced they had come from a smaller caliber weapon, probably an AA gun no larger than 3-inches in diameter. The gun was certainly big enough to ruin the *Aeneid's* day, but its accuracy was too far off to be of any immediate concern. Weston wondered how often the enemy gunners had trained on real targets.

The *Aeneid's* guns continued firing, their crews ignoring the enemy shells. They were disciplined and well-trained, from the men in the magazine belowdecks feeding the ammunition hoist, to those working the guns on deck, to Berry and his assistant. They carried out their duties under fire with coolness and professionalism, like this was just another drill.

"Aircraft preparing to take off, sir!" one of the lookouts reported.

Weston instantly brought the binoculars back to his face. The light from the burning buildings allowed him to see much of the installation in silhouette. A plane was indeed beginning to taxi to the runway airstrip, the outline of its tail fin and its spinning propellers distinct against the flames. It must have been on standby, an emergency sortie ready to take off at a moment's notice.

If that was the case, it was likely to be loaded with bombs.

"Stop that plane, Mister Berry!" Weston called out between the cacophony of the gunfire. "Shift your fire to the end of the runway!"

Weston almost regretted giving the order, because it seemed an eternity before the corrections were made and the guns were firing again. He watched with concealed uneasiness as the plane drove to the end of the runway, turned around, and immediately accelerated for takeoff. It would be airborne in seconds, and it seemed it had made it. Then, both six-inch guns fired simultaneously. The first shell burst just behind the plane, and Weston dared to hope that the shrapnel from the blast would do the job, but the aircraft continued accelerating unabated. The second shell missed by an even greater margin. There was not enough time to reload the guns and adjust their aim. It seemed the plane was going to make it into the air. But then, as Weston watched, the airplane suddenly veered hard to the right. At near takeoff speed, it immediately began to wobble out of control, its wings angling wildly until one struck the ground causing the whole aircraft to spin tail over nose like a giant boomerang. An instant later, its full fuel bladders erupted transforming the tumbling aircraft into a rolling ball of fire that left a long streak of burning fuel across the dark field.

"Nice work, Mister Berry!" Weston gave the gunnery officer a thumbs-up, convinced that the plane must have run over a crater in the runway left by one of the previous shots. Berry was grinning excitedly, apparently just as surprised and relieved by the lucky break.

But there was little time for elation. The enemy shore battery fired again. This time the shell struck the water, skipped once and detonated five hundred yards off the beam.

Weston knew he would have to pull the plug soon.

Fires raged on Matsuwa. The buildings had been severely damaged. From the fate of the enemy aircraft, he could only assume the runway had been adequately marred to make it unusable for the time being. The *Aeneid* had done her part. Now, all that remained was for

MacCullen and his men to destroy the fuel depot and finish the job.

Scanning the dark foothills beyond the burning air base, he saw no fires on the slope, no signs that the scouts had completed their mission, and he began to wonder if they had even managed to reach their objective or if they had all been captured or killed.

Another shell struck the water, just two hundred yards off the port bow.

"All ahead standard," Weston ordered into the bridge microphone, then turned to Berry. "I'm going to give those enemy gunners a harder target to hit, Mister Berry. Continue firing. Try to knock out a few of those parked planes near the hangars."

"Aye aye, sir."

The *Aeneid* could not stay up much longer, but her presence on the surface with guns blazing was crucial to keeping up the ruse that one of her shots had destroyed the fuel depot. If the submarine dove now, and the depot were to explode later, the Japanese would surely suspect an infiltration and scour the island for the scouts.

Another five minutes of the barrage resulted in more fires and more destruction ashore. Weston conned the *Aeneid* through several turns to throw off the enemy gunners whose aim was getting better, one shell even whizzing over the bridge.

*Where the hell was MacCullen?*

The prospect of failure crept into Weston's thoughts. If the scouts had met with disaster, if the fuel depot was not destroyed, and the *Aeneid's* guns had not damaged the runway as much as he had hoped, then this whole mission would be for nothing. Weston slammed his fist down on the rail in frustration. There was nothing he could do about it now. He was about to give Berry the order to secure the guns when one of the lookouts sang out.

"Explosion on the mountain, sir!"

Weston instantly brought the binoculars back to his face. A wave of relief came over him as he steadied his field of view on a giant inferno in the foothills beyond the airbase. Several blasts flashed in rapid succession, flames rising higher and higher until the whole side of the mountain was lit by an ominous orange glow. As expected, he could not see the fuel depot which was still hidden by a ridgeline, but he could see the giant flames licking up from the opposite side, indicating a massive fire raged where the fuel depot had once been.

"They did it, Captain!" Berry exclaimed triumphantly.

Weston nodded, allowing a small smile. There was no time to waste. Every second on the surface was another chance for the enemy gunners to get lucky.

"Secure the guns! Clear the decks! Clear the bridge!"

Like play actors exiting a stage, the gunners prepared the guns for sea, secured the ammunition hoists and scrambled below. Within a matter of seconds, what had been a deck teeming with two dozen sailors was deserted. After the last man had left the bridge, Weston took one final look at the destruction on the island.

The *Aeneid* had left her mark. Who knew how many Japanese had been killed in the onslaught, but if this did not draw the Japanese destroyers away from La Perouse Strait, he did not know what would. He could still see the radio tower in the glow of the blazes. It appeared undamaged. Hopefully, the enemy commander was using it at this moment to send desperate messages for help.

He looked once again at the fires burning near the mountain and wondered where MacCullen, Greathouse, and the other scouts were at this moment. Probably already making their way to the north coast for pickup. They had all done their duty. Now it was time to take care of their own.

The klaxon rang throughout the compartments below as Weston dropped down the ladder and pulled the hatch shut behind him. In the conning tower, he was met by the faint smiles of the watchstanders and a nod of satisfaction from Townsend. The relief on their faces reflected his own, and he allowed himself to breathe easier for the first time in several days.

"Let's get out of here," Weston said, then leaned over the hatch to call down to Hudson. "Make your depth one hundred feet, Joe."

As the bow planes dug into the sea and the hull angled downward, a massive blast split the silence of the room, rocking the hull and sending a violent shudder through every frame. Weston felt the deck displace several inches beneath his feet and would have been pitched into the outboard had he not been holding onto the ladder rungs. Other men who had not been prepared found themselves thrown into the bulkheads to be painfully pressed against protruding valve handles or the sharp corners of electrical boxes. Light bulbs burst in the overhead, and cork insulation rained down like snowflakes.

The explosion had been so loud and so close that Weston wondered if it had been internal to the hull. Just as soon as it had started, the shaking subsided, and the *Aeneid* continued the dive, though a little faster than Weston would have liked.

"Do you have control of her, Joe?"

Hudson's upturned face looked pale, as if he was still mentally recovering from the shock of the nearby explosion. "Aye, sir, I have control. We're going to overshoot by about ten feet."

Weston nodded, then turned his attention to the men in the conning tower. No one was seriously hurt. Monk, who had been standing by the TDC, had a laceration on his forehead and was sent below to the corpsman as damage reports began coming in over the phone circuits. The damage was light. Only a few burst light bulbs and a couple of leaking flanges.

After the *Aeneid* was on depth and clearing the area at standard speed, Townsend made his way over to Weston.

"What the hell was *that*, Captain?" he asked in a hushed manner. "That was no light coastal gun."

Weston turned to Finkelman on the sound gear. "Have your hydrophones recovered? Are you picking up anything out there?"

The sailor shook his head. "Nothing, Captain. No contacts."

"That didn't even hit us, and it shook us like a half dozen depth charges," Townsend said doubtfully. "It had to have come from a large caliber weapon. There has to be a destroyer up there somewhere, something we didn't detect. Are you certain your gear is functioning properly?"

"Yes, sir," Finkelman replied. "It all checks out. If there are any ships up there, they aren't making any noise."

Searching his mind for an answer, Weston considered the possibilities. Had one of the bombers managed to get airborne without him noticing and drop a bomb on the *Aeneid* as she was diving? Perhaps it had been an inbound plane, intending to land at Matsuwa. Or, maybe, it was another shore battery, something much more significant than an anti-aircraft gun. But if the enemy had something that big on Matsuwa, why had they waited so long to turn it on the submarine? And why had Weston not seen it during the day?

"Keep a sharp ear out, Finkelman," he said. "Report anything you hear, no matter how trivial."

"If it was a destroyer,..." Townsend said apprehensively.

Weston nodded bleakly. If there was an undetected warship up there, it might create a problem when the *Aeneid* surfaced on the other side of the island to pick up the scouts.

"Let's go get our passengers, XO. Give me a good course to the pick-up point."

# 20

# RIGHTEOUSNESS

*La Perouse (Sōya) Strait*

*IJN Hamakaze*

In the relative comfort of the *Hamakaze's* navigation bridge, Ando sipped his tea as the rain lashed the windows like a fire hose. The storm had descended on the strait as the sun had set, miring the squadron in patchy moments of showers and fog and frustrating any efforts to search for periscopes or surfaced submarines.

The sonar repeater pinged dully above the din of the darkened pilothouse. A mile off either beam, the other two destroyers, seldom visible through the fog, drove on a parallel course, their sonars also pulsing the depths to regain the contact they had lost.

It had been one of the most promising contacts yet. Three hours ago, a substantial sonar return had been detected near the center of the strait, moving slowly to the east. The *kaibōkan* had been the first to discover the anomaly. They had converged on the contact immediately, dropping two patterns of depth charges before the weather changed suddenly and the contact disappeared from their scopes. No flotsam or oil had been sighted, and so it was assumed the contact had not been sunk. By all estimates of its speed and heading, the contact had been moving east, directly into the sector patrolled by the destroyers. Now, it was up to the *Hamakaze* and her sisters to find the potential enemy submarine and sink it.

It had been one of the few moments of excitement in the little fleet for many days, and the *Hamakaze's* men had welcomed it with eagerness. Ando had sensed their heightened focus, their strong desire to fulfill their purpose here, no less fervent than his own. But, after searching for more than an hour, they had come up with nothing.

"It seems we have encountered another whale, Captain Ando." Yamada was suddenly standing beside him. A casual smile adorned the admiral's face, hiding the disappointment he must have felt.

"Possibly, Admiral," Ando replied. "Still, there is hope."

"It is fading quickly, Hitoshi."

Yamada glanced back at the chart table where Kawaguchi fidgeted. The ASW officer was more outwardly frustrated than anyone.

"I am afraid," the admiral said softly, his eyes shifting to the streaming windows.

Ando did not know how to respond to that. Especially, since the admiral's demeanor of late had been that of a man resigned to his fate – the honorable end for a disgraced samurai.

"Afraid of what, sir?" Ando finally ventured.

"I am afraid I have let young Kawaguchi down," Yamada said sullenly. "As I have let you all down. He will not be able to avenge his brother, and we have lost an opportunity to strike a severe blow to our enemy. I had hoped my final act in the emperor's service would be one of renown and legend, but that is not possible now. The things I taught you all those years ago at Eta Jima, Hitoshi, seem to have become irrelevant in the face of new technology."

"What do you mean, sir?"

"We have enough ships and aircraft guarding the strait. If the Americans have slipped through, then it is very likely they have developed a new means of evading our sonar."

Ando was reluctant to remind the admiral that enemy submarines had been elusive since the war's start and that the Americans had not gotten better at hiding. The Imperial Navy had simply not developed adequate sonar systems and tactics to find them.

"They could still be out there, sir," Ando said reassuringly. "We cannot give up now."

"No, Hitoshi." Yamada sighed as he stared out the rain-streaked glass with despondent eyes. He looked fatigued. His shoulders sagged visibly as if all the vivacity he had exhibited over the past few days was finally taking its toll on his aging body. When he spoke again, it was as if he were in a trance, as if resolved to one certain outcome. "Excuse me, Captain. I must retire to my cabin. Please pass the word that I am not to be disturbed."

Yamada turned on his heel and nodded to the flag lieutenant who stood nearby. The expressionless lieutenant came to attention and then fell in step behind the admiral to follow him out of the room. It was clear to Ando what the admiral intended to do. He would retire to his stateroom and proceed with that barbaric ritual, that act of utter madness, to preserve his honor. He would change out of his uniform into a simple kimono and then ceremonially disembowel himself with the short sword while his aide stood by with the *katana* to fulfill the role of *kaishakunin*, charged with decapitating him immediately after the fatal cut.

Ando gritted his teeth in frustration. The single-mindedness of Yamada irritated him. Yamada was an officer of the Imperial Navy, most of whom considered themselves more culturally advanced than their Imperial

Army counterparts. As Japan had burgeoned out of its feudal shogunate past, the two services had developed at different rates. The navy had gone from simple coastal sail craft made of wood to large ocean-ranging aircraft carriers made of steel in a matter of a few decades. Out of necessity, to keep up with the giant leaps in technology, the naval service had been forced to adopt a more pragmatic view of the samurai traditions. The army, on the other hand, had not. While such outdated ideas as *seppuku* and the equally suicidal and ineffective *banzai* charge were commonplace in the army, Ando found it shocking that a refined naval officer such as Yamada would succumb to such madness.

This was his mentor, his teacher, his inspiration, the man whom he had revered as a cadet, as a junior officer, and all those years rising through the ranks. He desperately wanted to reach out and grab Yamada's arm, to stop him from this lunacy, to talk some sense into him. Surely, the high command had better use for him than this.

"Admiral!" Ando said urgently, then composed himself for the benefit of those around him. "Forgive me, sir. Please wait."

Yamada stopped and looked back at him with annoyed surprise as Ando crossed the room to face him.

"Do not dishonor me, Captain," Yamada muttered such that no one else in the room could hear. "I go to my death gladly. We live under the august grace of our divine emperor. My life is insignificant."

Ando was surprised to hear such words from Yamada that could have come straight out of the *Kokutai no hongi*. But before he could reply, a sailor appeared on the bridge saluting and bearing a paper in one hand.

"What is it, petty officer?" Ando prompted.

"Radio has received an urgent message for Admiral Yamada, sir."

Yamada appeared momentarily flummoxed, as if it strained him to be yet again diverted from his intended path. It was several seconds before he regained his composure and took the message from the sailor. Yamada's eyes widened as they scanned each line, his hands nearly shaking by the time he finished reading and crumpled the paper into a ball.

Having already infringed on his personal relationship with Yamada, Ando did not press him to reveal the contents. Instead, he crossed to the chart table and pretended to review Kawaguchi's plot, allowing Yamada to be alone with his thoughts.

"Captain Ando," Yamada finally said in an even tone. "Please join me on the signal bridge."

Ando obeyed without question, following Yamada up the ladder into the driving rain.

"You may go below to the pilothouse," Ando said to the signalmen on watch, sensing that Yamada wished to speak to him alone. "I will call for you if you are needed here."

The signalmen dressed in hooded rain gear saluted gratefully, then bowed and disappeared down the ladder leaving Yamada and Ando alone with water streaming down their faces.

"What is it, Admiral?" Ando said after a long moment of silence passed between them. He had to raise his voice over the sound of the *Hamakaze's* bow crashing heavily through a swell.

"Proof of my failure, Hitoshi." Yamada's creased face stared out to sea. He held up the crumpled message, now soaking wet. "This tells me Matsuwa is under attack."

"Matsuwa?" Ando replied bewildered.

"It is under bombardment by an enemy submarine!" Yamada snarled. "No doubt, it is one of the Yankee subs we have been searching for, delivering a parting blow as it leaves our home waters. Not only has the enemy escaped our trap, now they taunt and insult us."

Ando gulped. Was it possible? How could the enemy have made it through the strait undetected?

"But Admiral," Ando protested. "Our ships and aircraft have been covering this strait day and night. We have had no sightings, no contacts to speak of other than the one a few hours ago. Surely, this must be a different submarine."

Yamada shook his head. "We must assume the enemy submarines have slipped past us."

Ando was still not convinced of that, but he made no further argument. "If they have, and one has already made it to Matsuwa, the rest could have made it to the Pacific by now."

"Perhaps. Perhaps not. The high command has left it up to me."

"What have they left up to you, sir?"

"A difficult decision, Hitoshi." Yamda paused, still looking out at the water. "I can keep the squadron here, plying these waters for the enemy, hoping they have not already passed beneath us, or," the admiral looked at Ando, "or, I can disperse the fleet and send them to the Kuril passes in the hopes we can stop at least one of the enemy from reaching the Pacific."

"There are a dozen passages through the Kurils, sir. They could be headed for any one."

"Some are easier traversed than others, Hitoshi. The Americans will choose those."

Ando considered the admiral was probably right. The smaller passages were heavily mined. Many were monitored by magnetic loops. They could be bottled up by two sub chasers, or a few aircraft. The larger passes would be much more appealing to the enemy. They were much broader and deeper than La Perouse Strait, giving a submerged submarine ample room for maneuver and escape.

"Have we received a weather report from the Kurils?" Yamada asked. There was a sudden vibrancy in his manner, a fire in his eyes, as if the old warrior was awakening within him.

"Yes, sir. Two hours ago. The low-pressure system is pushing north. The skies over the Kurils are clear. Visibility is excellent."

"Perfect conditions for hunting submarines, wouldn't you say, Hitoshi?"

Ando nodded. "Certainly much better than what we face here, sir."

With the rain pelting the brim of his hat, Yamada stood silent for several seconds, as if considering his options. No longer did he appear solemn and morose. If anything, he seemed invigorated. Ando knew, at that moment, that his mentor did not intend to go through with the *seppuku* – at least, not for the moment. Though the news from Matsuwa was bleak, it had given Yamada one thing he had not had before – a positive sighting of the enemy. Up until that message, the American submarines might just as well have been ghosts haunting his dreams. Now, he had a firm contact. He knew where one of the enemy subs was, and now there was a possibility of saving face, of preserving his honor, if he could locate and sink just one of the enemy before they escaped into the Pacific.

Yamada turned to face Ando, his eyes filled with the same confidence they had exuded in the previous days.

"Prepare a new message to all ships, Captain! The Yankees will not slip through our fingers so easily!"

# 21

# AN ALL-FIRED HURRY

*La Perouse Strait*

*USS Sea Dog*

Floating with the current, the *Sea Dog* crept along the ocean floor in silence, the submarine's keel hovering just a few fathoms above the rock-strewn sand. The water here was shallow, less than two hundred feet, shallow enough that if the submarine stood on end with her bow touching the seabed, half of her hull would stand high and dry above the surface.

It was as silent inside the hull as it was outside. After nearly eight hours submerged with the air conditioning plant secured, the sweltering crew sat or lay throughout the stifling compartments where even the bulkheads streamed with moisture. Only the watchstanders moved about, constantly wiping their brows with already sopping rags.

In the conning tower, Prewitt rose to his feet and made his way over to the chart table where his executive officer was keeping tabs on the submarine's dead reckoning position. Amid the pencil lines on the paper were droplets of sweat that had run off the XO's temples.

"I put us near the half-way point, Skipper," the XO said, placing the point of a pair of dividers on the mark that represented the *Sea Dog's* position.

Prewitt wiped his brow and nodded. "Then that means the other two boats are already approaching the exit."

The XO nodded grimly, both men understanding that was an optimistic appraisal of the situation. Two hours ago, the sonar had picked up distant explosions far ahead, very likely a depth charge attack on the *Finback* or the *Pintado*. They had only been encouraged by the fact that the shellacking had not lasted long, assuming that was because the enemy had lost contact, and not because the targeted submarine had been destroyed. Ever since that brief few minutes of turmoil, the sea had been unsettlingly quiet, except for the incessant pinging in the distance. The pinging grew steadily louder as the *Sea Dog* crawled along with the current, a constant reminder that the most dangerous waters still lay ahead.

Prewitt wondered if they were heading into a trap. Perhaps the Japanese had drawn a great steel net across the exit, and the *Sea Dog* was driving straight for it. Maybe, at this very moment, an enemy destroyer was directly above them, drifting with the current and listening, waiting for just the right time to unleash a mass of depth charges. Or perhaps the *Sea Dog* was headed into an uncharted minefield.

The minefields at the entrance to the strait had been avoided with conservative use of the FM sonar. But now that the enemy was closer, Prewitt had ordered the mine-detecting sonar secured. Using it was too much of a gamble. Any sound emission from the *Sea Dog* might be picked up by the enemy's passive hydrophones.

The speaker in the overhead intoned a sound like faint static. It was raining again up there in the world above.

The sound was reassuring, almost soothing, in sharp contrast to the ominous echo-ranging. Prewitt had considered taking advantage of the weather conditions, of surfacing and driving at top speed on the diesels, trusting in the fog and rain to hide the *Sea Dog* from the enemy warships. But the squalls were too intermittent for that. More than likely, they would clear suddenly, and the submarine would find herself in the middle of the enemy fleet with all searchlights pointed at her.

"Do you have any idea where that pinger is?" Prewitt asked. He had to pull his mind away from too much speculation.

"Just a rough triangulation based on our movements," the XO replied. He used a pair of dividers to mark the distance between two points on the chart. "I'd put it at four thousand yards. It's been moving, too, so there's probably a lot of error in that." The XO gestured to the sound operator. "Anderson can probably give you a better range."

Prewitt turned to the sound man, expecting an answer, but the sailor did not seem to have heard what the XO had said. Anderson was listening intently to his headphones, minutely adjusting the dial that controlled the steerable hydrophone.

"Hold on!" he said, raising a hand to one earpiece. "I'm getting high-speed screws, Captain! Lots of them! Like the whole fleet just got underway."

"Coming from the channel ahead of us?"

"Yes, sir," Anderson squinted his eyes at the azimuth indicator on his control gear. "Multiple contacts, spanning zero eight zero to one one zero."

"Are they moving to attack one of the other boats?"

"I don't know, sir. I don't think so. They're not pinging anymore. They're just moving in an all-fired hurry."

For several tense minutes, Prewitt did not know whether to remain at silent running or to order up more speed to try and push through while the enemy ships were making so much noise. The sounds of the swooshing propellers were just audible over the loudspeaker. Like every other man in the compartment, he could not help but stare at Anderson, waiting for the next report.

"Those warships are heading away, sir!" the sailor finally reported. "Screw noise is fading rapidly. I'm hearing destroyers and escorts up there. There must be a party somewhere, Captain, because they're moving out. I think they're leaving the area."

"Well, what do you know?" the XO said exultantly. "It looks like ComSubPac came through for us, after all. The diversion must have worked, praise the Lord Almighty!"

A few men cheered without thinking and were immediately silenced by a scathing glare from Prewitt.

It could be an enemy trick. What better way to tempt a submarine into coming to the surface? Just about any captain would prefer a quick run on the surface over this snail-like crawl. But Prewitt was not going to fall for it.

"Steady as she goes, steersman," he ordered firmly, sequestering much of the excitement in the room. They had made it this far. They could not afford to let their guard down now.

But after an hour had passed with no echo-ranging, and the noise of the distant ships had diminished to the point that it was hard for Anderson to pick it out over the sound of the rainfall, Prewitt finally allowed himself to think that a lucky star was indeed shining on them.

"Screw noise is fading much faster now, sir," Anderson reported. "I'd say they're at least twenty miles away. They're going in different directions, some to the east, some to the north."

Prewitt exchanged a hopeful glance with the XO. It was a miracle. Unless the Japanese were playing a very clever trick, they were withdrawing their entire fleet from the strait. He wondered if the captains of the *Finback* and *Pintado*, wherever they were in the depths ahead, were forming the same conclusion.

"How the hell did ComSubPac pull that one off?" A man said down in the control room, voicing Prewitt's own thoughts.

Somehow, ComSubPac had done it. They had drawn off the enemy ships. Prewitt did not know how. He did not care. All that he knew was that the enemy was gone, and he was going to take advantage of it.

"All ahead standard," he said. "Let's get out of this damned strait, gentlemen."

"Amen to that, sir!" the XO affirmed with a wide grin.

# 22

# MOMENT OF TRUTH

## *Matsuwa Island*

The infinite field of stars was slowly supplanted by gray hues as the first hints of dawn approached. Looking up, Greathouse and the scouts could see the first beams of sunlight reflecting off Mount Matsuwa's snow-capped peak. The lowlands remained shrouded in darkness, but not for long. Soon, the dark veil that had hidden the scouts on their trek around the eastern side of the mountain would lift, exposing them on rocky terrain that offered little cover.

To the south, beyond the mountain's shoulder, thick columns of smoke rose into the sky to be dragged by the wind out over the sea. It was a testament to the destruction visited upon the Japanese last night, and Greathouse felt much satisfaction every time he glanced over his shoulder to gaze upon it. It was but a small measure of retribution for his comrades lost on Attu.

The mission had been a success. The fuel depot had been completely destroyed. There had been some delays, which Greathouse attributed in his mind to MacCullen's poor leadership, but the charges had been set, and every single tank had gone up in a crescendo of successive explosions that had produced a fireball massive enough to singe the scouts' eyebrows as they had watched from a mile away. The sight of the mountainside bathed in burning fuel had been dazzling, as if the volcano were spewing lava down its slopes, but it paled in comparison to the destruction down below. From the foothills, the scouts had watched the carnage unfold around the airfield as shell after shell from the *Aeneid* had exploded amongst the clustered buildings and aircraft creating mass havoc. The Japanese garrison had been taken entirely by surprise. With his binoculars, Greathouse had seen stunned enemy troops and airmen stampede from the burning buildings and scramble in all directions, by and large ignoring the attempts of their officers to gain order. In the light of the raging fires, he had seen one

Japanese officer emerge from a structure wearing nothing but his infantry tunic as if he had been caught on the john. The bare-assed fool waved his sword above his head threatening the men running past him, but none of them stopped. Who could blame them? Men were dying everywhere, some covered in burning fuel, some maimed, some blinded by the flames. Those on fire scampered wildly for some means of relief while their fuel-soaked comrades fled in terror lest they, too, burst into flames.

But all had not been chaos and confusion. Clusters of men had stood fast and fought the fires despite the dangers, and many paid the full price for their bravery. Greathouse had seen one such group directing a firehose onto a burning building when a six-inch shell landed in their midst, blasting them into shards of flesh. Another dozen men trying to push a burning plane away from a hangar were obliterated when a bomb under the aircraft's wing exploded. It had appeared that most of the other aircraft were severely damaged or destroyed as well. Greathouse had only observed one plane attempt to take off, and that plane met its end at the end of the runway as a tumbling ball of fire.

It had been a good night indeed, Greathouse considered, though he lamented the loss of Myers. He still believed the private's death could have been prevented had MacCullen acted sooner, and he did not intend to back down on that assertion when and if they ever reached home again. If MacCullen thought he could drum him out of the regiment without a fight, he had another thing coming. The asshole lieutenant might have connections at the top, but Greathouse had connections, too, where it really mattered, among the sergeants. His peers at regimental headquarters would never let that incompetent shirker lead men ever again. He would see to that.

But Greathouse tried to pull his mind away from the administrative troubles that awaited him stateside. First things were first. First, they had to get off this rock.

On the trek north, they had made good time, thanks to a freshly-constructed gravel road that just happened to be going in their direction. The road had been an unexpected convenience. It was the same road they had discovered earlier, the branch forking off from the fuel depot road. Like the relocated fuel depot, the road had not appeared on any of the charts of the island, but it was there, and so they had taken it, greatly accelerating their progress.

Throughout the night, the road had led the scouts on a winding journey through a myriad of valleys and ridges along the mountain's lower slopes, many of which would have taken hours to cross otherwise and would have prevented them from making their pickup time. The road was Heaven-sent, a stroke of good luck for MacCullen who had misjudged the ruggedness of the terrain when he had committed to a 0600 rendezvous with the *Aeneid*. Still, the lieutenant appeared more disturbed by the road than thankful for it. On several occasions he had commented on its excellent quality and how he could not understand why the Japanese would build it here. Having earlier brushed off the road's existence, MacCullen now seemed obsessed with determining its purpose.

On one occasion during the night, the scouts had been forced to scramble off the road as several Japanese trucks came barreling out the darkness behind them, their path lit by a single dim headlamp in the leading vehicle. Hiding in a ditch beside the road, Greathouse and the others had watched with fingers on triggers as the convoy had passed them, listening to the gears grind on each truck as it handled the steep grade.

"They can't be looking for us going that fast," Houston had commented after the trucks had driven by. "Where the hell does this road go?"

"Keep quiet!" MacCullen had silenced him harshly. "There could be foot patrols out there. Let me worry about the damn road!" The lieutenant had seemed more frustrated as they discovered more road in front of them.

Now, in the dim light of dawn, the squad reached the north side of the mountain where the road finally came to an end – or rather, it took an abrupt left turn uphill and disappeared among the crags and crevices of the volcano's higher slope. The squad stopped for one last rest before their final push to the north shore, less than a mile away, an easy cross-country march.

They downed the last drops of water in their canteens as they stared out at the dark expanse of ocean in the distance, wondering where the *Aeneid* would appear. MacCullen was the only exception. He stood apart from the group, his binoculars trained on the mountainside. Cleary, he was still perplexed by the road. As MacCullen studied the winding highway, Greathouse studied him, wondering what harebrained ideas were swirling inside the young officer's mind.

Then, surprisingly, MacCullen turned to Greathouse and gestured for him to join him.

"The Japanese are building something up there, Sergeant," MacCullen said evenly, as if they had not been at odds with each other for the last several hours. "They are either building something, or they already have built something. I'm sure of it."

"Is that so, sir?"

"Look at that foundation, Sergeant." MacCullen pointed excitedly. "This isn't a simple patrol road. The Japanese have built it to support trucks carrying heavy loads. There has to be a new construction of some kind up there."

"Maybe the Japs are fortifying the mountain, sir," Greathouse offered. "Maybe they're putting pillboxes up on that slope like they've done on other islands."

"Possibly." MacCullen shook his head. "But I don't think so. This road runs up the northern slope, but the only beach that can support landing craft is on the south side of the island. It doesn't make sense to build fortifications here. It has to be something else."

There was something in MacCullen's eyes that Greathouse had seen in many officers before him — something he did not like.

"Time's a-wastin', Lieutenant," Greathouse said guardedly. "Shouldn't we be moving along? The sub will be looking for us."

"There is something up there, Sergeant," MacCullen said steadfastly. "I'd bet my bars on it. I want you to send Martinez and Bell up to take a look."

Greathouse bit his lip from saying what he wanted to say. "That's not a good idea, sir."

MacCullen looked at him blankly. "I did not ask your opinion, Greathouse. Do it, now."

Greathouse did not move. "That road goes up the slope quite a ways, sir. It's switchbacks all the way up. It could go on for two miles or more. If we send the boys up there, they might not make it back in time for the rendezvous."

"They're scouts, aren't they? They're trained for this!" MacCullen was clearly irritated.

"It isn't our mission," Greathouse replied succinctly.

"It isn't what?"

"That up there ain't our mission, sir. We came here to destroy a bunch of fuel tanks. We've done that."

"I decide what our mission is, Sergeant!"

"Commander Weston didn't say anything about doing a reconnaissance."

"He's not here, Sergeant! And he didn't know about the road. If he did, then I'm sure he would agree with me, though his opinion would be of no concern." MacCullen's lips pursed in a contemptuous smile. "I'm surprised that you of all people would use a naval officer as a crutch to avoid your duty. Perhaps you're not the blood-and-guts man I took you for."

Greathouse scowled. He had had all he could take. "You'll refer to me as *sergeant*! I earned it long before your cowardly ass ever put on a uniform!"

"Damn you! You'll not speak to me like that!"

"I'll speak to you any way I damn well like!" Greathouse kept his voice low so that the others could not overhear the heated exchange. "This isn't a game, sir. It's not some exercise for you to win a ribbon. The things you pulled in Africa aren't going to happen here!"

MacCullen was brimming with anger. "You know nothing about what happened in Africa."

"I know you turned yellow. I know you damned near got your whole platoon wiped out. Oh, I know about you, *Lieutenant*!"

MacCullen's face was suddenly contemplative. "Major Nash thought he did, too. He was wrong, just as you are."

"Is Commander Weston wrong, too, sir?" Greathouse prompted. "He knew about you, too. Before we left the sub, he told me to make sure you didn't do anything stupid over here. Now, I'm following his orders, and I'm stopping you from doing something very stupid. I ain't sending my boys up that mountain. If you want to find out what's up that road, you'll just have to go yourself." Greathouse paused before adding sharply, "With all due respect, *Lieutenant*."

Their eyes were locked for several seconds, Greathouse's set and determined, MacCullen's jittery and uncertain. The lieutenant's poise was quickly fading as if he was suddenly consumed by something welling up inside of him. He averted his eyes and did not look at Greathouse.

"Come on, sir, what's the matter?" Greathouse continued brazenly. He could not help but chide the young officer. "Don't have the stomach for doing something you want these boys to do? Kind of like in Africa, isn't it, sir? I heard you came away with a bronze star for that one. Only cost you your whole platoon. Why don't you go up there and win yourself the next one, because you ain't paying for it with the blood of these boys."

"Damn you to hell!" MacCullen said under his breath. "You don't know anything."

"I know that you're a coward."

"I am not a coward!"

Greathouse raised his eyebrows and looked down at MacCullen's boots. "You've been double-timing it pretty easily on this march, Lieutenant. Hard to believe you were down with trench foot a few days ago. Lucky that came along, wasn't it? Otherwise, you'd have been butchered with the rest of your platoon."

"Is that the story you've told them?" MacCullen gestured to the other scouts.

"I didn't need to. They've got eyes."

"You don't know what you're talking about, Sergeant. No matter what you think, it didn't happen like that. I didn't desert my men in Africa. And I didn't choose to remain behind at Attu, either."

Greathouse shot him a dubious look.

"I'll admit I did not have trench foot, Sergeant," MacCullen said with a conceding nod, somewhat struggling to get the words out. "But it was not my idea. As I said, you don't know what you're talking about."

"I call things like I see them, sir. Seems to me, there's only one word for a man claiming to get trench foot the night before an operation!"

"What would you call that man if he was simply following orders?"

"Orders?" Greathouse said with bewilderment. "What orders?"

"The orders given to me by Major Nash aboard the *Aeneid* when we were still en route to Attu."

Greathouse looked at him perplexedly.

"I was given orders, Sergeant," MacCullen explained. "I acted on those orders. I had no choice."

"What the hell are you talking about, Lieutenant? Are you trying to tell me Major Nash ordered you to get trench foot?"

MacCullen nodded.

"That's complete bullshit! I don't believe it!"

MacCullen looked back at him gravely. "Rumors have a life of their own in the army. They travel faster than official correspondence and convey less truth with each telling. Like you, Major Nash had heard stories about my time in Africa. I do not know from whom, possibly my own platoon sergeant. I know the men of my platoon despised me. They, at least, despised my methods. In any event, Major Nash made this discovery on the voyage to Attu and confronted me with it. He claimed to have lost all confidence in my ability to command, and that the men under me did not trust my leadership. I explained to him that the stories of my time in Africa had been exaggerated. I even gave him the names of half a dozen officers that could corroborate my side of the story and prove, without a doubt, that I had not done these things. But the major was not interested in discovering the truth. He said the truth didn't matter at this point, that the men under me did not trust me to the point that it might jeopardize our mission on Attu. He had already made up his mind. I was to remain behind." MacCullen paused and clenched his jaw as if reliving the frustration of that moment. "Of course, I begged him to let me go. I pleaded with him. Told him my name had already been smeared in Africa. That this decision would destroy my career. Not to mention, the shame of it all. So, the all too generous major made me an offer. To save face, I could feign an injury. He would back me up and ensure the company medics did, too."

Greathouse gasped, dumbfounded and disbelieving. Not in a million years would he have believed such a story, had he heard it third hand. But now, looking into MacCullen's steady eyes, he saw no trace of deceit. As much as he despised the pompous bastard, he believed he was telling the truth.

"So, you see, Sergeant. I had little choice. I did what I had to do for the company and the mission." MacCullen glanced over at the other scouts who were still out of earshot but curiously watching the exchange between the two men. "Major Nash and all the medics took the truth to their graves, and so now I must suffer a lifetime of whispers and doubts, the man who stayed behind while his company was butchered on Attu." MacCullen looked at his watch, took one final look at the road leading up the slope, and then let out a long sigh. "Forget about the reconnaissance, Sergeant. You are right. We will proceed to the rendezvous as planned. Get them moving."

# 23

# GUNS AND WATER

*Off Matsuwa*

*USS Aeneid*

The *Aeneid* surfaced a mile off the north coast of Matsuwa. Weston was the first on the bridge, followed immediately by Townsend and the lookouts who pressed binoculars to their faces to scan their assigned sectors.

"There they are, Captain!" Townsend announced before the water had finished gushing into the sea from the decks below. He pointed at a spot on the dark shoreline. "I see their signal."

Within seconds, Weston found it, too – a tiny flashing light near the water's edge. It was still too dark to see any distinct features along the coast other than the white foam of the waves crashing on the rocks, but the blinking code was the correct one. The scouts had to be there.

"Lots of breakers there, XO," Weston said. "Are you sure you're up to this?"

"Don't worry, skipper," Townsend replied with a chuckle as he glanced down at the deck where several sailors were preparing the raft for launch. "We've been over this. I've got experience with these rafts. Remember, I spent a year assigned to the navy divers when I was an ensign. I know these boats in and out, and I know how to handle them close-in to the shore. You send anybody else, they'll likely capsize the thing."

"If you say so, XO," Weston said casually. He did not like the idea of sending his most experienced officer on such a dangerous excursion, but Townsend was right. Handling small craft in rock-strewn, agitated waters was an art form all to itself, and Townsend was the best pick for the job.

"We'll be back before you know it, Captain," Townsend said reassuringly as he donned a helmet and life vest.

"Make sure you don't stop to sightsee."

"On that rock?" Townsend flashed a grin. "I wouldn't think of it, sir."

Weston watched as Townsend crossed to the aft cutout and took the outboard ladder down to the main deck where the boat handling party had already inflated the raft and lowered it into the sea. Two taut lines held the bobbing black ellipse tightly to the submarine's side as gentle waves slapped against the hull. It was still quite dark, but Weston could make out enough, and he could clearly see Townsend's khaki uniform among the various blue dungarees and black sweaters. One by one, three sailors, hand-selected as the best oarsmen in the *Aeneid's* crew, entered the wobbly craft followed finally by Townsend himself. All four looked somewhat like commandos in their bulky vests and navy gray helmets. Several oars were then handed to those in the raft, more than its current crew could use. The extra oars would be used by the scouts after the pickup to assist in the pull away from the shore.

With a final wave at the bridge, Townsend ordered the lines cast off, and the ungainly raft drifted away from the *Aeneid*, the men inside immediately digging their oars into the water, leaving white splotches on the surface as they turned the craft and headed for the shore.

Weston checked his watch. The round-trip was expected to take one hour, one hour in which the *Aeneid* would be sitting on the surface as the light of day rapidly approached. Once again, he prayed the airfield on the other side of the island had been put out of commission by last night's bombardment. The last thing they needed was a Val bomber screaming out of the sky from the scattered gray clouds above them.

"Excuse me, Captain."

It was Berry. He had just come up to the bridge from the main deck, taking the same ladder Townsend had used to descend. Berry had been supervising the boat handling party, and now that the boat was away, there appeared to be something else on his mind.

"What is it, Lieutenant?"

"I was just thinking, sir," Berry said with some reluctance. "Since we plan to stay on the surface, wouldn't it be wise to man the guns? We never know what might come around that headland, maybe that sampan we saw last night, or maybe a Jap gunboat."

Weston smiled inwardly. Spoken like a true gunnery officer, always looking for the chance to employ the guns he and his divisions worked so tirelessly to maintain.

"If anything comes around that headland, Lieutenant, I intend to dive, not take it on in a gunfight. Go ahead and get your men below. I want the main deck secured in case we need to get down fast."

"Aye aye, sir," Berry replied, walking away and descending the ladder back to the main deck almost dejectedly, like a boy told he could not go out and play.

It almost made Weston chuckle out loud. He could remember a time when he was not too different from Berry. In his years as a junior officer, he had been eager for battle, eager to fight any enemy, regardless of the risk. As he watched the small raft move incredibly slowly across the water, only some fifty yards away now, he wondered if he was being just as reckless now by sending

Townsend, his most capable officer, on such a hazardous assignment.

"Bridge, control," Monk's voice intoned over the speaker. "Recommend commencing the turn, sir."

"Bridge, aye," Weston replied. In Townsend's absence, Monk had taken his place on the chart desk in the conning tower and was carefully marking the *Aeneid's* position as she cruised parallel to the coast at seven knots under the lee of the towering Mount Matsuwa. The plan was to drive in a long racetrack pattern around an imaginary point that would keep the submarine as close to shore as possible while remaining in waters deep enough – just barely – to dive.

Weston's intuition told him the turn was a bit early. Not a big deal, but he wanted to wait before giving the order to make sure Monk was keeping a proper accounting of the ship's position and not entirely relying on the automatic trace provided by the DRT. He pressed the intercom button again and was just about to call down for Monk to take another visual navigational fix, when, out of the corner of his eye, he saw something on the side of the enormous mountain before him. Tiny puffs of smoke about half-way up the volcanic slope. Three of them, distinct and separate, like three jets of gases escaping the hot caverns hidden beneath before an eruption. But Matsuwa was dormant. The realization of what the gas jets were came to Weston a half-second later, and he had a moment to be struck by an icy cold horror before the ocean around him erupted.

*Kaboom!...Kaboom!...Kaboom! Kaboom!*

Three giant explosions ripped the air apart around the *Aeneid* as three great columns of water flew skyward marking the spots where the large shells had hit. The bridge, the deck, everything was covered in a thick mist and spray as the sheets of water fell back to earth, drenching Weston as if he stood under a giant fountain. The detonations had been close, the shock waves nearly knocking him off his feet. He heard shrapnel striking the metal weather shield around the bridge. Above him, a man cried out in pain.

"All ahead flank! Right full rudder!" Weston shouted down the open hatch to the steersman below who rapidly threw the wheel over, ignoring the torrent of water spilling through the opening.

It was not until the spray had subsided that Weston could ascertain the damage. As the waters receded through the scuppers, he saw a shoe floating upon the foam. When it finally came to rest on the deck, he nearly retched. It contained a severed foot. Looking up, he saw blood trickling down the periscope shears, and his eyes followed it to the source of the gore. The port side lookout was slumped in his perch, either unconscious or dead. He had been struck in the shin by a piece of flying metal. The deadly shrapnel had taken his foot right off and had continued into the hull just behind him, painting the side of the periscope mount red. The other lookout had already moved around the housing to help the wounded man, while others stood by on the bridge to receive the sailor's bleeding body. Weston desperately wanted to lend a hand, but he fought the urge to do so. The men knew what to do. They would take care of each other. He had to take care of the ship.

The deck surged forward as the *Aeneid's* 2,700-ton hull felt the thrust of the accelerating screws. The rudder began to bite into the water, heeling the ship to starboard. They had to turn to a new heading, and fast.

If the enemy shells had not managed to bracket them, they had come awfully close. That meant the Japanese gunners on the side of that mountain would need only make a simple correction to place their shells directly down the periscope shaft.

"Report damage!" Weston ordered into the 1MC.

Checking forward, Weston did not see any apparent damage. No men should have been forward when the shells hit, so he was not alarmed to see the deck clear. As he rushed to the aft coaming, his mind raced with a dozen thoughts. Why had the intelligence not mentioned the big guns on Matsuwa? Why had the Japanese put them here? Why on the north side of the island? Were there others on the south side? Had that been the source of the massive explosion the *Aeneid* had experienced last night just after diving?

When Weston reached a point where he could see the main deck clearly, his knees nearly gave out. At least a half dozen men had been on deck before the blasts. Now, only half that number remained, and two of those were dead, their bodies mangled and sprawled beneath the aft gun mount. The men had been savaged by a large piece of flying shrapnel, one deadly piece that had passed through both men's torsos. Only their bloody dungaree-clad legs identified them as human beings. The gun itself had taken damage, too. A giant gash had been gouged into the barrel near the breech end, probably created by the same projectile that had killed the sailors.

Only one man remained alive on the deck below. The young sailor wandered about aimlessly, apparently in shock, but otherwise unharmed. Weston recognized him as the eighteen-year-old fireman Bertowski. The increasing light of the dawn allowed Weston to discern at least two more bodies floating face-down in the sea off the starboard side. One wore khakis.

*Berry.*

Weston had spoken to the young gunnery officer not three minutes ago. He would never talk to him again. Berry would never make it back to that sleepy farm town in Iowa. He would never live to receive the bronze star that Weston had nominated him for after the last patrol. His body would float away and never be seen again. Gone without a trace. Food for the fish. Nothing for his loved ones to bury. Nothing over which to say a prayer.

"Yates!" Weston called to the quartermaster of the watch. "Go down there and help Bertowski before he walks over the edge. Get him below, and get things secured down there!"

"Aye, aye, Captain!" Yates replied, removing the spare binoculars slung around his neck and dropping them on the deck before scrambling for the aft ladder, his middle-aged frame moving as nimbly as an eighteen-year-old's.

The ship was turning faster now, the speed surpassing ten knots. The guns had not yet fired again, but it was only a matter of time. Weston had to get the ship out of danger. He had to steer unpredictably, give the enemy gunners a challenge while he waited for each compartment to report that the pressure hull was sound enough to dive.

At that moment, he remembered the boat in the water. Amid the horrific sights and his urgency to get the ship moving, he had momentarily forgotten that Townsend and three crewmen were still in the raft...unless the enemy salvo had sunk them.

Looking off the port quarter and not finding what he wanted to see, an instant sensation of loss and regret flooded over him. Townsend and his men were lost like the others. But then the remaining lookout above stretched out an arm to point a few degrees to the left of where Weston had been looking.

"I have them, sir! Just off the starboard quarter."

Weston found them, too, though the starboard quarter became the starboard beam by the time he did, due to the *Aeneid's* sharp turn.

"There they are!" Weston announced, unable to contain his own excitement at seeing the small black raft and its crew, just blurry dots from this distance. He had missed them in the gray light of dawn. Thankfully, the lookout had not. Reaching over the press of men lowering the wounded man through the hatch, Weston's hand found the microphone talk button. He kept his eyes glued to the small black dot on the sea.

"Rudder amidships! Steady as you go!"

"Rudder amidships, aye," answered the steersman. "My rudder is amidships, sir."

"Very well."

The ship slowly steadied on its new course, the bow pointing just to the left of the rubber raft.

"Come on!" Weston shouted to no one in particular. "More speed! More speed, damn it!"

"Speed by log, fifteen knots, sir," came the steersman's voice again. The sailor had obviously heard Weston's frustrated outburst through the open hatch.

There was nothing anybody could do. It took a set amount of time to get a 2,700-ton submarine up to maximum speed, and while the *Aeneid's* diesel engines were practically brand new, she was an old ship. Her lines were not as sleek and hydrodynamic as the more modern fleet boats. On the surface, she moved through the water like a true pig boat.

"Bridge," Monk's voice intoned over the speaker. "Captain, this course takes us straight into the rocks in two thousand yards. Recommend slowing, sir."

"Recommendation noted, Mister Monk. Steady as she goes! And have the small boat handling party standing by at the conning tower side hatch." Weston would not think of sending men topside when the *Aeneid* was at top speed. The water would crash over her bow sweeping anyone off like flies. Even now a dash of spray doused the aft gun deck and the two mangled bodies which no one had had the stomach or the time to remove. "We'll slow just before we reach the raft. Keep them in view, boys. They're getting closer. Just a thousand yards to go. Keep going!"

Weston kept watching the figures in the little raft through his binoculars. The light was better now, and he could see them much clearer. They were desperately rowing for the submarine. Was that Townsend in the front waving one khaki-sleeved arm? It had to be. Townsend was waving while the others rowed. He was waving at the *Aeneid,* and it took only a few seconds for Weston to discern what his XO was trying to communicate. The body language was clear even from this distance in the man he had come to know over four war patrols and special operations. Townsend was waving, but not for the *Aeneid* to come pick them up. He was waving them off, signaling Weston to forget about them and save the ship. And now Weston also realized that the raft was not rowing toward the submarine, but away from it. Townsend was still driving the raft toward the rocky coast and certain capture or death.

"All compartments have reported in, Captain," Monk's voice sounded over the speaker. "No apparent damage to the pressure hull. We can dive at any time, sir."

For an instant, Weston felt a tinge of guilt and the eyes of those on the bridge watching him. Was he really jeopardizing the *Aeneid* and the eighty-seven men aboard her to save four men? Was he doing his duty as a captain, or was he too afraid to let go of Townsend after seeing so many of his men already killed and maimed? But, in his heart, he knew there could be no question. How many subs had ventured into coastal waters, running under blazing Japanese gunfire to rescue downed airmen? Those cases were no different from this one. Townsend and those three sailors were just as worthy of saving as any pilot.

"The guns have fired again, Captain!" Ensign Weaver, the junior officer of the deck, announced suddenly.

Weston tore his eyes away from the raft long enough to look at the mountainside. He saw smoke there as before, but not as much. Had only a few of the guns fired? He received an answer two seconds later when a massive column of water shot up well before the *Aeneid's* bow, missing her by at least five hundred yards, but still close enough to make everyone on the bridge duck behind the coaming as the shockwave of the explosion rippled past.

"They can't hit a moving target so easily," the lookout announced triumphantly.

But Weston was not sure there was anything to rejoice at. The enemy gunners were playing it smart, using only one gun at a time to determine the range and increase their firing rate. And now he could finally see the towering water column in its entirety and judge the real power of the enemy guns. They had to be large bore pieces, at least equivalent in size to the *Aeneid's* own weapons. Weston never once considered taking on the coastal battery in a slugging match. The enemy had too many advantages. They had the high ground. They had more guns. And they did not have to contend with a rolling deck and thus could rely on their shells to land consistently.

Again, a puff of smoke appeared on the mountain, and again a column of water rose from the sea, but, to Weston's surprise, this one was farther away than the last one had been. How could that be? The enemy gunners had a clear, birds-eye view of the ocean below. The *Aeneid* and her curving white wake would be clearly visible, as would the fall of their own shots. Were the enemy gunners that incompetent? Or were they...?

Weston swallowed hard.

*They were going after the raft!*

The Japanese up on that mountain had shifted their aim to the raft. Undoubtedly, they had concluded it was of some value since the *Aeneid* was putting itself in danger to reach it.

Weston had little choice. The only way he could turn the enemy guns away from the raft was to turn the ship around and head back out to sea.

"Left full rudder!" he grunted into the microphone. Through his binoculars he could see the men inside the raft clearly now. He could see Townsend's face beneath the gray helmet staring intently back at the *Aeneid* and saw him raise a fist in triumph as the submarine turned hard to port and pointed her bow out to sea. Clearly, the XO agreed with his decision and now turned away and dug his own oar into the water to help the others pull for the island.

Satisfied that the Japanese gunners would quickly lose interest in the raft, especially since its occupants would certainly be captured once they reached the shore, Weston focused his efforts on getting the *Aeneid* ready to dive.

He pressed the intercom button. "Secure the boat handling party. Give me a sounding."

"Sounding eighteen fathoms, sir," came the reply a few seconds later.

"Continuous ping on the fathometer. Let me know when it hits twenty!" Weston turned to the men on the bridge. "Clear the bridge!"

As the lookouts dropped from their perches to go below, Ensign Weaver still had his binoculars to his face. "The guns have fired again, sir!"

"Hurry! Get below!" Weston shouted as the men filed down the hatch. "We've got shells inbound!" He crossed to the other side of the bridge to get out of their way and to prompt Weaver to take cover. But before Weston could pull the mesmerized ensign down behind the coaming, something instinctive made him glance back at the raft. At the precise moment that he found the tiny craft, a thousand yards off the stern filled with elbows and oars urgently rowing, two shells impacted the water.

They did not strike near the *Aeneid* as Weston had expected. They hit the water near the raft throwing up great geysers that completely obscured the little craft from view.

"No!" Weston exclaimed, bringing the binoculars to his face and praying for a miracle. But when the spray subsided, the surface was clear. The raft was nowhere to be seen. It had been obliterated from the face of the sea. Weston searched for any sign of flotsam, bobbing heads or flailing arms, for any indication someone might have survived.

"Bridge, Control," the speaker squawked. "Sounding twenty-two fathoms!"

Weston did not respond. Instead, he continued to search. Eventually, Weaver acknowledged the report for him, but Weston hardly heard it. As he scanned the water's surface, images of Townsend's wife and newborn child back in San Francisco filled his mind. He had only met Betty Townsend on a few occasions, and each time her eyes had communicated with him without speaking. *Bring my husband home…bring my husband back to me.*

But that would not happen now. A young widow and a fatherless child would have to deal with their grief. George and Betty Townsend had been together for many years. Betty had moved with him wherever the navy had sent him, had been part of the navy wives' circles at each new duty station, and had waited the agonizing months between his brief shore leaves. That life to which she had devoted her heart and soul for so long was now gone. Not only had she lost her husband, she had lost her social link with the wives of the other officers. She belonged to a new group now, an ever-growing number of navy widows.

Weston suddenly felt an overwhelming sense of guilt. Would she blame him? Would the loved ones of the other dead sailors blame him, too?

Suddenly, Old Yates was at his shoulder, speaking lowly and respectfully, but firmly. "They're gone, sir. We must dive."

Torn with an unexpected flood of emotion, Weston wrenched himself back to his duties.

"Get below!" he said to Yates and Weaver. Reaching for the diving alarm, he pulled on it twice. "Dive! Dive!"

In five seconds, he had followed the other two men below, pulling the hatch shut behind him. The deck was already angling downward. At the *Aeneid's* present speed the bow planes bit sharply into the sea pushing her down quickly.

"Sixty-eight feet…sixty-nine…seventy…seventy-one — " Hudson reported from the control room.

But the depth reports were abruptly cut short by two massive explosions. The hull lurched to one side, tilting the deck several degrees, tossing men and unstowed equipment to the decks. Weston felt himself thrown against the port bulkhead, his shoulder coming into contact with the jagged corner of an electrical junction box. It felt like someone had hit him with a hammer. Weaver, who had been inspecting the hatch, fell into him an instant later, body-checking Weston into the bulkhead with such force that he could not breathe. Men cried out in pain and terror as the main lighting went out. The *Aeneid* continued to roll to the port side, and the downward angle grew ever steeper.

With little gentleness or care, Weston thrust the ensign off him and groped his way to the control room hatch under the dim emergency lighting.

"She's not righting herself, Joe! One of the port side tanks must be open to the sea. Counter-flood to starboard! Hurry!"

Weston knew that if one or two of the auxiliary ballast tanks on the port side had been holed by that last salvo, as he suspected they had, seawater was now rushing into the compromised tanks throwing off the critical balance that kept the *Aeneid* from capsizing. The only quick way to counteract the weight pulling down the port side of the submarine was to flood an equal amount of water into tanks on the starboard side.

"Flooding Aux 4A!" Hudson reported.

Almost immediately, there was a noticeable effect. The deck slowly began to tilt back toward center. The counter-flooding had worked. The only problem was, the *Aeneid* was now much heavier, and she was going down fast. The depth gauge was rotating at an alarming rate.

"Ninety feet!...Ninety-five feet!...One hundred!..."

"Get control of your depth, Joe! Blow bow buoyancy! Blow safety!"

"They're blown, Captain! The momentum's driving her down!"

"All back full!"

But as the steersman ordered up the new engine order, the ship struck something hard, something substantial. The deck jolted beneath Weston's feet as if the entire ship had suddenly moved up several feet. Then, the hull, which had been traveling through the water at nearly ten knots, came to an abrupt stop. Men and equipment flew through the air. Weston tried to hang on to the railing around the control room hatch, but the abnormal jolt shook his hand free and sent him lurching forward into the steering station, knocking the steersman there into the wheel and striking his own head on the forward bulkhead. The solid steel knocked him senseless.

Moments later, Weston began to come to his senses. Somehow, in his half-conscious state, he sensed that the deck was tilted again, this time to the starboard side, but there was no more movement, no rocking. The *Aeneid* had obviously run aground and was now at rest on the ocean floor. He felt an odd pressure against his eardrums and wondered if one of the compressed air lines had ruptured. Men groaned all around him in the darkness. Distant voices called for help in the passages and compartments below. And there was something else, too – a high-pitched, steady sound that took him several seconds to identify, but one that he knew all too well. It was the sound of water entering the pressure hull.

*A powerful, unbroken stream of water...*

# 24

# THE GUNS OF MATSUWA

*Matsuwa Island*

*Matsuwa Fortress Heavy Artillery Regiment*

By the spring of 1943, the Japanese high command secretly understood the war in the Pacific was not going their way. They knew it was only a matter of time before the Allies attempted a move on the home islands. In the event the enemy chose to invade Japan from the north, the Imperial General Staff had determined that the twenty-kilometer-wide passes north and south of Matsuwa were likely to be used by any Allied fleet attempting to breach the Kurils. To address this threat, coastal guns were placed on the island. They were large weapons, six 15-centimeter/50-caliber naval guns salvaged from an *Agano*-class cruiser that had foundered on a shoal in the South China Sea over a year ago. The guns had been converted for land use and shipped to Matsuwa in complete secrecy, along with an entire naval construction battalion. Within two months, the workers had completed the road network winding its way up the steep slopes of the mountain. Two months after that, they had finished the massive concrete bunkers that would house the weapons. Finally, the guns themselves had been installed, an enormous undertaking in which one of the seven-meter-long, 8000-kilogram barrels had nearly been destroyed when the truck towing it lost control and drove off the road, plunging down the slope and dragging the trailer with it. A half-dozen men were killed and the truck was wrecked, but the giant gun survived the fall intact. Eventually, when the work was finally finished, one gun emplacement had been constructed on the southern slope of Mount Matsuwa and another on the northern slope. Both emplacements were identical, each housing three guns in a single concrete bunker separated into two chambers, one containing the magazine and the other containing the guns. The structures were reinforced to protect from both air and naval attack. The guns were recessed within a slit-like eight-foot-high embrasure that ran along the entire front face, allowing an extensive range of motion while protecting them from anything but a direct hit. At two thousand feet above sea level, the guns could fire their 45-kilogram projectiles over twenty kilometers away. Any ships attempting to enter the Sea of Okhotsk using the passes on either side of Matsuwa would find themselves under a hellish storm of high-explosive and armor-piercing shells. For all intents and purposes, the guns were indestructible.

This impressive feat of engineering, this great accomplishment, did not appear in the Tokyo newspapers, nor was it announced on the public radio broadcast. It was kept secret lest the Japanese citizenry become aware that the war was shifting from an offensive posture to a defensive one. Like the losses at Midway and Guadalcanal, the people were kept in the dark, left to think all was going Japan's way. Meanwhile, the gun crews on Matsuwa drilled for the moment they would have to combat an armada of American battleships cruising past their little island.

At the gun emplacement on the northern slope of Matsuwa, Captain Haruto Fujimoto of the fortress heavy artillery regiment stood at the aperture looking down at the expansive ocean below him and the patch of bubbling water closer to the shore. Even though the three massive guns beside him were separated by intervals of ten meters, the bunker felt cramped and stuffy, its oily, cordite-filled air uncomfortable to breathe. Brushing away some lava rocks and pebbles that had jostled loose under the concussion of the last barrage, Fujimoto climbed out onto the lip of the embrasure to get some fresh air and have a better look at the seascape below. Every time the guns were exercised, a little bit of the mountain above came crumbling down. Fujimoto often wondered if one day the percussion might bring the whole mountainside down on them. But, for now, it had only been light rubble, just enough to keep his men busy between drills cleaning up the mess.

Though he and his men manned one of the most remote outposts in the empire, Fujimoto took his job seriously. He prayed for the day he would be transferred to China, or Burma, or the South Pacific, where the real action was, but, until then, he would make sure the guns of Matsuwa were never caught off guard. If any enemy ship ever came within range, he would make sure it was sent to the bottom.

There was always the prospect of something happening. Never in his wildest dreams had he expected the opportunity that had presented itself this morning. As the darkness had retreated across the sea, he and his men had been stunned to discover a surfaced enemy submarine less than two kilometers offshore.

Presumably, it was the same sub that had attacked the airfield last night on the other side of the island, and Fujimoto felt especially thrilled to repay it with some of its own savagery. Most of the men in his company had been at the airfield at the time of the bombardment, and many had died under the falling shells.

Before the attack, they had been enjoying one of those rare pleasant times that came only once a month, when the freighter *Seisho Maru* arrived with fresh supplies from the homeland, an ample amount of *sake*, and the *ianfu* – the comfort women. For most of the afternoon and well into the evening, the officers of the garrison had performed the *kampai* routine countless times, draining cup after cup, while reminiscing of old campaigns and delighting in the company of the women. The women had been as lovely as ever, serving food, playing music, dancing, and seeing to every need and desire. All had been dressed like geisha girls, though Fujimoto suspected most were Korean. Whatever the women's nationalities, Fujimoto and the other officers had been sad to bid them farewell. A few hours after sundown, the women had returned to the *Seisho Maru* in preparation for the ship's planned departure early the following morning.

It was not long after that when the first enemy shells screamed overhead, startling Fujimoto and his comrades out of their inebriated stupor. At first, they thought the base was under attack by an American cruiser or destroyer squadron, such as those that had gallivanted around the Pacific in the early months of the war, shelling Japanese-held islands at will, always remaining one step ahead of the carrier fleets sent to deal with them. Then the word reached garrison headquarters that the base was under attack by a single submarine. The bold enemy had torpedoed the *Seisho Maru* and was now cruising along the coast, firing away with two large deck guns.

Angered by the submarine's cowardly attack on those defenseless women, Fujimoto quickly rounded up his men with the intention of manning the southern gun emplacement to defend the island, but he was stopped by the garrison commander who reminded him the guns were to be kept a secret and were not to engage any enemy vessels unless expressly directed by the high command. That order came half-way through the raid when the garrison commander's radio pleas were finally answered by Tokyo. They were to engage and sink the enemy submarine using all means at their disposal.

The bomber squadron commander was the first to respond. With most of his squadron wrecked, he personally piloted an undamaged plane to get aloft and strafe the enemy, but he went down in flames before even getting airborne. Fujimoto then led his own artillery troops from the safety of their bomb shelters to make a mad dash for the trucks. Seven of them did not make it, struck down by flying shrapnel from an enemy shell. Once the loaded trucks were clear of the base and racing up the treacherous road to reach the gun emplacement high on the south side of the mountain, fortune smiled once again on the enemy. Riding in the lead vehicle, Fujimoto saw the fuel depot in the hills suddenly explode. A lucky shot. A stray enemy shell, probably a ricochet, deflected at just the right angle to fall into the narrow canyon and detonate among the volatile tanks. The place went up like a tinderbox, one tank after another exploding and throwing burning fuel perilously near the road. After a harrowing drive, Fujimoto and his troops reached their guns. But, by the time the battery was ready to fire, the submarine had fallen silent. From the high emplacement, it was just visible as a dark sliver on the sea, cruising about three kilometers off shore. It was clearly departing the area, its mission accomplished. Fujimoto's gunners managed to get off only one shot before the submarine submerged beneath the waves.

The enemy attack had devastated the airfield. Half of the buildings had been destroyed by blast or fire. At least a third of the fifteen planes there had been lost and most of the others damaged. Even if the aircraft had remained untouched, the airstrip had been rendered unusable, pockmarked by at least a dozen craters. It would take several days to repair.

Realizing the enemy might attempt to pass north of the island on its way back to the open Pacific, Fujimoto had decided to split his company by platoon. Two platoons had remained at the south gun emplacement, while Fujimoto loaded his third platoon back into the trucks to make the long drive around the mountain to the gun emplacement on the northern slope. He had thirty men with him – hardly enough to operate the three big guns effectively – but they had managed. If the enemy were foolish enough to show themselves, Matsuwa's guns would be ready for them.

Never had Fujimoto expected his efforts to come to fruition. He certainly had not expected to see an enemy submarine sitting within point-blank range of his guns as the light of dawn lifted the curtain of darkness off the seascape. As shocked as he had been, he had not squandered the opportunity. After firing the first salvo, Fujimoto had noticed that the submarine had dispatched a small boat or raft of some kind, perhaps filled with spies intending to gain further information about the island's defenses. Whoever they had been, Fujimoto had seen to it that they did not make it to the shore. On his orders, his expert gunners had blown them from the water, the giant shells leaving no trace of them. But when Fujimoto's gunners turned their aim back onto the fleeing submarine, he cursed himself under his breath for choosing to sink the raft first. The sub had been close to the shore, too close to dive, or so Fujimoto had thought. He had assumed the enemy would need to drive at least another kilometer away before diving, the water being too shallow near the coast. But the crazy Yankee captain had submerged his ship despite the risk, and, once again, Fujimoto found himself shooting at the submarine only as it was diving out of sight.

But this time, fortune was with Fujimoto. His guns had scored a hit. An expanding patch of oil remained on the surface in the precise spot where the submarine had disappeared, and the patch had been growing steadily for the last few hours. Without a doubt, the enemy submarine was still there, unmoving, sitting on the bottom only a few dozen feet below the surface. Whether it was destroyed or just licking its wounds, there was no way for Fujimoto to tell. But he did know that if the sub tried to come up again, his guns would be waiting. As soon as he spotted a periscope or a dark shape near the surface, he would open fire, and there would be no escape this time.

The artillery platoon's radio operator walked with purpose across the emplacement and climbed out of the embrasure to stand on the concrete lip with his officer. Fujimoto returned the soldier's salute.

"What is it, Corporal?"

"A radio message from the garrison commander, sir. The high command has received your report of this morning's action, and they congratulate you on sinking the Yankee submarine. They urge you to be ever vigilant in the coming hours. More enemy submarines may attempt to escape past Matsuwa."

*Perhaps they did not read my report thoroughly,* Fujimoto thought with mild amusement. This enemy sub was not trying to escape, it was trying to land spies or saboteurs on Matsuwa. But, no matter. Let the high command spin it any way they liked. If there were other subs out there, and they came within range of his guns, he would turn them into steel coffins, just as he had that submarine down there in those shallow waters.

"Very well, Corporal. Have the crews stand ready for another gun drill."

Before the corporal could acknowledge the order, his eyes suddenly grew wide as if he had seen something beyond Fujimoto's shoulder. The corporal opened his mouth to speak but never got a word out. His head recoiled violently, and then the side of his head burst in an explosion of blood, painting the freshly scrubbed concrete embrasure and Fujimoto's tunic in red. The corporal's lifeless body fell over the edge, spun head over heels and impacted the rocky slope twenty feet below with a sickening thud.

"Alarm!" Fujimoto shouted as he dove back inside the bunker for cover. "To your rifles!"

The men of his platoon looked up from their duties with confusion, their faces reflecting their bewilderment as to why they would need their rifles here. In their haste to leave the airfield last night, only a handful had bothered to bring them. Most were armed only with field bayonets which they had only ever used as digging tools.

Fujimoto saw them hesitate and quickly drew the 8-millimeter *Nambu* pistol from his belt. He fired it once out the embrasure. "Do as I say, now! Hurry!"

They did not need to be told twice. The men who had brought rifles ran for their weapons while the others drew out their bayonets. They instantly took up positions behind the massive guns, clearly wondering from which direction the threat was expected. As Fujimoto crouched behind one gun with his men, he finally had a moment to think clearly, to consider precisely what had just happened out there on the ledge.

The corporal had been hit by a bullet — a sniper bullet. That much was obvious. But who had fired it? Had the enemy landed another group of commandos before dawn, and the raft he had destroyed had contained a second group? That had to be it! But why would they be here?

Fujimoto did not have to ponder the question for very long. *They had come to destroy his guns! Why else would they be here?*

As Fujimoto waited there with half his men pointing their weapons toward the embrasure, and the other half pointing their weapons at the single door in the rear wall, the only other way in or out of the bunker, he felt helpless. He had no idea what he was up against.

How many enemy were out there? Aside from a rifle, what kind of weapons did they have?

Fujumoto knew the more he waited, the more time the enemy had to move in closer. Had he expected a ground attack, he would have summoned a platoon of riflemen from the other side of the island to dig in on the slopes above. But now there were no friendly troops out there to defend the bunker, and that gave the enemy a decided advantage.

There were voices outside, English voices. No, they were American, for sure. While Fujimoto was attempting to translate what they were saying, an arm appeared in the embrasure, dangling from the roof. It held a small satchel that was emitting smoke.

Fujimoto raised his pistol and fired at the dangling limb, but before he could perfect his aim, the arm swung and released the satchel such that the pouch fell into the bunker. The next moment, the arm was withdrawn, leaving the satchel sizzling on the concrete floor.

"Soldier!" Fujimoto pushed the wide-eyed young man next to him toward the simmering satchel. "Throw it outside. Hurry! The rest of you, get down!"

The young soldier was a new recruit, the greenest and most inexperienced man in the platoon, which is why Fujimoto had chosen him. The wide-eyed and confused private simply did as he was told. He ran toward the satchel, scooped it up from the floor, took two steps toward the embrasure, but got no farther.

It exploded in his hands.

The blast disintegrated the soldier, the concussion instantly deafening Fujimoto and pressing his body to the floor. Two men that had not taken shelter behind the sturdy guns were flung across the room, their bodies smashed against the far wall. A severed leg landed on the floor two steps away from Fujimoto as the air was sucked from his lungs. The massive concussion had knocked him senseless. When he opened his eyes, the entire room was filled with blinding dust. He could not see or think straight, nor could he will his legs to move.

As the dust cleared, several heavily-armed, fatigue-clad men swung inside the bunker through the embrasure and began gunning down his men. The enemy commandos methodically moved throughout the room putting a spray of bullets into each dazed artilleryman. The din of sub-machine gun fire was barely audible in Fujimoto's ruined ears, but in his mind he thought he could clearly hear the cries of his men. Then, a stinging pain, multiple pains, shot up his back. The boot of an enemy soldier appeared before his eyes, and he saw the smoking muzzle of a sub-machine gun. Blood gurgled in his mouth and throat, and each breath was more difficult than the last.

Suddenly realizing that he, too, had been riddled with bullets, Fujimoto kept his eyes locked open, doing his best to play dead. When the gunfire finally ceased, all his men were prostrate and unmoving.

The enemy soldiers slung their weapons and immediately went to work. How many were there? Four…, no five. They ignored Fujimoto entirely as they set about like factory workers, using his own men's dollies to haul powder bags from the magazine and place them in strategic spots around each gun mount. They talked little and moved quickly, evidently well-trained in how to disable a gun of any size.

As Fujimoto's mind faded in and out, he saw the commandos rig devices to the powder bags – detonators. When their work was finished, they assembled in the center of the room, one of them stepping over Fujimoto to join the group. They still did not realize that he yet lived.

Breathing shallowly, Fujimoto felt that he might pass out at any moment, but he was cognizant enough to feel that his right hand, now folded under his body, still clutched his pistol.

The ocean breeze was slowly clearing the smoke and dust from the room. Fujimoto could see a pair of men conversing while the others waited. The two appeared to be in charge. One was broader in the shoulders than the other and seemed somewhat older. The other was thinner and had more boyish features – likely, a young officer. Which one would be of more use to the Americans in the war ahead? Fujimoto had but one final chance to strike a blow for the emperor.

As the commandos filed toward the embrasure and began climbing out, the two leaders were the last to depart. The first one slung his weapon, reached for the hand of someone on the roof, and was pulled up and out of sight.

Now, only one remained.

Fujimoto had to move quickly. It took an incredible amount of energy just to withdraw his arm from under him, and finally to bring the pistol up. With his hand trembling, he struggled to steady the weapon on the unsuspecting commando. When the arm reappeared to assist the last man up, Fujimoto fired, squeezing the trigger multiple times.

*Crack!... Crack! Crack! Crack! Crack!...*

He heard the vibration of each report in his head and kept squeezing until the magazine was empty. Then, with all his energy spent, the pistol fell from his hand. Through blurry eyes, Fujimoto saw the commando wince and clutch his abdomen. The man staggered, teetering on the edge of the embrasure as if he might fall, but then two arms reached down from the rooftop and grabbed him by the rucksack, quickly hoisting him up and out of sight, leaving Fujimoto to wonder if any of his bullets had struck a fatal blow.

With the commandos gone, Fujimoto was the only one alive in the bunker. All around him lay the bodies of his men contorted in their death throes. Pools of blood covered the floor, the red boot prints of their attackers everywhere. Even with his vision blurring in and out, Fujimoto spied the detonators the enemy commandos had placed on the nearest gun, two devices, each appearing to be affixed with a timer. Perhaps he could disable them. Glancing down the line, he did not see any similar devices on the other guns – at least, none that he could make out from where he lay.

Had they set just these two detonators, intending for the powder bags around the other guns to ignite in a chain reaction? If that was the case, then he could foil their efforts if he managed to disable just these two devices.

With every last bit of strength he could muster, Fujimoto pulled his body toward the gun. His legs did not seem to work, and so he was forced to drag himself across the floor, leaving a smear of blood behind him. It seemed an eternity before he was finally beside the gun. The detonators had been attached to several powder bags jammed in the gun's open breech, and the gun had been trained as far to the left as its stops would allow, such that it now pointed inside the bunker, overlapping the barrel of the gun next to it.

Fujimoto reached up with both hands to grab the steel ladder rungs and heft his bleeding body onto the gunner's platform. After gaining the platform and resting for several seconds, he rolled his body closer to the breech, each revolution invoking immense pain as his wounds pressed against the grating. Finally, he was within an arm's length of the detonators. He looked up and saw the small clock-like faces, each with one red arm ticking away, slowly rotating toward a distinct black mark. He could barely breathe now, his lungs wheezing and gurgling with every breath. Reaching out, he pressed the only switch he could see on the first device, hoping it would not set it off instantly.

The arm stopped rotating.

Encouraged by this and mustering all the energy he had left, Fujimoto reached for the switch on the second device and pressed it.

The arm stopped rotating, and the ticking stopped.

*He had done it!*

A smile of contentment crossed Fujimoto's bloody lips as he collapsed back onto the grating. He had already abandoned any hope that he might survive. The closest help was on the other side of the island, more than an hour away by truck. He was losing so much blood that he would be dead within minutes. But he had, at least, foiled the enemy's plans. His guns had been saved that they might sink more enemy ships. When the garrison troops arrived, they would find his body here on the platform, beside the stopped detonators, and they would deduce what had happened. The base commander would communicate Fujimoto's last valiant act to the high command, and he would be hailed as a hero, perhaps posthumously awarded the Order of the Golden Kite, and his family honored above others.

Fujimoto lay back and let out a great sigh. He could now go where the spirits reside, content that he had performed his duty to the last.

But the transcendental journey to his heavenly slumber was suddenly interrupted when he felt a vibration on the metal platform beneath him. Then he felt another, as if someone was walking on it. Turning his head ever so slightly, he saw a man standing on the platform, not two steps away, staring down at him with a blank expression. Though the man's face was covered in dark paint, Fujimoto could tell that he had Anglo features. He wore the fatigues and slouch hat of one of the enemy commandos.

Apparently, the man had returned to investigate when he had not seen the expected result. He carried a sub-machine gun in one hand, which he casually pointed at

Fujimoto, though Fujimoto got the impression he was not going to use it. After looking into his eyes for a long moment, the commando strode over to the breech, removed the detonators and moved them to a powder bag situated on a much higher spot – a spot Fujimoto would never be able to reach in his present condition.

As the man worked, Fujimoto briefly lost consciousness. When he came to again, the man was gone, but the two detonators remained. And there was that light *tick...tick...tick* of the timers that somehow Fujimoto's deafened ears could hear over all other sounds.

There was nothing he could do now. He closed his eyes and focused his thoughts on the *kami* of the wind whistling through the embrasure, the surf crashing far below, and the sleeping power of the mountain. He thought of his ancestors, his family, and the emperor.

The next instant, the timer stopped, the detonators fired, and Fujimoto and everything around him disintegrated in a blinding flash of light.

# 25

# NO MORE RUMORS

The wave crested above Greathouse's head, threatening to dash him against the jagged, half-submerged rocks. He noticed it only just in time to swim against it with one arm while towing his semi-conscious companion under the other arm. Both men just made it over the wave's frothy top before it crashed down behind them, dragging them back several feet and obliterating the few yards of progress they had made. Like two corks bobbing on the sea, they were thrust in whatever direction the sea threw them, struggling to breathe amid a surface covered with ice-cold, salty froth.

They came so close to one jutting rock that Greathouse had to thrust off the rough submerged surface to keep from smashing into it, severely scraping the bottoms of his feet in the process. When they were away from the rock, he immediately began swimming again, dragging the dead weight of the other man behind him.

After a few agonizing strokes, Greathouse tried to get a good look at his surroundings, but the waves were so high, and he was so low to the water's surface, that he could only see his immediate proximity and the dark peaks of the rocks surrounding him. He saw that one corner of his visible horizon was free of rocks, and so he swam in that direction with all his might, hoping it would lead to the open sea.

"Houston!... Bell!... Martinez!... Wilcoxon!" he shouted as the wild surface agitation slapped him in the face.

"Here, Sarge!" one voice called, and then another.

Greathouse could not tell where the voices were coming from, nor could he see his men whom he knew were also swimming against the angry surf, but he assumed they were faring better than he was. Like him, they had cast away their weapons, rucksacks, boots, blouses, and anything else that might have proved to be an encumbrance. But while they had only themselves to worry about, Greathouse was pulling the only wounded member of the squad, Lieutenant MacCullen.

A swirl of seawater carried a streak of blood past Greathouse's face. The blood had come from one of the three bullet wounds across the lieutenant's torso and right thigh. Greathouse deduced that at least one of the bandages he had taken great care in applying to MacCullen's wounds must have been carried away.

"Still with me, sir?" Greathouse said between breaths.

A slight nod of the young officer's doused head and a squeeze of one hand on his shoulder were the only responses, but they were enough. None of the bullet wounds were near his lungs, and so his breathing seemed to be somewhat normal, and that was one good thing. But two of the wounds were low across his abdomen, and Greathouse guessed he was suffering from internal bleeding. But there was nothing Greathouse or any of the scouts could do except bandage the wounds and get the lieutenant to someone who could treat him, like the corpsman aboard the *Aeneid*. And so Greathouse swam and swam, struggling to get beyond the waves, beyond the wild coastal surf that wanted to draw him back. He did his best to keep MacCullen's mouth and nose above the surface, but it was nearly impossible, and he heard the lieutenant cough up seawater several times.

"Stay with me, sir!" Greathouse said again, gathering his strength and pushing and thrusting as best he could, focusing on kicking his legs in the long, controlled, powerful strokes he had learned in training. Of course, when he had done this during training, he had not just hiked several miles across a mountain range the night before, climbed up a mountain to attack an enemy bunker, and then back down that mountain, dragging a wounded man who was, for all intents and purposes, dead weight.

As Greathouse kept reaching out for the next stroke, one after the other, the chaotic events of the morning replayed in his mind.

Earlier that morning, the *Aeneid* had arrived on schedule, at the designated time and place. After the submarine had acknowledged their signal, Greathouse and the others had prepared to be picked up, placing all their gear in a single bag to be discarded into the sea.

They had watched with expectation from a rocky outcropping as the raft had pushed off from the submarine and began moving toward them. As the little craft had drawn closer, they had seen the faces of the four men manning it, their oars rising and falling with urgency.

And then,…all hell had broken loose.

Several heavy bangs had echoed down from the mountainside followed by three large waterspouts erupting near the submarine. Greathouse and the scouts immediately turned their binoculars onto the smoking slope far above them, and it was not long before they made out the lip of a concrete structure partially recessed into the mountainside.

The scouts watched in horror as the shore battery proceeded to blast away at the submarine, momentarily targeting the little raft, which was promptly blown to smithereens. The *Aeneid* tried to get away, turning around and heading out to sea at top speed, but the enemy guns caught her just as she was submerging. Three giant columns of water hid the submarine from view. When the guns finally fell silent, and the spray cleared, there was nothing left on the surface but bubbles and oil.

For several long minutes, the scouts stood there on the rocky shore, staring at the empty patch of sea where their salvation had disappeared. It was at that moment that Greathouse's eyes met MacCullen's. There was no triumph in the lieutenant's expression, no contempt, or even anger, only regret. And Greathouse felt regret, too, and guilt. He wondered how things might have played out had he not stonewalled MacCullen and had just sent Martinez and Bell to recon the road as ordered. Had they discovered the gun emplacement earlier, they would have been able to flash the danger signal, instead of the *All Clear* message that had lured the submarine so perilously close to the shore.

How many men had died because he had let his preconceived notions of the lieutenant override his military discipline? Would he have hesitated to send Martinez and Bell up that road if Major Nash had given the order?

In any event, Greathouse was determined to give MacCullen his complete support now and to ensure that the others did as well.

"Break out the gear and saddle up!" MacCullen ordered, breaking the trancelike stare of the scouts at the empty sea.

Fortunately, they had not yet thrown the bag containing their equipment into the surf.

"What are we going to do, Lieutenant?" Wilcoxon asked sourly.

"Whatever the hell the lieutenant wants, soldier!" Greathouse interjected hotly. "Now, do as he says before I put my boot up your ass!"

As the scouts donned their rucksacks and weapons once again, Greathouse made his way over to MacCullen.

"Listen, lieutenant," he said slowly, feeling almost ashamed, as if he needed to get something off his chest. "About what happened before…About the way I acted. I didn't mean to —"

"How many detonators are left, Sergeant?" MacCullen cut him off sharply, clearly indicating he did not want to discuss it.

"Two, sir."

"Good. Have them checked out and carried by separate men in case we run into trouble."

"What are we going to do, lieutenant?" Greathouse asked in a professional, respectful tone, not a skeptical one.

MacCullen looked up at the bunker on the mountainside still shrouded by the smoke discharged from the giant muzzles. "We're going to take out those damn guns!"

And they had done just that. They had pulled from deep within them, assembling the strength to climb that mountain, moving from crevice to boulder. Assuming the bunker had been the destination of the convoy of trucks they had seen on the road last night, and realizing it took at least two dozen or more men to work such heavy guns, the scouts knew they were grossly outnumbered and could not win a firefight in the open.

Thus, they took extra care to remain out of sight, avoiding the winding road whenever possible. It took them at least three full hours to make the climb, MacCullen insisting on taking the lead the whole way up. The higher they climbed, the better vantage they gained on the ocean below, and the more dismal the slick of oil looked where the *Aeneid* had gone down.

The attack on the gun emplacement was straightforward enough, not too different from the countless bunkers they had practiced on during the months of maneuvers in the deserts of Texas. With no guards posted outside, they made their way around the bunker to the steep slope behind it and then advanced downhill directly towards the half-buried concrete roof. The only moment of uncertainty came when the Japanese officer suddenly appeared on the escarpment, his head poking just above the roofline of the bunker. The enemy officer faced the sea. Had he turned around, he would have easily seen the entire squad of scouts, minus Martinez, crawling across the roof. Posted further up the slope with his rifle, Martinez covered the approach. He kept the enemy officer in his sights until the soldier appeared. When the soldier turned to face the officer and saw the approaching commandos out of the corner of his eye, Martinez put a bullet through his skull. The enemy officer then disappeared inside the structure before Martinez could get off another shot.

It was not as clean as they had hoped for, but it allowed them to put the satchel charge they had kept in reserve to good use. When they believed all the Japanese were dead, they rigged the bunker for destruction. Two detonators were set, a primary and a back-up. The whole thing went like clockwork, right up to the moment Lieutenant MacCullen got hit.

Expecting the bunker to blow within seconds, they hustled the wounded officer to safety. MacCullen demanded they leave him behind, but they ignored his remonstrations. Hunkering behind a boulder for cover, they waited and waited, but nothing happened.

And so Greathouse went back to the bunker, slipping back inside through the embrasure. He discovered the Japanese officer still alive and the detonators switched off. After relocating the devices, he looked long and hard into the wounded officer's eyes. Strangely, he felt an unexpected tinge of sympathy for the man.

Greathouse hated the Japanese for Pearl Harbor, for starting this damn war, for lost comrades on Bataan, Attu, and many other battlefields. But when he saw the eyes of that Japanese captain up close, he did not see a monster or a savage. He saw a warrior, like himself, doing his duty. He saw honor and bravery.

Perhaps that was why he had not bashed in the man's skull as he had intended to. He had simply left. It had certainly been no mercy. If the Japanese officer had not died of his wounds within the next few minutes, then he had surely gone to meet his ancestors when the bunker went up like a Fourth of July fireworks show bringing half the mountainside down on top of it.

Those guns would never fire on American ships again.

Now, as Greathouse continued his one-arm stroke through the water with MacCullen on his back, he could not get the eyes of that Japanese officer out of his mind, no matter how much he tried. Perhaps, now being so close to his own death, he was seeing the last terrible acts he had committed on this earth, the last sins before going to meet his Maker.

"Come on, Sarge!" Houston called. "We're just ahead of you."

Greathouse struggled to keep MacCullen's head above water, as well as his own. He kept pulling, swimming toward the open sky. But then another wave suddenly appeared ahead of them. In a matter of seconds, it picked them up and set them back to where they had been before. Once again, he was surrounded by rocks and thrashing desperately to avoid being smashed by them. It seemed his every movement was in vain.

"Houston!" Greathouse called between mouthfuls of saltwater. "I need help! Houston!"

There was no reply. The unencumbered soldiers could be a hundred yards away now, past the surf and swimming more rapidly out to sea. Greathouse could barely hear anything above the waves crashing against the rocks. Then he felt MacCullen's hand squeeze his shoulder.

"You have to let me go, Sergeant," the lieutenant uttered feebly.

"Not a chance, sir! We're both going out there and finding that sub! Just you hang on. It'll only be a little longer." Truthfully, Greathouse did not know if he could manage the feat of strength alone, nor did he know if the *Aeneid* was indeed out there.

This whole crazy foray into the dangerous coastal waters was predicated on one man's belief that he had sighted a periscope about a mile out. Granted, that man was Martinez, the man with the best eyes in the squad, but it had still been an enormous leap of faith for the rest of them. Twice Martinez claimed to have spotted a periscope, and both times he had been the only one to see it.

"It was there, Sarge. I swear it!" Martinez had exclaimed as they had all stood on the coastal rocks scanning the sea.

The other three soldiers had balked at him, but the final decision had been up to Greathouse.

"The way I see it," he had said to the four exhausted soldiers. "We can wait here for the Japs to find us, or we can go out there. If the sub's out there, it'll be watching for us. They've got no more rafts aboard, so we'd have to swim anyway. We'll have to do our best to make it to them, and hope they see us."

He had not added that MacCullen's condition was grave and that the lieutenant had no chance unless they got him aboard the sub soon, but he had seen in their expressions that they fully understood.

Now, as the unending waves kept setting him back, Greathouse was not sure he had made the right decision. Why had he not simply left MacCullen on the road? The Japs would have eventually found him. They would have either bayoneted him or given him medical care, but at least he would have had a chance.

No, he quashed that musing. It would have been the bayonet, for sure. This *was* their only chance – MacCullen's only chance – and Greathouse just prayed the sub really was out there, and not a wreck on the sea floor.

"You have to let me go, Sergeant," MacCullen repeated in his ear. "I'm too heavy for you."

"No, sir! You hang on back there!" Greathouse did not know why he was so adamant about keeping the lieutenant alive when his chances were already so slim. Perhaps it was guilt, the guilt he felt for jumping to conclusions about a man who had turned out to be not such a bad soldier after all. He did not know if those stories from North Africa were true. Possibly, they were. But one thing was certain. On the island of Matsuwa, Lieutenant MacCullen had proven to be among the bravest of the company.

Greathouse felt a sudden press against his shoulder. It was not the feeble squeeze of MacCullen's hand he had felt before, but a push, a violent push, and he felt his arm start to come loose across the lieutenant's chest. MacCullen was trying to push away from him. He was trying to force Greathouse to let him go.

"Damn it, sir! Stop!" Greathouse yelled between waves slaps. "I can't keep us afloat if you're not still."

"I know," MacCullen replied quietly, and with one gathering of strength wrenched Greathouse's arm from his chest and pushed himself away. The waves between the rocks were unpredictable and violent, and within seconds the two men were separated by several yards.

"Damn it, sir! Swim this way!"

"Save yourself, Sergeant," MacCullen said while spitting out copious amounts of seawater. "Save the men…go on…"

"Lieutenant!" Greathouse shouted.

But MacCullen's face had already been swallowed up by the waves.

"Lieutenant!" Greathouse thrashed the water, looking for any sign of MacCullen, but there was none. The officer had sunk out of sight. If he had not yet drowned, he was probably, at this moment, being bashed to death by the press of the waves against the rocks.

There was no use looking any longer. Lieutenant MacCullen was dead.

Now free of the encumbrance, Greathouse turned his back on the rocks and swam as hard as he could for the open sea. It took much exertion, but he eventually made it past the surf, and the resistance from the sea eased considerably. Reaching the crest of a swell, he saw four bobbing heads about fifty yards ahead of him. He began to swim towards them, and though he was relieved that all four of his men had made it, there was no sign of the *Aeneid*. He was faced with the prospect that he might have led his men out here into the open ocean to die in the freezing water. It would not be long before hypothermia did them all in.

"Where's the lieutenant, Sarge?" Bell had asked through chattering teeth when Greathouse finally caught up with them.

Greathouse did not answer, and Bell did not ask again.

With the sun now high in the sky, the exhausted sergeant felt the contrast of its warm rays on his face and the ice-cold water enveloping his aching body. He held up his wrist to check his watch, but the watch was missing, now replaced by a long red scrape. It had likely been ripped off as he had grappled with the rocks.

No matter. He guessed it was about noon. Better not to have a watch. Knowing how long they had been treading water would only add to their misery. He wondered just how long they could survive out here. His extremities were already numb.

"Look!" Martinez exclaimed as the group crested another swell. In that brief moment while elevated just a few feet, they had been able to see more than their immediate surroundings. There was a disturbance in the water not twenty yards away.

Greathouse stretched his neck and thrashed wildly trying to see over the waves as the succeeding swells took them up and down. At first, he thought the disturbance just foam from a cresting wave, but then he saw the persistent feather of spray and the distinct broomstick-like pole sticking out of the water. It was moving slowly, perpendicular to their position.

"We're over here!" Greathouse shouted, waving his hands wildly. He did not know if the submarine's sonar could hear his voice, but he shouted anyway. "Over here!"

The rest of the squad joined in, a collection of flailing, splashing arms, making every disturbance they could to get the attention of the individual looking through that periscope. It seemed like they waved their arms for an hour, though it had been only minutes before a long field of bubbles appeared on the water's surface. The jutting bow of the submarine broke through. It was not the sleek, angled bow Greathouse remembered, but a mangled twist of steel, crunched like a tin can. As more of the deck was revealed, he saw that one of the bow planes was distorted, too, pressed to the hull at an odd angle, as if smashed by a giant steamroller. Then the rest of the *Aeneid* appeared, its long slender shape rising from the water like a wounded sea creature. The submarine was not quite riding on an even keel, tilting slightly to port, clearly exposing a large jagged hole in the outer hull just aft of the dented conning tower.

For a moment, Greathouse just treaded water, taking in the sight of the sub with relief and apprehension. He was mesmerized at the damage it had suffered. He knew little about submarines, but he was amazed that it had managed to rise again. He could only imagine what it must have been like for those locked inside that steel tube when it had come under fire.

Men appeared topside with lifelines. Soon, all five men had been fished from the water and Greathouse was standing before Weston on the main deck, shivering as several towels were thrust into his hands and placed over his shoulders.

"Good work, Sergeant," Weston said, though he did not smile.

The *Aeneid's* captain seemed preoccupied. Judging from the damage Greathouse had observed, he could guess why.

"Thank you, sir," Greathouse replied with a grin. "You're a sight for sore eyes."

Weston nodded. "As are you." He hesitated before asking, "Lieutenant MacCullen? Private Myers?"

Greathouse shook his head gravely.

"I see." Weston seemed dulled by the news, as if it was just another tragedy to add to an already tragic day. Then, he seemed to snap out of his malaise and patted Greathouse on the shoulder. "Well, go ahead and get below and change out of those wet clothes. The corpsman's waiting in the wardroom to give you all a once-over."

"Yes, sir."

Turning on his heel, Weston headed back toward the conning tower, but Greathouse called after him. "Sir?"

The captain turned back to face him.

"The lieutenant did good, sir," Greathouse said solemnly. "I wanted you to know that, in case anything happens to me."

Weston gave an understanding nod. "Thank you, Sergeant. Anything else?"

"Just one more thing, sir. Seeing as how I'm the senior man now, if any letters need writing, I'd be glad to…I'd be glad to…" Greathouse choked back the words. He could not say any more.

Weston smiled sympathetically. "I understand, Sergeant."

# 26

# PAYBACK

The *Aeneid* drove northeast under the early afternoon sun. Matsuwa and its towering mountain filled the seascape astern. Patches of cloud dotted the sky, periodically shading the wind-swept bridge where Weston stood pondering the damage the submarine had sustained, the tense hours of the morning spent on the bottom, and how lucky they had been to raise her.

"Bridge, Control," the speaker squawked. It was Hudson's voice. "High-pressure air compressor up and running, Captain. Air charge in progress."

"Very well."

*That was good*, Weston thought. It had taken much of the reserve air to get the ship off the bottom. The sooner the air banks were recharged the better.

Feeling the dizziness return, Weston reached out for the railing to steady himself. His head still throbbed from the hard knock. His disorientation was not helped by the fact that the ship was still listing to port. Now that the diesels were running, there was enough power to use the pumps, and Hudson was using them to slowly remedy the odd angle. For now, the crew would just have to contend with a tilted deck, which made groping through the narrow passageways quite a challenge.

It was, in all truth, the least of their worries.

After the uncontrolled crash dive that morning, the *Aeneid* had come face-to-face with the hazards of operating in shallow waters. Traveling at just under ten knots, the submarine had collided bow-first with a submerged rock formation, crumpling the outer hull near the bow and sending a powerful strain through her girders from stem to stern. Miraculously, the pressure hull had not been compromised, though mounted equipment and machinery had dislodged in many compartments, pinning sailors to the deck and threatening to crush the life out of them.

There had been one fatality, a machinist's mate in the number two engine room who had careened head first into a protruding valve stem. Like a medieval war axe, the unforgiving steel had bashed in the man's skull. A good third of the crew had reported some kind of injury, everything from broken bones, to electric shock, to lacerations and bruises.

The *Aeneid* had spent hours on the bottom, while the crew inspected for damage and repairs were made. There had been a few tense moments, when it finally came time to attempt an ascent. Two auxiliary tanks had been blown dry with no movement of the depth gauge needle. Only after the third tank had been half-emptied did the submarine finally nudge free of the rocky bottom and begin climbing toward the surface. Almost immediately, Hudson and the men on the planes had trouble getting control of depth. It was apparent from the start the bow planes had been damaged, which only made the ascent more challenging. Broaching the surface meant falling under the enemy guns once again. Hudson had resorted to extreme measures, and only through a combination of flooding and blowing tanks, along with some extremely proficient handiwork by the sailor controlling the stern planes, had he managed to steady the ship at periscope depth.

Anxiously training the periscope on Matsuwa, Weston had expected to see the shore battery there preparing to resume the barrage. Instead, he had gasped in amazement at the sight of smoke and dust billowing from the mountainside. The gun emplacement had been destroyed, a fresh landslide marking the spot where it had been. He had suspected it was the scouts' handiwork, and immediately began to wonder how the hell he was going to get them off the island without a raft. Several observations later, as he had turned the lens onto the rocky coast to search for the commandos, he had been surprised to discover five heads bobbing in the water just this side of the surf.

Now, after picking up Greathouse and the others, the *Aeneid* was fleeing the scene at best speed, her main engines simultaneously powering the dual shafts and recharging the batteries while she attempted to open the distance to Matsuwa. With no way of knowing the extent of the damage to the airfield, other than Greathouse's succinct report — *the damn thing went up like the Fourth of July, sir* — Weston had to assume it was operational.

A dash of white moved along the northwestern horizon. Leveling his binoculars, Weston checked that the three sampans sighted nearly an hour ago were still there. The ribbed sails of the small vessels gleamed lustrously whenever the sun fell on their part of the seascape. The sail craft were too far away to bother with, but it was almost a certainty they were sending out regular radio transmissions with the *Aeneid's* position.

"Keep an eye out for aircraft," Weston called up to the men in the lookout perches. "Remember, the SD radar is O.O.C."

The air search radar antenna was one of the critical pieces of equipment that had been damaged by the shrapnel that had struck the conning tower. That meant human eyes would be the only means of detecting incoming planes.

Looking out on the forward deck, Weston saw two figures standing on the bow, a good sixty feet away. One was Chief Hines, and the other was…Weston skipped a breath. For a moment, with the shimmer of the sun on the water partially obscuring his view, he thought the other man was *Townsend.*

*But, no. It couldn't be. Townsend was dead.*

Closing his eyes briefly, Weston opened them again and squinted through the glare. He could see much clearer now. His throbbing head was playing tricks on him. It was not Townsend, but Lieutenant Monk, now the *Aeneid's* acting executive officer. The lieutenant and the chief were inspecting the damaged bow plane.

Weston took a deep breath, startled at the momentary lapse. If he continued to hallucinate like that, Monk would soon be the ship's acting captain, as well. Townsend was gone, like so many others. And now, he must add Lieutenant MacCullen and Private Myers to the casualty list.

Two more deaths on his head.

But he could not keep thinking like that. He had done his best with what was available. Nowhere in the intel reports had there been any mention of heavy shore batteries. It was no one's fault. The deaths had been unavoidable, just another tragedy of war. But that did not make him feel any better.

Soon Monk was on the bridge, reporting his findings to Weston.

"The fuel leak was from number 5 fuel ballast tank, Captain." Monk read from his notepad. "I estimate we lost about five thousand gallons. As you know, aux tank number 2 has a large hole in it, so we can expect it to fill to capacity whenever we dive. The number three main engine is out of commission. Chief Underwood tried cross-connecting the cooling systems, but we can't isolate the leak with the crossover valve open. We'll have to keep it shut until the pipe's been patched." He moved his finger to the next item on the list. "The main induction piping is damaged, as well. It's full of seawater. We're draining it now, but we're going to have to draw air in through the hatches until it's dry. Some seawater made its way into number one battery. We've pumped it out, but the hydrogen levels down there are creeping up, so I've ordered the battery hatch propped open. The electricians had to jumper out two cells..." Monk continued reading off the list in order of severity until, finally, he got to the minor damage, and that was where Weston interrupted him.

"Can we dive, Stu?"

Monk screwed up his face. "I'd rather we didn't, Captain. Not until we get that seawater piping patched. We're down to single valve isolation, and we're seeing some leak by on that valve. If we go deep, we're taking a big risk."

"What speed can you give me?"

"We can place the third main engine on the line now. So, I'd say fifteen knots, with two mains driving the motors and the other main and the auxiliary generators charging the battery."

Weston nodded and forced a smile. "Thank you, Stu. Keep me posted."

"Aye, aye, sir," Monk said tiredly before heading down the bridge hatch.

Weston turned to the junior officer of the deck. "Alright, Mister Weaver. Let's bring on another diesel."

"Aye, aye, sir."

As the new engine was started and began its warm-up cycle, its clamor joining the cacophony of the other two, Weston put his binoculars to his face and scanned the skies around Matsuwa. The features of the volcano were no longer distinct, now fading to gray in the light haze. Still no planes.

Weston was beginning to think the airfield had indeed been destroyed. Why else would the enemy not have squadrons of search aircraft darkening the sky?

Yates stood beside the binnacle, a cigarette dangling from his lips as he polished the lenses of the TBT unit. The old sailor looked as casual and content as could be, as if the *Aeneid* were cruising just outside Pearl Harbor. Weston beamed inwardly. There were some sailors, like Yates, who were not fazed by anything. Revered by the junior sailors, they were more comfortable at sea and in combat than they were ashore. They were completely at peace with whatever Poseidon had in store for them, whether it be a safe passage or a watery grave.

*What would the Navy do without such men?* Weston thought. *What would I do?*

Pharmacist's Mate Stanley, the ship's corpsman, emerged from the hatch at Weston's feet. He looked worn and exhausted. After doctoring the wounded for the last several hours, Stanley's shirt was stained with the dried blood of his patients.

"How bad is it?" Weston asked hesitantly.

"Thirteen broken bones, Captain," Stanley replied wiping sweat from his brow. "Mostly wrists. I just set the last one. They should heal ok if they stay on light duty for a while. Four concussions. I've got those men under observation. I've sewn about a thousand stitches in all, if you include our army friends."

"How are they? How is Sergeant Greathouse?"

"They're fine, sir. He's fine. Those rocks made a mess of his feet, but I think he'll be up and around by the time we get home."

Stanley had said it so matter-of-factly, as if there was no doubt in his mind they would reach Pearl Harbor – as if he was confident they would be able to hold this battered sub together on the two-thousand-mile journey half-way across the Pacific.

"Give Mister Monk a full report so that he can modify the watch bills accordingly." Weston smiled reassuringly. "And get some rest. You've got a lot of patients to tend to over the next couple of weeks."

"Aye, aye, Captain," Stanley replied wearily.

As the tired corpsman descended the ladder, Weston wondered if the *Aeneid* would ever reach Pearl Harbor, let alone Midway, in its present state.

He checked his watch. *1300 hours*. Five hours to sundown. Five hours until he could even think about breathing easier.

"Bridge, radar," the speaker squawked suddenly. "SJ contact, bearing two one zero."

Luckily the surface search radar was still operational. Weston marched briskly to the aft end of the bridge and pressed the binoculars to his face. He turned to scan the seas astern. Studying the horizon for a long minute, he saw nothing but the hazy northern slopes of Mount Matsuwa ten miles away.

"Radar, Captain. We've got land on that bearing. Is it possible you're seeing clutter?"

"No, sir," came the firm reply. "It's not that. It's something beyond the island. Something moving!"

"Holy shit!" one of the lookouts yelled in alarm. "Warship, off the port quarter, sir! Twenty thousand yards! She's coming around the headland!"

Again, Weston ran his field of view along the northern coast of Matsuwa, scanning to the right slowly and steadily. Then he saw it, a gray mass driving around the north side of the island. Even from this distance, there was no question what it was. It was a Japanese destroyer, and it was moving with great urgency. Its two swept stacks spewed ever-expanding lines of black smoke that angled sharply astern and made it appear to be flying effortlessly across the water.

The enemy destroyer had apparently been tipped off to the *Aeneid's* presence. It had carefully approached to within a dozen miles using the island as a screen. As Weston watched, it cleared the rocks and made a sharp turn to the right, its broad silhouette quickly narrowing to a slim bow and superstructure, its two smokestacks converging into one. Like a bounding lion chasing its prey, its bow dipped and rose through the waves as it headed directly for the *Aeneid.*

"Peter, Mary, and Joseph!" Yates muttered at his shoulder. "She's moving fast, sir!"

Weston pressed the microphone talk button. "Sound general quarters! Keep the gun crews belowdecks." He then turned to Weaver. "Start passing bearings to the TDC, Ed. Let's get a good solution on her."

Moments later the 1MC squawked with Monk's voice. "Man battlestations!"

The fourteen-bell gong rang throughout the ship, and the crew raced to their stations. Within seconds, Weaver was peering through the TBT and regularly pressing the transmit button to send bearings to the conning tower below. The bearings would be plotted on Monk's chart and entered into the torpedo data computer. The solution might prove useful in the event Weston decided to send a torpedo in the enemy's direction.

As additional lookouts filed up the hatch, Weston considered his options. Escape on the surface was impossible. He pegged the enemy warship for a *Kagero-*

class destroyer. It was designed to cruise like a gazelle, while the *Aeneid* moved more like a cow. He estimated the destroyer was moving at nearly thirty-five knots compared to the *Aeneid's* fifteen. That meant the distance between the ships was closing by one mile every three minutes. Soon the *Aeneid* would be within range of the twin-mounted naval guns on the destroyer's bow — probably 5-inch/50-caliber pieces.

A running gunfight was also out of the question. While the destroyer's guns were smaller in caliber by one inch, it had vastly more of them, with two more twin gun mounts on its stern. Moreover, the destroyer's guns were encased in armored turrets, protecting the gunners from the elements and any flying shrapnel, while the *Aeneid's* gunners would be out in the open.

If the aft gun had not been out of commission, Weston might have considered using it to lob shells at the destroyer, not so much to score a lucky hit as to force the enemy to perform evasive maneuvering. To bring the forward gun to bear, the *Aeneid* would have to turn slightly in either direction, and that would only allow the destroyer to close faster.

How he wished some wise engineer had thought to place a smoke generator on the *Aeneid* that he might throw out a smokescreen to cover their retreat.

"Bridge, SJ," the speaker intoned. "Range one eight oh double-oh."

"Very well. Keep the reports coming. Control room, what's the depth here?"

A pause, then Hudson's voice replied. "Over a thousand fathoms, sir."

It was just as Weston had expected. He had practically memorized the charts of the area. He depressed the intercom button again.

"How are the air banks looking?"

"Just below sixty percent capacity, sir."

It was not ideal, but it would have to be enough. There really was no other choice.

"Lookouts below!" he shouted. "Clear the bridge!"

He could imagine Monk's face down in the control room as the lookouts began dropping into the compartment. There was no guarantee that if the *Aeneid* dove she would ever come back up again. So much water had been pumped on and off over the last hour to keep her at an even keel, there was no telling how heavy she would be when the main ballast tanks flooded.

"Muzzle smoke, Captain!" Weaver announced nervously. "The destroyer's firing her bow guns!"

Four seconds later, a whistling sound filled the air as two shells screamed overhead and threw up geysers in the sea one hundred yards beyond the *Aeneid's* bow.

*Close*. Weston thought. *The gunnery officer on that Jap destroyer knows what he's doing. Can't afford to let him have another shot at us.*

"Bridge, radar. Range one seven oh double-oh."

"Secure the TBT and go below," Weston said to Weaver, who immediately obeyed.

Again, the destroyer's twin gun mount fired, spewing out a jet of white smoke. Weston pulled the diving alarm, not waiting to watch the fall of the shot.

"Dive! Dive!"

The next moment the main ballast tank vents opened, shooting spray into the baffles as sea pressure forced air out of the tanks. Taking one last look at the sea, the island, and the sky, Weston wondered if he would ever see them again.

Dropping down the ladder, he closed the hatch behind him.

# 27

# PUNISHMENT

The conning tower was hushed, as if Weston had just dropped into the scriptorium of a monastery. With the diesel engines secured, the submarine's spinning shafts were now being powered by the silent batteries. The men were at their stations, some just roused from their bunks, some injured and wearing bandages, all intently focused.

Two loud whacks resonated through the hull, followed by a long rumble. Two more close shells.

"I need to bring in water forward to get her down, Captain," Hudson called from below. The absence of functioning bow planes was taking its toll on the dive.

"Very well."

"Flood negative to the mark," Hudson could be heard commanding the trim manifold operator. "Flood bow buoyancy."

Within moments, the added weight had the desired effect. The deck tilted downward, and the depth gauge began to show progress.

"Eighty…eighty-five…ninety…ninety-five…one hundred…" Hudson reported. "Easy on the stern planes. Watch your bubble."

With the ship now completely submerged, they had a few minutes' grace period before the destroyer was on top of them, and Weston intended to make use of it.

"Take her down to two hundred feet, Joe."

There was a pause and a tentative glance from Hudson's upturned face before the diving officer acknowledged the order. "Two hundred feet, aye, sir."

Weston ignored the wide-eyed looks from Monk and the others in the conning tower. He understood their apprehension. The *Aeneid* had suffered much damage from the earlier shelling and grounding. It was very likely there was damage that had not yet been discovered. Taking her that deep was a big risk.

*But she would hold*, Weston kept telling himself. *She must hold!*

"Right full rudder. All ahead full. Come to one three zero."

He would dive deep, make one substantial maneuver, one quick sprint to the right, driving at top speed away from the spot where the *Aeneid* had submerged, hoping the enemy would assume she was still on her original heading.

"Steady on one three zero, sir," the steersman announced.

"Very well."

Hovering over the chart table with Monk, Weston looked at the overall picture. The dead reckoning position of the destroyer showed it should be about ten thousand yards away now. Assuming it drove straight for the *Aeneid's* diving spot, it would be overhead in a matter of minutes. If they were lucky, it would drop its first depth charges at top speed, estimating the *Aeneid's* position based on her lingering wake. If they were very lucky, the resulting explosions would blank out the destroyer's hydrophones for another couple of minutes, giving the *Aeneid* more time to get farther away.

But that did not happen.

"She's slowing, sir," Finkelman reported as he directed his hydrophone toward the sound of the warship's screws. "Bearing two four zero. She's slowing significantly, Captain."

"All ahead one third. Rig for silent running."

If the destroyer truly was reducing speed, then its captain was acting prudently. Rather than waste his depth charges on a blind run, or drive headlong into a spread of torpedoes from the *Aeneid's* stern tubes, he had decided to proceed cautiously. Clearly, he was not in a hurry.

It was the last thing Weston could have wished for.

"Let's hope for a thermocline, Skipper," Monk commented.

Weston knew that was unlikely. He had already glanced at the bathythermograph on the opposite bulkhead. The windowed device contained a carbon-coated card on which a stylus drew a line representing the water's temperature as the *Aeneid* dropped lower into the depths. But the submarine had nearly reached the ordered depth of two hundred feet, and the card still showed a roughly straight line. No thermocline. No layer of cold water in which to hide from the probing sound waves.

*Ooooohweeee!….Ooooohweeee!...*

The first sonar pulses intoned over the speaker on Finkelman's panel, the bone-chilling sound echoing across the depths like the song of a distant whale.

"ASDIC, Captain," Finkelman said unnecessarily. "She's looking for us."

Every man watched Finkelman as if he were the keeper of knowledge, the only one who could interpret the eerie pulses, but they all knew what the sounds portended.

"Left full rudder. Come to zero six zero." Weston had chosen the reciprocal bearing to the destroyer as the *Aeneid's* new course. If there was no thermal layer to protect them, he could at least make sure the submarine's hull was presenting the smallest aspect to the enemy's sonar transducers.

The sound pulses continued, one after another, for several long minutes. It was difficult to keep an accurate count of them, but one thing was certain – they were getting louder.

Weston considered taking the boat deeper, but concern about the hull's integrity made him hesitate.

"To all compartments," he said to Reynolds on the phone set. "Inspect for leakage."

Reynolds relayed the order and was soon receiving replies. Using a grease pencil, he checked off each compartment on a board as they reported in. The men below were probably glad to have something to do to take their mind off the interminable wait, and those daunting sonar pulses.

"All compartments have reported in, sir," Reynolds said. "No new leaks to report."

Weston nodded, then leaned over the hatch. "Joe, take her down to two hundred fifty feet."

"Two five zero feet, aye, sir," Hudson replied reluctantly, then turned to the men at the ships control panel. "Five degrees down."

The deck angled downward as the *Aeneid* descended. Every man in the conning tower except the steersman and Finkelman kept his eyes glued to the bathythermograph, almost willing it to show any indication of a thermocline, but the trace continued in a straight line.

The pinging grew much louder now. The apprehension was evident on the men's sweat-streaked faces. Finkelman did not have to report that the destroyer was closing. They all knew it.

Then, there was a distinct change to the sound of the echo-ranging.

"She's shifting frequencies, Captain," Finkelman reported. "She's holding steady on a constant bearing. I think she's got us."

"Left full rudder," Weston commanded. "All ahead full."

There was no use remaining silent any longer. If the enemy sonar had detected the *Aeneid's* football field-length hull, it would not lose contact now, not without some miracle intervening. Weston's only option was to try to induce the enemy captain to change course and possibly over-correct before dropping his depth charges.

"She's turning with us, sir," Finkelman reported. "Still on a constant bearing."

*Damn!* Weston cursed inwardly, though he kept a calm exterior. "Go to three hundred feet, Joe. Fast!"

Hudson immediately gave orders to flood the auxiliary tanks, and the depth gauge began to move much more quickly. The rapid pinging was now interlaced with the *swoosh-swoosh-swoosh* of the enemy's propellers.

*It would not be long now.*

The pinging then abruptly stopped, and the expected report followed soon after.

"Splashes, sir!"

"All compartments, brace for depth charge attack!"

The *Aeneid* was moving deeper, but would it be deep enough? It seemed an interminable wait with the deck tilted at an angle, as the enemy depth charges, each packed with hundreds of pounds of explosives, dropped ten feet every second. The men remained silent. Only Reynold's voice could be heard, speaking lowly into the headset as he alerted the various compartments to the unimaginable terror that was just moments away.

Their lives had been cast like a set of dice. If the wrong roll came up, the depth charges would crack the hull open. Those in the ruptured compartments would be the lucky ones. They would die quickly. Those in the intact compartments would have an agonizing wait for their own dreadful fates, as the battered hulk that had once been their ship sank deeper and deeper into the dark abyss. Pressure would increase with each passing foot of depth, and they would have to listen as the wrenching steel groaned and whined around them. They would have to watch as the hull compressed under the enormous strain, rivets popping, girders snapping as the angry sea fought to get inside. Finally, in one violent and terrifying instant, the remaining compartments would crumple like a tin can.

A horrible end, indeed.

How could one prepare for that? Was it possible to prepare?

The men stared at the overhead, some with eyes closed, some grabbing a tight hold of the nearest pipe or ladder rung. Then, came the dreaded clicking noise as the plummeting depth charges armed themselves.

*Kablammm!....Kablammm!-Kablammm!....Kablammm!*

# 28

# ALL SHE CAN TAKE

In rapid succession, the charges detonated, the earsplitting blasts closer than any Weston or any other man on board had ever experienced, as if they were just a few feet on the other side of the steel skin of the conning tower. For an instant, the bulkheads seemed to snap as though they were made of rubber. Men were thrown across the room. Light bulbs shattered. Cork insulation rained down. The hull quivered as if a giant sea creature had the *Aeneid* in its maw and was shaking the life out of it before devouring it. It seemed the shaking would never stop. When it finally did, Weston found his lower back aching from an impact with the corner of the TDC panel. All the bulbs in the room had burst, leaving a single battle lantern as the only source of light, and this was held on the ship's heading repeater by the steersman, who had managed to remain at the wheel throughout the violent jolting.

The acrid odor of smoke floated on the air.

"Maneuvering is answering all stop, sir," the steersman reported.

"Very well," Weston replied. He knew that something had to be seriously wrong with the engineering plant if the supervisor in the maneuvering room had changed the ordered bell on his own. Glancing at the depth gauge in the weak lighting, Weston saw that the needle had surpassed three hundred feet. "Watch your depth, Joe!"

"Aye, sir," came the unsettled reply from Hudson below.

Weston found Reynolds in the darkness still wearing the phoneset. "Find out what's going on in the maneuvering room. I need to know what speed they can give me."

"Aye, sir," Reynolds replied, somewhat nasally.

At that moment, Weston realized the periscope assistant was holding a greasy rag against his nose. Blood was dripping from his chin, and his right eye was swollen from a savage impact. He looked like a prize fighter after fifteen rounds.

"Are you alright?" Weston asked.

"I'm fine, sir," Reynolds said with forced confidence.

Something dripped from the ceiling onto Weston's head. Grabbing a battle lantern, he shined it onto the overhead to discover water trickling from the lip of the periscope fairing. It formed a steady stream as it curled its way down the gleaming trunk and disappeared into the dark well below.

"Looks like the lubber's line for the bearing transmitter is leaking," he said. "Someone get to work on it."

"We're on it, sir," Monk said, grabbing the ensign from the TDC to help him.

The phones began to buzz as compartments called in damage reports. Reynolds took them all, repeating them aloud.

"The after torpedo room reports the port side stern tube gland is leaking water into the motor room bilge. They're working on it. Chief Hoffman is back there in charge of the damage control efforts. He says they hear a loud clacking noise whenever the rudder is used. He's checked the steering apparatus inside the hull and can't find anything wrong. He thinks there's damage to the upper shaft bearing outside the pressure hull. All weapons are secure. Minor injuries."

No sooner had Reynolds finished talking than Hudson called up from the control room.

"We're heavy aft, sir. I'm having trouble maintaining a zero bubble."

"We've got flooding aft," Weston confirmed. "Use the pumps if you have to."

"Aye, aye, sir. Pumping four thousand pounds from aft trim to sea."

Weston was reluctant to give permission for use of the pumps. Should the destroyer pause in its active search and listen, it was likely the pump noise would be heard, but the submarine was in trouble. The angle on

463

the deck was growing sharply, and the trim pump could counteract it quickly by moving fifteen hundred pounds of water per minute.

"Maneuvering reports arcing in the cubicle, Captain," Reynolds continued. "One of the panels caught fire. The fire is out. Mister Chapman is back there checking out the damage."

That would explain why the bell order had been changed. Weston could picture Lieutenant Ezra Chapman, the ship's engineer, giving orders back in the maneuvering room. Chapman had made the right call. An out of control fire in the main bus cubicle would be the virtual nail in this iron coffin.

A minute passed, and the angle on the deck only continued to grow, now at almost seven degrees up.

"Take the conn, Stu," Weston said to Monk. "I'm going below."

Skipping every other rung on his descent to the control room, Weston stepped off the ladder and wedged himself into a position behind Chief Gallagher who was working the trim manifold under the glimmering light of several lanterns.

"What's going on?"

"Trim pump's not responding, sir," Gallagher replied. "Neither is the priming pump."

"Go down there and check it out, Chief. Mister Hudson, take charge of the trim manifold."

Gallagher nodded and quickly moved to the hatch in the deck leading to the pump room. With a flashlight in one hand, he promptly descended out of sight. Moments later, his head and shoulders reemerged.

"Pump room's flooded, sir. We've got a leak down here. At least two feet of water in the bilge. The power panel's dripping wet. Must have tripped a breaker."

"Get it isolated, Chief. Take whoever you need with you."

"Aye, aye, sir."

Gallagher waved his hand summoning a pair of sailors to follow him and then disappeared back into the pump room.

"The bubble's still going up, sir!" Hudson reported, pointing at the gauge. "We're at ten degrees now!"

"Blow aft trim to sea," Weston commanded. "Flood bow buoyancy."

Hudson manipulated the switches on the trim manifold, not quite as deftly as Gallagher who knew the panel like his own reflection, but proficient enough to get air moving into the tanks within seconds. A sibilant noise passed through the piping in the outboard, as high-pressure air blasted into the aft trim tank, displacing the water there and pushing it through a myriad of piping out into the ocean.

Weston did not like stealing from the precious air reserves, but he had no choice. There was also a tactical danger that went with using air to expunge water from the tanks. It was possible some air would escape out into the sea, expand on its way up, and leave a significant disturbance of bubbles on the surface for the enemy to see.

As the water was pushed from the aft trim tank and more was brought in near the bow, the up angle began to stabilize, but it did not return to zero.

"Maneuvering reports water rising in the motor room, sir," Reynolds called from the conning tower.

"We've got to save the motors," Weston said. "We've got to get the water out of there!"

"How can we do that without pumps, Captain?" Hudson asked anxiously.

Weston considered for a moment. "We do it by hand. We'll form a bucket brigade!" He turned to Weaver standing wide-eyed at the back of the room. "Grab every spare man you can, any man not actively involved in maneuvering the ship. Line them up and start transferring water to the forward torpedo room bilge. If we can transfer enough to keep the motors uncovered, we just might take the angle off her in the bargain."

Dozens of men were summoned from the crew's mess and the other spaces, some even taken off of minor repair jobs to join the long line. It stretched hundreds of feet, from the motor room, up the ladder to the maneuvering room, all the way forward through both engine rooms, the crew's quarters, the crew's mess, the control room, the officer's passage, and finally the forward torpedo room, where the passed buckets were emptied into the bilge. It was a long and cumbersome process, with a continuous stream of sloshing buckets going forward and empty ones returning aft.

Hudson kept glancing at the bubble indicator, looking for any indication of progress. At the back of his mind, Weston knew it would all be for naught if the flooding aft was not brought under control. There were moments when his impulse was to rush back there and take charge, but he knew he would only get in the way. Chief Hoffman was a ten-patrol veteran. He would have the repair efforts well in hand and did not need the distraction of his captain looking over his shoulder. If Hoffman could not stop the leak, no one could.

"Passing three hundred fifty feet!" Hudson announced restlessly. "We're past test depth now, Captain, and she's still sinking out!"

Before Weston could respond, Monk's voice called down through the conning tower hatch. "More echo-ranging, Captain. High-speed screws approaching fast. He's making another run on us."

Forcing himself to take a deep breath, Weston met eyes with Hudson. "Let her go deeper, Joe. Maybe we'll get under those depth charges."

Hudson complied, though he was clearly not happy about it. The hull could fail anywhere from a few fathoms to several hundred feet below test depth. There was no way of knowing.

Within seconds, the echo-ranging was audible through the hull. The men of the bucket brigade cast their eyes upward as they worked. The buckets began moving faster, as if it might somehow help the *Aeneid* escape the approaching danger. Splashes were heard on the surface, and again the agonizing wait started. Finally, the cluster of charges detonated. A strong vibration traveled through the hull, but the rattling was not nearly as intense as the first pattern had been. The charges had gone off too shallow.

The *Aeneid's* descent had saved her from punishment this time. But Weston knew it was a double-edged sword. The farther the submarine ventured into the deep, the more the sea pressure intensified. The enormous force pressing against the hull contracted it. Visually, the change was almost imperceptible, but, taken over its three-hundred-foot length, it had the effect of reducing the submarine's overall displacement, thus reducing its buoyancy. In short, the *Aeneid* got heavier the deeper she went, which meant even more water would have to be removed to achieve neutral buoyancy again.

"We're passing four hundred feet, Captain," Hudson said with clear frustration. "Stern planes are on full dive, and I'm having trouble keeping her at eleven degrees up. She wants to go more. The buckets aren't working, sir. I need speed!"

Weston took three seconds to consider the implications of giving bell orders. The main electrical buses were still being evaluated by the engineer. Any surge of current might spark another fire, and then they would have another problem to deal with. It was risky, but the only other alternative was to blow the main ballast tanks dry, and that would send the *Aeneid* straight up to the surface and into the waiting guns of the enemy.

Weston turned to the nearest sailor wearing a phone set. "Call back to maneuvering. Inform the engineer to prepare to answer all bells."

Hudson seemed to fidget as Weston waited for a response, the depth gauge inching farther beyond the fixed red needle at the *Aeneid's* test depth. Finally, the sailor on the phones acknowledged.

"Mister Chapman reports, ready to answer all bells, Captain."

"All ahead standard," Weston called up to the conning tower. "Rudder amidships."

He kept his fingers crossed as the new order was rung up, felt the pulsation through the deck and watched the needle on the speed indicator slowly rise. As the *Aeneid* approached four knots, the water flowing across the stern planes finally began to take effect. The angle started to come off.

"Better?" Weston asked Hudson.

"That will help, sir." The diving officer's tone expressed the relief they all felt. He began giving orders to the planesman. "Ease off on the stern planes five degrees. Let's see how she holds."

Through some skillful manipulation of the planes, the deck was soon near level, and the *Aeneid* was moving through the water at six knots, being held on depth by her speed.

There were smiles on the faces of the junior sailors in the room, but the veterans knew they were somewhat misplaced. Everything on a submerged submarine was a trade-off. Running at this speed would create noise that the destroyer might hear, in addition to rapidly depleting the batteries, which would reduce the time the *Aeneid* could remain submerged.

Eventually, the unrelenting human conveyor belt, transferring ten pounds of ballast from aft to forward with each slopping bucket, began to pay off. Hudson was able to hold the bubble steady with less and less help from the stern planes until, finally, the *Aeneid's* speed was reduced to an energy-conserving three knots. The flooding in the after torpedo room had been reduced to a minor leak, and the water level in the motor room had been lowered to the point that it just lapped over the deck plates.

The destroyer continued to prowl overhead, alternately echo-ranging and listening. Weston kept a wary eye on the course indicator, satisfied as long as it pointed somewhere to the east, away from land. With the rudder making noise whenever it deflected in either direction, he would only use it if absolutely necessary. Any minor course corrections could be made by spinning the *Aeneid's* two screws in opposite directions.

With the significant leaks now under control, the exhausted men of the bucket brigade were dismissed to their normal stations. Creeping along through the dark depths, the *Aeneid* remained rigged for silent running, holding steady at four hundred feet, her hull popping and groaning periodically from the enormous sea pressure.

Some thirty minutes passed with no depth charge attack.

After fixating his mind for the last hour on ways of keeping the ship afloat, Weston was mentally drained. He could feel the contusion on his head throbbing. Climbing the ladder to the conning tower, he looked at the chart desk, instinctively expecting to see Townsend's face looking back at him – the exchanged hopeful glances they had often shared when they could not voice their anxieties about the ship's situation in front of the crew. But instead, it was Monk's face that he saw, unsure and looking to him as to a father.

Snapping out of it, Weston came to terms with the harsh reality of it. He was on his own. He would have to manage this without his right-hand man.

Hovering over the water-stained chart, Weston reviewed the lines of bearing Monk had drawn representing the enemy's movements. Finkelman had tracked the destroyer around the azimuth as it made a great circle around the *Aeneid's* position. The warship had performed three complete orbits, only echo-ranging periodically, and remaining somewhere between five hundred and a thousand yards away. It had not changed speed or given any indication of another attack for quite some time.

"Maybe we've stumbled into a thermocline, Captain," Monk said hopefully. "Maybe he's lost us!"

If the *Aeneid* had reached a thermocline, they would never know. The Bathythermograph sensor was inoperative, one of the many systems damaged in the first depth charge attack.

Moments later, Monk's overly optimistic assessment was proven wrong.

"Destroyer's speeding up, Captain," Finkelman reported. "She's turning towards us!"

Over the speaker, the echo-ranging suddenly increased in frequency, growing louder and louder as the destroyer drove at top speed toward the *Aeneid's* position. As before, the echo-ranging suddenly stopped.

"Four splashes this time, sir," Finkelman reported.

"Not again," a man muttered down in the control room.

Visualizing the four explosive cannisters tumbling through the depths, Weston prayed they were set too shallow, like the last ones.

*Kablamm!!!*

The first explosion was faint. The hull did not even shake. The depth charge had gone off shallow. A few men exchanged smiles of relief, and Weston dared to hope that the destroyer had lost them and was now blindly dropping its weapons.

Two seconds later, that hope faded when the second depth charge exploded.

*Kablamm!!!*

This time, the concussion sent a rumble through the hull, instantly quashing any levity in the room. Like the first charge, the second charge had gone off too shallow, but there was no question it had detonated closer – much closer. Weston could not help but grimace. The Japanese bastard had staggered his pattern. He knew where the *Aeneid* was but not her depth. And so, he had set his charges to go off at variable depths, hoping to catch her wherever she was. That meant the next ones would be set to go off even deeper.

"Two more to go," Finkelman said, unnecessarily voicing the thoughts of every man in the compartment.

Perspiring faces stared at the overhead as if they could see through the metal skin of the pressure hull and follow the deadly bombs falling towards them. The excruciating seconds passed, and then the inevitable moment came. The dull click of the arming triggers sounded, and every man braced for the horror they were about to endure.

*Kablammm!!...Kablammm!!*

# 29

# LOYALTY

## IJN *Hamakaze*

The *Hamakaze* steamed in a straight line at an even twenty-four knots as the sea beyond its stern erupted in two massive explosions. From the signal bridge, Ando watched the masses of bubbles churn to the surface in two distinct spots. The roiling continued for several seconds before it finally ceased amid the destroyer's white wake. He had ordered variable depth settings for this pattern of depth charges to prevent the enemy submarine from escaping by changing depth at the last moment. The last two charges in the salvo had been set to go off at the maximum depth setting of one hundred forty-five meters.

"An excellent run, Captain!" Yamada said with delight from the other side of the signal bridge. "My compliments to Lieutenant Kawaguchi! A fine ASW officer you have there."

"Thank you, Admiral. I agree." Ando smiled. "But only time will tell if this pattern scored a hit."

"We have the enemy, Ando," Yamada said with a wide grin, clearly energized by the hunt. "He slipped past us at La Perouse, and he mocked us with his attack on Matsuwa, but he did not count on the coastal defenses there. He is damaged, and now he will pay the ultimate price for his arrogance."

Ando smiled as he watched Yamada stare aft. The normally stately posture of the admiral was gone, replaced by the rail-gripping excitement of an academy cadet. Ando was glad to see him so, especially since, for most of the journey from La Perouse, Yamada had sat brooding in the corner of the pilothouse, staring through the glass at the sea as if deep in thought.

Last night, shortly after receiving the radio message informing him of the attack on Matsuwa, Yamada had ordered the fleet to disperse to the various exits from the Sea of Okhotsk, leaving only a few sub-chasers behind at

La Perouse Strait. Each destroyer and *kaibōkan* had been given assignments chosen explicitly by the admiral based on the ship's speed limitations. The *Hamakaze*, the fastest in the fleet, had been given the farthest assignment, the already hot zone around Matsuwa. Surmising that the submarine attacking Matsuwa was the first to escape the Sea of Japan, and that the others would be only a few hours behind it, the admiral had ordered his warships to run at top speed to beat the remaining enemy subs to the passes and stop them before they reached the Pacific.

It had been a long shot, and though Yamada had given the orders with outward enthusiasm, Ando knew better. As the *Hamakaze* had steamed through the night, Yamada had withdrawn into an increasingly contemplative state, as if he did not really expect any of the deployed units to meet with success. Then, early this morning, when the radio began to buzz with reports of an American submarine caught on the surface by Matsuwa's shore batteries, and that the sub was damaged and potentially sunk, the admiral had come alive again.

"Make all speed for Matsuwa, Captain Ando," he had said with urgency. "I want your top speed. Overboost the boilers if you must."

The *Hamakaze* had already been traveling above full speed, around thirty-four knots, for most of the night, and there was little to be gained by pushing her harder. It would burn much more fuel, but Ando had obliged his admiral without question. And so, the boilers had built up more steam, and the screws had turned until it seemed the vibrations through the ship would shake her apart. For the duration of the morning's high-speed run, Yamada had stood alone on the signal bridge with a fixed smile, ignoring the dousing spray as the bow plowed its way through the swells.

The *Hamakaze* had reached Matsuwa in record time, traveling the eight hundred kilometers from La Perouse Strait in just under thirteen hours. And now, after miraculously catching the crippled American submarine on the surface attempting to limp away, and then forcing it to dive, a definite kill seemed within the admiral's grasp. The enemy was down there somewhere, not far away, likely damaged. If this latest spread of depth charges had not struck the killing blow, another salvo surely would. It was only a matter of time. The enemy sub could not get away.

After dropping the first two patterns, Ando had used a tactic from the admiral's own playbook. He had let up on the submarine for half an hour, driving the destroyer in a large circle, as if he had lost sonar contact, hoping to coax the submarine into coming shallow for a reckless torpedo shot. In reality, Lieutenant Kawaguchi's sonarmen had never lost the enemy. The American sub made such a considerable clamor they did not even need echo-ranging to track it. Kawaguchi's men listened as metal ground against metal, tanks flooded or were filled with air, and hand tools were liberally used. They had even heard raised voices from time to time – the sounds of a crew trying to save their ship and themselves. The sub had not come shallow, but each circle maneuver had allowed Kawaguchi and his men to refine the sub's location for the next drop.

*Now, to see if any of the charges found their mark.*

"Full starboard helm," Ando said into the voice tube. "All ahead standard."

The *Hamakaze* made a tight circle in the ocean until her bow pointed back at her wake, where the last charges had been dropped.

"Zero your helm," Ando ordered.

Looking down upon the main deck, he could see the depth charge handling parties eagerly leaning out over the railing to search for any wreckage or oil. But when the destroyer drove over the drop location, there was none to be found.

Ando considered ordering another pattern dropped immediately on the same spot but decided against it. Better to do it slowly and methodically.

"Tell Lieutenant Kawaguchi to continue his search," Ando said into the voice tube. He could imagine the lieutenant hovering over the chart table, gritting his teeth as the sensitive listening equipment recovered from the undersea explosions and he worked out a new enemy position. Desperate to kill those who had killed his brother, Kawaguchi was as obsessed with finding the enemy as Yamada was, almost to the point of having a nervous breakdown.

Last night, shortly after the admiral had dispersed the fleet, Kawaguchi had nearly lost his wits. Convinced that Yamada was incompetent for allowing the enemy submarines to escape the Sea of Japan, Kawaguchi had reproached the admiral in person, making his opinion known in a most disrespectful manner. Kawaguchi had committed this affront on the bridge in front of several sailors. Ando had not been on the bridge at the time, but when he heard about the incident, he immediately admonished Kawaguchi and ordered him relieved of all duties. That is, until the admiral himself had come to Ando's stateroom requesting that Kawaguchi be reinstated. Yamada, who should have been incensed at the upstart lieutenant, was not offended and said he preferred to work with men who were passionate about fighting the enemy. If anything, he had taken the reprobation to heart. As much as Ando had tried to convince him that internal matters among the ship's crew were his to sort out, and that insubordination could not be permitted under any circumstances, Yamada had insisted that Kawaguchi not be punished. And so, reluctantly, only hours before reaching Matsuwa, Ando had acquiesced and had restored the lieutenant to his position.

As much as Ando did not like it, he had to admit, Yamada and Kawaguchi were much the same. Or, rather, Kawaguchi was Yamada's necessary instrument for victory. There were not two men aboard more bent on getting the enemy. For Yamada, honor was at stake. For Kawaguchi, revenge.

Within minutes, sonar was reporting a sizeable submerged contact off the port beam, and Kawaguchi requested both Ando's and the admiral's presence in the pilothouse. As the three officers looked over the chart, Kawaguchi showed the enemy's current position, only a few hundred meters from the last drop location.

"The submarine must have increased speed and gone deeper," Kawaguchi said, as if in explanation for the failure of the previous depth charge pattern. "On the passive sonar, my men are picking up noises similar to what they heard earlier. Repairs are in progress down there. It is possible that our attack has caused flooding, forcing the enemy to increase his speed to keep from sinking."

"Excellent, Lieutenant," Yamada said, looking pleased.

"Thank you, Admiral." Kawaguchi's tone was almost apologetic, as if he now regretted his earlier defiance. "I believe the tactic of staggering the depth setting is a good one, sir. But I would like to propose a slight alteration."

"Go on," Ando said.

"I am confident in the ability of my men to track the enemy submarine. I am also confident that, if given the conn, I could drive the ship directly over the enemy and drop at the precise moment we are on top of her. I propose, on the next run, we drop our charges at staggered depths, with most set to go off deep, as before. Only, this time, we fire two charges from the throwers and drop twelve in rapid succession off the stern racks."

"Fourteen in one spot?" Ando exchanged glances with Yamada. "Fourteen of our seventy-eight remaining charges? You are that confident?"

"I am, sir," Kawaguchi said boldly, standing up straight and facing his captain.

Yamada was nodding. "I agree with the lieutenant, Captain. You have contact on the enemy now. It is not guaranteed that you will have him an hour from now."

Ando sighed. In his mind, hunting submarines was a game of *shōgi*. He preferred the slow and deliberate approach, not expending munitions unnecessarily. But the opinion of Kawaguchi, the most recent graduate of the anti-submarine school, could not be discounted. And how could he argue with Yamada, the legend?

"Very well." Ando nodded. "You may take the conn, Lieutenant."

Kawaguchi took the conn while Ando and Yamada stood aside and observed. From the chart table, Kawaguchi called out rudder and speed orders, while updates on the contact were passed from the phone talker to the quartermaster and then instantly drawn on the chart for the lieutenant to analyze.

"Come left two degrees," Kawaguchi ordered the steersman. And then, moments later, "Come right two degrees."

With the nearest shoal water several kilometers away, Kawaguchi was only concerned about the *Hamakaze's* position in relation to the sonar contact. Carefully and skillfully he guided the destroyer through several minute corrections, accounting for the estimated movement of the enemy, until the ship was finally driving directly for a rendezvous with the small circle on the chart representing the area of uncertainty around the target's location.

Not satisfied with the first pass, Kawaguchi directed the ship to continue past the mark without dropping any charges. Frustration was evident on his face, but he remained focused, not even glancing at the senior officers watching him. After a run of about five hundred meters, and another sweeping 180-degree turn, he again lined up the *Hamakaze's* bow to bisect the small circle on his chart. This time, he was satisfied with the results.

"Stand by racks and launchers!" he said to the phone talker who quickly relayed the orders to the crews on deck. "Six charges from each stern rack. One charge from each launcher. Set depth on the first two charges in each rack to one hundred meters. Set depth on all remaining charges to one hundred forty-five meters. Charges are to be released simultaneously with no delay."

Within seconds the sailor reported, "All racks and throwers standing by, sir."

"Secure the sound heads!"

The lieutenant was committed now. With no further assistance coming from sonar, he would have to drop the charges based on the information already on the chart and his own calculations.

"Come left one degree." He made a final correction, holding his finger at a specific spot on the chart while he watched the stopwatch laying on the table before him. "Ready...release charges!"

The deck rumbled as the launchers fired, throwing the explosive-packed canisters fifty meters off both quarters. At the same time, one depth charge after another rolled off the stern racks, sinking into the destroyer's frothing wake.

Thirty seconds later, the first four charges rumbled through the deep, transforming the ocean's surface into a snow-white field of bubbles stretching some two hundred meters across the *Hamakaze's* wake. Another ten seconds passed, and there was another rumble, this one lasting much longer than the first as the eight remaining charges went off in rapid succession. The ocean astern appeared to rise, momentarily bubbling up in a massive disturbance as if a volcanic vent had burst open on the ocean floor.

Ando and Yamada ascended to the signal bridge to observe the impressive upheaval. When the roiling seas finally subsided, the scene above the surface was once again placid and serene. Ando felt the warm sun on his face, heard the squawking seagulls flapping their wings above the masts, watched the clouds drift overhead. The feeling was divine. But he knew, far below the surface, the enemy was experiencing something entirely different. He could only imagine the terror of being on the receiving end of those massive blasts, with the sea pressing in all around.

"Captain, sonar hears the sound of rushing water, several surges!" Kawaguchi's excited voice intoned from the tube several minutes later, after the sound heads had stabilized. "I think the sub's compartments are imploding!"

Ando exchanged glances with Yamada, whose ear-to-ear grin matched the excitement of Kawaguchi's voice.

"Good work, Lieutenant," Ando said. "We will go back and see what we can find."

Taking the conn back from Kawaguchi, Ando maneuvered the *Hamakaze* back to the area where the mass of depth charges had been dropped. Even before he saw anything on the surface, the aroma of diesel fuel was thick in the air. Then, the men on the main deck were pointing enthusiastically at something in the water. More men gathered around the bow and pointed as well. As the ship drew closer, and the sun's glare off the water no longer blinded him, he finally saw what had stirred such excitement in his men.

The sea for several hundred meters around was covered in a sheen of diesel fuel, its unique chemical properties breaking up the reflected sunlight into a myriad of colors. Amid the fuel was a mass of flotsam — crates, wooden planks, canisters of food, life jackets, and a number of other items one would expect to find on an ocean-going vessel.

A resounding cheer rose from the deck. The men at the guns and anti-aircraft batteries soon joined in until they were all raising their hands and shouting in unison, *"Banzai! Banzai! Banzai!"*

"We have sunk her, Hitoshi!" Yamada said with a bright-eyed grin, looking as though he might join in the ovation. "Kawaguchi has done it! You have done it! *Banzai!*"

Ando tried to maintain his composure. Someone had to. But the celebration seemed well-placed. There was enough wreckage to confirm that the American submarine had been sunk. The *Hamakaze* could add another kill to her battle record. Kawaguchi had his revenge. And the admiral had preserved his honor. "It is I who should be complimenting you, Admiral," Ando said finally. "It was your rapid deployment of our forces that allowed us to catch the enemy before he escaped. I trust that some of our fleet will meet with similar successes in their own patrol areas."

Yamada's smile slowly faded to a reflective countenance. "I am content with this one victory, Hitoshi. I will be remembered for this. To end with a victory is all an officer can ask for. Is it not? To have been a good and valuable servant to the emperor is all a true samurai could ever desire."

Ando stared at Yamada in amazement. Could it be that he still intended to commit *seppuku*? Was his sense of duty and honor so entrenched that it would not permit him to go on, even with this partial victory?

"Surely, with the sinking of this submarine, and the one we sunk two weeks ago," Ando ventured, "the enemy will avoid the Sea of Japan in the future. You will be honored by the high command for this, Admiral. My officers and men – indeed, the officers and sailors of the entire fleet – look up to you and respect you. They are encouraged by your example."

Ando was attempting to get across to the admiral that his continued service would be far more valuable to the empire than his death, but he could tell by Yamada's expression that there was no swaying him from his intended course.

493

"As I said, Hitoshi, I am content," Yamada replied, eyeing him with patient gratitude. The admiral then took a long look around the horizon, as if taking in the sights and sounds of the sea one last time. "I will retire to my quarters, Captain. I wish to see the after-action report within the hour, so that I may append my signature to it. Until then, I do not wish to be disturbed."

After a long pause, during which Ando knew in his heart the admiral was going to his stateroom to prepare himself for that final samurai act, Ando nodded reluctantly. "Yes, Admiral. I will have Lieutenant Kawaguchi prepare it at once."

With the exultant men still cheering on the decks below, Admiral Yamada turned on his heel and walked away. But before he reached the ladder, the voice tube intoned again.

"Captain, this is Lieutenant Kawaguchi." The lieutenant's voice sounded unsure, even unnerved.

"Go ahead, lieutenant."

"Passive sonar detects no further noise from the enemy submarine, sir, but…" Kawaguchi's voice faded as if he were also conversing with someone beside him.

"Go on," Ando prompted.

"Sonar holds the enemy sub bearing two two five, sir."

Ando exchanged glances with Yamada.

"It has not moved, sir." Kawaguchi's voice lacked its earlier conviction. "We cannot determine its depth. I believe it to be a lifeless wreck, sinking to the bottom, but…"

"But you cannot be certain." Ando finished his sentence for him.

"No, Captain, I cannot," Kawaguchi admitted. "But, with all the fuel and debris in the water, it is the only thing that makes sense." Kawaguchi paused before adding, "The men on deck have even reported sighting a body in the water, sir. The sub must have been destroyed."

Unless, thought Ando, the enemy captain was extremely coldhearted, and was playing a very old trick.

"You think the enemy is playing possum, Captain?" The admiral was beside Ando again, voicing his very thoughts.

"It is possible, sir."

"Then how do you explain all of this?" Yamada gestured to the giant patch of fuel and debris all around the *Hamakaze*.

"There is a lot of fuel here, and that is odd considering how low on fuel the sub must be after an extended patrol in the Sea of Japan. But perhaps this sub carried reserve fuel tanks of some kind."

"And the sounds of flooding Kawaguchi's men heard on the sonar?" Yamada asked reluctantly as if he did not want to believe Ando's hypothesis.

"The flow noises could have been the submarine ejecting debris from her torpedo tubes. I would not put it past any Yankee captain to discharge the bodies of his dead men – or even his wounded men, for that matter – if it might enhance the ruse."

"Then we must know the truth, Captain."

"Yes, sir. We will remain here and continue our search. If we lose contact with the wreck, then we will know it has indeed sunk. We should hear additional noises as its more robust tanks implode at extreme depths. If we do not...if it does not drop away, or if it moves even the slightest bit in any direction, we will resume our attack."

Yamada nodded. "Very well, Hitoshi."

It was clear that the admiral was hesitant to put a hold on the crew's celebration or to cast doubt on what he had thought a certainty only moments before, but if Ando had learned anything about Yamada over the years, he had learned that the admiral valued duty and honesty over all else.

The sinking would need further confirmation.

The phone circuits quickly spread the word around the ship, and the cheering diminished as the crew went back to their stations. Returning to the pilothouse, Ando and Yamada did not converse. Kawaguchi remained on the phone with sonar waiting for any movement of the enemy.

"Starboard helm, ten degrees," Ando ordered. "All ahead two thirds."

Once again, Ando would drive the *Hamakaze* in a giant circle and wait and observe. Kawaguchi would be able to establish a good triangulation range on the target, and they would see whether the submerged contact was indeed dead or alive.

After a half hour of steaming, Ando approached Kawaguchi's plot.

"What is your conclusion, lieutenant?"

Kawaguchi stood up to face him looking frazzled and embarrassed. "The enemy is still there, sir. There has been no change in her position, and passive sonar is detecting more gas noises. It could be air escaping from ruptured tanks," he paused, then added reluctantly, "or it could be the enemy is using high-pressure air to keep from sinking out." Kawaguchi fidgeted, as if the knowledge that the enemy was still afloat, still alive, gave him great physical discomfort.

"Do not worry, lieutenant," Ando smiled. "That sub is not going anywhere."

"I am sorry, Captain, Admiral." Kawaguchi bowed to Ando and Yamada. "May I recommend dropping another full pattern on the same spot, maximum depth setting?"

"No, lieutenant," Ando said. "I do not think so, this time."

"But, sir, I know precisely where he is!" Kawaguchi said sharply, bordering on an outburst. "One more pattern will sink him, for sure! We must drop now! Surely, you agree, Admiral."

Kawaguchi may have been expecting support from Yamada, but there was none in the cold expression that stared back at him, and Ando knew he would not have to reprimand the young officer. Yamada was about to do it for him.

"You will stand at attention, Lieutenant!" Yamada snapped. He was no longer the gentle old sailor from the glory days of the past. He was the rigid instructor at Eta Jima again. Ando had to fight back a grin when

Kawaguchi's jaw drop in utter fear as the admiral now revealed his wrathful side for the first time. "You will do as you are told, without question! You will set an example for the sailors!"

"Yes, Admiral," Kawaguchi replied promptly from the arrow-straight stance he had assumed, eyes staring past the glaring admiral's shoulder.

"You will accept the loss of your brother as any officer or sailor in the Imperial Navy is expected to do. You will serve your captain, your fleet, and the emperor with complete attention and professionalism."

"Yes, Admiral." Kawaguchi remained at attention, clearly disconcerted by the dressing down.

"There are many ways to fight a submarine, Lieutenant," Ando said, after getting an approving nod from Yamada. "The enemy is damaged. They are low on electrical power, low on air, low on morale. The sound conditions are perfect for our sonars. They cannot escape. We could drop large patterns as you suggest, and we might get lucky, but I am counting on their environment to kill them, not our depth charges. I would prefer to conserve ours, that we may use them to harass the enemy over the next several hours. We will ping them incessantly and drop an occasional depth charge to keep them guessing, to let them know they have not eluded us. When they have reached their physical and mental limits, they will have to come to the surface, if they still can. If they do, then we will ram them, or they will die under our guns. If they do not, no submarine can remain submerged longer than forty-eight hours without depleting all battery and oxygen reserves. At that point, we will know they are all dead."

"I understand, Captain," Kawaguchi said stiffly. "Please accept my apologies, sir, for my hasty outburst."

Ando nodded. "You may return to your station, lieutenant."

Kawaguchi strode quickly to the chart table. A simple nod was the only response from Yamada, and that was all Ando needed. And so, the *Hamakaze* continued to circle the sonar contact, echo-ranging continuously, until another thirty minutes passed, and something finally changed.

"Contact is moving north, sir," Kawaguchi announced. "At three knots."

"All ahead standard," Ando ordered. "Stand by racks. Two charges. Depth set to maximum."

Again, using course corrections from Kawaguchi, Ando drove the *Hamakaze* over the enemy position. One charge rolled from each stern rack, and again contact on the enemy was not restored until several minutes after the subsequent detonations.

"Contact has turned, Captain," Kawaguchi reported. "It is now moving east at four knots."

The *Hamakaze* sped for the enemy position, driving at full speed, the sonar shifting its ping to the attack frequency. But, this time, Ando did not order any depth charges dropped.

"To confuse them, Lieutenant," Ando said in response to Kawaguchi's puzzled look. "It is a psychological game now. On each successive pass, they will hear us coming and wonder if we are going to drop them a gift or pass on by. It will drive them mad with fear."

The lieutenant turned back to his table, apparently disagreeing with the tactic, but holding his tongue.

*Have patience, Lieutenant,* Ando thought as he and Yamada exchanged amused glances. *The enemy's punishment has only just begun.*

# 30

# NAMES AND FACES

*Sea of Okhotsk*

*120 nautical miles east of La Perouse Strait*

*USS Sea Dog*

The bow of the *Sea Dog* broke the surface as dusk settled on the empty sea. Soon her diesel engines came to life, her crew welcoming the fresh air drawn in after the long transit through the strait and beyond. For hours on end, they had breathed nothing but recycled air. The oxygen levels had gotten so low that one could not even light a match.

But that was over now. They had made it. La Perouse Strait was far over the horizon astern. The storms had moved on, the sea was clear, and the night was peaceful.

"Do not radiate on the radar or the radio," Prewitt said into the bridge microphone. "We've come this far. We sure don't want to give the Japs anything they can use to get a head on us."

Even coming to the surface was risky, of course, thought Prewitt. An enemy night patrol plane might spot the *Sea Dog's* white wake on the dark sea. But the batteries needed recharging, and it was a chance they would have to take.

The passage through La Perouse had been surprisingly uneventful and easy – almost too easy. The fleet of warships that had been staunchly guarding it for the past several days was gone, leaving behind only a handful of sub-chasers and smaller craft that had not managed to detect the *Sea Dog* as she cruised beneath them on the outbound current.

The sounds of the enemy warships departing had filled the earphones of the sound operator all day – a mass of churning screws heading off in multiple directions, continually fading. Wherever they were going, they were going in a hurry. They were certainly going too fast to do any effective searching. Prewitt and his XO had come to the same conclusion, that the enemy had given up on La Perouse Strait and was now dividing up their fleet to cover the passes through the Kurils. While the *Sea Dog* and her pack mates were not out of the woods yet, with the enemy fleet dispersed, they would have a much easier time making their way through that last obstacle between them and the Pacific Ocean.

Considering they still had a two-week voyage to reach Midway, the fuel situation made the question as to which pass to take an academic one. Taking the southern passes would expend the least amount of fuel. And so, as per the pre-arranged plan, the *Finback* and the *Pintado* would make for the passes on either side of the island of Urup, one of the southernmost islands in the chain, while the *Sea Dog* made for the pass just south of Simushir Island, the next major island north. Sonar indicated some of the enemy warships were heading for those same passes, but the waterways were wide, and the chances were good the three submarines would make it through.

"Bridge, XO," the intercom squawked. "We've plotted a course for Simushir, Captain. Recommend coming to course zero eight five. A standard bell will put us in a good position to run through the strait in the early morning hours, while it's still dark."

"Very well. Come to course zero eight five. All ahead standard."

As the *Sea Dog* turned, leaving a disquieting white curl in the ocean behind her, the bridge speaker squawked again.

"Captain, XO." There was a measure of reluctance in the executive officer's voice this time. "Just before we went to standard speed, Anderson picked up more explosions on his sound gear. Off to the northeast. Very distant, just like they were an hour ago." There was a long pause. "He thinks they're depth charges, Captain."

Prewitt stared at the darkening horizon to the north where there was nothing but sea and sky. Sonar had picked up several explosions earlier in the afternoon while the *Sea Dog* was submerged and quiet. The explosions had been distant, like a drum beating on the other side of a vast canyon. They were quite possibly several hundred miles away, their echoes propagating through natural sound ducts in the ocean depths that formed under certain environmental conditions.

Coincidentally, last night, at least one set of high-speed screws from the enemy fleet had faded in the same direction of the explosions. Prewitt had ordered the quartermaster to draw a line of bearing on the chart in the same direction, and it had pointed directly to the northern islands of the Kuril chain – more specifically, to the island of Matsuwa, over three hundred miles away. If Anderson's keen ears were right, somewhere up there, a submarine was on the receiving end of a depth charge attack.

It could not be the *Finback* or the *Pintado*, not unless one of those captains had decided to take his boat on a reckless, fuel-consuming tour of the Kurils. So, it had to be another submarine. But what would an American submarine be doing up there? Shipping through the northern Kurils was sparse at best, too sparse for ComSubPac to post a submarine there.

Or perhaps…this was the diversion ComSubPac had arranged. Had they used one submarine as bait to clear the way for the wolfpack? Had it come down to a simple mathematical equation? Risk one submarine to save three?

As Prewitt grew more and more convinced that was the case, he began to wonder which boat had been given the dangerous assignment. Which one of his peers, or even friends, was on the receiving end of that barrage while his boat and the others quietly slipped through the enemy's fingers? Faces and names filled his mind, each one of them too high of a cost in his own judgment. Could he, or any man aboard for that matter, live with themselves should they discover their comrades had died so that they could live?

After a long moment spent staring out into the darkness, Prewitt hit the intercom talk button.

"XO, this is the Captain. Pick up the JA phone please."

The JA phone circuit was more secure than talking over the 7MC, which was broadcast in several compartments throughout the boat. He did not want to spread any unnecessary rumors until he had a firm idea of their options.

As Prewitt put the phone to his ear, the XO's voice came on the other end of the line.

"XO, I want you to rerun our fuel numbers. And make sure you account for every last gallon. We need this to be dead nuts on."

# 31

# DISCIPLINE

## IJN *Hamakaze*

The dark sea rumbled astern of the *Hamakaze* as another pair of depth charges sent shockwaves through the deep. In the darkened pilothouse, Ando watched a sailor near the status board erase the number *48* and replace it with the number *46* using a grease pencil. It was the number of depth charges remaining in the *Hamakaze's* inventory.

Kawaguchi's voice could be heard from within the blackout curtains drawn around the chart table, talking to the sonar operators on the phones. The admiral sat in a chair on the far side of the room calmly drinking tea and staring out at the sea beyond the steersman's shoulder.

"She's turned again, sir," Kawaguchi reported when sonar contact was regained. "Heading southeast now at approximately three knots."

In his mind, Ando had formed an imaginary face, that of the enemy captain. He had met many American naval officers at various port calls and naval conferences before the war. Some of them had been submarine officers. He wondered if he had ever met that man down there, enduring inhuman punishment under the *Hamakaze's* depth bombs.

*There can be only one winner of this game, my friend,* Ando thought. *And it will not be you.*

The routine had gone on for hours. The *Hamakaze* would make a run on the sound contact every twenty minutes, sometimes dropping charges, occasionally firing off a gun mount, sometimes doing nothing at all. And after each run, the enemy was always there, often heading in a different direction. This had continued for the rest of the afternoon and late into the night, with the destroyer's powerful searchlights sweeping incessantly across the dark seas for any sign of bubbles, flotsam, or a periscope.

The gun and depth charge crews worked in modified shifts to sustain the burden of the extended time at general quarters. Even the pilothouse watchstanders and those in the engineering plant changed out twice, allowing fresh sailors to relieve those weary from a long day of changing course and answering bells. An exception to this was the men in the sonar room. They were kept at full manning, with the mess attendants delivering meals and plenty of hot tea to their stations. Ando, Yamada, and Kawaguchi were also exceptions. Choosing to remain focused on the hunt, they never left the pilothouse and often discussed with one another the attack or feint to be used on the next run.

As morning broke on the following day, and the sun once again revealed the distant island of Matsuwa and the empty sea, the radioman of the watch brought a message to Yamada.

"It seems our ships posted at the other passes have had no contacts," the admiral said after reading it. "Nothing at all."

Kawaguchi could be heard cursing under his breath from behind the blackout curtains.

Yamada smiled, clearly appreciating the young officer's passion. Handing the clipboard back to the radioman, he turned to Ando. "This news makes our mission here that much more significant, Hitoshi. We must not fail!"

"We will not, sir," Ando reassured him. "Our tactics will work. The sub must be nearing the end of its air reserves. Their batteries must be near depletion. If anyone's still conscious down there, they will have to come to the surface sometime today."

"Of course," Yamada agreed, taking a sip of tea.

Again, Ando pictured the American captain in his mind, and he found himself somewhat marveling at his adversary. After all these hours, after all the depth charges, after all the close calls, that submarine crew was still fighting, still holding their ship together. What kind of man did it take to lead men under such circumstances? Ando glanced at Yamada in his chair, and then at Kawaguchi behind the curtain. He wondered if they, in their desperation to sink the Yankee, had ever entertained such thoughts.

"We are ready for our next run, Captain," Kawaguchi reported.

"Very well. Full starboard helm. Ahead full."

As the *Hamakaze* heeled over to port and picked up speed, Ando could not stop thinking of the enemy captain, one hundred meters below him, struggling to keep his ship afloat. Ando was sure he would never know the name of the man he was going to kill, but Ando decided that he admired him, all the same.

# 32

# DAMAGE

*Depth Four Hundred Feet*

*USS Aeneid*

Day had turned to night, and the night back to day, in the world above, but the *Aeneid's* crew knew only darkness.

Weston groped his way through the knee-deep water in the motor room, holding onto steel stanchions and anything else within reach to keep from swaying on his feet. The air was fouled with the aroma of seawater, sanitary tanks, and a trace of toxic chlorine gas. Somewhere, the seawater was touching a hot electrical circuit. There were enough grounds throughout the ship that the batteries were likely putting as much power into the sea as they were into the electrical grid.

With the air conditioning plant secured, the moisture in the air had grown so thick that the interior of each compartment looked like a foggy London alley. Like the bulkheads, Weston's face streamed with perspiration. His uniform was drenched with a mixture of seawater, grease, and sweat.

Two shirtless men were working in the outboard, attempting to patch a motor lube oil line. Their bare skin was bruised and scraped from turning wrenches in virtually inaccessible spaces. With the oxygen level as low as it was, they moved lethargically, like images in a slow-motion film. Weston, too, felt as though he was moving in slow motion. Carbon dioxide absorbent had been deployed to combat the rising $CO_2$ levels, but he knew that, too, would soon not be enough. If the seemingly endless stream of depth charges did not soon kill them, the toxic gases building up inside the hull surely would.

The Japanese destroyer continued to make high-speed runs overhead, as it had for the last twenty-eight hours. In that time, the *Aeneid* had withstood more than sixty depth charges, and there was no let-up in sight.

At the aft end of the motor room, Weston found Lieutenant Chapman and Chief Hoffman standing in the watery bilge.

"What's the status back here?" Weston asked them.

"We're still taking on water, Captain," Chapman replied, his face and disheveled hair dripping with sweat. "My electricians are trying to stay on top of the grounds. We've managed to stop the leak from the tube bundle, but the water level in the motor room is still rising. Chief Hoffman just figured out the starboard shaft seals are leaking past the gland."

Hoffman, the chief motor machinist's mate gave a confirming nod. He held a giant crescent wrench in one hand and a flashlight in the other. Covered in bilge water and grease after crawling on his hands and knees to find the leak, Hoffman looked exhausted but not defeated. He was a die-hard veteran of the boats, one of the iron men who kept them afloat under nearly impossible conditions.

"It's a bitch to get to, Captain," Hoffman said wearily. "It's right where the starboard shaft goes through the fairing."

"Can you isolate it, Chief?"

"Not without securing the shaft."

*That would be a problem,* Weston thought, considering the *Aeneid's* rudder was out of commission. For the last several hours, he had been using both shafts to steer the ship. He had just come from the after torpedo room where a half dozen men covered in hydraulic fluid were working vigorously to get the rudder back into operation. But then, the ability to steer the ship was not a high priority at the moment, since, wherever the *Aeneid* maneuvered, the destroyer seemed to have no trouble finding her.

"If it's any consolation, Captain," Chapman said. "I'm not sure how much longer the starboard shaft is going to last. The motor's vibrating excessively. We think those last depth charges knocked one of the commuter segments loose. And we're also hearing a thump with each revolution of the shaft. Chief thinks the main thrust bearing is damaged."

Weston smiled weakly. "That settles it then. Pass the word to the conning tower. We'll be stopping the starboard shaft and answering bells on the port shaft only."

"Aye, Captain."

Satisfied that things were well in hand here – or as much as they could be – Weston slogged his way to the ladder where the bucket brigade had reformed to remove water from the motor room bilge. The exhausted men passed each bucket languidly, as if each one weighed one hundred pounds. They seemed to welcome the brief interruption as he disrupted their chain, climbing the ladder up to the maneuvering room. Making his way forward through the cramped passage, he negotiated the long line of men. Most of them were too tired to stand.

It was stifling. It was miserable. There were repairs of some kind going on in every compartment as he passed from one to the next. In many places, deck plates had been taken up to access leaks, forcing him to step carefully over the open chasms.

The men eyed him as he passed by, their expressions a combination of defiance and resolve. They would not be broken. They had trained for this, and they were prepared. They would do what needed to be done. They had patched the ship back together many times before, performing miracles before his eyes – and they could do it again.

The words of Weston's PCO instructor resounded in his head. *Ask men to go above and beyond what they think they are capable of, and they will surprise you…and themselves.*

He was proud of every one of them. There were no loafers, no snivelers, no quitters. Despite all they had endured, despite seeing the bodies of two of their own, Petty Officers Cooper and Allen, loaded into the torpedo tubes and ejected with the debris in a vain attempt to convince the enemy they had been sunk, none had given up. Even Sergeant Greathouse and several of his scouts were in the line passing buckets.

They were his crew – his men.

Sending up the bodies of Cooper and Allen like they were so much discharged garbage had not been an easy decision, and it still unsettled Weston to think about it. Both men had been aboard for more than a year, part of the *Aeneid's* mainstay of veterans holding the others together. Cooper had been killed in the collision with the ocean floor yesterday morning. Allen had died after being crushed by a dislodged panel during one of the closer depth charge attacks. And it had been Allen himself who had come up with the morbid suggestion as he lay dying on the mess room table with Weston, the corpsman, and many others hovering over him. The sailor had grunted out his final wishes, stating that he wanted his corpse to be used to save his comrades. It had been a commendable and noble gesture, but it had all been for naught. The Japanese had not fallen for the ruse.

Weston checked his watch. *1715.* The *Aeneid* had been submerged for nearly thirty hours. How much more could the crew take? Even iron men had a breaking point. If they did not, then the ship certainly did.

In all his war patrols, Weston had never encountered such a persistent enemy. He had expected the destroyer to either run out of depth charges or give up, but it was still up there, hounding their every move, waiting for the inevitable moment when they must surface. And that moment was coming soon. Weston was not sure the Aeneid could hold out until dark, when they would at least have a chance of escaping. The toxic air would kill them all before then.

Soon, he would have to make a decision.

As he reached the forward engine room, two explosions sounded outside, rocking the hull and knocking tools off of catwalks to splash and clatter in the bilges below. The blasts had been close, the noise deafening, but none of the men in the compartment had even flinched. They were numb to it now. Most simply ignored it, or gave the finger to the overhead, as if the Japanese could see the gesture.

Between the sleeping diesels, Weston found Chief Underwood, the chief motor machinist's mate who took care of the *Aeneid's* four main engines and two auxiliary generators. The gaunt-faced chief looked up with mild interest as Weston approached.

"How are your engines, Chief? Will they come through for us when we need them?"

After wiping his face with an oily rag, Underwood flared an inquisitive eyebrow, followed by a toothy, almost crazed grin. "Aye, sir. They'll be ready. Just you say when, Captain."

Continuing, Weston entered the crew's mess, where injured men occupied nearly every seat. The more seriously injured lay on the tables. At one of these, Stanley busily dressed a wound, not even noticing his captain. Weston decided not to disturb him and nodded encouragingly to those who made eye contact with him as he passed through. Many seemed embarrassed to be there, as if they wished to be at their stations helping their shipmates.

Upon reaching the control room, Weston was met by Hudson.

"We're holding steady at four hundred feet, sir," Hudson reported. He gestured at the open hatch to the pump room, through which the voices of several sailors could be heard conversing as they worked. "Trim pump's back in operation. The drain pump should be soon. The electricians are drying out the armature with heat lamps right now."

"Good. What's our reserve air pressure?"

"Minimal in all air banks, sir. To be honest, with all the water we've taken on, I'm not sure we've got enough air left to blow us to the surface."

"Thanks, Joe." Weston patted him on the shoulder. "Keep things together down here."

"Aye, sir."

Weston climbed the ladder to the conning tower, each rung a chore in his oxygen-deprived state. Monk, Finkelman, and the steersman were the only ones in the compartment, the rest having been sent below to assist with the damage control efforts.

"Answering ahead slow on the port shaft, Captain," Monk said. "The rudder is still inoperative. We're turning slowly but steadily to the right."

"Understood. Where's our friend?"

"Still there, sir," Finkelman reported. "He's making a wide turn off our port beam, getting ready for his next run."

Weston stared at the chart for a long moment, contemplating the myriad of lines Monk had drawn and then erased to keep abreast of the destroyer's position. To any casual observer, the dozens of lines drawn over one another resembled a confused high school geometry student's homework, but to one trained in plot tracking, they made perfect sense. And Weston saw something in those lines, a possible opportunity, and he wished Townsend were beside him to affirm his deduction.

"What are you thinking, Captain?" Monk asked timidly.

"I think this Jap has been hounding us for so long that he's getting sloppy." Weston pointed to a cluster of lines on the chart and then to the imprint of several other erased lines. The patterns were nearly identical. "After his run, he turns left in a wide arc, slows down to search for us for about ten minutes, and then starts his next run. He's not using unpredictable maneuvers like he was before."

Monk groaned out loud as he realized he should have noticed the same thing several hours ago. It was an oversight Townsend never would have made.

"Sorry, sir," Monk said feebly.

"I want you to plot out a projected track for the destroyer and for us, Stu," Weston said, ignoring the apology. "Plot out at least thirty minutes into the future. Use a speed of fifteen knots for this portion of the track, where the destroyer slows between runs to listen."

"Aye, sir."

Monk may have been inexperienced at deciphering lines of bearing on a chart, but he was certainly adept at plotting. The lieutenant worked like a master draftsman at lightning speed, measuring off distance with a pair of dividers, drawing out the tracks with parallel ruler and compass, and then annotating the time in five-minute increments. When he was finished, he moved aside for Weston to analyze it.

Sweat dripped from Weston's forehead onto the paper as he examined the projected positions of both ships, the destroyer's resembling a giant racetrack, the *Aeneid's* a wide circle. And he found what he was looking for, at a position marked with the time *1745*.

He checked his watch again. It was *1725*.

Twenty minutes. *Not much time*, he thought. *But if they hurried, they might just make it.*

He grabbed the 1MC microphone from the bulkhead and pressed the talk button. "This is the captain." His voice echoed through the compartments below. "Listen carefully. I want all torpedomen to lay to the forward torpedo room. All other hands can continue with damage control and repair efforts, for the time being, but stand by to go to battle stations on a moment's notice. Carry on." Ignoring the bewildered look from Monk, Weston leaned over the hatch to the control room. "Can you control your depth, Joe?"

"I think so, Captain."

"Can you bring her up to one hundred feet in less than ten minutes, and hold her there?"

"I can try, Captain."

"Good enough. Stand by to come shallow. Wait for my command." Weston turned to Monk. "Mister Monk, get Reynolds up here. I want you on the TDC. And pass the word to the forward torpedo room. Make tubes one through four ready for firing in all respects!"

# 33

# HONOR

*IJN Hamakaze*

The sun sank toward the perfect horizon, bathing the glittering sea in yellow hues. Ando strolled the signal bridge in his heavy coat to protect against the brisk, late afternoon breeze. The cold air stung against his lips and ears, but it served to revive him after the four hours of sleep he had allowed himself. During that time, he had relinquished the conn to Lieutenant Kawaguchi, who had followed Ando's general order to wear down the enemy with run after run, dropping one or two charges as the solution seemed appropriate. Now, the *Hamakaze* had a little more than a dozen depth charges remaining.

*It would be enough*, Ando thought confidently. The sonar was still tracking the enemy sub. It would have to come up before long, within the next couple of hours by his estimate.

"Good evening, Admiral," Ando said as he approached the starboard side of the bridge where Yamada, similarly bundled in a bridge coat, gazed out at the white-capped sea.

"Hello, Hitoshi. I trust you slept well."

"It was very short, Admiral, but perhaps it will improve my performance this evening, when it is needed most."

"Is Kawaguchi still down there?"

"No, sir. I have sent him to his stateroom and have ordered him to get at least four hours of sleep." Ando smiled. "But I do not think he would have left unless I had ordered him to."

"He is a most devoted officer. His kind will be invaluable in the coming days." Yamada's tone was solemn, and it was clear he had been contemplating the future of the empire.

"I think we can manage without Kawaguchi for a few hours," Ando said, remaining cheerful. "The sonar room supervisor is manning the plot in his absence."

"It would be a shame if the lieutenant was asleep when the submarine is finally confirmed sunk."

Ando smiled. "Kawaguchi made me promise to wake him at the first sign of a change in the sound contact."

"I am sure he did." Yamada chuckled. He seemed suddenly in a better mood, as if the talk of the imminent victory had broken him out of his melancholy reflections.

"Captain, this is Sub-Lieutenant Osaki," a nervous voice came over the tube. "Sonar contact established. Ready for the next attack run. Recommend turning in two minutes."

"Very well, Lieutenant." Ando turned to Yamada. "We have not dropped charges in the last two passes, Admiral. Shall we wake up the Yankees now?"

Yamada smiled and nodded.

"Stand by racks!" Ando said into the voice tube. "Set depth to maximum. One charge each rack."

But instead of an immediate acknowledgment, there was only silence. After a long pause, Osaki's voice finally responded. "Captain, Sub-Lieutenant Osaki again." The junior officer sounded agitated, uncertain. "Sonar reports many odd noises coming from the enemy contact. Request to go to the sonar room, sir, and listen for myself."

"Go ahead, Lieutenant." Ando exchanged glances with Yamada. "Report to me when you have something."

"It could be they have sunk out and are breaking up," Yamada said hopefully.

"It could be. Or it could be they are finally coming shallow." Ando leaned towards the voice tube. "All lookouts be on the alert for periscopes or disturbances on the surface. Train all gun mounts to port. All gun crews stand by!"

The destroyer's three turrets slowly rotated until the long gun barrels were trained over the portside railing.

The helmeted sailors in the anti-aircraft mounts also turned their 25-millimeter weapons at the sea.

Every man expected to see a periscope or conning tower emerge at any moment. But then, Osaki's voice intoned again, this time over the bridge intercom speaker, calling from the sonar room. "Captain, multiple torpedoes in the water to port!"

The next instant, one of the lookouts pointed and confirmed the report. "Torpedoes, five hundred meters off the port bow!"

"Full starboard helm!" Ando said before finding the incoming weapons in his own binoculars. "All ahead flank with immediate overboost!"

A heartbeat later, he saw them. Four thin lines of bubbles on the surface, reaching out like long fingers for the *Hamakaze's* hull.

"All guns commence firing at incoming torpedoes!" he ordered.

Instantly, the guns on every deck erupted, spewing smoke and flame and thrashing the seas to port. The bridge vibrated with each salvo from the main turrets.

The percussion was earsplitting, deafening Ando such that he could not hear what Yamada was trying to say to him over the cacophony.

"…cannot see…" was all he heard. Ando assumed the admiral was telling him that the incoming torpedoes were obscured from view by the mass of smoke and spray produced by the *Hamakaze's* broadside. It was a concern, but Ando did not intend to address it just yet.

When alerted to incoming torpedoes, a destroyer always had a good chance of escaping if it followed well-established evasive protocols. Ando's brief glimpse of the torpedo wakes before the fusillade had given him a good judgment of their general course and speed. He had always had an eye for such things. The *Hamakaze* had accelerated quickly and was responding well to her helm, having already turned nearly ninety degrees away from her previous course. He waited just a little longer, until he believed the torpedoes were somewhere amid the shell-thrashed seas directly astern.

"Rudder amidships! Cease firing!"

Now, he would get an idea of their position, and see whether he should continue turning to starboard or maintain course. As the seas subsided, the wakes soon materialized again. Three of the torpedoes were moving far away to port. They would pass harmlessly up the port side. But the fourth – the fourth was going to present a problem.

Realizing he had slightly misjudged the *Hamakaze's* set and drift, Ando followed the thin line of the fourth torpedo as it slowly converged with the destroyer's wake and was finally lost from view, a ribbon of white amid the churning seas.

If he maneuvered now, and the torpedo was deflected to either side by the immense forces of the destroyer's propeller wash, he might inadvertently drive the ship back into the torpedo's path. If he did nothing, it was possible the weapon could drive straight through the agitation and explode under the stern.

One of the signalmen near Ando watched nervously while subconsciously fingering a finely embroidered strip of cloth in one hand. It was a *senninbari* – a belt of a thousand stitches – woven by the women of the sailor's home village and meant to bring him good fortune in battle. Ando had never been very superstitious, but, right now, he wished his entire crew had such a talisman.

Yamada cast Ando an anxious look. As an old destroyer captain, the admiral clearly comprehended all that was going through Ando's mind. He looked as though he wished to say something, but he did not. This was Ando's ship to fight – his decision to make.

At last, Ando made up his mind. He did nothing.

Several nerve-wracking seconds passed with every man gripping the rail in anticipation of impending doom, until finally one of the lookouts called out. "Torpedo passing up the port side, sir!"

Ando crossed to the port side of the bridge in time to see the bubbling wake draw a straight line in the ocean not fifty meters from the *Hamakaze's* beam. The helmeted men on the deck below pointed with relief and astonishment as the enemy weapon steamed farther away.

The torpedo had missed.

Ando adjusted his cap and smiled. The long night of repeated depth charge runs had finally paid off. The submarine captain was desperate now. With his air supply dwindling, he had come shallow and had done the only thing he could do – fire a spread of torpedoes in a last-ditch effort to save his ship. He had been lucky all night evading the *Hamakaze's* attacks, but his luck had finally run out.

From his high point on the signal bridge, Ando could easily see the spot where the four torpedo wakes converged. The submarine was there.

"Now, it is our turn, Admiral," Ando said to Yamada, and then leaned over to the voice tube. "Full starboard helm. Stand by racks!"

There would be no playing dead or evading this time. Now, the Yankee submarine would die.

# 34

# SURFACE AND DIE

*Depth One Hundred Feet*

*USS Aeneid*

Inside the conning tower, every man waited as they listened to Monk count down the seconds to impact. He had already completed the countdowns for the first three torpedoes, and now he reached zero for the fourth as well.

No impacts.

Weston tried to remain optimistic. The countdown was wrought with error. After all, he had fired the salvo from one hundred feet, using only sound bearings, shooting when the *Aeneid's* tubes were pointed at the destroyer's projected position and trusting that the correct gyro angles and spread had been transmitted from the TDC to the torpedoes in their tubes. It was possible the TDC solution was off by a few seconds. There was still a chance that one of the weapons could score a hit and cripple the destroyer, if not sink it.

But now it was thirty seconds past zero, and there were still no detonations.

"All fish still running hot, straight, and normal," Finkelman reported. "They're diverging from the destroyer. That tin can's turned away to the right. I think he evaded them, Captain."

"Damn!" Weston slammed his fist into his open palm. The destroyer must have been farther away than he had thought, or he had estimated the wrong speed. Either way, the torpedoes were gone, and now there were four wakes on the surface pointing back to the *Aeneid's* position.

"Passing course north to the right," the steersman announced. Without an operational rudder, the sailor had little to do but control the engine order telegraph. With only the port shaft rotating, the *Aeneid* was in a slow, constant turn to the right.

The thought entered Weston's head that the submarine might swing around far enough to bring the stern tubes to bear, but the chances that the destroyer would drive in the same direction long enough for a good firing solution were nonexistent now.

"Watch your depth, Joe!" he shouted down to Hudson as he noticed the depth gauge rising past ninety feet.

"I can't stop the ascent, Captain!" Hudson's upturned face replied. "We've gained some buoyancy coming up. She's expanded."

"Then flood auxiliaries!"

Hudson gave the orders and soon the sound of rushing water resounded throughout the ship as the variable ballast tanks were filled. Weston watched the depth gauge closely. The needle slowed but did not stop. The ship was still rising.

"We're still going up, Joe!"

"I know, sir. But the air banks and the batteries are critically low. If I bring in any more water, we won't be able to get it off. We'll sink out!"

*So, this is it*, Weston thought. The moment had finally come. The *Aeneid* must surface or make one final dive. It was a choice between certain death in the crushing depths or an equally certain death under the enemy's guns.

Weston looked around the compartment at the faces staring back at him, and he knew they reflected the feelings of every man on board. They were all tired of evading, and so was he. If this were the end, then they would meet it facing the enemy.

He grabbed the 1MC microphone off the bulkhead. "This is the captain. I know you men have been itching for your chance to hit back at the Japs. Well, now's your chance. Stand by to man battlestations surface. Gun crews stand by to man the forward gun. Engineering, prepare to emergency start the diesels, and get that damned rudder fixed as fast as you can!" He paused, knowing he was asking men who were on their last leg to run another mile. "This is it, gentlemen! The Japs have got us cornered and on the ropes. Let's give them one hell of a fight!" He released the button and leaned over the rail. "Get us up fast, Joe. Use all the air you've got left."

"Aye, Captain!"

The sibilance of high-pressure air forcing its way into the main ballast tanks filled their ears. Men were already moving around in the control room below, donning helmets and breaking out gear. Weston could imagine the line of gunners forming beneath the deck access hatch in the crew's mess amid the injured sailors and guessed some of those wounded sailors were volunteering to go topside to help man the guns.

He waited until the depth gauge needle rose past seventy feet, then pressed the microphone button again. "Battle surface!"

The lookouts began climbing up into the conning tower, instantly packing the compartment to standing room only. Suddenly, Quartermaster Yates was beside Weston, placing binoculars around his neck like a medieval squire helping a knight don his armor. The old sailor gave him an encouraging wink.

"We'll give 'em hell, Captain."

Weston could only nod. Something in the veteran sailor's eyes communicated that he knew the truth – that they were, in fact, going to their deaths. But there was no resentment there, no regret. Yates was resigned to his fate, as it appeared they all were.

"Forty-seven feet…" Hudson called out. "Forty-six…forty-five…"

"Man the bridge," Weston commanded the sailor standing on the ladder rungs just beneath the closed hatch. "Watch it. We've got a slight positive pressure in here."

The sailor spun the hatch wheel, cracking the hatch open slightly and allowing the ship's internal pressure to vent before releasing the catch to avoid being launched through the small opening like a projectile from an air gun. The open hatch let in the oxygen-rich sea air, instantly reviving those in the conning tower as if they had been injected with caffeine.

Weston was the second man on the bridge, groping his way to the coaming as the frothy seawater drained through the scuppers. The lookouts were right behind him, instantly climbing up the dripping masts to take their stations. Moments later, the long barrels of the six-inch guns and the wooden planks of the gun decks rose out of the sea.

The destroyer steamed less than a thousand yards off the port beam, presenting its starboard profile. It was moving swiftly and was apparently alerted to the *Aeneid's* presence, because its three main gun mounts were already rotating ominously to point at the surfaced submarine.

"Man the gun deck!" Weston yelled down the hatch.

Like a swarm of ants, men burst from the deck access hatch, some wearing helmets, some not, some shirtless, some even in their skivvies, all of them streaked with sweat, oil, and grease. They ran to the forward gun, the gunners taking their seats, the ammunition handlers cracking open the hoist port while the gunners' assistants removed the bracket and plug from the muzzle.

As the preparations continued on the gun deck, Weston took three seconds to examine the enemy warship. It was so close that he could make out every line and fixture through his binoculars. From the blue-clad Japanese sailors pointing wildly at the *Aeneid*, to the individual flags fluttering from the masts, to the lifeboats on their davits, to the rust-streaked drain ports along the hull. It was unreal to see it in such detail after so many hours hearing only its screw noise and sonar pings. The menacing warship was ready for battle. The long gun barrels of its main batteries blended in with the armored casings behind them as they zeroed in on the *Aeneid*. No elevation was needed. The shots would be point blank.

Suddenly, the sea astern of the *Aeneid* came alive with dancing geysers as the destroyer's AA guns opened fire, riddling the water with 25-millimeter shells. The staccato sound of the rapid-fire weapons reached Weston's ears seconds later, but were soon drowned out as the *Aeneid's* diesel engines came to life. The engines stuttered at first, but then fired up to normal operating speed, purring away as they produced power for the submarine's single working shaft.

"Ahead full!" Weston said into the microphone.

A burst of AA shells zipped by directly above, prompting Weston to look up and check that none of the lookouts had been hit. The whizzing projectiles had seemed mere feet above his head. They must have passed within inches of the lookouts, and he quickly decided there was no reason to have them up there. Enemy planes were the last of their concerns right now.

"Lookouts, shift your watch to the bridge!" he shouted over the chugging diesels.

Now under diesel power, the *Aeneid* was accelerating, heading nearly parallel to the destroyer's course. Weston checked the swing of the bow. It was not fast enough. They were sitting ducks. He grabbed the 7MC microphone. "Engineer, what's the status of that rudder?"

There was a momentary pause during which Weston could imagine Chapman struggling to get to the 7MC microphone in the maneuvering room amid the repair activity all around him.

"Hydraulic line's fixed, Captain," Chapman's voice finally answered. "Recharging the accumulator now. You'll have the rudder back in ten minutes."

*We don't have minutes,* Weston thought. Until that rudder was restored, the *Aeneid* could not take evasive maneuvers. She was the perfect target, her constant right turn too slow to throw off the enemy gunners. They had only seconds before the enemy's main batteries would open fire. He could not understand why they had not fired yet.

For their part, the *Aeneid's* gun crews did their best to ignore the lethal AA shells impacting the hull and tearing gouges in the wooden deck. The gunners were already training the forward gun out over the port side, rapidly spinning the azimuth and elevation handwheels. The *Aeneid's* constant turn would complicate their aim, as would the shroud of mist and spray stirred up by the enemy shells.

Weston suddenly noticed Weaver beside him fumbling with a phone set while trying not to drop a range finder he held in the other hand. With Berry dead, the ensign was now the de facto gunnery officer. It was no wonder he was panicking. He was less than a year out of the academy – a twenty-two-year-old kid.

"Take it easy, Eddie," Weston said calmly. "You've qualified to stand this watch station. Now just follow the procedures."

Weaver took a deep breath before his face formed an unconvincing smile. "Aye, Captain."

"Load with high-capacity rounds, super-quick fuse. Tell your gunners to aim for the destroyer's bridge. And make every shot count!"

Weaver had just begun to relay the orders when the destroyer's entire main battery – all six five-inch guns – erupted in a simultaneous salvo. The fifty-pound shells screeched overhead as if to unzip the sky and smashed into the sea one hundred yards to starboard, the detonations throwing up one-hundred-foot spouts of white water. They had missed, but just barely. The enemy gunners needed only to make a slight elevation correction, and they would have the *Aeneid* in the next salvo.

As Weston contemplated this, the forward deck gun fired. It sounded feeble compared to the destroyer's massive broadside. Every man on the bridge watched expectantly for a hit, but the gunner had fired on the downroll, probably startled by the explosions behind him, and the shell splashed harmlessly into the sea, two hundred yards short of the target.

"Reload, quickly!" Weston shouted down to the gun deck, though the men there did not need to be told. They had already loaded another one-hundred-pound shell and were ramming new powder bags into the breech when he spoke.

*Really, it did not matter how fast they moved*, Weston thought morbidly. They were decidedly outgunned. The next inevitable barrage from the destroyer would send the *Aeneid* to the bottom.

But then, as he watched the enemy guns, expecting to see them erupt with that fatal salvo, they suddenly began to rotate. Quite inexplicably, the gun barrels swiveled away from the *Aeneid*, swinging around 180-degrees, from the starboard side of the destroyer to the port side. At the same time, the destroyer began a sharp turn to the right, toward the *Aeneid*. At first, Weston thought the enemy intended to ram him, but then the heeling destroyer swerved back to the left as if maneuvering to evade something. None of it made any sense.

Until the next moment, when a miracle happened...

# 35

# FOR THE EMPEROR

*IJN Hamakaze*

Ando had known the enemy submarine was coming to the surface. The groggy-eyed but eager Kawaguchi had made it to the bridge in a matter of seconds and had quickly gotten his men back under control. Seconds ago, he had reported sonar hearing air noises consistent with a submarine blowing its main ballast tanks, and so Ando already had his binoculars trained out to starboard when the undersea vessel broke the surface a half kilometer off the beam.

The visible damage to the sub was shocking. There were a dozen large dents in the hull and conning tower. One deck gun was mangled and out of commission. And one bow plane appeared to be cocked at an odd angle. Judging from its wretched state, Ando wondered if the enemy sub was trying to surrender. His mind was instantly swept away by the implications of such an achievement, and the rewards it would surely bring – not for himself, but for Yamada.

"Your tactics have worked, Hitoshi!" Yamada said excitedly, his tanned and weathered face breaking into a wide grin. "You have forced them to the surface. You may destroy them now!"

But as the main batteries waited for his command to fire, Ando hesitated. What a propaganda boon it would be to capture an American submarine with all its code books and technology, and several valuable prisoners. Yamada would no longer be the dishonored commander who failed to complete his entire mission. He would return home a national hero revered by the high command and admired by his fellow flag officers. With such a success, the high command would have to relinquish him from his vow. They would not be able to resist the temptation to use him as a propaganda and recruitment tool – *the World War I legend who captured an American submarine in today's great war.* And Yamada, the dutiful naval officer and servant of his country and emperor, would not refuse.

"What are you waiting for, Captain?" Yamada said, fidgeting anxiously beside him.

Ando turned to look back at him. Capturing the enemy sub would save the admiral's life. Reluctant to accept the imminent suicide of his mentor, Ando ruminated on this for several long seconds. That is, until men appeared on the submarine's deck and began training the forward gun toward the *Hamakaze*.

*Are the Americans crazy enough to engage me in a gun duel?*

There was no chance of capturing the submarine now. If the Americans wished to die, he would oblige them.

Downhearted, Ando leaned over to the voice tube. "Commence firing, all batteries!"

The next second, the first salvo crashed out, vibrating the deck and displacing the hull to port by several inches. Columns of water shot up just beyond the submarine. The shells had missed, but not by much. His gunnery officer would be sending the appropriate adjustments to the gunners in their turrets. The enemy would be destroyed in the next salvo. Ando saw Yamada gripping the rail in anticipation of that moment.

Then, Kawaguchi called from the voice tube. "Captain!" His voice sounded apprehensive, almost struck with horror. "Sonar has detected torpedoes to port! At least two, sir!"

"It has to be the torpedoes we just avoided, Lieutenant," Ando replied calmly, certain of the mistake. "I'm sure it will be some time before they run out of fuel."

There was a pause. "No, sir. I do not believe so!"

At that moment, Ando heard Yamada gasp. The admiral had crossed to the port side and was pointing out to sea. "Torpedoes to port, Hitoshi! Incoming torpedoes to port!"

"Full starboard helm!" Ando said into the tube before dashing to join Yamada by the rail.

When he looked out at the blue water, he felt a chill creep down his spine. Not one hundred meters off the beam were two arrow-straight wakes. They were moving at high speed, and they were lined up to impact the *Hamakaze's* bow.

"All batteries engage torpedoes, port side!" he shouted.

As the *Hamakaze* turned sharply to the right, Ando tried to make sense of this odd turn of events. Had the American torpedoes doubled back somehow? Did the Americans have homing weapons like the Germans? Or was it…?

The *Hamakaze's* turn quickly placed the incoming weapons astern, but her high speed, now nearing thirty knots, had set her far to the left, like a race car fish-tailing around a sharp bend in the road. She was still in the torpedoes' path, only now they were headed for her starboard quarter.

"Full port helm!" Ando ordered in desperation, hoping to correct his error, but he knew it was too late.

The white streaks drew closer to the stern, disappearing in the churning foam beyond the fantail.

"Sound collision!" Ando shouted into the voice tube.

Alarm bells rang out below, and men scrambled to close any open watertight doors throughout the ship.

Then, the bubbling wake of one torpedo emerged on the port side, driving up the beam. It had missed. Some of the signalmen on the bridge let out a cheer, but Ando and Yamada did not. The second weapon was not yet accounted for.

The next instant, it exploded beneath the *Hamakaze's* fantail.

Every man on the bridge was knocked off his feet as the destroyer's stern was momentarily lifted out of the water and then came crashing back down into the sea. A column of steam and fire erupted setting off the depth charges in their racks and incinerating the men there in a thunderous ripple of massive explosions that tore the destroyer's stern apart. Ando felt himself thrown against the railing. There was an enormous pressure on his ears and an immense wave of heat against his exposed skin. Then he was flat on the deck. A choking darkness had descended all around him, and he could not breathe.

The last thing he heard as he lost consciousness was his men screaming in terror.

# 36

# THE LEGEND

When Ando came to, the toxic fumes he had inhaled instantly forced his body into the uncontrollable convulsions of a coughing fit. The wind had shifted, blowing some fresh air over the signal bridge and allowing him to finally breathe somewhat normally. After taking a moment to collect his senses, he realized that the deck on which he lay was severely tilted. He examined himself, moving his arms and legs, and determining that he had not been severely wounded. Just bruises and scrapes. Apparently, some piece of the superstructure had shielded him from the brunt of the blasts.

Many others on the bridge were not so fortunate.

Looking around, he saw that several of the signalmen were dead, some of them savaged grotesquely by flying shrapnel. In one corner lay a severed head still attached to its helmet by the fastened chin strap. Ando recognized the face as one of the gunners from the aft AA mounts. The blast had thrown the man's head several dozen meters forward of his battle station.

Struggling to stand, Ando felt soreness in every muscle in his body. It was as if he had just hiked to the top of *Fujisan*. Another gust of wind removed the lingering smoke from the bridge, temporarily allowing him to look aft, and his heart sank at what he saw.

The aft quarter of the ship, from the fantail all the way to the number two gun mount, was totally gone, missing, replaced by an expanse of flotsam, bodies, and churning bubbles. A massive fire raged around the number two smokestack, but it seemed to be slowly quenching itself as the hull slipped further beneath the waves. Judging from the angle of the deck, Ando surmised the bow was hanging high and dry above the surface. What was left of the ship was slowly sliding backward into the sea as the blast-wrenched watertight doors belowdecks failed one after another.

There was no saving her. The *Hamakaze* – his ship – was finished.

Ando found Yamada near where he had last seen him. The admiral was conscious, propped up on his elbows, with his legs outstretched unnaturally beside him. His legs were clearly broken. His hat was gone. His hair and uniform were white with ash. A trickle of blood streamed from his mouth.

"We will get you help, Admiral," Ando said, kneeling beside him.

"No," Yamada said weakly, shaking his head. "No. No." It seemed *no* was all he could manage to say.

There was a rustling near the ladder. Ando heard voices. Fallen obstructions were being lifted out of the way as men tried to gain access to the signal bridge. Soon, Sub-Lieutenant Osaki and several sailors materialized from the smoke.

"Captain!" the young officer called, running to his side to help him. "The ship is sinking, sir!"

"Understood," Ando said, waving off assistance. "See to the admiral."

Obeying, Osaki and the sailors tried to lift Yamada from the deck, but the admiral resisted their every move. "No! No!" he said repeatedly, then demanded, "Where is Lieutenant Kawaguchi?"

Osaki hesitated before responding, "Kawaguchi is dead, sir."

Upon hearing this, Yamada seemed to lose all animation. His face turned skyward. His bloodshot eyes were watery as they stared at the billowing smoke above, the giant black cloud expanding into the sky, dwarfing the sinking ship beneath it. Yamada appeared numbed, mesmerized, uncaring, and older than Ando had ever seen him look before.

When Osaki and the sailors made another attempt to lift him, Yamada once again batted their hands away.

"No! No!" he kept shouting through blood-stained lips.

Finally, Ando stepped in. "It's alright, Lieutenant. I will see to the admiral. Take care of the rest of these men, and pass the word to abandon ship."

"Yes, Captain."

Osaki and his men took up the burned and battered signalmen who still breathed, and soon disappeared down the ladder, leaving Ando and Yamada alone. An alarm blared on the decks below – the signal to abandon ship. The hull lurched once as a compartment below the waterline ruptured and was instantly filled with the sea, resulting in an even steeper tilt on the deck.

Ando knelt beside Yamada, but the old flag officer did not look at him. His soot-covered face simply stared skyward at the bubbling black column, his eyes jittery as they watched the ash and smoke ascend into the heavens. It was as if he were watching the fleeting hopes of the empire being swept away on the ocean wind.

"Admiral," Ando said. "The ship is sinking. There is not much time. We must get to the lifeboats."

Yamada did not seem to have heard him. "It is a good way for a warrior to die, is it not, Hitoshi?" Yamada said weakly. "To die in battle – the *bushido* code, the way of the samurai."

Ando pressed his hand to the admiral's shoulder. "We must go, sir."

"You must go, Hitoshi. I must remain here." Yamada reached out a bloody hand and squeezed Ando's wrist. "I am sorry for your ship. She was a fine vessel, and her crew were exceptional sailors. You fought her well. Lieutenant Kawaguchi…" the admiral started but could not finish, and Ando could not tell whether it was from his wounds or overwhelming grief over the young officer's loss.

"I will see that Kawaguchi is properly honored, sir. I will see them all honored."

"Of course." Yamada's lips formed a weak smile. "Now, go, my student. Your country and your emperor still need you. I wish to rest here for a while."

Ando choked back a tear for the first time in a very long time. The savage war had largely desensitized him to death, but now, as he stood up to leave his teacher, his mentor, his friend, he felt the sudden weight of all those losses, all the sorrow he had sequestered over the years.

It was difficult to stand on the angled deck, but Ando came to attention as best as he could and bowed to Yamada. "It has been my distinct honor, Admiral."

The dying admiral nodded his head appreciatively. "Farewell, Hitoshi."

# 37

# LET THEM GO

## *USS Aeneid*

A pillar of black smoke marred the sky a mile off the *Aeneid's* starboard quarter. Beneath it, sat the Japanese destroyer, dead in the water, broken and burning. The explosion of moments before had been enormous, the shockwave massive enough to be felt by those on the submarine's deck.

Weston had watched with disbelief as the giant column of water and flame had shot skyward from the destroyer's stern, sending a violent shudder through the 2,500-ton warship as if its steel hull and girders had been constructed of cardboard. The first blast had been immediately followed by a series of rapid explosions, likely the destroyer's depth charges or torpedoes going off. Pieces of debris and shrapnel had splashed down as far away as the *Aeneid*. When the bubbling cloud of smoke was drawn downwind, allowing Weston to see the extent of the damage, he knew the battle was over. The destroyer was no longer a threat. The warship's stern was entirely missing, nearly to her number two stack. The half of the ship that remained was quickly settling into the water from the stern. The sharp angled bow that had cut through the waves so speedily now stood still, pointing skyward like some artistic monument. Blue-clad sailors ran about frantically on the tilted deck, no longer concerned with the submarine, only with saving themselves.

The *Aeneid's* guns were now silent. Weston had ordered a general cease-fire, partly because the enemy warship was sinking, and partly because he was not sure the submarine's feeble hull, in its current state, could withstand many more recoils of the heavy six-inch gun.

While the men around him celebrated exuberantly over the enemy's demise, Weston was doing his best to keep a cool head. He had ordered the lookouts back to their perches to scan for aircraft. He had ordered the gun crews below, much to their displeasure, but he had agreed to let the entire ship's crew rotate through the bridge, five at a time, to see the destruction of the enemy warship and to revive themselves with some fresh air.

After all they had endured over the past twenty-four hours, he could not have refused.

"What do you think happened, sir?" Weaver asked hesitantly after things had somewhat settled down topside and the groups of spectator crewmen were cycling through the bridge. "Do you think there was some kind of accident on the Jap destroyer?"

Weston smiled. The ensign was young and inexperienced and seldom got to look through the periscope. He had certainly never seen the tell-tale signs of a torpedo explosion, of which Weston was intimately familiar.

"Captain, JK," Finkelman's voice came over the speaker. "I'm picking up CW from a QC, sir."

"What does that mean?" Weaver asked, unabashedly at first, but then, after seeing Weston's expression, realized that he should know its meaning. The ensign would have some reading to do on the voyage home.

"It means we're not alone, Mister Weaver," Weston said with a hint of reproof in his tone.

At that moment, one of the lookouts sang out, and young Weaver had his answer.

"Submarine surfacing off the starboard bow, sir, four thousand yards!"

The mystery of the destroyer's demise was solved.

It took a few seconds for Weston to find the new arrival in his binoculars. The black, gray, and white camouflage patterns effectively hid the vessel in the glittering expanse of blue ocean. Finally, he found it and saw what he had expected to see — a fleet submarine running parallel to the *Aeneid's* own course. Within a matter of minutes, light signals were passing between the two boats. She was the *Sea Dog*, and it had been her torpedoes that had arrived in the nick of time to save the *Aeneid* from certain destruction.

*Can I assist?* and *Well done!* were two of the blinking messages Weston had not needed Yates to decode for him.

As the two submarines slowly closed the range with each other, the blinking messages identifying the spare parts each needed so that they could be ready to exchange them when they finally came together, Weston turned over the conn to Weaver and walked aft to stand alone – or as alone as one could be on a submarine bridge.

There were still two thousand miles to go before they reached Midway, and there was still much to be done, but he needed a quiet moment to himself now that the immediate ordeal was over. Lighting a cigarette, he leaned on the rail and looked across at the sinking destroyer. She was almost down now. Just a few feet of the bow section remained above the waterline. The sea surrounding it was littered with floating debris, patches of burning oil, and lifeboats filled to capacity.

He suddenly felt exhausted. The faces of Townsend, Berry, Cooper, Allen, and all those he had lost stood at the forefront of his thoughts. The ship would sail on. The *Aeneid* would live to fight another day, but things would never be the same.

He would never be the same.

"I suppose they'll make it, sir," a voice said beside him.

Weston turned to see Greathouse leaning on the rail next to him. The big sergeant's face was expressionless as he stared out at the distant boats full of Japanese sailors.

"I suppose they will," Weston replied warily, half-expecting Greathouse to suggest that the lifeboats be machine-gunned, as he had after the sinking of the freighter en route to Matsuwa. Back then, Greathouse had displayed unreserved satisfaction at the fate of the enemy. But this time, Weston noticed, there was something different in the sergeant's demeanor. It was not sadness, nor even sympathy for the defeated enemy, but perhaps an acceptance – an acceptance that there must be injustices and suffering in war, and that true satisfaction can only come at the war's end, when the soldiers and sailors on both sides no longer had to kill one another. It was an acceptance Weston realized he himself would be wise to adopt if he were to be of any use to his crew, his ship, or his loved ones back home.

"Alright, you damned bilge rats!" Yates snarled from the forward end of the bridge. "Time's up! Get your stinking hides below so the next five can come up and have a gander!"

Taking one last look at the enemy, Greathouse gave a small nod and then turned away, joining the file of men waiting to go below.

# 38

# BENEVOLENCE

*Three days later*

*Matsuwa Island*

Ando rode in the passenger's seat as the truck bumped along the mountain road. An army corporal next to him drove the vehicle while several soldiers and laborers filled the benches in the open back. The truck was headed to the north side of Matsuwa where the soldiers and laborers would be added to the dozens of men already working on rebuilding the destroyed coastal battery.

Ando was here for a different reason.

During the long and dull drive, he found himself looking out at sea to the east, where, about twenty kilometers away, he could see the patch of ocean where his ship had gone down, taking most of his crew with it. His mind drifted to the events of the past three days. It was all just a blur, really. There had been so many things to do. There were still so many things to do. Truthfully, he had not wanted to come along on this ride today. His mind was with his surviving crewmen back at the airfield, but the grim task that lay ahead was his, and his alone, to fulfill.

The horror of that moment, when the *Hamakaze* had gone down, was still fresh in his mind. Forty-seven of her crew had made it to the boats. Others had not been able to get off in time and had leaped into the sea only to get pulled under by the suction forces created by the massive ship as it sank beneath them. Many of those bobbing heads had disappeared and were never seen again.

After floating in the open boat for several hours, many more men died of their wounds, most of them covered with horrible burns. By the time the small boats from Matsuwa finally arrived to rescue them, thirty-six of the *Hamakaze's* crew remained alive. In the three days they had now spent on the island, four more had succumbed to their wounds, leaving only thirty-two survivors – just thirty-two out of a crew of two hundred forty.

Feeling the guilt of a survivor, and that of a captain who had led his men to defeat, Ando had worked tirelessly over the past three days to see to the comfort of his remaining crew. The medical staff at the airfield was already up to their elbows in injuries. It was all too easy for them to put the naval personnel at the end of the line, but Ando had made sure his men were given adequate attention.

The local garrison was still working around the clock to clean up from the naval bombardment, but they had managed to restore the damaged runway to service. The garrison commander had offered to have Ando flown back home to Japan – ostensibly out of professional courtesy, but most likely because he did not like the idea of a senior naval officer interfering with the operation of his infirmary. Ando had refused, choosing to remain with his men. He would travel back to Japan with them, in whatever means of transport the navy provided, but he would not leave without them.

At the last turn in the road before it ascended the mountain slope, the driver brought the truck to a stop where a camp of several field tents had been erected near the shoreline. Here, Ando got out, and the truck continued on up the road.

As Ando made his way down the rocky path to the camp, he noticed a score of laborers fishing items from the water and moving them to piles on the dry shore. There were heaps of mangled boxes, splintered crates, and an assortment of other unidentifiable objects. The laborers' noses and mouths were covered with bandanas, and they seemed to be giving a wide berth to a separate collection of items covered in white sheets and laid out in neat rows.

"Ah, Captain Ando!" An army lieutenant bowed and saluted as Ando approached. "You received the message I sent this morning. Thank you for coming, sir."

Ando nodded. The message had arrived at the first light of dawn as he had eaten breakfast with the garrison commander. There had been a storm in the night. Heavy winds and high seas from the east had washed several items ashore – items that Ando needed to identify.

"I have asked for trucks for them, sir," the lieutenant said respectfully as he directed Ando towards the neat rows. There were twenty-three white sheets in all. A pair of boots or bare feet protruded from each one. "I suppose they could be laid to rest here," the lieutenant continued solemnly, "we could cremate them, sir, and then arrange for a boat to take them back out to sea. It is up to you, sir."

Though the lieutenant was respectful and polite, a cluster of soldiers who were overseeing the laborers stood nearby with bayoneted rifles conversing and chuckling amongst themselves. They displayed little reverence for the gathered dead, nor did they stiffen or make any attempt to suppress their merriment as Ando walked past them. The rivalry between the services was in full force, their disdain for the Imperial Navy evident.

The sheets were pulled back one by one, and Ando identified them. He knew them all. Kuyama the bosun, Ohno the radioman, Ichikawa the steward, Koga the Machinist's Mate, and nineteen others. The icy cold temperature of the water had preserved them well. As

Ando stated each name, one of the Koreans wrote it on a tag that was affixed to the body.

When the morbid task was finished, Ando noticed two other bodies that had been separated from the others, as well as from each other. One was covered in a white sheet and was carefully laid out. The other was a mangled corpse that had been discarded in a ditch as if it had been thrown there.

The lieutenant drew back the sheet on the first body, revealing the cold, pale visage of Admiral Yamada. His legs were oddly angled as before, but aside from that Ando could see no wound. The admiral's face was calm in death, his eyelids slightly open, his lips slightly parted, as if frozen in the moment the afterlife was revealed to him.

"We expected you would desire special treatment for this one," the lieutenant said, after allowing a moment of respectful silence. "That is the uniform of an admiral, is it not, sir?"

Ando took a deep breath and stared out at sea. The surf curled over the rocky shore, and several gulls floated on the brisk ocean breeze. It was a peaceful place, where any sailor might wish to rest.

"They will be buried here," Ando finally said.

"The admiral, too, sir?" the lieutenant asked.

Ando nodded. "That is the way he would have wanted it."

"As you wish, sir."

"What about that one?" Ando said, pointing to the body in the ditch. Now that he was closer, he could see that it was not Japanese, but Anglo. The dead man wore the olive drab fatigue pants of an American soldier. On the collar of his tattered shirt was a single silver bar. An officer, Ando deduced, but a very junior one, perhaps no older than his own Lieutenant Kawaguchi. Both had been too young to die.

"This was no doubt one of the Yankees who destroyed the battery up there," the officer gestured to the north slope of the mountain where a company of men, just small dots from this distance, worked with shovels and pickaxes to dig out what remained of the gun emplacement. "He washed ashore with the others.

Now my men will use his rotting corpse for bayonet drill."

The lieutenant grinned widely, apparently expecting to please Ando with the remark, but Ando did not return the smile.

"We have moved beyond such barbarism, Lieutenant!" he said admonishingly. "We *must* move beyond it! We live in a different world now. If we do not acknowledge that, if we do not understand that, then we are truly finished."

"He is a Yankee devil, sir!" The lieutenant retorted, suddenly aghast.

The army officer eyed Ando with something like contempt, leaving Ando to wonder how long it would be before his words made it to the ears of the garrison commander, and then perhaps to his own superiors, but he did not care.

"This man was brave," Ando said firmly. "He was a warrior, like you, serving his nation. He will be given a proper burial. Bury him here."

The lieutenant was clearly not pleased with the order, but he bowed curtly and then strode away to give orders to the workers.

Ando looked on Yamada's features one last time before pulling the sheet back over them.

*Goodbye, my teacher. On this rocky shore, on this cold isle in the shimmering sea, may your spirit find peace. Rest with the samurai. Rest with honor. Goodbye.*

# 39

# THE SILENT SERVICE

*Three weeks later*

*Pearl Harbor*

The Skipper's Lounge was a private bar in the submarine base officers' quarters, closed off entirely from the main bar. It was a place where the submarine aces of the Pacific War could exchange sea stories and tactics and generally relax with their fellow captains without worrying about proper decorum. Picture frames and plaques on the wall displayed the tonnage leaders, a few newspaper articles of interest, images of sinking ships shot through periscopes, and even a few rare photos in which the famous captains of the deep appeared with Hollywood celebrities.

Around a table in one corner of the bar sat four officers with loosened ties and rolled up sleeves. They drank, smoked, and chatted casually. Many toasts were offered, not so much with boisterous merriment as with relief that they had survived and were here to tell the tale. An occasional chuckle made its way from that corner table to the bar where an older man, an admiral, sat pretending not to be eavesdropping on their conversation.

"Another one please, Juan," Rear Admiral Giles said to the attendant behind the bar after draining the glass.

"Yes, sir," the bartender replied with a smile.

Giles had not come here to listen in on the party in the corner. He had, in fact, just stopped by for a drink before heading over to Ford Island, where he would board an R4D Skytrain that would take him on the first leg of a long journey to his next assignment, down in the Southwest Pacific theater. It had only occurred to him who the men were after seeing the four submarines tied up at the waterfront on his walk over here. The boats had not been there three days ago, the last time he had made that walk – and now he had put two and two together.

All four boats had looked like they had been through the wringer, with barnacles and rust aplenty. All four had come close to watery graves. Repair crews were already swarming over them, preparing them to go back out as soon as possible.

Two weeks ago, upon hearing that the submarines of *Wolfpack 351* had arrived at Midway, Giles had allowed himself a moment of personal satisfaction, that his Sea of Japan operation had been a success, as well as the diversion that had allowed the three trapped submarines to escape. He had not passed up the opportunity to stop by the chief of staff's office and watch him eat crow. But, after that, he had moved on. His plate was too full to linger on the past. There was always another operation in the works, more intelligence to sift through, another mission to plan.

Giles stole a glance at the distant table as he lit a cigarette. He knew who the four men were, though he had never met them. They certainly did not know him, and that was probably best. It would undoubtedly disrupt their repose if they knew the one who had quite literally sent them to hell and back was sitting only a few feet away.

A fresh glass of beer was placed before Giles, and he took a long swig, feeling the bite of the drink as it went down his throat. He remembered reading the initial patrol report on *Wolfpack 351*. After escaping through La Perouse Strait, the submarines *Pintado* and *Finback* had made their way past the Kurils without major incident and had made it to Midway with a few puddles of fuel left in their tanks. After burning up most of her remaining fuel in a high-speed, all-night run on the surface to save the beleaguered *Aeneid*, the *Sea Dog* had not had sufficient fuel left for the journey home. Only after a harrowing fuel transfer from the *Aeneid* in heavy seas did she have enough to get her to Midway.

*Pintado*, *Finback*, and *Sea Dog* had suffered little damage other than the normal wear and tear of equipment. The *Aeneid*, however, was a different story.

That old V-boat had been battered to hell. Giles knew little about the inner workings of a submarine, but judging from the *Aeneid's* appearance, it must have taken a small miracle to sail her back to Midway, and then to Pearl. She had suffered so much damage that ComSubPac had declared her unfit for sea. Once the Pearl Harbor repair crews had a few weeks with her, and she was deemed sound enough to cast off from the pier again, she would head back to the mainland for an extended period at the Mare Island Naval Shipyard – and her crew would get some much-needed shore leave.

Giles examined the men at the table again, wondering which one was the captain of the *Aeneid*. *Oh yes*, he thought, *that must be him* – the brooding one who only mildly laughed at the jokes. That was the face of a captain who had lost men in battle.

For just an instant, Giles toyed with the thought of going over there, introducing himself, and congratulating those men. He wanted to meet the *Aeneid's* captain, in particular, to thank him for performing his mission in such an exemplary way – and, more importantly, for allowing Giles to save face with ComSubPac. His salvaged reputation with the submarine admiral would be beneficial for future operations.

But, then, Giles reconsidered. It was better that he did not know these men personally.

Perhaps his next notion for winning the war would require sending one of them out to do something extremely dangerous, something against all the odds — *another suicide mission*, as they liked to call them.

Giles checked his watch. He had to get going if he wanted to catch the boat to Ford Island.

"Juan." Giles waved over the bartender.

"Yes, sir."

"You see those men in the corner?"

"The four skippers, sir?"

"Yes. I want you to set them up with anything they want. All the beer they can drink. All the food they can eat. Understand?" Giles took his travel money from his wallet, nearly two hundred dollars, and subtly passed it to Juan. "This should cover my tab and theirs."

"Yes, sir," Juan smiled as he took the cash. "That will be plenty. What should I tell them?"

"Tell them…" Giles stopped as he got up to leave, glancing one last time at the four captains. "Tell them nothing." He smiled. "See you next time, Juan."

"Goodbye, sir."

# HISTORICAL NOTE

This story is purely fictional. However, it is based on a few historical events that may be of interest to the reader. On May 11, 1943, the US submarines *Narwhal* and *Nautilus* – both V-boats, like the fictional *Aeneid* – landed an elite force of 245 U.S. Army scouts on Attu just before the American invasion to retake that island. They were not massacred as were the scouts in this story, but the subsequent fight to take Attu was both fierce and costly, resulting in one of the highest casualty rates in the Pacific War. In the three-week operation, the Japanese and the weather inflicted more than 3,829 casualties on the 7th U.S. Infantry Division, including 549 killed. The Japanese garrison was annihilated, many in a suicidal banzai charge in the final days of the battle. Of the estimated 2,600-man Japanese force, only 28 surrendered. The Americans recovered and buried the remains of 2,351 Japanese soldiers. For anyone wishing to read more about the invasion of Attu and the war in the Aleutians, I highly recommend *The Thousand-Mile War: World War II in Alaska and the Aleutians* by Brian Garfield.

Admiral Yamada and his World War One past are also fictional. While it is true that Japanese destroyers operated in the Mediterranean during the Great War, and one was indeed damaged by an Austro-Hungarian U-boat, there are no records of any U-boat sinkings by Japanese destroyers.

I have borrowed the name *Hamakaze* for my fictional IJN *Kagero*-Class destroyer. The real *Hamakaze* participated in several naval battles in the South Pacific, including the Japanese victory at the Battle of Kolombangara. In the Bismarck Sea, on January 10, 1943, the *Hamakaze* was one of three Japanese destroyers credited with sinking the *USS Argonaut*, another V-boat, which went down with all hands after a concerted depth charge and gun attack. The *Hamakaze* finally met her end in April of 1945 when she participated in the final sortie of the Japanese fleet – Operation *Ten-Go* – a suicidal attack against the overwhelmingly superior Allied fleet supporting the Okinawa invasion. She was sunk along with most of the ships in her task force, including the famous battleship *Yamato*.

I have also taken some liberties with the general chronology of the war, moving up by several months the first penetration of U.S. submarine wolfpacks into the Sea of Japan, but this did occur. The logic of such a risky excursion for such meager results was debated long after the war's conclusion. Two American submarines, the *Wahoo* and the *Bonefish*, were lost with all hands in the Sea of Japan, the *Wahoo* while attempting to slip past the anti-submarine defenses at La Perouse Strait. In 1995, a monument of peace was erected on nearby Cape Sōya dedicated to the men of the *Wahoo* and the crews and passengers of the five Japanese ships she is believed to have sunk. In 2006, the remains of the *Wahoo* were discovered at the bottom of La Perouse Strait confirming her fate and her final resting place.

The Japanese-held island of Matsuwa in the Kurils was indeed bombarded by American submarines and planes during the war and was used as a diversion to pull Japanese anti-submarine forces away from La Perouse Strait. On July 14, 1943, the *USS Narwhal* bombarded the airfield and hangars with her six-inch guns and received some unexpected return fire from shore batteries that had not been previously sighted. While the *Narwhal* completed her mission and lived to fight another day, the U.S. submarine *Herring* was not so fortunate. On June 1, 1944, after sinking the merchant ships *Hiburi Maru* and *Iwaki Maru* anchored off Matsuwa, she was sunk by gunfire from Matsuwa's hidden shore batteries. *Herring* went down with all hands. Her remains were only recently found, discovered by Russian divers in 2016.